TANGLED LINES

JEFF DOWNING

BLUE SHEPHERD

Blue Shepherd Publishing
PALM HARBOR, FLORIDA

Blue Shepherd Publishing - Florida

www.blueshepherdpublishing.com

Printed in the United States of America

Library of Congress Control Number: 2018900015

Tangled Lines / Jeffrey S. Downing
ISBN 978-0-9996878-0-2 (Paperback Edition)

ISBN 978-0-9996878-1-9 (Hardcover Edition)

ISBN 978-0-9996878-2-6 (eBook)

Formatting and Cover Design by Damonza / Damon Freeman

Visit the author's website at www.jeffreydowning.com

No man ever steps in the same river twice, for it is not the same river and he's not the same man.

—Heraclitus

In memory of
DEA Special Agent William H. "Billy" Yout
1947 – 2004

Acknowledgments

The setting for this fictional story is Allentown, Pennsylvania and surrounding areas of the Lehigh Valley—my birthplace and, despite living away from it for many years, the place I still fondly refer to as "home." I chose this location because of my familiarity with the area and, of course, because of the Little Lehigh River, which features prominently in the tale.

My great-great-great-grandfather Joseph J. Downing, Sr., emigrated to the United States from England in 1845 and settled in Allentown in 1870. He served the City on the Common Council for the Police Department, a Committee of the Allentown City Council, for many years beginning in 1884. More than 60 years later, my great-uncle John L. Deily began his career as a police officer with the Allentown Police Department where he served with honor and distinction for more than 40 years before retiring as a Lieutenant Detective in 1989 at the age of 67. My grandfather, Roland B. Downing, retired in 1979 after serving 27 years as an Alderman, Justice of the Peace and District Magistrate in Allentown.

Despite the fictional accounts in this book of a rogue Allentown Police Department narcotics unit, I have nothing but the deepest respect for the honorable men and women of the APD, who, with courage and integrity, keep the citizens of the city safe every hour of every day.

There are many people who have contributed to the success of this project. First, my wife Vickie, I thank for her loving support and encouragement, especially in the book's infancy. "Did you write the next chapter?" really did help me to keep writing, sometimes very late into the night.

My deep appreciation to my friend Brian Weakland, an award-winning journalist, author, screenwriter and accomplished attorney, whose cogent suggestions for the manuscript as he read "the next ten chapters," were inspiring. "I have good news and bad news," he told me. "The good news: Tangled Lines is a wickedly good page-turner with intriguing characters in amazing settings. The bad news: you've wasted thirty years of your writing life in your silly day job."

Next, to my friend and colleague Assistant United States Attorney Roberta Bodnar, my gratitude for her helpful suggestions and input and continued efforts to motivate me to "publish this thing."

My "beta readers" all read the book and gave supportive and valuable feedback. My thanks to Cindi Marshall, Marissa Marshall, Jerry Thompson, Wendy Tudor, Gary Zino, Carol Zino and retired Assistant United States Attorneys Kathy Peluso and Don Hansen.

Some have asked whether any parts of the book are true. That answer is, of course, no. This is a work of fiction. However, after more than 35 years of experiences in the criminal justice system, it would be difficult to say that some parts of the book, while completely fictitious, have not been inspired by actual events. As for any technical aspects of the book, when necessary I relied on the expertise of two very experienced federal agents—both of whom I have worked with extensively over the years. My sincere thanks to my friends Special Agent Walt Lanier of the Bureau of Alcohol, Tobacco, Firearms and Explosives, who also spent many years with the Georgia Bureau of Investigation investigating homicides, and Supervisory Special Agent Sheldon Burkett of the United States Drug Enforcement Administration.

Along this journey, there are so many others who have encouraged me to finish and publish this work so they could finally read it. My thanks to them all. Here it is. Enjoy!

Prologue

All I could see was the river. It was always that way.

It was fast—swelled from the hard Pennsylvania rain the night before.

I was with my grandfather. My mom's dad. I was seven—almost eight. It was our day. I just wanted to fish.

My grandfather—Jim Herbster—or Pap as I called him, directed his light yellow 1967 Ford Galaxie off the main road and rambled down the gravel and dirt pathway to a makeshift parking area behind a white cattle barn. The car slowed then came to a stop near the end of the parking area where a new silver 1969 Buick Electra was parked.

"Come on Pap," I shouted joyfully from the front passenger's seat, "let's go fish."

Pap got out of the car and methodically scanned the landscape along the nearby river. Directly in front of him an old concrete bridge crossed the fast-moving water. Thick, partially rusted steel pipes created the bridge railings with three horizontal cross pipes. I had heard stories about some of the fine trout my grandfather had landed from the far bank of the open river just upstream from the bridge. To his right, slightly downstream from the bridge, the cascading rapids raced over a field of smooth limestone rocks, the turbulence eventually subsiding further downstream where the river made subtle bends here and there.

I anxiously watched. Pap was always cautious, maybe even overprotective, when we were near the water. I sensed he was unsettled. Maybe the swift current made him that way.

A sound—something I didn't hear—caught his attention. He looked left toward an old gray stone building with a matching gray shingled roof, a single door and a lone window to its right. A small red brick chimney protruded through the right side of the roof. Situated within a few feet of the river, Pap called it an old spring house—used to cool fruits and meats before the availability of ice delivery and, eventually, electric refrigeration.

Further upstream, to the far left, some seventy-five to a hundred yards, I could see the looming crown of a fifty-foot tall weeping willow tree. A light breeze brushed the graceful, sweeping branches. Beyond it, around seventy-five feet or so, stood another majestic willow. It was there, between the willows, Pap learned to fish with his father and where he taught me how to fish.

"Come on Pap," I interrupted his survey of the river. "Open the door."

My grandfather had carefully placed our two fishing rods in the passengers compartment of the car. The rods laid diagonally between the outer edge of the seat and the window. Until the rods were out, I couldn't get out of the car—at least not through the passenger's door.

Pap opened the front passenger's door to extract the rods.

"Just be patient," he counseled me.

My mother had often told me that patience was a virtue, but it wasn't one of *my* virtues.

The rods now freed from the vehicle, I jumped out of the car.

"Open the trunk!" I hollered.

Pap pushed the key into the lock on the trunk and opened it. I reached in, grabbed our dark green metal tackle box and began to walk away.

"Hey . . . what are we going to fish with?" Pap asked. "Get the worms."

I turned and headed back to the trunk where I grabbed a weathered Maxwell House coffee can half-filled with dirt and earthworms.

I turned toward the river.

"Hold on a minute," Pap called. "The lines are all tangled up." My grandfather looked at the fishing line on his rod and my small Zebco matching rod and reel fitted with a red and white bobber. The tangled lines pulled me back from my anticipation of the river. I stood by, impatiently waiting for Pap to unsnarl them, finally deciding to sit on a nearby log.

I could hear the river. I could even smell it. Pap finally pulled the rods apart.

"Well, come get this," he called to me, holding my fishing rod. "I'll carry the tackle box." I stepped back to the car, handed him the tackle box and grabbed the small rod.

"Can we fish now Pap?" I started walking ahead of him.

"Between the two trees?" I asked, referring to the open area between the two huge willows. I looked back for his approval. He nodded and pointed in that direction which made me walk faster.

As we walked through the grass approaching our spot, gusts of the summer wind blew against my face and bent the tops of the random clumps of high grass guarding the borders of the water. Up ahead, I saw some commotion near the bank of the river. A man, on his knees hovering over the small, seemingly lifeless body of a young child.

"Stop! Come back here," Pap called with sufficient urgency. Curious, I hesitated, then turned toward my grandfather. I felt his firm grip on my shoulder.

"Wait here," he instructed. Pap's voice never trembled but it did then.

I watched him run toward the awful scene. The man pushed on the child's chest and slapped his face. The child's body was soaking wet. He didn't move. I knew he had fallen in the river.

"Please help me! My son! He's not breathing! He got pulled under the water! Please help me!"

I saw Pap look to his left, where a football field away toward the road was a small house. He looked back at me. The distress on his face frightened me more.

"Get back away from the water!" He motioned to me. "Back!" I was frozen. My feet couldn't have moved if I wanted them to. I tried to look at Pap, but couldn't take my eyes off the boy. I heard Pap when he yelled again. "Sit down and stay right there. Don't move. I'll be right back."

For a second, Pap watched helplessly as the man tried desperately to get the child to breathe. He took off running, as fast as I had ever seen him run, in the direction of the small home. About halfway there he stopped and looked at me, then continued to the house. The owner had heard the disturbance and had already called the police.

"Thank God," Pap cried out. Out of breath, he tried to run back to the river. By the time he reached the scene at the water, I saw the black and white pattern of a police car with its single red, cherry-topped light driving rapidly toward them. A cloud of flying turf billowed from behind the car. Within seconds, the car reached them and a young Allentown Police Officer jumped from the car.

"Please help us!" Pap shouted over the cries from the dying boy's father.

The officer rushed to the young boy on the ground, rolling him over and grasping him from behind, trying feverishly to pump the water from the boy's lungs. He put his ear to the child's mouth listening for breath, or any sound. He tried again to get the boy to breathe. His efforts were futile.

"Oh my God!" the child's father cried. "Oh my God! No!"

After several minutes, the officer stopped and gently laid the child onto the grass.

"I was just fishing over there." The man motioned toward a point beyond the far willow tree. "He was supposed to stay on the bank." The man reached down and cradled his son's head and upper body. "He was playing with his ball. It must have gone into the water and he went in to get it."

Pap had told me more times than I could remember to never go into the river. Never—no matter how calm it looked—and for good reasons. The river bottom between the two willows was very shallow for the first ten feet off the bank. Just past the shallows was a steep drop off and a wide crease of deeper water, deceivingly calm on the surface, but with a fast undercurrent. Several deep holes on the silt bottom were hidden in that short stretch of the river.

"He must have slipped off the ledge and got pulled under," the man spoke through his tears.

The officer put his hand on the man's shoulder, trying to console him.

Pap looked at me. I had never seen him cry before. I stood up as he approached. He kneeled to hug me. I felt his heart pounding as he turned me away from the sight of the dead boy.

The officer had retrieved a blanket from his patrol car and covered the body.

Part of me wanted to run away from the river and never come back there again. But I loved that river. It was my favorite spot.

"Are we gonna fish today Pap?" I asked quietly.

"Not here . . . Not today."

One

"POLICE! SEARCH WARRANT! Police! Search warrant!"

Masked figures banged on the door of an early 20th century twin home on east Front Street in the center of the city. Armed with a search warrant for the home of Luis Cordero, the six Allentown Police Department narcotics detectives tried to gain entry. Four detectives flanking the sides of the front door shouted again, "Police, search warrant! Open the door!"

No one responded.

Two detectives covered the back door.

Pausing for just a few seconds, they listened for any activity inside. Hearing none, they yelled again, "Police, search warrant!" Then again in Spanish, "policia, policia!"

The detectives knew Cordero was home. They had surveilled him to his residence earlier that morning. His 2010 victory red Camaro SS was parked in front of the two-story brick frame home. The six-a.m. wake-up call was a result of Cordero's crack cocaine trafficking in the city. An undercover narcotics detective had purchased crack from Cordero several days earlier from the area directly in front of his home. During the deal, Cordero sent one of his workers into his house to get the crack the undercover detective purchased. District Magistrate Roland Benjamin signed the search warrant last night.

Fearing Cordero and anyone else in the residence might be destroying cocaine and other evidence, the entry team waited no longer. Detective Thomas Gallon, a former college linebacker poised to the left side of the front door, utilized a black steel battering ram against the door. Striking the door just below the lock, he took it off the hinges. Three detectives followed the shattered door into the residence. With guns drawn and each detective wearing a thick ballistic vest, they entered the front room. Black ski masks concealed their identities.

At the same moment the detectives broke through the front door, the back door crashed open and Cordero tried to make a break for it. He was going nowhere. One of the two detectives waiting outside the back door slammed his 9mm Beretta handgun into Cordero's ear.

"Don't move or you're dead!" he shouted.

The other detective did the same.

"Get down! Get down!" she demanded. "Let me see your hands!"

They pushed Cordero face down onto the ground.

In the meantime, the entry team, led by Detective Chip Meyers pressed forward, sweeping the house for occupants, room by room.

In the front, upstairs bedroom, Detective Sergeant Rocco Morales found Mariela Cordero, the suspect's wife, cowering behind the bed.

"Show me your hands," he demanded. "Enséñame tus manos!"

Mariela threw her hands in the air.

"No shoot! No shoot!" she shrieked.

Morales pointed his gun at her head. "Get down! Now!"

Mariela dropped to her stomach and stretched her arms out in front of her. Morales handcuffed her.

"All clear," Meyers announced over the radio after clearing the second bedroom. Morales heard Meyers coming down the hallway. A few seconds later Meyers walked into the front bedroom.

"You okay in here, Rock?"

"We're good," Morales answered. "Get Piper up here to search her."

Meyers called on the radio for Detective Kathy Piper, "Kat, I need you in the front bedroom."

"The toilet's running. The upstairs one," Meyers informed Morales. "She must have flushed the shit while her boy tried to beat feet."

Morales pulled Mariela to her feet. Detective Piper walked in, grabbing Mariela's arm to push her against the wall to pat her down.

"She's clean," Piper assured them after a cursory search. "Not much you can hide in just a nightgown."

"What did you flush?" Morales asked.

"Nothing," she responded, lowering her head.

"Nothing, huh? We'll see about that."

Morales snatched Mariela by her long thick black hair and quickly forced her down the hallway to the small bathroom. A tub and a single-sink vanity lined the left side of the room. The toilet was tucked into a small alcove on the back right, directly across from the sink.

Morales pushed her toward the toilet.

"You didn't flush anything?" he growled, shoving her head toward the toilet. "Really?"

Morales pulled her head up and stared into her face.

"No!" she protested, struggling to loosen the detective's grip on her hair.

"No?" Morales tensed his right arm and shook her. He turned, pulling her with him. He forced her face toward the mirror directly above the sink behind them. "You're a fucking liar."

"You're hurting me," she cried.

"I knew you could understand me, you bitch. What did you flush?"

"Nothing," she said defiantly.

Morales pulled her closer to the sink, paused, then violently slammed her face into the mirror, shattering glass and slashing Mariela's pretty face. Blood splattered on the sink and poured from her broken nose. Morales shoved her head into the sink, mashing her face into the bloody porcelain bowl and shards of glass.

She sobbed hysterically.

He yanked her head back turning her bloody face toward him.

"Well, if you didn't flush it you must have stashed it somewhere else," he snapped.

Morales stood behind her and pulled her nightgown up and over her back. She pushed back. Her resistance was met with yet another slam of her face into the sink. With his left hand pinning her down, Morales used his teeth to remove the black glove from his right hand, then forced his fingers inside her.

She tried to scream as he violated her.

"I guess you didn't hide it there either, you fucking whore." Morales shoved the battered, distraught and still handcuffed woman to the floor.

"Everything good, Rock?" Meyers asked, approaching the bathroom doorway.

"Yeah." Morales stretched his glove onto his hand. "Charge this bitch with resisting arrest too," he said, walking toward the door. "She copped to flushing the shit but then she tried to fight me."

Morales gave Meyers an evil smirk.

"That was a really bad idea." Morales looked back at Mariela still trembling on the cold tile floor.

"I guess it was," Meyers replied, his thinly-veiled objection to beating the shit out of a handcuffed woman duly noted.

Downstairs, Luis Cordero sat handcuffed on the couch in the front room. He had been advised of his *Miranda* warnings and refused to speak without a lawyer.

In the upstairs, back bedroom in a shoe box Meyers discovered a pound of crack cocaine broken down into smaller amounts and packaged in small Ziploc baggies.

With Meyers upstairs, Gallon and Morales searched the kitchen. Inside the oven, Morales discovered a large brown grocery bag, rolled closed at the top.

"Look what I found," Morales said, holding the bag up in front of him and rocking it from side to side.

Gallon walked over to the kitchen table where Morales had placed the bag. Both of them peered inside.

"There must be thirty grand in here," Morales said, dumping the packs of cash onto the table.

Gallon counted the stacks. Each one was five-hundred dollars—in mostly twenty-dollar bills—folded in half and secured with a rubber band.

"Looks more like $35,000 plus to me," Gallon replied, counting the stacks back into the bag.

Morales smiled at Gallon and slapped him on the back.

"I call that a good payday, pal," Morales said.

"Amen," Gallon replied.

"Let's get those two pieces of shit out of here," Morales said, referring to the Corderos.

"Amen to that too, brother."

Two

The Little Lehigh River rolled east through the southern stretch of Lehigh Parkway just outside of Allentown, Pennsylvania. The cool May morning had excellent trout fishing written all over it. The river wound through the residential areas of the Parkway—mostly homes owned by wealthy doctors and lawyers—and then through some of the most beautiful, wooded scenery in the east. In an almost mile long expanse, the river was posted as "Fly Fishing Only Waters." There, anglers throwing artificial flies from fly rods, rather than worms or other live bait from baitcasting reels, found their solace—and amazing wild brown trout. Trout caught in these waters were released to be caught again another day. Unlike other areas of the Little Lehigh that were heavily fished by other fishermen who ate their catch, this little piece of heaven was quiet, peaceful and only lightly occupied by fly anglers. If there was a place near the city to escape, this was it.

On this exquisite morning, the light misty rain had almost subsided, leaving a clean, fresh smell in the air. The fragrant aroma of the surrounding bushes and trees, blooming wildly in the young Spring, added to the experience.

An older man walked up the dirt path next to a stretch of water where he saw a lone fly fisherman wading just off the near shore. The far bank was inaccessible because of the tall, thick shrubs and vines. On the near bank, he approached an enormous weeping willow tree. Another of equal size lined the bank some twenty-five yards upstream.

"Catch anything?" the older gentleman asked, walking to the edge of the stream where Thax Colby stood in his waders, focused on the fly he had tossed upstream from his position. Thax looked up, momentarily taking his eyes off the slowly drifting fly.

"Oh, same thing I usually catch." Thax chuckled. "An eyeful of this gorgeous place and occasionally a good close glimpse of one of those brownies that wants to admire my fly as he swims by it." Thax cast his fly back upstream. The fly dropped as softly as a small leaf on top of the water.

"I know that's not true," the gentleman replied. "Old Ronnie down at the house tells me you're the best fly fisherman he's ever seen and from all my conversations with him over the years, I know *he* thinks *he's* the best he's ever seen."

The old man wore a tan fishing vest over a long-sleeve brown plaid flannel shirt. His olive-colored hip waders were dry. A brimmed fishing hat sheltered his timeworn face and short powder-white hair. He cradled the cork grip of an eight-and-a-half-foot bamboo fly rod in his right hand just above the antique looking reel. He looked down the small pathway running beside the stream to a 19th century stone building, an old spring house, no bigger than twelve feet by twelve feet. One sturdy oak door led to a well-stocked fly shop most of the locals patronized. The proprietor, Ronnie Gerhart, was a fixture—there for twenty-five years—and an institution along the Little Lehigh. Ronnie had fished nearly every fly water on any serious angler's bucket list, but would trade them all for the Little Lehigh.

"Best trout waters *anywhere*," he would proudly say. And nobody could doubt him.

"Well," Thax said, again flipping the size 14 Royal Wulff fly upstream another twenty feet, "Old Ronnie can say what he wants, but that won't put a fish on that fly." Thax smiled.

A native Pennsylvanian, Thax had grown up in the Lehigh Valley. At six feet two inches, 195 pounds, his athletic, former marathon runner's physique was mitigated by the stress of his job and the passing of the years. His deep blue eyes and rugged face made his graying brown hair look more "distinguished."

Occasionally, a passing fisherman along the bank would approach another while they were fishing, as the old man did, then would move on. The gentleman just stood there watching as Thax picked up his drifting fly with the rod tip and threw it further toward his target near a rock ledge on the far side of the stream.

"There are some *big* brownies over by those rocks," the man said to Thax. "Just don't wade too far to the middle. There are some *huge* holes out there. People have drowned right there."

"I know," Thax said gratefully. "I've been fishing this part of the stream since I was a boy."

Thax threw his fly in the direction of the rocks.

"I'm sure you do," the man said, quietly acknowledging that he was probably quickly becoming a pain in the ass.

Thax was there to fish and relax—one and the same for him, but the man reminded him of his grandfather, who taught him to fish when he was a young boy. He looked over at a weathered green, wooden park bench on the other side of the path. Seeing that no one was there, he reeled in his line.

"Moving to another spot?" the man asked.

"No, I think I'm gonna take a break for a few minutes," Thax responded, walking to the bank of the river.

"Can you sit for a while?" Thax inquired.

The older man walked across the path toward the bench. Thax followed. They sat next to each other on the bench.

"So," Thax asked, "how did *you* do this morning?"

"I caught a couple small ones. Nothing to write home about."

"Well, that's pretty good," Thax said. "You're not done for the day, are you?"

"Yep. It's time to head home. The wife lets me fish all day, every day except Sunday. On Saturday I try to get home by eleven."

Thax sensed a sadness in the man.

"I guess Saturday isn't your best day then, is it?" Thax tried to get the man to smile.

"Well," the man said softly, "my wife is sick, been sick for a long time, and when I'm there with her she's happy. But she knows if I fish, then I'm happy and that makes her happier."

"Sounds like you found a good one." Thax nodded.

The man sat quietly for a moment.

"We've been married fifty-two years. I'm not sure what I would do without her."

"Do you live nearby?"

"We live in one of those townhouses on the other side of Fish Hatchery Road. Nice place," the old man said. "I can walk to the river in five minutes, but it usually takes me fifteen minutes to get home if you know what I mean."

"I understand," Thax replied. "It's always hard to leave this place."

The man stood up and reached for his rod he had set up against the side of the bench. "It's been nice to talk to you."

Thax stood up and put his hand on the man's shoulder.

"I guess you better get going. I don't want you to get in any trouble because of me." He tried again to get the man to smile. He did.

"Hey. Ronnie didn't tell me your name." The man reached out his hand. "I'm Bob Freeman."

"Thax Colby." Thax gripped Bob's hand. "It's been very nice to talk with you."

"Likewise," Bob replied.

"Thax, what do you do when you're not fishing?"

"I'm a federal prosecutor. I put bad guys away."

"I guess you have good job security."

"Sure do," Thax said. "Take care, Bob."

"You too," Bob replied, "and be careful."

Thax watched the man wander off down the path. Just then a fifteen-inch brown trout jumped out near the rock ledge on the far side of the stream. He walked toward the water armed with his fly rod. Wading into the water, he felt a buzzing in the left front pocket of his fly fishing vest—the unmistakable vibration of a cell phone. He thought for a second about not answering it. It was Saturday. He was relaxing. There was at least one amazing wild brown trout right out there. The vibration stopped.

"Hallelujah," he said out loud.

Within seconds the phone vibrated again. Thax reached inside his vest and unzipped the waterproof pocket on the left side, grabbing the phone. The caller ID displayed the name Chris Campisano, a Drug Enforcement Administration Special Agent and one of his best friends.

"Dude, it's Saturday."

"I know. I know," Campisano said excitedly. "You know I wouldn't call you if it wasn't important . . . Are you catching anything?"

"How in the hell can I catch anything when my fly isn't in the water? I'm talking on the damn phone."

"I need to see you. *Tomorrow*," Campisano said.

"Tomorrow's Sunday."

"Oh. It is? Thanks for reminding me. What time?"

"What's going on?" Thax asked.

"I can't tell you over the phone. I'll be at your office at eleven o'clock."

"Okay, Christopher. This better be good."

Three

If Chris Campisano had not been a DEA Special Agent, he would have been the next man cast as James Bond. His athletic build, jutting jaw line and light olive complexion, from his Sicilian heritage, made him the consummate head turner for the ladies in his office—and everywhere else in the world. Despite his usual gentle demeanor, he was also one of the toughest federal narcotics agents around. With fifteen years of experience, there were few better investigators in his agency.

Campisano had the respect of every law enforcement officer he had ever worked with. In his third year on the job, while working undercover buying heroin, the drug trafficker he was dealing with put a gun to his head and threatened to blow his brains out. Backup agents started to move in when the then young agent calmly told the trafficker, "that's really gonna slow down our deal." The trafficker, perhaps amused, put the gun down and finished the deal. Backup agents were stopped by the field supervisor right before they kicked in the door to the trafficker's business to save their brother agent. The next day, Campisano found a new quote pinned to the cork board above his desk. It read: "Ten feet tall and bulletproof."

Campisano had worked for many years with Thax when Thax prosecuted drug traffickers. While Thax was now prosecuting public corruption cases, they remained close friends.

"Who let you in?" Thax asked as Campisano stuck his head around the doorway into Thax's office. Thax's office was on the third floor of the federal courthouse at 5th and Hamilton Streets in center city Allentown.

The United States Attorney's Office took up the entire floor. The Drug Enforcement Administration was on the first floor.

"Are you on DEA time?" Thax asked, looking at the clock on the wall of his cluttered ten by twelve-foot government office. It was almost eleven-thirty.

"Sorry, cowboy, I got held up at church." Campisano flashed a smile.

Thax stood up from behind his desk and shook hands with his friend. Campisano sat down in one of the two chairs facing Thax's desk.

"What's going on?" Thax asked.

"Well, I don't want to say this has nothing to do with drugs because that wouldn't be true. I'm not sure if this is anything, but—"

"I've heard that before," Thax interrupted. "Just spill it."

"All right. Have you ever heard anything about anybody in the narcotics unit over at Allentown P.D. being dirty?" Campisano looked for a reaction from his friend. He got none. He continued.

"You know I'm working with your colleague, Jen Stuart, on a case that's going to trial in a couple of weeks. She's still pretty green but I think she's gonna be okay—after I get done helping her out of course."

"I'm listening." Thax settled into his chair.

"Okay, so Geoff Moser from our office, this was originally his case, but when he transferred up to Green Bay—"

"He went to Green Bay?"

"He says he's got family up there. Give the guy a break. I think he's a Packers fan." Campisano paused for a moment. "Are you going to let me tell you about this or not?"

"All right, keep going," Thax said.

"Anyway, APD has a couple of guys who work on our task force. Steve Dailey and Chip Meyers. They both seem like decent guys. They come over to our office and work some cases with us and they do their own thing with their unit at APD. About four or five months ago, an undercover detective from the State Police, who is also on our task force, makes a couple of small buys of coke from a guy out in Fogelsville. It's small stuff so everybody thinks the case will go to the DA to prosecute. When we hit the house to arrest this dirt bag, we hit a home run—bunch of dope, guns and what looks like about forty to fifty thousand in cash. Obviously, it's not this bad guy's first day at the ranch so when we figure out how much time we can hit him with over here in federal court, Jen agrees to indict him on federal charges.

"So here's Moser's DEA-6," Campisano said, tossing a copy of the DEA report of investigation onto Thax's desk. Thax sat forward and picked up the report.

"In the report, it says Detectives Dailey and Meyers found $15,000 in the bedroom where all the cocaine was seized. A couple of our other agents, Steve Yout and Lance Connolly, found another $27,000 in an old cooler in the garage. The main bad guy, Warren Robinson, admitted the dope was his. Everybody is thinking he's done. Now, when he gets over here in federal court facing a couple of decades in prison, all of a sudden he claims he didn't make any post-arrest statement and whoever says he did is lying. Anyway, now he wants to go to trial and Jen is gonna shove this up his ass and, of course, she wants to use the pictures of the money as evidence."

Thax listened.

"So I get the pictures and I'm getting ready to give them to Jen. Turns out this bad guy likes to be organized and, as you can see in the DEA-6, Yout, who's a great agent, actually counted two of the rubber banded stacks of money right there in the garage and both of them were exactly a thousand dollars. I looked at the photo of the money Yout and Connolly seized. They pulled it out of the cooler and laid it out on the garage floor. You know how I am. I counted the stacks. There's twenty-seven there—twenty-seven times a thousand—"

"I can do the math, Christopher."

"And twenty-seven thousand is what they turned in."

"Right."

Campisano took two eight by ten inch photos from a folder. "I pulled the photo of the money Dailey and Meyers seized. They laid the money out on the bed to take the photo. The stacks of money look identical to the ones taken from the garage. I counted them. Here Thax, you count them." Campisano handed Thax the photo.

He studied it carefully. "How much did they say they seized?"

"Fifteen thousand. Why? How many stacks do you count?"

"Twenty-three. Twenty-three stacks."

"Now do you see my problem? Where did the other eight go?"

"How could this happen?" Thax asked. "I thought you guys had all kinds of checks in place to account for money."

"We do," Campisano replied. "If money is seized it's photographed right where it is and it's put into a self-sealing bag. It's sealed. The bag is initialed by the two agents who put the money into the bag. When they get back to the office, the same two agents who seized the money take the sealed bag to the non-drug evidence agent. It goes into the vault and then to the bank. They count it at the bank and they cut us a cashier's check."

"How much was the check for the money Dailey and Meyers turned in?" Thax asked.

"$15,000 exactly."

"So they *were* all thousand dollar stacks." Thax rubbed his neck. "So how could these guys take the money, Christopher?"

"Well, there's only two ways they could have done it. Either they took it right there at the scene before they bagged it, which would be way too risky . . . almost impossible with everybody around—"

"Or," Thax interrupted.

"Or, after they got back to the office they took the bag over to one of their cubicles, opened the bag, took what they were going to steal, and put the rest of it in a new self-sealing envelope, which they would both have to initial again. That's the only way."

"Son of a bitch," Thax muttered.

"I know. Both of these guys had to be in on it. This really pisses me off, Thax. So I go to Dailey and I ask him about it. I show him the pictures. He's got no explanation except he says he doesn't know anything about the packs all being a thousand bucks. They didn't count any of them at the scene. He tells me he remembers them all being different sizes."

"Well you can see that's bullshit looking at the photo," Thax snapped.

"I know," Campisano agreed. "I asked him if he could explain why we got a cashier's check for exactly $15,000 for the money he and Meyers turned in."

"And why the other pack was exactly $27,000?" Thax interrupted again.

"Exactly. He didn't have an answer for that either. I didn't even bother talking to Meyers. I knew at that point I wasn't getting anywhere, so I had to let my Group Supervisor know right away."

"Who's the GS in your group?"

"Tommy Campbell."

"Well, you definitely have a problem." Thax shook his head. "What's DEA doing about it?"

"Well," Campisano explained, "Dailey and Meyers haven't been back in our office since then and Tommy was going to take this to someone at APD Internal Affairs. I wanted to run this by you before he talked to APD. I mean, we've never had any problems with them, ever. I hate that I think I can't trust them now."

"Well, let me think about this. I hope Jen doesn't need these guys as witnesses," Thax thought out loud.

"We don't need them to testify. That won't be a problem," Campisano assured Thax. "Moser saw the money when Dailey and Meyers laid it out on the bed. He's just going to have to make a trip back here from Green Bay."

"Well, I need to talk to Jen. We may have bigger problems than whether we can get a photograph into evidence. That whole case is compromised if this is true. Do you guys have any other cases where Dailey or Meyers seized money?"

"Pending cases?"

"Pending or past. I don't care. Any time they seized money."

"Are you asking me to investigate, because you know I'm already on it."

"Just keep this really quiet for now. Can you do that, please?"

"Consider it done, cowboy. I'm a pro, remember?"

Thax got up from his chair and walked out of his office with Campisano. As they approached the office entry-exit door, Thax slapped his friend's back.

"Nice catch Christopher. Be careful with this."

Four

Chrissy Barnes was almost never late, except for weddings, which she hated. On this morning as she navigated her way across westbound Interstate Route 22 from New Jersey into Allentown, the usual snags and snares of rush hour traffic enveloped her. She hated this drive, but loved living in Jersey where she was closer to the beach.

"Sacrifices," she'd tell people. "Everyone's got to make some."

As the lead reporter for the local cable station—Valley 10 News—Chrissy usually enjoyed her pick of stories and always worked the best breaking news. Today was one of those days.

As she aimed her old midnight blue Jeep Cherokee between an eighteen-wheeler and a slowed local bakery truck she realized traffic was not moving at its usual death crawl today—it was just not moving at all.

"Dammit," she screamed, hitting her brakes. "What the hell is going on here."

She took a breath and glanced down at her silver Tiffany watch. It was eight forty-five. The clock on the radio corroborated her tardiness. In the distance, just three miles away, she could see the growing skyline of the city. As traffic inched forward, the old Pennsylvania Power & Light building, symbolic of downtown Allentown came into view. The federal courthouse, her destination, was just four short city blocks from there.

Chrissy loved this city but still dreamed of the day when she would seek out a better market and a prized network news position. But for now, Valley 10 News was her home. Chrissy was a southern, country girl, born and raised in Forsyth, Georgia—a small town about fifty miles south of

Atlanta. After high school, she studied at the local community college for a semester to appease her parents until realizing Forsyth was just too small a world for Christine Penelope Barnes. With her parents' blessings, she transferred to the University of Florida in Gainesville. There, she received her B.A. degree in journalism—and a minor in fraternity boys.

Chrissy was the picture of brains, beauty and athleticism. While on her way to the Florida Keys after graduation, she and her two closest sorority sisters stopped to savor a gourmet lunch at Jackson's on Clearwater Beach, a local hangout for Tampa Bay's rich and famous. On this day, the sunshine state's junior senator Ryan Stokes was enjoying a relaxing day among his constituents. The young legislator was caught off guard by Chrissy's wit and charm during a brief encounter inside the restaurant. Later, as Chrissy and her sisters left the parking lot a Florida State Trooper on a motorcycle pulled her over.

"What did I do?" an exasperated Chrissy asked the young trooper.

"Nothing ma'am. Senator Stokes would like to know if he could call you."

Call he did. Just two days after graduation Chrissy accepted a job offer as the junior Senator's deputy press secretary. Chrissy did a U-turn—from the Keys of course—and a week later headed for Washington, D.C.

Chrissy enjoyed an excellent reputation as the Senator's deputy, a job she cherished until the call of her real love—investigative reporting—led her away. At the time, she was in a serious relationship with a young CEO who lived in Bethlehem, a neighboring city of Allentown. She easily slipped into an open reporter position with Valley 10 News in Allentown, a locale where, as she would put it, "there's always something ready to pop."

Chrissy inched closer and peered at her watch again. Eight fifty-five. *I'm not going to make it,* she thought. She moved to the far right lane, the exit lane to downtown Allentown. With traffic stopped, she reached for her rear-view mirror, turning it toward her. She gazed into it, adjusting her short blonde hair. She snagged a tube of lipstick from her purse. While negotiating the exit ramp, she covered her full lips and threw the lipstick back into her purse. "Finally," she exclaimed. "Some breathing room."

Chrissy navigated down Seventh Street where she hung a left onto Hamilton Street. Two blocks down she hung a tight right and slid her trusty

Jeep into an open space. With her purse and Starbucks coffee in hand, she headed for the courthouse.

"Sorry. No time for you Mr. Parking Meter," she quipped.

It was two minutes after nine. Chrissy was late for the sentencing of a local stock broker who had bilked his clients out of several million dollars. She had reported on the investigation from the beginning and didn't want to miss the finale.

Making her way through security, she flirted with John Regis, her favorite Court Security Officer.

"How's Big John today?" Chrissy smiled widely.

"You look great today Chrissy!"

"Gotta run. I'm late. See you on the way back buddy." She waved, heading for the elevators.

Chrissy pushed the elevator call button several times. A young lawyer stood waiting.

"I guess that doesn't make it move any faster," she said, receiving a pleasant smile from the man. She returned his smile.

When the doors opened Chrissy, looking down at her watch and casting aside all elevator etiquette, headed for the doors. As she did, Thax Colby stepped out of the elevator. Thax and Chrissy collided just outside the elevator doors, sending her coffee flying. She tried to dodge Thax and the hot java moving in her direction.

"Damn," she said under her breath, moving backwards from the crash site.

"I'm so sorry. Are you okay?" Thax asked, reaching to help her.

Chrissy wore a sleek navy suit with a short skirt and a white blouse. Matching navy heels completed the outfit.

"I'm fine . . . I'm late and I smell like a latte, but I'm okay," she said, examining her suit for coffee. "It's why I love navy blue," she joked.

Thax had seen Chrissy around the courthouse before but they had never met.

"My name's Thax, Thax Colby," he said, extending his hand. "If there's any coffee on there, please let me pay for your dry cleaning."

Chrissy looked at her watch then at Thax. His blue eyes pierced through her. He handed her a slightly dog-eared business card. "That's me."

"I think the suit is fine, but my poor coffee . . ."

Chrissy looked at the wet area on the short gray carpet beneath her feet. "I would let you buy me coffee sometime if you want to." No one had ever accused Chrissy Barnes of not being forward.

Thax looked at the beautiful woman in front of him and smiled. "Okay. It's a deal."

"Perfect," Chrissy said, reaching to call the elevator. "How's ten-thirty? Starbucks down the street?"

"Today?" Thax said quizzically.

"But of course." She beamed. "There's no guarantee for tomorrow."

The elevator doors opened. Chrissy paused this time to see if anyone exited. After a second, she stepped in, turning to look at Thax.

"Starbucks. Be there!" she mouthed, winking at him as the doors closed.

* * *

"So, what's your story Colby?" Chrissy asked. "No wedding ring? Divorced?" She leaned closer. "I know you can't be gay," she inquired, acting serious. "*Please* tell me you're not gay."

Seconds earlier Chrissy and Thax sat in a booth at the Starbucks just down the street from the federal courthouse.

"Do you always meet men by tossing coffee on yourself," Thax asked playfully, ignoring Chrissy's questions.

Chrissy was happy. She liked Thax immediately. She sipped on her coffee. "So what kind of cases do you prosecute?"

"Mostly public corruption cases. I still do some drug cases now and then, but mostly corruption."

She focused her eyes on his. "What are you working on now?"

"Well, the thing about public corruption cases, as I'm sure you probably know, is we really have to fly under the radar," Thax continued. "You know I can't talk much about that."

"I know. I knew you couldn't talk to me about anything that you're doing. I'm a half-decent investigator, so if there's anything you think I can help you with, anything, I'm happy to do it," Chrissy replied. "You know I broke the story a few years ago on the former tax collector in Lehigh County who was embezzling money. I had some good sources. I'm serious. I love this stuff."

"I have a sentencing next week on a cop over in Bethlehem. The guy was writing speeding tickets on Friday afternoons targeting Puerto Rican drivers. With the drivers that didn't speak good English he explained that he would have to take them to jail for the weekend unless they posted a cash bond. They asked how much and he asked 'how much do you have?' Whatever they had was enough. He took their money *and* wrote them a ticket. They showed up in the District Magistrate's court to pay their tickets and after they did they wanted their bond money back. The judge says, 'what bond money?'" Thax laughed.

Chrissy looked puzzled. "Tell me you're kidding. Are people really that stupid? Is this cop that stupid? What did you charge him with? It's not a federal crime to be stupid, is it?"

"No," Thax said, "we'd have to have a lot more federal prisons. The cop was charged with a civil rights violation. He'll probably get a couple of years."

Thax finally drank some coffee. He liked it lukewarm anyway.

"So," Thax asked, "does your boyfriend know you have coffee with men you hardly know?"

Chrissy looked at Thax lifting her left hand. "No boyfriend. No ring . . . You never answered *my* question."

Thax looked down at his coffee then back at Chrissy. "I was married for a few years many years ago but she couldn't deal with the life of a federal prosecutor. We met in law school and worked together in the DA's Office in Harrisburg for a few years. Her daddy had lots of money and she couldn't understand why I wanted to keep doing this and not travel all over the world with her, so she took off."

Chrissy sensed that Thax was uneasy talking about his past, and tried to change the subject.

"I'm sorry. I didn't mean to open an old wound," she said.

"It's okay. The last I heard she was living in some huge home out in Montana. She doesn't even fly fish," Thax tried to make a joke.

"Well . . . I think I need to go find a story," Chrissy changed the subject. She took another swig of her coffee.

Thax's phone vibrated. It was Campisano. "I need to go too," Thax said, "but I really don't want to." He let the phone ring until it stopped.

Chrissy walked with Thax to the exit doors. He reached for the door and opened it for her. They walked back toward the courthouse. When they got to Chrissy's Jeep, she turned and extended her hand to Thax.

"Until I see you again, Mr. Colby."

Thax reached out and held her hand.

"I hope that's soon," he said, slowly releasing her hand.

Thax's phone rang again.

* * *

Thax answered his cell phone while ascending the steps in front of the U.S. Courthouse and Federal Building.

"Talk to me, Christopher."

"Hey. I got some good info. Where are you?"

"I'm just walking into the courthouse."

"I'll be up in your office in fifteen minutes. Do you know Shea Barrows from the FBI?"

"Of course I know her. Why?"

"Because I'm bringing her with me. I'll explain when we get there. See you then." Campisano hung up before Thax could say anything further.

Five

Campisano knocked on the closed door to Thax's office.

"Come in," Thax shouted.

Campisano walked in with FBI Special Agent Shea Barrows. Thax walked from behind his desk to greet them.

"Thax, I guess you know Shea."

Thax gave Barrows a hug.

"Hey Shea, it's been too long. How have you been?"

"Good, Thax. It has been a while."

"Have a seat." The agents sat in the chairs across from Thax's desk.

Barrows was a seasoned FBI agent, having started in the Bureau almost twelve years earlier. After graduating with honors from USC, the California girl attended Stanford law. Nearly every big firm in California swooned over her, including Baker Botts, one of the top firms in California and the country, and where her father was a senior partner. Much to her father's chagrin, she had other plans. She applied for a special agent position with the FBI and was accepted into the next academy class. Barrows was a natural beauty. Her long, wavy strawberry blonde hair contrasted with her fair porcelain skin. A spate of faint freckles littered her cheeks and the bridge of her nose. Although she had given up triathlons after the birth of her second child, she was still in better shape than most women—or men—ever would be.

"Well, what's going on?" Thax asked, getting down to business.

"Shea called me about something that I thought was *really* interesting. I'll let her tell you, but just so you know, I've briefed her on our investigation."

Thax's eyes darted toward Campisano. His invitation for the FBI to join the investigation was unusual. The DEA and FBI didn't always play nicely together.

"Relax," Campisano said. "She needed to be completely on board. We've worked together before."

"That's fine," Thax said. "Now tell me what's going on."

"Two weeks ago, I was the duty agent, which you know I love because I get all the flipping crazies calling on my day. So I get this call from a guy who lives out in the West End, out on 31st Street."

"That's Whitehall Township. Not Allentown," Campisano interjected.

Barrows shot Chris a quick look.

"Anyway," she continued, "this guy tells me some cops came to his house with a warrant and searched it and that they left a dead fish in his house. I take his information and ask him what cops he was talking about. He says he doesn't know. I ask him if they left a copy of the warrant and he says they didn't. Just told him they had one, showed him a piece of paper and searched his house.

"Oh, and did I mention they left a dead fish," Barrows said sarcastically. "I almost asked him if he had the tin foil in his head adjusted lately . . ."

Thax was amused at the story.

"But then I asked him why he called the FBI and he said he told his neighbor about it and his neighbor, who is a retired Customs agent, told him to call the FBI." Barrows rolled her eyes. "I told him I would check it out and get back to him."

"I assume there's more?"

Barrows continued. "It turns out the guy who called, his name is John Karopolis, and he's owned a diner in the area for many years. He's got no criminal record and he told me he's never been in any trouble. Anyway, I thought it was worth taking a ride out there to talk to him some more."

"And," Thax said anxiously.

"I went to his house. Nice house. Nice neighborhood. He tells me a bunch of cops showed up at his house at seven in the morning. They all wore black ski masks. They knocked on his door and told him they had a search warrant. He asked to see it and they flashed him a piece of paper that looked like it said warrant on it, but they never gave it to him. They pushed their way in and shoved him down on his sofa. Made him sit there while they searched his home."

"Who were the cops? Do we know?"

"Since it's Whitehall Township, I called a friend I have in Vice and Narcotics just to ask if they had done a warrant in that area lately. He told me they hadn't. I called the State Police and asked them the same thing. It wasn't them either. That's when I called Chris. I thought maybe it was DEA. I didn't know who else would be doing a search warrant in that area."

"I'm starting to get a really bad feeling about this." Thax sat forward in his chair. "Keep going."

"Now my curiosity is really up. So I asked about the dead fish. The guy tells me that a few hours after they left he smelled something fishy and it gets worse. These a-holes took a frozen fish out of his freezer and stuck it under the refrigerator!" Barrows's voice cracked.

"Why this guy? Why his house? Did they take anything? Was there anything, any dope in his house?" Thax fired off a flurry of questions.

"That's what I asked," Barrows answered. "At first, he didn't want to tell me. I guess he was embarrassed about this whole thing. This guy's been a model citizen all his life, but his son Jimmy, not so much. Jimmy Karopolis has been dealing drugs most of his adult life, almost ten years. He's got a long rap sheet. Been in State prison twice for drug trafficking."

"Does he live with dad?"

"No," Barrows said. "I'll let Chris tell you this part."

Campisano looked at a small flip notepad he sometimes carried for notes. "I called the secretary at the District Magistrate's office, the judge who would have signed a warrant for this area. I told her we were working on a drug investigation and were trying to find out if the judge had signed a search warrant for a home on 31st Street. She told me they had no record of any recently in that location. Then I checked the Lehigh County jail records. Four days before this happened, Jimmy Karopolis got popped by the Allentown P.D. narcotics unit for slinging cocaine down in Jordan Park. When they first booked him his bail was $5000. When Shea interviewed him, the dad said he went to the arraignment and told his son not to worry, that he would get the money to post his bail. He'd just as soon kick the kid in the ass—but it's still his son. He said there were other people there in the courtroom, but he didn't recognize anybody. It looks like APD added a bunch of other charges right after the arraignment. Jimmy's bail was upped to forty-thousand dollars cash."

"Don't tell me," Thax interjected, "dad had the forty grand at his house when the cops came in, but not after they left."

"Exactly," Campisano answered.

Thax pursed his lips. "I don't suppose our friend saw any of the cops' faces?"

"Actually," Barrows paused, "after they walked out, Karopolis was terrified and he wanted to make sure they were gone. So, he peeked out the front window and saw one of the guys who had taken his ski mask off."

"Can he ID him?"

"I have a guy at the Department of Highway Safety who owed me a favor. I got some DL photos of the guys I know are in the APD narcotics unit and Karopolis is pretty sure the guy he saw is Joshua Schick."

"*Detective* Joshua Schick, Allentown P.D.," Campisano said.

"Pretty sure?" Thax asked Barrows.

"We did a nice photo lineup, Thax. I think his words were, 'ninety-eight percent that's the guy.'"

"You call that 'pretty sure?'"

Barrows nodded.

Thax stood up.

"All right, I need to run to court in ten minutes so let me think about this and I'll touch base with you guys tomorrow."

Barrows walked down the hall with Campisano following behind. Thax escorted them to the door of the U.S. Attorney's Office. At the door, Campisano turned toward Thax while Barrows continued to the elevators.

"This isn't gonna end up on the Valley 10 News tonight, is it?" Campisano asked quietly.

"What are you talking about?"

"I've got some big windows in my office and a great view of the front of this building." Campisano grinned. "Just screwing with you buddy."

Thax said nothing. As Barrows entered the elevator, Campisano hurried to catch it.

"Hey," Thax called to his friend.

Campisano stopped and turned toward Thax.

"Don't be an asshole," Thax joked.

Campisano laughed. "See ya, buddy!"

Six

LOGAN BRANFIELD WAS the popular mayor of the City of Allentown. Reelected for a second four-year term more than three years earlier, he claimed responsibility for a revitalization of the downtown area as well as a relatively prosperous business climate. A proud graduate of the University of Pennsylvania and Harvard Law School, he practiced law in the city for years before winning the mayoral election by a landslide. His wife, Dana Holmes Branfield, a former Miss Pennsylvania, played the part of the trophy wife as well as any woman could. On paper, Branfield was a star—a rising one—and he hoped to carry his popularity to the Governor's mansion in Harrisburg in the coming election. He was a ladies' man and a fervent philanderer—too many mistresses to count. None of that, however, could help him now.

Standing on the tee of the 18th hole of the Allentown Municipal Golf Course this Saturday morning, he found himself two strokes down to his playing partner, Richie Sokol. The 172-yard par-three was one of the toughest holes on the course. A large, deep swale ran from tee to green, banking from right to left, leaving any shot short of the green in deep rough to the left or worse—in one of the two enormous sand traps dutifully guarding the front left half of the green. Many a duffer had been lost in this cavernous beach. Sokol had pushed his tee shot to the right of the green, into a thick band of tall evergreens lining the adjacent fairway. Despite finding trouble on this hole, most golfers would have been envious of the quality of either man's game. Both consistently shot scores in the high-seventies.

Branfield placed his ball on the tee and, gripping a six-iron, stepped behind the ball to line up his shot.

"What do you say we go double or nothing on the whole game, Richie?" the mayor asked brazenly. "Huh, Richie? It's just another thousand bucks!" The mayor stood behind his ball, waiting for Sokol to take the bait.

Richie Sokol didn't like to lose at anything. His career with the Allentown Police Department ended suddenly when he was shot in the chest and the right leg while serving a search warrant on a drug house. The first 9mm slug was stopped by his vest, saving his life. Another bullet tore through his knee, crushing bone and tearing muscle in its path. At the time, Sokol was a lieutenant in charge of the narcotics unit. Unable to rehabilitate quickly, he had no choice but to retire on a medical disability. As luck had it, the mayor—Logan Branfield—had just fired his old bodyguard and Sokol, even with his limp, was the man for the job.

Sokol looked down range at the thick trees his ball had apparently nestled into.

"That means if I make a bogey you need a hole-in-one. You sure you want to lose all that money?" Sokol asked defiantly.

The mayor asked again, "Do you want the fucking bet or not?"

"Let's do it boss," Sokol said, waving his right hand toward the hole inviting the mayor to finally swing.

Branfield addressed the ball and swung. The pin was placed in the front of the small green. His shot headed directly at the hole landing a few yards short of the green, but then kicked straight left into the bunker.

"Goddammit!" he cursed.

Sokol chuckled under his breath. "Get in the cart. Let's go see where my ball is."

Sokol drove the golf cart to the tree line where he found his ball in a clearing between two of the large pines. He had a straight clear chip shot to the green. Sokol was a big, strong man—much more so before his injuries, but his short game was his forte. His ball lay just twenty yards from the hole.

"Hey boss. How about an extra thousand that I get down in two from here?" Sokol said, taunting his friend.

Sokol didn't like to lose. Branfield detested it.

"Why not make it an even five Richie? Why not?" Branfield talked faster. "Why the fuck not. Let's make it five thousand that you can't get down in two from there. You don't need to say anything. I know you're in. Just hit the fucking shot."

Sokol took a few practice swings and struck the ball perfectly. The ball rolled eighteen inches from the hole. Sokol smiled confidently but said nothing. He marked his ball with a dime.

The mayor walked into the front sand trap and hit a great shot onto the green, three feet from the pin. Branfield's next shot—a short putt—stopped inches from the hole. As he tapped his ball into the cup he stepped directly between Sokol's ball marker and the cup, then twisted his foot tearing up the green.

"What the hell . . ." Sokol looked at the mayor in disbelief. "What the hell did you do that for?"

"To teach you something you already know." Branfield leaned forward, his face inches from Sokol's. "I own every fucking inch of this city and everything in it, including this golf course and this green. Don't *ever* bet against me Richie. Now pick up your fucking ball and let's go. Even-Steven." The mayor walked off the green toward the cart. Sokol stood and watched, still dazed at the mayor's behavior. He finally got to the cart and got in to drive. The mayor put his left arm in front of Sokol's chest.

"I need more Richie. I need more. I've got a big house, three cars, two kids and a wife that wants nothing but the best. There's a lot of fucking money out there to be made!"

Sokol shook his head resolutely. "I hear you, boss."

"When I'm governor and you're the Commissioner of the State Police, we'll look back on this day and laugh our asses off." Branfield looked out over the golf course from their elevated position on the course. "Yes we will Richie. Now, let's get these clubs in the car and get a sandwich and a cold beer . . . Commissioner Sokol," the mayor cheered.

"Yes, sir. Let's do that."

* * *

By noon, Thax had landed a couple of beautiful rainbow trout in the lower pool downstream from his favorite spot between the two huge willow trees. The sun was now directly overhead casting small shadows over the

Little Lehigh. Thax waded under some low hanging branches and moved upstream. The overhanging willow and oak trees made it tougher to cast, but not for an experienced angler like Thax. He spied a good-sized brown trout rising to take a bug fifteen feet from his position. His cast was almost perfect. The fly drifted less than a foot and bam! The brownie hit it like a ton of bricks. Thax set the hook and played the fish for a few seconds before reeling him in. Reaching down to release the fish, he felt the vibration of his cell phone in his vest pocket.

"Are you kidding me?" he said to himself. "Can't a guy get some peace?"

In fact, Thax had a lot on his mind. The APD was a good department with so many great officers. Thax's uncle had served honorably and bravely with APD for four decades. The prosecutor had many friends in the department. It was distressing to think a whole narcotics unit could be dirty. The phone stopped ringing. He flipped his fly into a shaded area under some low hanging branches of a gray dogwood bush. The fly drifted downstream untouched. He looked at his vest pocket anticipating that Chris Campisano would call him back.

Thax enjoyed another serene hour of fishing before deciding to pack it in for the day. Walking back up the path toward the old stone building, he saw two familiar figures sitting at the green wooden picnic table just outside the building. Thax smiled and shook his head as he approached.

"What? I don't call you back and you track me down," Thax said.

Campisano and Old Ronnie sat across the table from each other. Campisano faced the stream.

"See," Campisano motioned with his head toward Thax as he spoke to Ronnie, "I told you he'd be pissed."

"Who's pissed?" Thax asked. "I'm going to have to start fishing in a different spot."

"Okay, buddy," Campisano chuckled. "You've been fishing here since before I was born."

Ronnie struggled to get his mildly overweight body off the picnic bench, politely uninviting himself from the conversation. He headed for the door of the fly shop.

Before he got there, he turned toward Thax.

"How'd you do today?"

"A couple of rainbows and a nice brownie."

"I don't guess you were throwing tricos, were you?" Ronnie asked sarcastically, referring to a small fly pattern simulating a type of mayfly with a black body and small white wings. Ronnie advised everyone that sought his expert advice that the only dry fly they should ever fish with on that stretch of the river was a size 24 trico—a fly so small you could fit four or five of them on the tip of a finger.

"Nope. Caught 'em all on a Parachute Adams," Thax said, describing a much different fly than the trico.

Ronnie didn't say a word, retreating to the stone building.

"So you're trying to make friends with Old Ronnie, Christopher?" Thax slapped Campisano on the back as he got up from the bench seat.

"I just thought I'd catch you here. Shea called me last night. She served that grand jury subpoena yesterday. I told her I would let you know. The guy didn't want to say anything."

"Thanks," Thax replied. "We'll see about that."

Campisano walked with Thax the short twenty yards to the gravel parking area where they were parked. The lot was behind an old white cattle barn off Fish Hatchery Road. When they got to the parking lot, Thax said goodbye to his friend.

"Thanks again, Christopher. Next time I'll answer my phone and save you the trip."

Campisano shrugged.

"It wasn't me who called you. I was close by so I thought I'd catch you here," Campisano said, opening the door to his black Dodge Ram pickup truck. "Really," he assured Thax before he closed the door and drove off.

Thax opened the tailgate to his dark green Jeep Grand Cherokee and disassembled his four-piece fly rod, placing it in the cargo area. He removed his fly vest and retrieved his cell phone. He had a voice message:

"Hey, fly boy, this is Chrissy," she said in her best sultry voice. "I sure hope you didn't fall in the river since you're obviously not answering your phone. I thought maybe we could grab some dinner tonight or watch a movie or whatever . . . Call me."

Seven

Detectives Thomas Gallon and Chip Meyers were best friends since they met in the Allentown Police Academy almost seventeen years earlier. Gallon, the only black detective in the narcotics unit, had graduated with a degree in business from Louisiana State University where he also played outside linebacker for the Fighting Tigers. He had a full athletic scholarship and a solid GPA as well. What he didn't have was any ambition for business. He liked action, the kind he would never see in the business world.

During his last semester, after the football season, he worked as a part-time bouncer at a nearby bar and nightclub. He was much stronger than he looked, and he *looked* really strong. One night a local patron drank too much and went crazy in the bar breaking everything in his path. The manager called the Baton Rouge Police; just two officers responded. Fortunately, Gallon arrived at work just minutes after the officers had entered the bar. The patron, glassy-eyed and crazy, threatened to kill the officers if they approached. When they inched forward, the drunken man rushed them, causing one of the officers to land his heavy metal flashlight smack in the middle of the man's bald head. While time stood still for several seconds, the officers expected the man to crumble to the ground. That didn't happen. When the man felt the stream of blood rolling down his head onto his face he shouted, "Now I'm *really* mad!"

Without hesitation, Gallon pushed his way through the officers and gathering crowd and executed an All-American tackle on the man, knocking the breath out him. The officers, with Gallon's assistance, handcuffed the subject and reestablished the peace. Before he graduated, the Chief of the Baton Rouge Police awarded him a citation for valor and a job offer as a patrolman. Gallon's whole family lived in Allentown. He didn't like Louisiana all that much anyway, so after graduation he moved back and applied to be an Allentown cop.

Unlike Gallon, Chip Meyers always knew he wanted to be a cop. He could never explain why, not even on his interview for the police academy. He just wanted to be a cop. After graduating from high school, he worked for a few years in a local hardware store owned by Ed Mueller, a friend of his father's. Mueller's store on Ninth Street just south of Tilghman Street in Allentown was a short walk from Meyers's home. Mueller treated Chip well and taught him many useful skills. But the best benefit of the job was Mueller's daughter Kristin, who usually worked the cash register at the front of the store. On Chip's twenty-first birthday, he applied to the police academy. The day he received word that he was accepted for the next academy class, he asked Kristin to marry him.

Both Meyers and Gallon were aggressive but fair patrol officers. When two detective positions opened up in the narcotics unit seven years ago, then-Sergeant Richie Sokol hand-picked Meyers and Gallon to fill the slots. The first year in narcotics things were great. The guys in the unit were inseparable and the more experienced detectives taught the rookie narcs the ropes. Meyers loved the undercover work. Gallon preferred kicking in doors. Life was good and then, things started to change. Somehow the wheels were slowly coming off the tracks.

The bulk of the work for the narcotics unit involved making undercover buys from drug houses in the city to get probable cause for search warrants. Sometimes, the detectives would use confidential informants to purchase drugs from the dealers. After a few days, the unit would serve a search warrant, usually catching the dealer with drugs and money. It seemed, at times, there was no end to the amount of drugs or the large caches of money.

One evening, the day after the unit executed a search warrant on a cocaine dealer's home and seized a lot of cash, Meyers found a plain white envelope in the pocket of his jacket that hung over the back of his chair. Not knowing what it was, he opened it, finding a thousand dollars in cash.

There was no writing on the envelope. Meyers's heart raced. He closed the envelope and hurriedly put it in his top middle desk drawer.

What the hell, he thought. Meyers left the office without the envelope.

On the way home to his wife and young daughters, Meyers stopped at the Red Barn Bar & Grill for a drink. After a quick shot of whiskey, he started to dial Gallon's cell phone, then hung up. Meyers and Gallon shared everything but Meyers wasn't sure what this was and he decided not to involve Thomas until he knew.

The next morning, Meyers opened his top drawer to find that the envelope was gone. His panic subsided. He breathed a sigh of relief. He checked again to make sure the envelope hadn't been pushed back in the drawer. He said nothing to Gallon.

A week later, the unit hit another house with a search warrant, again seizing drugs and cash. The next day, as Meyers prepared to leave for the evening, he opened his top desk drawer to retrieve his keys. This time he found two white envelopes. He closed the drawer and looked around the office. Only Sokol and Detective Rocco Morales—the senior detective after Sokol—were still in the office. He opened the drawer and without taking the envelopes out, opened them slightly to see that both held at least a thousand dollars in cash. He left the envelopes in his desk.

The next morning—after a sleepless night—when he walked through the door, Sokol summoned him into his office.

"Close the door, Chip," Sokol instructed. Meyers complied.

"Have a seat." Meyers sat in an old padded metal chair. "There's been some information given to me that one of my detectives is stealing money during search warrants." Sokol sat on the edge of his desk just two feet from Meyers. "Do you know anything about that, Meyers?" Sokol leaned forward into Chip's personal space.

"No, sir," Meyers assured him.

"Well then, you certainly don't mind if I go check your desk, do you?" Sokol said roughly as he stood up and moved toward the door. "If I find that someone is stealing money, that will be the end of their career. I hope it's not you, Meyers." The young detective knew that what he feared was true.

Meyers stood up and reached for the door handle, blocking Sokol from the door.

"Boss, I'm not stealing money and there's nothing in my desk," Meyers said. Sokol stepped back.

"Go ahead, check it if you want to," Meyers nervously offered.

Sokol put his hand on top of Chip's on the door handle, stepping uncomfortably close to him.

"Chip, do you see all those scum drug dealers every day, driving fancy cars, living in nice homes, screwing their pretty little coke whores and buying anything they want?"

Meyers listened.

"It's good to be us, Chip." Sokol grinned. "Now get the fuck out of my office . . . and buy your wife something nice on the way home."

Chip Meyers was on the take.

* * *

Several years later, Richie Sokol was promoted to Lieutenant. Morales had been promoted to Sergeant running the everyday operations of the narcotics unit. Morales stuck his head into Sokol's office.

"LT, you coming out with us tomorrow?"

"What are we hitting tomorrow, Rock?"

"Should be a good paper, boss. The guy is a main player with the Avenue Locos," Morales advised, referring to a violent local street gang. "I'm expecting to find a lot of dope in that house. Come on LT, it'll be a good one."

"All right Rock, I'll go. But I'm going in first. I'm not sitting on the sideline until you clear it," Sokol said, smiling.

"Briefing at oh-five-hundred, LT. See you then," Morales said, walking out of Sokol's office.

* * *

The APD narcotics unit staged at six a.m. down the street from a home on Irving Street in East Allentown, south of Dieruff High School. Surveillance units confirmed that Diego Perez, the local leader of the Avenue Locos street gang was home. In the van transporting the detectives to the target home, the tension was palpable. Each detective visualized their assignment one last time, and even the most experienced detectives felt the rumbling butterflies in their stomachs.

"Go! . . . Go!" Lt. Sokol's command reverberated inside the van as it raced north on Irving Street. With the cover of darkness, the narcs bailed out of the van and ran toward the house.

"Police! Open the door!"

Sokol waited a few seconds before giving Gallon the thumbs up signal to breach the front door.

The old white door was nearly obliterated with one swing of the heavy battering ram. Gallon pulled away quickly as Sokol and Meyers charged through the doorway.

"Police! Search warrant!" they shouted.

Sokol and Meyers moved quickly into the house, their weapons trained on the area illuminated by their flashlights directly in front of them. In the pitch-dark living room, they immediately came under fire.

Three shots, fired as fast as the shooter could pull the trigger, rang out from behind a wall partially dividing the front room from a back dining area. The bright muzzle flashes gave away the shooter's position.

"Shit!" Sokol screamed as the first bullet slammed into the thick ballistic vest covering his chest. The second bullet whizzed past his head, lodging in the door frame behind him. Still reacting to the initial impact on his vest, the third bullet ripped through his knee cap and exited the back of his leg. He dropped to his chest, screaming in pain.

"I'm hit! I'm hit bad!"

Meyers dropped to the floor and rolled to his left while Gallon took cover behind the door frame. Fearing for his life, Meyers rolled back to his feet and fired five shots at the incoming gunfire. He dove for cover, waiting for return fire. Sokol, writhing in pain and bleeding badly, tried to lay still.

Meyers screamed toward the interior of the home.

"Police! Drop your gun! Put it down now! Now!"

Gallon had retreated behind the wall. He knew Sokol was down. Stammering into his radio, his heart beating through his chest, he called for help.

"Officer down inside. Officer down."

He switched from his secure radio that broadcasted only to the narcotics unit to the general radio frequency.

"Officer down! 10-44! Officer down at six-five-nine North Irving Street! I need an ambulance now," Gallon's voice quivered.

Meyers knew Sokol was in trouble. Leaving his cover position, he crawled across the floor to where Sokol lay. Sokol was losing blood and going into shock.

"Hang on, LT," Meyers begged. "Where are you hit?"

A street light from across the street provided just enough light through the open doorway for Meyers to see the blood pouring from Sokol's leg onto the wooden floor. It also left them dangerously visible and exposed to the shooter. Meyers covered Sokol and continued to face the area from where the shots were fired.

Sokol grabbed Meyers's shirt sleeve, then passed out.

While Meyers covered Sokol's position, reinforcements arrived at the front door. Sgt. Morales and Detective Dailey flanked the entryway. There hadn't been a sound from deeper in the house since Meyers had returned fire.

Meyers signaled to Dailey who crawled through the door to where Sokol and Meyers lay on the floor. "Get him out of here," Meyers shouted. *Fuck the rules for a gunfight,* he thought. He fired five more shots toward the threat position covering Dailey as he pulled Sokol to safety. Morales yelled from the cover of the front door.

"Diego. Get your hands up, now. We're coming in."

The smell of gun powder wafted through the air. There was no sound—only the ringing in Meyers's ears.

Diego Perez had been dead for almost three minutes, killed instantly by Meyers's return fire. Lt. Sokol owed his life to Chip Meyers.

* * *

Chip Meyers sat next to Richie Sokol on a concrete and wood park bench in Trexler Memorial Park in the West End of Allentown, just a mile from Meyers's South Whitehall Township home. The 100-plus acre park was bequeathed by the family of General Harry C. Trexler, to the city of Allentown in 1934. General Trexler, a former Brigadier General of the

Pennsylvania National Guard, maintained a summer home on the land that now provided this beautiful expanse of nature for the city residents.

"I'm really scared, Richie," Meyers said. "These feds don't play around."

Meyers handed the folded grand jury subpoena to Sokol. Despite his recent move from the narcotics unit to the Mayor's office, Sokol remained the unit's de facto leader.

"Listen, Chip. You tell these guys nothing. There's no way they're onto us. This is some goddamn fishing expedition they're on." Sokol looked at the subpoena and handed it back to Meyers.

"Tell them to shove it up their ass!" Sokol said, raising his voice.

A passing runner glanced in their direction. Sokol glared at the jogger who quickly moved along.

"I know, Richie. But why me? Why are they targeting me?"

Sokol put his hand on Meyers's shoulder and looked him right in the eyes. "Chip, you listen to me. First it's you, then it's me. These guys have nothing. If they did we'd be in handcuffs. This is so much bigger than just you or me. You know that. We all have to keep this together."

"I hear you, Richie," Meyers said. "It'll be fine. I guess I needed to hear you tell me that. I don't want to be the only swinging dick that gets jacked up on this."

"Nobody's getting jacked up on anything," Sokol assured him. "Nobody did shit so there isn't anything to talk about anyway . . . right?" Sokol nodded.

Both men knew that was a bunch of shit. The APD narcotics unit was dirty from head to toe. The unit didn't just steal money from drug dealers and their families; after they stole it they used it to get whatever they wanted. Sokol knew there could be no chink in the armor.

"Go see this guy tomorrow." Sokol handed Meyers a business card. "Bill Kelly. He's a friend of the mayor's. A great lawyer. He'll get you through this grand jury thing without any mess. Just don't tell *him* shit either. If he asks, tell him you don't know why the fuck you got the subpoena."

Meyers took the card, looked at it then stuck it in his pocket.

"Call him. He'll be expecting your call."

"All right, Richie. Thanks."

Eight

CHIP MEYERS'S HAND trembled as he poured another glass of Scotch from the half-empty bottle on his desk. Slouching in his chair, he lifted the glass to his lips. He fumbled through some papers on the desk until he pulled one from a small manila folder. A green glass banker's lamp on his desk provided the only light to the otherwise dark home office. He leaned forward and focused on the one-page document. He lifted it off the desk, set it back down, then took another drink. The Allentown Police narcotics detective was inconsolable.

How the hell did this get to this point, he thought.

He looked at the document again, this time picking it up and holding it up to the light in front of him. Just a week earlier, life was good. Things were good at work and at home. Then the FBI agent showed up in his driveway last week with the federal grand jury subpoena. The female agent wasn't rude but got straight to the point. The feds were investigating corruption allegations in the police department and they wanted his cooperation. Meyers told the agent he knew nothing. That's when she dropped the subpoena on him. The subpoena required him to appear tomorrow to testify.

How could I have been put in this position? he wondered. *Who told them about me?* It's not that he knew nothing. Since the first day he took those envelopes, he had become a full partner in the corruption of the narcotics unit. He knew a lot. He just couldn't believe they were on to him. *What was going on? How could they know? Was someone in the unit talking?* Meyers had been agonizing over this for days and each day closer to his grand jury appearance made him worse.

Earlier that day, he had talked to attorney Bill Kelly. Kelly's plan was for Meyers to "take five" in the grand jury—to refuse to answer questions based on his Fifth Amendment right against self-incrimination. While he sat in Kelly's office, the attorney called the federal prosecutor, Thax Colby, to tell him Meyers would refuse to testify. That's when Colby told Kelly that Meyers would be compelled to testify by a grant of immunity, which would make self-incrimination impossible—he would not be able to hide behind the Fifth Amendment privilege. Now Chip's options were to lie and go to jail for perjury, refuse to say anything and be jailed for contempt, or the unthinkable—tell the grand jury what he knew. *At least the FBI agent hadn't served him at the office in front of everybody,* he thought.

Meyers finally broke down and told Gallon about the subpoena. Gallon knew what he and the other detectives in the unit had bought into when they started taking money.

"I knew someday someone was gonna start asking about this shit," Gallon told Meyers. "Who are they gonna believe, some piece of shit drug dealer or me?" Gallon asked. "As long as it's them against us and not us against us, everything is okay."

Meyers knew his friend was concerned—for Meyers and for everyone else.

Meyers wondered if anyone else in the unit got a subpoena. No one was talking if they did. If Sokol knew someone else got served with a subpoena he hadn't given that up.

Meyers took another drink of his Scotch and stared out the window. The moon was full, casting its light over the city. He closed his eyes hoping the Scotch would dull the torment and anguish he felt. In his self-imposed darkness, he heard a faint noise in the hallway outside his office.

"Dad," his fifteen-year-old daughter Katie whispered, sticking her head through the office doorway. "It's just me. I can't sleep."

Meyers looked at the small digital clock on his desk. It was twelve-thirty a.m. He tried to stand up, but stumbled catching himself on the arm of the chair.

"Are you sick, Dad?"

"No baby, Dad's fine. Why don't you get a drink?"

Meyers barely managed to make it to the kitchen. He steadied himself against the kitchen counter while Katie got a drink of water.

"There you go, sweetie. See you in the morning," he slurred. He kissed his oldest girl on the head and watched her disappear into her room down the hall. Tears welled up in his eyes. *How did I get myself into this mess?* he thought. *What a disgrace I will be to my family.* Two hours earlier he had kissed his wife Kristin goodnight. She knew something was wrong all week but he couldn't involve her in this. She never asked about the extra money and he never shared anything about it with her.

He stumbled back to his chair and fell into it. He gulped the last of the whiskey in his glass, then poured and downed another couple of ounces.

On the desk, his cell phone vibrated. He pulled it closer and recognized the number.

"Hey," he answered.

"Just checking on you. You okay?"

"This is pretty messed up, man."

"Look, you keep this shit to yourself. Nobody will get hurt. They got nothing unless someone talks."

"They're forcing me to talk," Meyers raised his voice.

"Hey. Don't say that shit. They can't *force* you to say anything."

"I don't know, man. I feel like a trapped rat. I'm in a box and I have nowhere to go."

"Listen, if anybody thinks you're gonna talk they'll come at you hard and fast. And there's nothing anyone can do to help you. Tell me you're not talking tomorrow and I'll say goodnight."

"Don't worry, man," Meyers answered. "Dead men can't talk." Meyers hung up.

He poured a few more ounces of Scotch into his glass and chugged the rest of it. He poured and drank another. From the top right drawer of the desk he pulled out a Colt blue steel .357 revolver. He laid it on the desk and reached for the bottle.

From the same drawer he retrieved a key—the key to a small credenza behind him. After fumbling to open the locked door on the front of the credenza, he located a blue, eight-and-a-half by eleven-inch spiral bound notebook. He grabbed it and closed the door.

Struggling to stay awake, he managed to set the notebook in front of him on the desk. Before he could open it, his upper body wavered from intoxication. He braced himself against the edge of the desk. His blurry eyes closed momentarily as he struggled to maintain consciousness. Then, forcing his eyes to open, his drunken gaze settled on the loaded firearm.

Nine

Kristin Meyers reached her arm across the bed for her husband. The covers on his side of the bed were undisturbed. Not even half awake, she looked at the digital clock on her night table. It was almost five-thirty a.m. If Kristin had not been wearing the earplugs she used every night because her husband was a serial snorer, she may have been awakened by the sound of a single shot from a handgun forty feet down the hall. Instead what she heard when she removed the earplugs was soft, muffled sobbing.

She rolled out of bed and grabbed her robe from the bottom of the king-size bed. The noises from down the hall grew louder. Through her bedroom door she saw light at the end of the hall near the home office. On the floor, in a fetal position, was her daughter Katie.

"Oh my God, Katie," she cried, running to her daughter. "What wrong?"

Katie was distraught and couldn't speak.

"What are you doing here? Why are you up?" Kristin probed for the reason for her daughter's distress. "Are you hurt?"

"Chip! Chip! Please help me!" she called, her voice growing more frantic as her daughter became less responsive. Kristin rushed to the door of the office looking for her husband.

"Chip!" she yelled again as she walked through the door.

Instead of a response from her husband, she saw her husband in his chair with blood everywhere and part of his head gone.

"Oh, no, God. No! No! No!" Kristin cried inconsolably.

She ran toward her husband, but could see from his lifeless body and the damage to it that he was dead. She backed out of the office, unable to take her eyes off Chip's body. She knew Katie had seen him. Her ten-year-old daughter, Erin, walked from her bedroom into the hall.

"What's the matter, Mom? Why are you crying?" Erin asked.

Kristin pulled Katie toward Erin, who continued to walk closer to them.

"Erin," Kristin tried to compose herself, "stay there. Don't come over here."

* * *

Like most other days, South Whitehall Township Detective Cole Hatten was awakened at five-thirty a.m. by a crazy German Shepherd he affectionately named Judge. Judge was a reliable alarm clock as Hatten didn't own a real one. After a quick fifty-yard walk with his dog, Hatten brewed a pot of coffee which he usually polished off while scanning the local news rag. A quick shower for him and a Milkbone and pat on the head for Judge, and he would be off to take on another day.

Hatten, now forty-eight, still lived in the same house he grew up in several miles west of Allentown. There were advantages and disadvantages to working as a cop in an area Hatten knew so well. On more than one occasion he arrested someone he grew up with or knew from school. A twenty-five-year veteran of police work, he began his career as a patrolman with the Allentown Police Department. After almost five years there, he earned his detective shield and worked in homicide. When the opportunity arose several years later to work with a smaller department in the township, he took it. Initially it meant going back to working in a uniform, which Hatten didn't mind at all. When one of the two homicide detectives retired six years ago, he was tapped for the slot.

Before he finished his second cup of coffee, his cell phone rang. It was his dispatch office calling.

"Where? Who called it in?" he asked. "I'll be there in fifteen."

* * *

Hatten made his way through the three marked South Whitehall Township patrol units and the yellow police tape outside the well maintained single story ranch home at 3771 Kensington Way a half mile west of the city. He reached into his jacket as he walked up the sidewalk to the front door where two uniform patrolmen stood. In a small department, everyone knew each other but Hatten pulled his badge from his jacket, snapped it to a lanyard and pulled it over his head so the gold shield hung from his neck onto his chest.

"What do we have, Kenny?" he asked the uniformed officer at the door.

"One down in the back office, Cole," the officer replied.

"Do we know who it is?"

"The wife identified him. Chip Meyers." The officer hesitated. "He's a cop in the city. Looks like a suicide."

"Anybody touch anything?" Hatten asked.

"Not a chance," the officer reported. "Just waiting on you and the coroner."

Hatten made his way from the front door toward the office near the back of the home. Walking into the hallway, he passed the family room where Kristin Meyers and her two girls sat on the couch quietly sobbing. Two uniformed officers tried to comfort them. He continued through the house and down the hall where he saw the officer at the door of the office.

"Morning." Hatten nodded. "Who responded to this?"

"I was the first one here, Cole," Patrolman Jake Young replied. "9-1-1 call came in about 5:40 a.m. Looks like the wife and older daughter found him."

Hatten looked into the office.

"Anybody been in there?"

"Just me. I went in to check him when I got here. He was obviously dead so I backed out and called it in. His wife says he's a detective with APD. Do you want me to contact somebody over there?"

Hatten thought for a second.

"Give me a few minutes in here to see what we have, then we'll get ahold of somebody."

Young nodded.

When Hatten entered the office, he saw Chip Meyers's body sitting in the high-backed leather chair behind a contemporary oak desk. The sun had risen enough to light the office through the windows on the wall to the right of where Hatten stood. Facing the scene from in front of the desk, Meyers's body slumped to the right in the chair and twisted slightly to the left. Hatten looked directly at an entrance wound on the right side of Meyers's head just in front of his right ear. On the wall to the right, following a pattern back to the chair, was splattered blood and pieces of Meyers's brain. Hatten walked around the desk to the left, being careful not to touch or disturb anything.

From the left side of the desk, he saw a .357 revolver still loosely clutched in Meyers's right hand. A green banker's light on the desk was still turned on. He observed a blue notebook and some other papers on the desk. A nearly empty bottle of Scotch whiskey sat to the right of the notebook, perhaps the liquid courage Meyers needed to end his life. The top of the desk was covered with blood backspatter, most likely from the entrance wound, he thought. He walked closer to Meyers's body. As often as he had to do this, it was never any easier. Hatten had to examine the body and the scene as a detective. He had to forget momentarily about the wife and young girls down the hall. His job was to determine what happened to this man—a brother police officer.

From behind the desk chair he looked at the exit wound. A large part of Meyers's head on the left side was gone from the top of his ear to the top of his scalp. This looked like a suicide.

He examined the papers on the desk. He searched for a note. He observed the blue notebook setting just to the left of the bottle of Scotch. With a pen he took from his jacket, he lifted the cover to see if there was anything written inside. There was nothing. On the far left side of the desk was a letter-sized manila folder. The folder was also covered with blood spatter. Cole lifted the edge of the folder with his pen. The top document in the folder looked like a subpoena. He examined it closer. The federal grand jury subpoena required the dead man in the chair to appear to testify today.

Hatten looked at his watch. It was a few minutes before seven o'clock. Chip Meyers would not be making his nine-thirty a.m. date with the federal grand jury. He read further. The subpoena had been issued by Assistant U.S. Attorney Thax Colby.

Hatten looked up to see Lehigh County Coroner Hilbert Chase walking into the room. Dr. Chase, a physically fit man in his mid-sixties, habitually adorned in his misty green surgical scrubs, walked past the officer at the door. Chase's distinctly European features were accented by his short salt-and-pepper hair and his not so well maintained bushy silver eyebrows.

"Doc," Hatten said with surprise. "I didn't expect the big boss today." Chase had a staff of deputy coroners who usually responded to death scenes.

"Hey, Cole. Well, I happened to be coming in this direction and you know I am an early bird so I thought I'd take the call. What do we have?" Chase asked, walking toward the body.

He surveyed the body from close up.

"Looks like a contact burn on the right side of his head." Chase observed the star-shaped entry wound. "Probably from that .357 there in his hand." He walked around to get a good look at the exit wound.

"The exit wound, slightly higher than the entrance wound. Consistent with an upward shot from the right hand."

Chase knelt to look at the gun in Meyers's hand.

"We'll bag those hands to test for gunshot residue," he told Hatten. "I don't see any signs of a struggle, do you Cole?" Chase continued without waiting for Hatten to answer. "Did he leave a note?"

"I didn't find any in here," Hatten answered.

"Looks like he numbed himself with that," Chase pointed to the whiskey bottle, "and turned his lights out with that," pointing to the gun in Meyers's hand.

"Give me a few minutes, Cole, and I'll get you an approximate time of death."

"I'll be back in a few," Hatten said, walking toward the door. A photographer arrived from the coroner's office.

"Glad you could make it," Chase chided the young man. Hatten quietly laughed at Chase's crotchety demeanor.

* * *

Hatten walked into the family room of the Meyers's home. Kristin Meyers sat holding her children. She had barely moved since he saw her almost twenty minutes earlier. Officer Sherry Krause continued to console them.

Officer Kent Newman approached the detective.

"What do we know?" Hatten asked.

"The wife says when she got out of bed she heard her daughter crying. The older daughter, her name is Katie, she woke up and walked down the hall where she found her dad dead. That's coming from Mom. No one has tried to talk to the kids yet."

"What else?" Hatten snapped.

"Well, there's no sign of forced entry. She says she knew he had killed himself when she saw his head and the gun. She tried to get the kids away and called 9-1-1. She said he's been really disturbed by something the last week or so but didn't share it with her. He was hitting the bottle pretty hard when she said goodnight last night . . . Oh, you know he's a detective at APD. Narcotics. She hasn't called anyone from there yet."

"I know." Hatten replied. "I'm gonna call there in a few minutes."

Hatten walked over to Kristin and her daughters.

"Mrs. Meyers, my name is Cole Hatten. I'm very sorry for your loss. We're going to do everything we can to find out what happened to your husband," he placed his hand on hers to comfort her. She sniffled, trying to gain her composure.

"Thank you," she mouthed.

"Do you think you can answer a few questions for me?"

Kristin nodded.

"Did you see the gun in your husband's hand?"

She nodded again.

"Is that your husband's gun?"

Kristin looked down and nodded. "He kept it in the office."

"Just one more question." Hatten knew Kristin was not doing well. "Did you know what your husband was supposed to testify about before a federal grand jury this morning?"

Kristin looked up, directly at Hatten.

"What?" She looked dazed. "Why would he do that?" Kristin asked, shaking her head.

"I don't know."

Hatten put a business card in Kristin's hand. "Call me if you need anything."

Hatten walked toward the hallway where Officer Newman stood. "Who's your Sergeant today?" he asked.

"It's Kyle Foster."

"Call him now. Tell him we have an APD detective down on a probable suicide and to wake the Chief. Then have him call APD and notify them ASAP. And this information, about an APD officer down, goes nowhere else. Understood?"

"Yes, sir."

* * *

Hatten walked into the office as the coroner's people were removing Meyers's body from the room. The photographer was finishing up with photos of the room and the desk area. Crime scene technicians from South Whitehall Township P.D. had arrived to recover and bag evidence.

"Doc, do you have a time of death for me?"

"Best I can do right now is probably between one and two o'clock this morning. I'll get to work on this one as soon as I can." Chase walked out the office door behind the collapsible ambulance gurney holding Meyers's body.

Hatten approached the crime scene technicians who were finishing their processing of the scene. The technicians, wearing gloves, were collecting items from the desk. One reached for the manila folder.

"Can I see that before you bag it?" Hatten asked. The technician handed Hatten a pair of latex gloves. He put them on and opened the folder.

Hatten looked closer at the grand jury subpoena. He took a pocket-sized notebook from his jacket and jotted down some information from the subpoena. He briefly looked through the other documents. Nothing else looked important.

He looked at the blue, spiral notebook. Carefully opening it, he examined it without moving it. He observed some small remnants of paper inside the metal spirals, the kind left behind when pages were torn from the notebook. He looked through the book, page by page, for the first ten pages. He found nothing.

"Make sure you get good pictures of all of the other documents in that folder," Hatten instructed the technicians.

* * *

"United States Attorney's Office, how may I direct your call?" the receptionist answered.

"Assistant U.S. Attorney Thax Colby, please. This is Detective Cole Hatten."

"One moment please," the receptionist replied.

"This is Thax Colby," Thax answered.

"Mr. Colby, this is Detective Cole Hatten from the South Whitehall Township Police Department. I'm in homicide."

"What can I do for you, Detective?" Thax glanced at the clock on his wall. It was eight-fifty a.m.

"Chip Meyers is dead," Hatten replied. "And, according to the subpoena on his desk, he was supposed to appear before a grand jury today."

Thax was stunned. "What happened? How did he die?"

"It looks like he killed himself."

Thax hesitated, collecting himself, "When did this happen?"

"This morning. At his home . . . Mr. Colby, I don't know what you've got going and mostly I don't care. But I thought you needed to know this right away. I don't know if this has anything to do with your subpoena but I didn't fall off the turnip truck yesterday either." Hatten paused. "I'm glad to help you with anything you need."

"Thank you, Detective. Let me deal with this here in my office and I'll be in touch."

"You know how to get me." Hatten hung up.

Thax looked up to see Campisano and Barrows standing in his doorway.

"What's up?" Campisano asked.

Thax hesitated. "Chip Meyers is dead."

* * *

Thax contemplated the news of Detective Chip Meyers's death. After a long discussion, he and Agents Campisano and Barrows agreed to meet the following day to discuss their strategy for the corruption investigation. Thax's cell phone rang. He recognized the number as Chrissy's.

"Hey there," he answered.

"Hey there to you, too. I'm on my way to South Whitehall. Did you hear about the police officer suicide?"

"I did hear something about that."

"I bet you did," Chrissy responded. "Seriously, do you know who this guy is? My sources are telling me he was an undercover narcotics detective from Allentown P.D. . . . Chip Meyers. Ever heard of him?"

Thax ignored the question. "What else are your sources telling you?"

"You didn't answer my question. Do you know this guy?" her voice tensed.

"Chrissy, you know I couldn't tell you if I did."

"You do know this guy! And there's more to it, isn't there? I can hear it in your voice." She probed for more.

"Just report what you know," Thax said.

"Listen mister, when you swap spit with me I at least hope you trust me enough to tell me what's going on. I'm not going to report anything you tell me if it's off-the-record."

Thax said nothing.

"Okay," Chrissy said, obviously frustrated, "I guess you don't know anything about it then."

Thax still said nothing.

"All right, Thax. I'm working late tonight so I probably *won't* see you later. I guess it'll just be you and your teddy bear tonight. Ciao!"

* * *

Chrissy stood outside the Meyers home in South Whitehall Township as the sun waned in the sky behind her. At the top of the six o'clock news the anchors cut to her.

"This is Chrissy Barnes for Valley 10 News with breaking news at the home of Allentown Police Detective Chip Meyers who apparently died at his own hands this morning, police sources are saying. Meyers, a narcotics detective for many years, lived in this home behind me with his wife and two young daughters. Allentown Police Chief Scott Butler called the death a horrible tragedy. Chief Butler said no one at APD had any reason to believe anything was troubling the experienced detective. Other law enforcement sources we spoke to on the condition of anonymity believe Meyers may have been the subject of an investigation by authorities, but could not confirm the existence or reason for an investigation. This morning the Lehigh County Coroner removed Meyers's body from the home where he lived for almost fourteen years. The coroner refused to comment on the case, but sources close to this investigation are telling us Meyers shot himself with his own gun early this morning. We will keep you updated as we learn more. This is Chrissy Barnes. Back to you."

Ten

DETECTIVE HATTEN STRODE down the main hallway of the old Lehigh County Courthouse Building to Coroner Hilbert Chase's office. A drab looking young man in the reception area verified Hatten's credentials and escorted him to Chase's office.

"Come on in Detective. Have a seat," Chase said, motioning for Hatten to sit in one of the uncomfortable looking metal chairs in front of his large metal desk.

"Nice digs, Doc." Hatten couldn't resist the sarcasm.

"I know. I know. But it's home." Chase played along.

Hatten sat as Chase opened a drawer from a solitary four-drawer gray metal filing cabinet behind his desk. He pulled out a file and sat in his equally cozy looking chair behind the desk.

"I guess you want to know COD, Detective?"

"What can you tell me?"

Chase opened the folder and looked at a three-page report.

"In English please, Doc. I flunked anatomy in high school," Hatten joked.

"Well, estimated time of death is between 1:00 a.m. and 2:00 a.m. Cause of death was a single penetrating gunshot wound to the right side of the head, entered just below and slightly forward of the ear. Exit wound on the left side of the head above the left ear. The velocity of the bullet and the gases, expanded his brain and blew out the top side of his head. Projectile was a .357 caliber which matches the gun found in the victim's hand."

"What else, Doc?"

"This was a pressed contact gunshot wound to the head. When the barrel of a handgun is held firmly against skin the gases from the muzzle force under the skin, causing it to balloon out and tear, leaving a starlike tearing wound in the skin around the entrance wound. That's what this was," Chase explained.

"And." Hatten waited for Chase to continue.

"And there was powder, gunshot residue on his right hand consistent with him firing the fatal shot. And there are no signs of any struggle—no scratches, open wounds, skin under fingernails. No defensive wounds of any kind."

"Anything else?"

"Your man blew his brains out. How's that for plain English?" Chase said abruptly.

"Doc, I'm sorry to press you like this. I just need to be sure. You understand."

"I do, Detective. There is one more thing. His blood alcohol was .29 percent. Probably drank that whole bottle of whiskey before he shot himself."

"Thanks, Doc. Can I get a copy of that report?" Hatten asked as he stood up to leave.

"Take this one." Chase handed the report to Hatten.

Chase stood up and shook Hatten's hand. "Call me if you have any questions."

* * *

"Are you expecting Detective Cole Hatten?" Abigail Sutton, Thax's legal secretary, stuck her head around the corner of the door into his office.

"I am. Can you please bring him back?"

A minute later Abigail showed Hatten into Thax's office.

"Detective, come on in," Thax met him at the door and shook his hand. "Please. Have a seat."

"Thanks for seeing me, Mr. Colby." Hatten sat in one of the chairs in front of Thax's desk.

"I wanted to let you know what's going on with the Meyers investigation. I don't know what you can tell me. I know you guys don't like to involve locals in your investigations. Believe me. I understand. I'm not asking you to do that Mr. Colby—"

"It's Thax," Thax interrupted.

Hatten nodded and continued.

"Thax, I obviously don't know why you subpoenaed Chip Meyers to the grand jury, but I'm guessing it wasn't to ask him if he copped a feel with his girlfriend in the ninth grade. I know you don't need to tell me why. What I need to tell you is that the coroner is calling this a suicide."

"Well, from what I hear that's what everyone is saying. Are you telling me it wasn't a suicide?"

"I can't tell you that, Thax. But I guess if I knew what you were after in the grand jury it might tell me if someone had a reason to kill Chip Meyers and make it *look* like a suicide."

Thax stared at Hatten. He wasn't permitted to tell him anything about the grand jury investigation.

"Do you have some reason, other than just a hunch, that Chip Meyers was murdered?"

Hatten opened a black faux leather case that held his iPad.

"I want to show you something." Hatten stood up and walked to the side of Thax's desk.

Hatten pulled up a picture of the blue notebook.

"Do you see this notebook? It was on the desk in front of Meyers when he died. Do you see the blood spatter on it, all over the front cover?"

Thax looked intently at the screen.

"This is the back of the notebook," Hatten explained, displaying a photograph of the plain brown backing of the notebook. "Do you see those marks?" Hatten asked, pointing to numerous small spots on the back of the notebook. "Those are blood marks. How did they get there?"

Thax looked closer.

"What I'm saying is, the notebook was on the desk, with the back against the desk top. Meyers shoots himself and blood spatter goes everywhere on the desk, but how did the blood get on the *back* of the notebook?"

"I'll tell you how," Hatten continued. "Somebody picked up the notebook and set it back down on blood spatter that was on the desk. It's the only explanation."

"Are you sure the crime scene people weren't just sloppy about this? I'm not saying they were—"

"No. Look at this picture." Hatten displayed a photo of the desk with the notebook still in place. "Look at the spatter to the left of the notebook. Do you see it? It's looks different than the spatter over there on the desk." Hatten pointed to an area on the other side of the manila folder.

"I think somebody killed Chip Meyers. The same person who moved that notebook."

"What was in the notebook?"

"Well, at first, I didn't think there was anything. I thought maybe Meyers was going to write a suicide note but there wasn't a pen or pencil anywhere on the desk," Hatten explained. "When I looked at the notebook at the scene, the only thing I saw was blank pages. It looked like some pages had been ripped out but there's no telling when or why.

My crime scene guys looked at every page and this is what they found on the second to last page in the notebook." Hatten displayed another photo of the page of the notebook. The page read:

Harlin 20,000 10/12 E.S.

"I have no idea what this means or if it means *anything.*" Hatten shrugged. "I thought it might mean something to you."

Thax grabbed a legal pad and scribbled down the notations from the notebook.

"Can you email me a copy of that?" Thax asked.

"Absolutely."

Thax thanked Hatten for the information.

"We'll keep in touch," Thax assured him as he walked him to the exit doors.

Eleven

Logan Branfield gazed out the large window behind his desk in his City Hall office. The sky was overcast. Branfield liked it that way.

"Damn shame about our detective," the mayor commented with an obvious lack of sincerity.

Richie Sokol stood to the right side of Branfield's desk, watching and listening. Two of the things he did best.

"Yes, it is, sir," Sokol replied. "He was a good man. I brought him to the narcotics unit years ago."

Branfield turned toward Sokol.

"Like I said, damn shame. Will you make sure his wife gets some nice flowers from me?" Sokol was the mayor's bodyguard but took care of everything like his chief of staff.

"Already taken care of, boss," Sokol assured the mayor.

"Good. I guess since he killed himself the family didn't want a full-blown police funeral." The mayor sat down in his beautiful high-backed leather executive chair.

"Well, the family usually likes to keep things quiet when a cop takes his own life. Embarrassment. Sign of weakness. No one wants to have to deal with all those questions," Sokol explained.

Sokol reached into his suit jacket and pulled out a white envelope. He tossed it on Branfield's desk.

"I can tell how heartbroken you are. Maybe that will make you feel a little better," Sokol said motioning to the envelope.

Branfield picked up the envelope and peered at the cash inside.

"A *little* better is right," Branfield said in a concerned voice. "Things a little slow out there in my city, Richie?" Branfield asked, holding up the envelope.

"Well, we have had a few bumps in the road this last week or so." Sokol glared at the mayor.

"I understand, Richie." Branfield tried to sound sympathetic.

"Every week can't be a good week, can it?" Sokol asked.

"Well, it can in my fucking city," Branfield scolded as he stuffed the envelope into the top left drawer of his desk.

"Thanks for the lunch money, Richie."

Branfield got up from his chair and walked over to Sokol. He put his arm around Sokol's shoulder and walked him to the office door.

"I've got some other business to take care of, Richie, so I have to kick you out now. I don't have anything to worry about here in my home city, do I?"

"No, sir," Sokol answered. "I think we're good."

"That's great, Richie, but I don't pay you to *think* we're good. Make sure we are."

Sokol opened the door leading out of the mayor's office. In front of him stood an attractive young woman holding a notepad.

"Have you met our new intern, Richie?"

Sokol nodded politely at the sultry, raven-haired college student.

"Come on in, dear." Branfield motioned to her, closing his office door behind them.

* * *

"What's our next move, Thax?" Campisano inquired. He sat on the front of his chair, anxiously awaiting Thax's response. Barrows sat next to him. The office door was closed.

"I can't believe this guy offed himself because of a grand jury subpoena," Campisano commented. "He could have just come in, been stand-up, and told us to go screw ourselves. It doesn't make any sense."

"Well, Detective Hatten doesn't think it makes sense either. The coroner ruled it a suicide but he's not buying it. At least that's what he's telling me," Thax said. "Hatten showed me a notebook that was on the desk in the office where Meyers died. There was blood spatter all over the desk. But somehow, a bunch of blood spatter got on the back of the notebook. He thinks someone might have moved the notebook after Meyers was killed."

"Does he have some reason why someone would do that?" Barrows asked. "What was in the notebook?"

"I don't know why he thinks someone would move it, but he did find something very interesting written on a page near the back of the book. Take a look at this." Thax handed the agents a copy of the page Hatten had emailed him.

They studied the notations on the page:

Harlin 20,000 10/12 E.S.

"What does he think this means?" Campisano asked.

"He has no idea, but he thought we should see it," Thax answered. "He said there were some pages ripped out of the notebook but no one could say when or why. This is the only thing written in it."

"Well?" Thax looked to Barrows who was already brainstorming, examining the entries.

"Okay." She looked at Chris then Thax. "Our theory is that the narcotics unit is stealing money from drug dealers. We thought Dailey and Meyers stole money from a search warrant. Then we have the 'fake warrant' at the Karopolis house. Well, what if 'Harlin' is a drug defendant and the '20,000' is money they took from him? Seems like a logical place to start."

Barrows had everyone's attention.

"What about the other notations?" Campisano asked.

"I don't know. I'm just thinking out loud, Chris," Barrows answered.

"Unfortunately, Lehigh County doesn't have public records access for criminal cases. We're going to have to go to the Clerk's Office to search this." Thax looked at Campisano.

"Don't look at me! I can barely send an email," Campisano joked.

"It needs to be you, Christopher. I'm sure there's some pretty clerk who would love to help a poor DEA agent look up some old drug cases." Thax chuckled. "The FBI over there is really going to raise some eyebrows."

"Okay. I'll get it done," Campisano relented.

"Good." Thax moved on. "I think DEA needs to push this issue of Dailey and the missing money with APD internal affairs. I don't know if it will shake anything out of the trees, but at a minimum it will put some heat on these guys."

"I'm on that too." Campisano nodded. "I'll get the Group Supervisor to send something over to Chief Butler and follow it up with a phone call. The more I think about that the more it pisses me off. The guy's a piece of shit. Don't worry, I'll get that going right away. What else?"

"I think we need to turn up the heat on Detective Schick. We've got enough with Mr. Karopolis's ID to at least take a run at him. Shea, I think you and I should have a chat with him."

"How do you want to do that?"

"I'm not sure yet," Thax answered. "Either individually or collectively, we've hit a big nerve with that unit. Meyers kills himself rather than show up at the grand jury? If that's what happened, he had to be feeling a lot of pressure from someone or a bunch of someones not to talk. If Hatten is right and this isn't what it looks like, then somebody *stopped* Meyers from talking, with a bullet. I want to put the fear of God into these people but we don't need any more bodies. I want people in handcuffs, not body bags."

Barrows and Campisano agreed.

"I'll call you tomorrow or Monday, Shea, and let you know where and how I want to do this."

"Okay, sounds like a plan."

The agents got up to leave.

"Looks like it's gonna rain all weekend," Campisano warned.

"What? You don't think I can fish in the rain." Thax laughed.

"I think you would probably fish in a hurricane, buddy."

"Amen . . . and I'm leaving my phone in the Jeep."

* * *

Detective Hatten rang the doorbell at 3771 Kensington Way. Kristin Meyers answered the door.

"Mrs. Meyers, I'm Detective Hatten. I don't know if you remember me?"

"Of course, Detective. Please come in," Kristin spoke in a soft voice, allowing Hatten into the house. She walked into the family room and sat on a floral-patterned wing back chair, inviting Hatten to sit in the chair next to her.

"Mrs. Meyers, I wanted to make sure you were okay and that you were being kept informed about things. Again, I'm very sorry for your loss."

Kristin didn't respond.

"I also wanted to tell you that I've spoken to the coroner and he's ruled your husband's death a suicide."

Hatten could see how difficult this was for her. Kristin broke down, then regained her composure.

"I just don't know why Chip would do this to us. We had such a good life. It's so hard for me to believe he would do this."

"I understand," Hatten said. He tried to comfort her. "I'm still investigating even though the coroner is done . . . Do you know of anyone who would want to hurt your husband?"

"He was a good detective. I'm sure there are a lot of people who he arrested, but none that I know of who ever threatened him," Kristin explained. "At least he never told me anyone threatened him."

"That was my next question."

Hatten reached into a folder he was carrying and pulled out a picture. He handed it to Kristin.

"Have you ever seen that blue notebook?"

"No. What is that?"

"This notebook was on the desk in the office," Hatten explained.

She looked at the photo again, shaking her head. "I've never seen it before."

"I know I asked you this the day I was here, but did your husband say anything to you about testifying before a grand jury? Anything at all?"

"No. What was that all about?"

"Well, frankly, I don't know. The feds don't share much about things like that, but I was wondering if he had mentioned it."

Kristin, still shaken, lowered her head and cried.

"My daughter, Katie, has nightmares every night," she sniffled. She grabbed a tissue from a box setting next to her on the chair.

"What kind of nightmares?"

"I haven't slept either unless I take one of those." Kristin pointed to a prescription bottle of Valium on the table in front of the couch, ignoring the question. "Every night I find her in the hallway outside the office, sobbing and shaking, and staring down the hall toward the back door. I think she's waiting for her dad to appear down there. It's horrible."

Hatten didn't want to impose much longer on the grieving family.

"Thank you for your time, Mrs. Meyers," he said rising from his chair. "If you need anything, please call me. I'll check back with you in a few days. I hope your daughter gets better. I'm sure she will as time goes by. I'd like to talk to her sometime when you feel she's up to it."

Kristin nodded as Hatten walked with her toward the front door. He stopped briefly and looked into the dining room. In the center of the table was a stunning floral arrangement of blue hydrangea, crème roses and white oriental lilies in a gorgeous cobalt blue glass vase.

"Those are really beautiful," Hatten said.

"They're from the mayor," Kristin replied.

"Beautiful," Hatten repeated.

"Thank you again, Detective," she said as Hatten walked out.

Twelve

A LIGHT, BUT STEADY, rain danced on the surface of the Little Lehigh River. July brought warmer weather to the Lehigh Valley but with it, more rain. Surely some summer picnics were cancelled and more than one family's plans for a day of fun at Dorney Park, the local amusement park, were dashed by the slow but constant downpour.

Thax found himself this early Saturday morning wading quietly under a canopy of willow and live oak trees stalking wild brown trout. When he arrived at the parking area near the weathered stone building, not even Old Ronnie had shown his face yet. The morning sun crept steadily above the horizon casting a glow over the surface of the river. A small rainbow appeared as the huge orange globe rose toward the clouds through the rain.

He enjoyed this time of day the most.

Thax fished from the concrete bridge upstream to the two giant willows. His morning was productive—two fourteen-inch brown trout caught and released. The trout were lucky. Few criminals caught by the prosecutor had enjoyed the freedom of release. By ten-thirty, he made his way out of the water and walked toward the parking lot. The rain was much lighter and broken. He stuck his head into the stone house to say hello to Ronnie.

"Morning, old man," Thax said playfully.

Ronnie, who was sitting at his work bench tying flies, looked up to see Thax. He looked over his shoulder, then behind him.

"Oh, you're not talking to me, Thax, are you?" Ronnie jabbed back.

"You're the only old man I see in here, buddy." Thax grinned. "Beautiful morning, huh?"

"If you're a duck, I guess. You catch anything?"

"Just a couple of nice brownies."

Ronnie shook his head and focused his attention back to the fly he was working on at the work bench.

Ronnie looked up at Thax. "Tricos?"

"As a matter of fact—"

"Good call, Thax—"

"—No." Thax couldn't resist the jab.

"No?" Ronnie asked again.

"Caught them with a Royal Wullf."

Ronnie sneered.

"That red floss band flashes when it hits the broken water buddy," Thax explained, referring to the small red band around the body of the Royal Wulff fly. The fly was originally created for rivers in New York's Adirondack mountains. Thax liked them just fine for these waters too, especially in the rain.

"Snaps those big browns right out of their holes," Thax boasted. "What can I say?"

Ronnie said nothing but continued working on tying the fly in front of him. Thax perused the array of flies in the small wooden display boxes.

"You just gonna let that pretty girl sit down there in the rain, Thax?" Ronnie spoke without looking up.

"What?"

"She was looking for you." Ronnie finally looked up.

Thax walked toward the door. "Why didn't you say something when I walked in here? How long has she been here?" Thax walked through the door and saw Chrissy's blue Jeep parked next to his in the parking lot. He looked downstream toward the concrete bridge. On the other side of the gravel roadway leading to the bridge was a green picnic table. On Sunday mornings, some of the local senior anglers would hold "church" meetings there. Their only prayers were for bigger fish.

Thax grabbed his fly rod and walked in that direction. A slow and steady rain had resumed. As he got closer he saw Chrissy sitting on the top of the table facing the river, with her feet on the bench seat of the picnic table. The light-blue jacket she wore over a T-shirt was soaked. Her blue faded jeans were drenched.

"And I thought those brown trout were the most beautiful thing on the river today," Thax spoke as Chrissy looked in his direction.

"Hey there," Chrissy responded. "Can't a girl get a little sun on the weekend?" She smiled.

Thax sat next to her on the table. He reached for Chrissy's hand and grasped it.

"How's your teddy bear?" Chrissy raised her eyebrows and squeezed Thax's hand.

"He doesn't miss you as much as I do. I'm pretty sure of that," Thax said softly. "Are you still mad at me?"

"No, Thax. I'm mad *about* you, not at you."

Chrissy turned and hugged him.

'Now . . . what are we going to do about it?" Chrissy asked pulling back enough to look into Thax's eyes. Thax looked at her then gazed at the river.

"I know there are things you can't tell me," Chrissy said. "Like stuff that goes on in the grand jury."

Thax turned toward Chrissy.

She looked serious. "What? You think you're the first prosecutor I've played around with?"

She had Thax's attention.

"Well . . . you are and I don't want to mess this up . . . but I don't want to be in the dark either."

Thax stood up and took a few steps toward the river. The rain had increased the flow over the turbulent slide of rocks directly in front of him. He stood and watched. Chrissy was quiet.

"Chip Meyers was a dirty cop. I was investigating him and some of the other detectives in that unit. I still am."

"Do you think that's why he killed himself?" Chrissy asked.

"I don't know. Why does a man—a seasoned veteran detective—blow his brains out when he can just come in and deny his involvement? The coroner says it was suicide, but I'm not buying that yet."

Chrissy got up and walked to Thax putting her arm around him. She knew how hard it was for him to share this information.

"It looks like this whole damn unit could be dirty," he said, exasperated. "Things are going to start getting really ugly, which is another reason why I was trying to protect you from all of it."

"Tell me how I can help."

"I need to show you something. I don't have it here. Chip Meyers had a notebook and I have a page from it."

Chrissy's eyes got big. "What's on it?"

"I have to show it to you, but . . . I'm dead serious. What I talk to you about . . . can never be a source of information for your work."

"And it never will be. I promise you." She leaned toward Thax and kissed him.

"Let's go." Thax tugged on Chrissy's hand as they started toward the parking lot. "We need to get you out of those wet clothes."

* * *

Chrissy tossed her wet jeans onto Thax's bathroom floor. The hot steam from the running shower filled the room moistening her already soft skin.

She pulled Thax close and kissed him.

"I thought you were going to take a shower," he said softly.

"Shut up and kiss me," she begged.

His hands cradled her face—brushing her drenched blonde hair behind her ears. He kissed her forehead, then her cheeks and finally her mouth. They kissed tenderly, then more urgently.

With his right hand he unsnapped her bra—a quick release he had perfected with his steady girl long ago in high school. He nuzzled Chrissy's face and kissed her again.

Pulling his T-shirt over his head, he threw it to the floor. His bare chest pressed against hers.

"Get these off," she whispered, pushing her hands down inside his jeans.

He quickly removed his pants.

He drew her body closer—but not close enough. It had never felt close enough. He caressed her sides and hips until his long fingers slid under the thin straps of her thong panties. He started to pull them down, then hesitated.

He searched Chrissy's face. Her soft emerald eyes told him to keep going.

Slowly, he pulled the thong down her legs, dropping to his knees. His soft sensual kisses swirled against her just below her navel. He grabbed her bottom and pulled her into him.

Her heart raced wildly.

Her body tensed.

She closed her eyes.

Her fingers shuddered as they stretched out through his hair.

"Come here," she moaned, slowly moving backward toward the vanity. Thax stood up, his hands tracing her body along the way.

She wrapped her arms around his neck and gave him a fiery kiss while tugging at his boxer-briefs until they dropped to the floor.

Her slender body arched back onto the vanity's granite countertop pulling him in. With her legs straddling his waist—her ankles crossed and locked behind his lower back—she squeezed him until he pushed inside of her.

"Take me to bed, fly boy . . ."

Thirteen

THAX WALKED THROUGH the door of his office and flipped the light switch. He took off his suit jacket and hung it on a government issued single-prong bronze coat hanger on the back of his door. He loosened his top button and tie. He was walking around his desk when his secretary, Abigail, stepped into his office.

"Chris Campisano called and wanted to know where you've been." Abigail looked amused. Thax glanced at his watch. It was eight twenty-five.

Abigail was dressed in her usual professional manner. Short skirt. Classy blouse. Very expensive Louboutin six-inch stiletto heels. Her shoulder length curly brunette locks bobbed when she turned her head toward Thax.

"He said he called earlier and no one answered," she continued.

Thax looked at his watch again, this time looking at Abigail so she would see him doing so.

"It's not even eight thirty. I didn't think they let DEA agents in the building before ten," Thax joked. The DEA agents Thax knew were not early risers.

"What did you tell him?"

"I told him you and I had been here for a while, but neither one of us must have had a free hand to answer the phone." Abigail smiled wickedly. Thax laughed.

Abigail was smart, sassy and sexy—a lethal combination—and she could hold her own with any of the cocky federal agents who passed her desk to flirt with her. She fended off more passes than an NFL defensive back.

"You're too funny." Thax smiled.

"I know." Abigail smiled and rolled her eyes. "Anyway, he's on his way up."

She turned her head to look down the hallway and found Campisano at the door. "Speak of the devil. I'll leave you two boys to your work."

Abigail moved aside to let Campisano walk through the door.

"Good morning," Campisano greeted Abigail with a smile. "I see your hands are free now," Campisano teased.

Abigail looked at Campisano and raised her right hand, flipping her middle finger. "This one is." Thax chuckled. Abigail closed the door behind her.

"What's going on?" Thax asked Campisano as he settled into his chair.

"Good stuff. Wait until you hear this."

"It must be if you had to tell me first thing. What is it?"

"Do you know Walt McConnell from ATF?"

"Sure I do. I've worked with him on a bunch of things before. A really good agent."

"Well, he and I were at a retirement party on Monday for Connie Andrews from DEA in Philly. We worked with her on a big investigation about five years back. Anyway, we're sitting at the bar after the party, shooting the shit, when he tells me this story about how ATF almost got into a shootout over in East Allentown a few months ago." Campisano leaned forward in his chair.

"So I said 'How the hell did that happen and why didn't anyone else hear about it?' And then he told me the story."

"Which I'd like to hear," Thax interjected. Campisano never told a story quick enough for Thax's liking.

"ATF had a confidential informant—a guy named Harman—who got approached by a guy named Danny Price. Price is a member of the East Side Boyz gang in East Allentown. They sell dope over there off Union Boulevard between Airport Road and Club Avenue. Price wanted to pick up some powerful hardware—AK-47s, AR-15s—whatever Harman could get him. So ATF does their homework on Price and it looks like he's got a felony conviction about eight years ago for burglary. He got probation for it. He has a couple of recent arrests for drugs but nothing that stuck, so he's still walking around gang banging."

Campisano had Thax's attention.

Thax brustled through some papers on his desk and grabbed a legal pad.

"So," Campisano continued, "Price is a felon and ATF is looking to pop him for being a felon in possession of a firearm. Harman makes a couple of controlled phone calls to Price, who is pretty savvy. He won't talk any shit on the phone. But they decide to reverse Price by selling him some AK's. Once he takes possession and pays Harman the money, they're going to arrest him. Case closed."

Campisano paused.

"Keep going," Thax said.

"Here's where it gets interesting. On the day of the deal, Harman meets with Price in Woodlawn Memorial Park on the East Side. Harman pulls up in his car with the guns and Price shows up in his car. Price waves Harman over and shows him a backpack with the money—three thousand dollars. Price hands the money to Harman who carries it back to his car. Harman then opens his trunk and Price comes over to check out the guns. Harman unwraps a blanket concealing the three AK-47s. Everything is good to go and Price carries the AK-47s in the blanket back to his car and puts them in the trunk. When Price starts driving away, ATF takes him down."

"Sounds like they burned their informant."

"That's okay. The guy was going to be relocated anyway. But that's not the problem."

"Well, what *is* the problem?"

"When the ATF agents jump out to arrest Price, all of a sudden there are other guys with guns jumping out of cars screaming and pointing guns at them. It's almost like Doc Holliday at the O.K. Corral. Everybody's screaming 'police' and pointing guns at each other. It's amazing no one got shot. Amazing."

"What the hell?" Thax asked in disbelief.

"When everybody puts their guns down and stops yelling at each other it turns out the other guys are APD *narcotics detectives*."

"Get the hell out of here."

"Walt, who is the senior guy for ATF on the scene, talks with their guy in charge. *Sergeant Rocco Morales,*" Campisano said. "Morales tells Walt that *Price* is *their* confidential informant and that they thought Price was buying guns from another bad guy—Harman. Morales explains to Walt that the narcotics unit doesn't usually get involved with buying guns but this time they did. He claims this all happened—Price getting contacted about buying some guns—while Price was cooperating with APD on some drug cases. Morales says it's a big misunderstanding, no one got hurt and 'let's just all go home.'"

"ATF didn't let Price go, did they?"

"Yeah," Campisano responded. "Sounds like they called the duty attorney in this office and whoever they talked to told them to let him go, that they would sort through it later."

Thax threw the pen he had twirling in his hand onto his desk.

"I know. That's pretty screwed up Thax."

"I'll find out who did that," Thax assured Campisano. "Son of a bitch."

"Well, there's more . . ."

"I'm sure APD *narcotics* has a record of that three grand in buy money being authorized to buy *guns*, right?" Thax said sarcastically. "This stinks, Christopher."

"Tell me about it," Campisano replied. "It gets better. Yesterday, I ran a criminal history on Price and I see he was arrested about five months ago by APD for possession of cocaine. There's a girl I went out with a few times who works down in records at APD, so I called her. I told her I was looking at this guy and asked her who arrested him. Turns out it was a patrol stop." Campisano pulled a police report from the folder he was carrying and handed it to Thax.

"Price was stopped for speeding on Hamilton Street down near Front Street," Campisano continued. "Just down the street from here. He acted like he was drunk, so the patrolman arrested him for DUI. When the officer patted him down he found a few small baggies of cocaine in his pockets. When backup units got there, they searched the car and found a digital scale to weigh the coke and almost forty-six hundred in cash stashed in a Wendy's bag on the back floorboard. When they asked Price about the money, of course, he told the officer he didn't know shit about it."

Thax skimmed the report while he listened.

"Did you get to the end of the report yet?"

"Not yet."

"Well, the cherry on top is that in Price's back pocket was a business card from . . . drum roll . . . Sergeant . . . Rocco . . . Morales," Campisano finished.

The men sat in silence for a few seconds.

"I want to talk to this patrol officer." Thax searched the report for his name. "Jack Sweeting."

Campisano grinned. He knew his friend too well.

"I knew you would. I have all his numbers. He works eleven p.m. to seven a.m. today. Downtown zone. Do you want to call him now?"

"I really do want to call him," Thax said, "but let's think this through."

"Okay, I'm listening."

"If we call this guy Sweeting, no matter what he tells us you know he's probably going to tell somebody in his chain of command that the U.S. Attorney talked to him about it. We didn't charge Price with the guns so why are we asking this officer about this little traffic stop? I guess we could say that's why we're asking about him, there *was* some cocaine seized—that's believable. What we could do is charge Price with being a felon in possession of the AK-47s—what my office should have done in the first place. Then, the guys from APD narcotics, if they are going to stick to their story, would have to stand up and testify for this piece of shit. It would draw them out and we could see how far they're willing to go. You and I know for damn sure that there are no APD narcotics reports leading up to this." Thax paused, then continued.

"Unless Morales or someone else wrote something after the fact. I guarantee there's no arrest plan and no authorization for that buy money to be used to purchase guns—that's if they have any paperwork on the money at all. It sounds to me like the narcotics unit was running protection for this guy Price to buy the guns or they were going to steal the guns for him. Either way, they didn't expect the guy selling the guns to be working for ATF. It doesn't sound very good."

Thax thought for a minute, then switched his focus to the entries in Chip Meyers's notebook.

"Did you get a chance to get to the Clerk's Office to see if there were any defendants named Harlin?"

"I did."

"Were you going to send me a post card about it?" Thax asked sarcastically.

Campisano ignored his friend's comment. He knew Thax was steaming mad about these bad cops.

"There was one defendant named Harlin," Campisano explained, pulling a copy of the defendant's State judgment from his folder. He handed it to Thax. "Robert Henry Harlin, convicted seventeen years ago for armed robbery. He died a couple of years ago in the State Correctional Facility at Chester."

"That's it?"

"One guy. That's it."

Thax spun around in his chair and looked out the window behind his desk.

For Thax, the quintessential public corruption case involved a quiet, cautious and surreptitious investigation culminating with a sniper shot—figuratively—between the defendant's eyes. Thax turned toward Campisano.

"We don't need to light a match on this thing. We just need to fan the coals that are already burning."

"You want me to call Sweeting, don't you?" Campisano asked to make sure he and Thax were on the same page.

"See if we can meet him later today. Don't tell him I'll be there. Just invite him to your office. And call Shea, she needs to know what's going on. But I don't want the FBI there for this interview. She'll understand why."

Thax looked at his watch and then at the clock on his desk. He needed to be in court in fifteen minutes. He walked to the door, grabbed his jacket from behind it, then came back to his desk to grab a case file.

"Call me in an hour," Thax said.

* * *

Thax walked into the DEA conference room where Campisano sat with Allentown Police Officer Jack Sweeting. Sweeting stood up when Thax walked in.

"Jack Sweeting." The officer reached out to shake Thax's hand.

"Hey Jack, nice to meet you. I'm Thax Colby." Thax shook Sweeting's hand. "I'm a federal prosecutor."

Thax sat down next to Sweeting.

"Jack, we're looking at a guy you arrested a few months back. The guy's name is Danny Price. Does that name ring a bell? You pulled him over down near Front Street and found some coke on him."

"Hell yeah, I remember that guy. He was a real piece of shit."

"How's that?" Campisano asked.

"Well, as I recall the guy was doing fifty something in a thirty-five zone. I lit him up and pulled him over. When I approached the vehicle, he had an attitude. Bad move. I can smell this guy's been drinking and I get him out of the car. He's drunk, so I hook him up. About that time my backup shows up. When I pat him down, I found cocaine in his front pockets. A couple of baggies. I don't remember the weight." Sweeting looked toward Campisano. "You have my report, Chris?"

"Yeah. It was a couple of ounces."

"What about the money?" Thax asked.

"It was like $4000, $4500, or something like that. Found it in a Wendy's bag on the floor in front of the back seat. I guess they're handing out money at fast food joints now," Sweeting joked. "The guy said it wasn't his, but we seized it as evidence anyway." Sweeting continued. "Unfortunately, if you're going to need the money to prosecute this guy, it's gone."

"What do you mean, it's gone?" Thax asked.

"Gone. Gone. Just like the cocaine."

"What are you talking about?" Thax asked.

"What I mean Mr. Colby, is all the evidence is gone. A couple of days after I booked this guy in, I got a call from the Sergeant in Narcotics. Morales," Sweeting stopped, thought for a moment, then continued. "I'm sorry, I forgot to tell you something else. When I searched this guy's pockets, he had a business card for Sergeant Morales on him. I asked this guy Price how he knew Morales and he wouldn't answer me. I thought that was strange. Anyway, so Morales called me and told me that the narcotics unit was taking over the case, which is fine with me, but they never did."

"What do you mean they never did?" Campisano pressed.

"I mean the case just went away. The guy was never formally charged." Sweeting looked perplexed. "You know, I've been doing this for a long time. I know those guys in narcotics sometimes make a guy like Price an informant, but the money and the dope, they get taken care of like they're supposed to be. They don't just disappear."

"Disappear?" Thax asked.

"Something didn't feel right to me on this so I went back and checked on the money and the cocaine." Sweeting reached into the front chest pocket of his crisply pressed blue uniform and pulled out a folded piece of paper. He unfolded it and set it on the conference table.

"This is the property record for that case. The money and the cocaine were signed out by Sergeant Morales for 'Court.' See that's the problem. This guy never went to court."

Thax pulled the paper toward him to examine it.

"This shows the money and the cocaine were signed out for court three days after Price was arrested. Is that what that says?" Thax wanted to make sure.

"That's what it says." Sweeting confirmed. "And it's never been returned."

"I guess we would have a hard time prosecuting Price without the evidence." Thax said, looking at Sweeting. "I'm glad we talked to you first."

Things were as good as they could get.

"Do you want me to try to track it down from Morales?" Sweeting inquired.

"No," Thax answered, "let us think about this and we'll get with you if we decide to pursue it. If you don't mind Jack, it would be good if we could just keep a lid on this for now."

Thax and Campisano stood up and Sweeting followed. They shook hands.

"Thanks again, Jack, for coming over. We appreciate your time. Be safe out there," Thax said as he walked Sweeting to the door.

"Thanks, guys," Sweeting said.

Fourteen

"NARCOTICS, SCHICK," DETECTIVE Josh Schick answered the phone on his desk.

"Detective Schick, my name is Shea Barrows. I'm an FBI agent here in the Allentown Office."

"Yes, ma'am, how can I help you?"

"Well, you can meet me at my office in fifteen minutes. I'm in the federal courthouse. First floor."

"What for? Is this about a case?" Schick asked, obviously caught off guard.

"I'll explain then. Oh, and Detective, I wouldn't tell anyone else over there in your shop where you're going," Barrows cautioned.

"And if I don't come?"

"That's fine too. Then I'll just come get you. How's that?" Barrows said calmly. Shea Barrows was not a pushover for anybody.

Schick was silent for a few seconds.

"What's this about?"

"Detective, you asked me that already. I'll see you in fifteen." Barrows hung up. She looked up at Thax. "He'll be here."

* * *

The receptionist led Detective Schick to an interview room in the FBI office. Schick had been an Allentown Police Officer for thirteen years—eight of them as a narcotics detective. He joined the APD after serving six years in the Marine Corps. He and his wife, Marlena, lived in a comfortable home in Macungie, a small town ten miles south and a little west of Allentown. The Schick's recently learned that after several years of attempts to have a baby by in vitro fertilization, Marlena was four months pregnant with twins. Schick had a lot to look forward to, but he had a bad feeling about this.

He walked in the open door.

"Detective Schick, I'm Special Agent Shea Barrows of the FBI." Barrows reached to shake Schick's hand. He didn't reach back. "Have a seat."

Barrows pulled out one of the four padded metal chairs that surrounded a wooden oval table.

"Who's that?" Schick barked pointing to Thax.

"Detective Schick, I'm Thax Colby. I'm a federal prosecutor." Thax didn't bother extending his hand. "Thanks for coming."

"Well, it didn't sound like I had a choice," Schick said, sitting down in the chair. He leaned forward with his hands folded together on the table. Thax studied his body language. Schick was clearly uncomfortable.

Thax pulled his chair next to Schick. Barrows sat across the table from Thax. Thax looked Schick in the eyes and hesitated a few seconds before he spoke.

"Detective, we are investigating some information that one or more Allentown detectives may be involved in stealing money from citizens. Do you know anything about that?"

"No," Schick replied smartly. "Are we done now?"

Thax continued.

"Detective, I haven't accused you of anything. My question is whether you know of or have heard of anything like that?"

"No. Nothing."

"I know you worked with Chip Meyers. Did you ever hear anything about him stealing money?"

"Chip Meyers was a good detective. He never stole shit," Schick answered defensively.

Thax remained calm but forceful.

"I didn't say he did. I asked if you'd heard anything about that."

"What do you mean stealing money?" Schick asked. "Do you mean, like when somebody is arrested, from their person?"

"No. I mean stealing money from someone's home. That kind of stealing."

"No. I don't know anything about that."

"How about during a search warrant, Detective? Do you know anything about detectives stealing money during search warrants?"

Schick shrugged. "I don't know anything. I think this is a big waste of time. Yours and mine. You know I'm a police officer, right?"

"Have you ever been involved in serving a search warrant outside the city of Allentown?"

"Why would I do that?"

"I don't know. That's why I'm asking. Does that mean the answer to that is no?"

"Never have. No reason to," Schick said tersely.

Barrows jumped in.

"Have you ever served a search warrant at a house on 31st Street?"

"That's not in the city," Schick answered. "I said I've never done that."

"Have you ever seen this house?" Barrows slid an eight by ten color photo of the Karopolis house across the table.

Schick picked up the picture and looked at it.

Without hesitating, Barrows slid another picture across the table to Schick. It was a picture of John Karopolis. Before interviewing Schick, Barrows had spoken with Karopolis who agreed to have his identity as a witness disclosed, if necessary, in investigating the theft of his money.

"How about this guy, have you ever seen him before?" Barrows asked.

Schick looked at the picture and leaned back in his chair.

"Have you seen this man before?" Barrows raised her voice.

"No." Schick glared at Barrows.

Thax jumped in. Sometimes with bad cops—like criminals—you got better results if you spoke their language.

"Well, Detective, he's seen you. When you and whomever else was with you went to that house on 31st Street with a bullshit search warrant and took money out of that man's home, you took your black ski mask off while you were standing outside. So don't lie to me."

Thax leaned closer to Schick.

"You've been sitting here for the last few minutes jerking me off,

Detective, and I don't like it. You want to go to federal prison? That's fine with me. I don't have any more time for your bullshit! Do we understand each other?"

Schick pushed back from the table.

"And another thing Detective, don't ever come into this courthouse again with that badge. My uncle wore that badge for forty years and was an honest, hard-working cop. You're starting to make me sick."

"I guess we're done here." Schick stood up.

"We're done today," Thax answered, "but we're not done."

Schick walked out the door toward the exit.

Barrows looked at Thax.

"Well, that went well," she said in a sarcastic tone.

"Now he knows we know. I hope he got a good night's sleep last night because he won't have another one any time soon."

Fifteen

A LONE STREET LIGHT illuminated the now scarcely used gravel parking lot of the old Carvel Ice Cream building on Hamilton Street in the far West End of Allentown. Many years earlier, a late summer Friday night would have found vehicles haphazardly maneuvering into the lot off the main road and families piling out of those cars to enjoy a frozen after dinner treat. The small white concrete building, dilapidated and covered with graffiti, was an eye sore, but unfortunately, not yet part of the mayor's revitalization project. Locals desperately hoped someone would soon buy the property and raze the ugly structure.

Richie Sokol drove his black MercedesBenz E350 Sedan into the lot and parked on the west side of the building. He turned off his lights but left the vehicle and the air conditioning running. It was a hot and humid evening. His passenger, Sergeant Rocco Morales, waited impatiently for Josh Schick to arrive. Moments later Schick's blue 2009 Dodge Ram truck pulled into the lot. The traffic along west Hamilton—old route 222—was relatively light for a Friday evening. Schick pulled up next to Sokol's car. As he got out of his truck, the passenger window on the Mercedes opened halfway.

"Get in the back." Morales motioned to Schick. Schick got in.

"Hey, LT." Schick reached forward to shake Sokol's hand. "It's been a while."

"Yes, it has." Sokol grabbed Schick's hand.

"Hey, Rock." Schick slapped his hand on Morales's left shoulder.

"Heard you had a conversation with the feds," Sokol said abruptly.

Schick paused, expecting a few minutes of bullshitting before getting down to business.

"This bitch FBI agent called me and told me to get my ass over to the federal building. I asked her what for and she wouldn't tell me. I told her I was busy and she would have to wait. She told me she would come make a scene at the P.D. if I didn't go, so I did."

"What did she want?" Sokol asked.

"Well she wanted to know if I knew about anybody at APD narcotics who's stealing money," Schick replied.

"Where the fuck did she come up with that?" Sokol asked.

"Richie, I don't know. Then they start—"

"Who's *they*?" Sokol interrupted.

"I got over there and there's a federal prosecutor there named Colby. They start throwing pictures in my face trying to intimidate me. I told them, 'who the hell do they think they are? I'm a cop.'"

"Is someone fuckin' talking?" Sokol looked pissed. He glared at Morales.

Morales shrugged. "They better not be."

"What kind of pictures did they show you?" Sokol asked.

"Well, that's where I think all this shit is coming from." Schick looked at Morales. "Do you remember that little Greek piece of shit, Jimmy Karopolis, who we've popped a bunch of times? He deals down near Jordan Park."

"Yeah," Morales replied.

"Remember months back when we did the rip of that bail money from his dad's house out in the West End on 31st Street?" Schick continued. "This prosecutor says the dad saw me there."

"Well, how the fuck can that happen? I assume you were wearing masks?" Sokol questioned. "How could he identify you if you were wearing your fuckin' mask?"

"I don't know. I don't remember taking my mask off. He said the guy saw me outside with my mask off. I just don't remember that."

"Jesus Christ!" Sokol turned forward in his seat in disgust. "Are you fuckin' serious?" He smacked his right hand against the steering wheel.

"I'm sorry, Richie. I didn't think—"

"Exactly Joshua, you didn't fuckin' think." Sokol interrupted again. He was steaming mad. He never called Schick Joshua unless he was.

"Well, it looks like we have a little problem then. You need to fix it. Now!" Sokol raised his voice.

Sokol sat in the deafening silence and shook his head in disgust.

"Does anyone have any other good news I can take back to the mayor—and hopefully, if no one fucks up—the next governor?" He looked at Morales, then at Schick. "Take care of this problem!"

"I will," Schick promised.

Sixteen

CHRISSY BARNES STOOD in the foreground of the picturesque park with the Delaware River as the backdrop. As usual, she looked sensational.

"This is Chrissy Barnes reporting live from the tip of Hugh Moore Park in Easton, Pennsylvania, where Allentown Mayor and gubernatorial candidate Logan Branfield has just stirred this crowd of almost five hundred people with an emotional speech about reducing crime in the State, specifically here in Easton, in the heart of Northampton County, where this city has recently seen a rash of violent crime. Just days ago, Erica Murtaugh, a young Lafayette College student, was brutally assaulted, raped, and senselessly killed in this very park. Branfield promised State funding for more police officers for the city as well as the establishment of a State Police Violent Crime Task Force office in the county if he is elected. As tragic as this horrific murder is, it could not have happened at a more critical time for Branfield, as recent polls show the electorate sees him as weaker on crime than his opponent. This tragedy has given him an opportunity to put his new 'tough-on-crime' position front and center. Branfield, who was once a five-point favorite in this race for the Governor's mansion, now holds onto a tenuous one-point lead according to the latest Harrisburg Patriot-News poll. Branfield's staff says that in the next few days, he will carry this message in a push westward across the Keystone State, hoping to change the public's perception of him on this critical issue and to swing the political momentum back in his favor.

"Live in Easton, this is Chrissy Barnes for Valley 10 News."

* * *

Chrissy headed east on South Delaware Drive out of Hugh Moore Park. A few hundred feet later, she banked her blue Jeep to the right onto South 3rd Street to cross the Lehigh River. She slowed to look at the amazing view. As she looked to her right, the powerful Lehigh poured over a man-made dam into the mighty Delaware.

Pausing for just a moment to admire the awesome view, she turned left onto Washington Street on her way to the Northampton County Courthouse. Chrissy lived ten miles from there in New Jersey, although lately she had given up her stressful commute for the comfort of Thax Colby's bed. While she usually avoided Easton, the Murtaugh killing was a huge story and nobody could cover a story like Chrissy Barnes. With her cameraman following behind her in the Valley 10 News van, she had set off to scope out the local courthouse, where, no doubt, the Murtaugh story would unfold as soon as the police captured the cold-blooded animal who had killed the young co-ed.

Chrissy maneuvered into an open parking spot a short city block from the court complex.

The Northampton County Courthouse was a striking civil war era, gothic style traditional courthouse. Six white stone Corinthian columns guarded the front entryway—each plinth topped with an ornate gold-ornamental finial. A gold-trimmed white cupola adorned the front center of the roof. Five two-story high windows provided natural sunlight to the lobby and the upper floors of the three-story structure.

Inside, Chrissy passed her purse through the magnetometer. A Court bailiff watched her pass through the metal detector.

"Whew!" she joked. "I just never know."

The Bailiff smiled back.

Chrissy spied the building directory on the wall in front of her. She was looking for the Clerk's Office. The directory listed the judges of the Court of Common Pleas, the District Attorney, Sheriff and finally the Clerk of Court. She scanned the directory.

"Clerk's Office, Room 103," Chrissy announced to herself. She started to walk away, then came back to the directory. A name caught her eye. Her heart fluttered.

"Holy shit!" she shouted.

The Bailiff and two young men, probably lawyers, turned and looked in her direction.

"Oh . . . I'm sorry," she said apologetically, putting her hand up to her mouth.

"Ho . . . ly . . . shit," she whispered under her breath.

Chrissy instinctively reached for her cell phone. No cell phones were the rule in most courthouses and she dutifully left hers in her Jeep. She walked briskly to the exit doors then down the steps. She was in a hurry. When she reached her car, she grabbed her cell phone and nervously dialed the phone.

* * *

Thax grabbed his jacket from the back of his door. He was heading out for a late lunch. His office phone rang. He decided to answer it.

"This is Thax Colby."

"Thax. It's Chrissy." She sounded strange.

"Chrissy, what's wrong?" Thax could hear she was out of breath. "Are you okay?"

"I'm fine." Chrissy tried to catch her breath. "I'm in Northampton County. At the courthouse."

"What's going on?" Thax sounded more concerned.

"Judge Harlin. *Judge Eugene Harlin.* It's the name in the notebook," Chrissy exclaimed.

Thax was silent.

"Thax, are you there?"

"I'm here. I'm trying to imagine what a judge in Easton has to do with our cops over here?"

Thax paused again.

"Do you want me to check anything else out while I'm here?" she asked.

"No. I just want you to come home."

"Home?" Chrissy asked.

"I'll see you tonight. I need to call Shea and Christopher. You're amazing."

Chrissy beamed. "I'm sorry, fly boy, could you repeat that last part."

"You heard me just fine. I have to go."

Seventeen

Detective Hatten knocked on the door at 3771 Kensington Way. He had come to speak with Katie Meyers—Chip Meyers's oldest daughter.

Detective Michelle Lambert came along for the ride. Ten years earlier, Lambert, a Boston native, came to the Lehigh Valley to study at Cedar Crest College—a private liberal arts college for women in Allentown's West End. Two weeks into her junior year, her father, a Boston cop, was killed when a suspect another officer had arrested managed to get ahold of the officer's gun inside the police precinct where Lambert's dad was starting his shift. The deranged suspect shot and killed Lambert's father and wounded two more officers before being killed by return fire. She knew the pain of losing a father. Upon her return to school, she found herself unable to resume her studies. She ended up at the police academy instead. After a few years as a patrol officer in South Whitehall Township, her skills at interviewing victims, mostly of sexual assaults, landed her a detective slot. She soon became the borough's chief sex crimes investigator. Emotionally toughened by her work but naturally sensitive, she knew how to gain the trust of a young witness. Unfortunately, she had spoken to too many.

Kristin Meyers opened the front door.

"Detective Hatten. Thank you for coming."

"Kristin, this is Detective Michelle Lambert."

Lambert shook Kristin's hand.

"I'm very sorry for your loss."

Kristin invited the detectives into her home. The area just inside the front door of the modest four bedroom, two and a half bath ranch home led to an open area with a quaint dining room to the left and a family room to the right. Hatten didn't know much about dining room furniture but he knew if he ever had an inkling to buy a dining room set, he couldn't afford this one. A leather sectional sofa and two wing-back chairs surrounded the sixty-inch flat screen centerpiece of the family room. The family room joined the open kitchen area at the end of the home. Hatten made note of the new looking stainless steel appliances.

"Please make yourselves comfortable," Kristin said, inviting Hatten and Lambert to sit in the family room.

"I'm sorry that I really don't have anything new to tell you Kristin," Hatten said. "I wish I did. When the coroner rules a death a suicide, I'm not supposed to keep looking at other possibilities, but my department has given me a little bit of time to investigate further. I'm really hoping your daughter might be able to help us with the time-line. How is she doing?"

Kristin leaned forward in her chair.

"She's not doing well at all. I know she's still mourning. We all are." Kristin reached for a tissue from a box on the table next to her. "She has nightmares every night. The first few nights, I found her in the hallway outside the office door, crying hysterically. She wouldn't speak. She kept staring down the hallway. The last few nights, when I get down to hold her, she's softly saying 'Daddy, Daddy,' over and over. I know she saw him in the chair."

"Katie's fifteen?" Lambert asked.

Kristin nodded.

"Mrs. Meyers, do you mind if we walk back to the office?" Lambert asked.

"Not at all," Kristin replied, rising from her chair. The detectives followed.

Kristin led the detectives through the open hall area between the dining and family rooms toward the back of the residence. They passed the master bedroom in the back left corner of the home. Katie's room was directly in front of them, next to the master bedroom. Down the hallway, the solid wall on the right side was adorned with framed family and baby pictures of the Meyers's daughters. They continued passing a bathroom between Katie's and Erin's bedrooms. Erin's bedroom, and the home office where Chip Meyers died, was separated by a hallway leading to the back door of the home—a single door with a partial window. The office was at the end of the hall on the back right corner of the home. Across the hall from the office door was an open walkway into the kitchen.

"Where is Katie now?" Lambert asked.

"She's in her room."

"And your younger daughter?"

"Erin. She's next door. Her best friend lives there."

Lambert stood in the hallway outside the office door.

"Tell me where you find Katie when she comes out here during the night," she asked.

Kristin pointed to the wall opposite the hallway leading to the back door.

"She sits there. Well, she doesn't sit. She curls up in a ball. But . . . right there."

Lambert sat on the carpeted floor of the hallway in the spot where Katie held her nightly vigil mourning for her father. Lambert could see the door to the office a few feet to her right. She could also see straight down the short hallway to the back door. Hatten walked to where Lambert sat on the floor and looked in each direction.

Katie's door opened.

"Katie," Kristin said, "come on into the kitchen."

Katie walked toward the detectives then walked with them to the kitchen where they all sat at the kitchen table. Lambert sat next to Katie.

Before her father's death, Katie Meyers had been a relatively happy fifteen-year-old girl. Kate Lauren Meyers had just finished tenth grade at Parkland High School where she was an honor student and co-captain of the girls' gymnastics team. But for a mild case of teenage acne, she was a good looking young girl with lots of potential.

"Katie, my name is Michelle. I'm a detective and I work with Detective Hatten."

"Hi. Nice to meet you," Katie replied softly.

"I'm so sorry about your dad."

Katie dropped her head and looked at the table.

"I lost my dad when I was a little older than you," Lambert continued. "Somebody he didn't even know hurt him and he never came home again."

Katie looked up at Lambert.

"What happened to him?"

"Someone shot him."

"I hate guns," Katie said, looking down again.

Lambert and Hatten had left their weapons in the car at Lambert's suggestion.

"Katie, do you know what happened to your dad?" Lambert asked.

Katie looked at Lambert, then at her mom.

"Mom said he shot himself." Her mother handed her a tissue.

"Katie, did something wake you the night this happened?"

"I guess I couldn't sleep. I don't remember what time it was, but I got up and when I opened my bedroom door, I saw a light coming from Dad's office. I walked down there and he was at his desk." She paused to wipe her tears. "Dad was drinking."

"What did you do then?"

"I went and got a drink of water. Dad came into the kitchen with me then I went back to bed. Something woke me up. I don't know what, but I walked back into the hallway toward Dad's office—" she stopped, crying harder.

"Did you see or hear anything?"

Katie put her head down. She was breathing faster.

"I don't know," she cried. "I don't know. All I remember is seeing Dad. I can't remember anything else!"

Katie got up and ran from the kitchen to her bedroom and slammed the door. Kristin got up to follow her.

"Let her go," Lambert said, reaching for Kristin's hand. "Just let her go. She'll be okay."

Lambert knew from experience that Katie was likely suffering post-traumatic stress disorder—a common occurrence after witnessing a death. Fear, guilt, and nightmares were normal. She knew pushing Katie too hard, too fast would only make things worse.

"I think we've made some progress." Lambert tried to comfort Kristin. Hatten nodded.

"Unfortunately, she's going to have flashbacks. Right now her brain is blocking it out. It's our coping mechanism. Just comfort her and give her time."

"I feel so helpless." Kristin said.

"It's going to be okay," Lambert assured her.

* * *

Chris Campisano stuck his head into Thax's office. Thax was just hanging up the phone.

"Christopher, what's up?" Thax motioned for him to come in.

Campisano sat down across from Thax. "I didn't want to deliver the bad news over the phone."

"What bad news?"

"Looks like Chief Butler is going to let Dailey slide on the missing $8000 bucks," Campisano said with disgust.

"Why? What did he say?"

"Well, I didn't talk to him. My supervisor, Tommy Campbell, spoke with the Chief and according to Tommy, the Chief's position is that while the story sounds 'a little funny,' he can't say Dailey actually stole anything. He says there's not enough proof that the money in the photograph isn't the same amount Dailey and Meyers turned in."

"Who are these people?" Thax scowled. "Do they seriously believe this nonsense?"

"I know the lieutenant in Internal Affairs thought the story was a bunch of horseshit. I spoke to him and he told me that IA wanted Dailey fired. They think he's a disgrace. They recommended to the Chief that he fire him. He's pretty pissed the Chief didn't do it. Tommy says the Chief is *thinking* about a two-day suspension."

"Yeah, he'll probably let him take the two days on Saturday and Sunday," Thax said contemptuously. "I really wonder what the hell is going on over there at APD."

"I know. It's crazy. So what do we do with Dailey now?"

"We wait."

They both paused, taking in Campisano's information.

Thax spoke first. "We need to talk more about Judge Harlin but I want to wait until Shea can be here. She had an emergency and had to fly to California. She should be back in a few days. I want to be really careful about how we investigate this."

"I agree. Oh, and tell the girlfriend that the Harlin thing was a nice catch." Campisano smirked. "I'd keep her just because of that."

"I just might." Thax smiled.

Eighteen

THE RISING SUN shining against the enormous oaks and willows along the banks, cast deep, long shadows upstream on the water of the Little Lehigh. Thax quietly pursued his prey—native brown trout. For Thax, from a purely strategic point of view, the early morning was the best time of day to fish this part of the river. A fly fisherman's shadows could easily spook a fish, as much as any other interruption or distraction in the water. Fishing upstream in the morning, on this section of the river, allowed the cagey angler to use the shadows, already thrown on the water by the big trees, as cover to move without detection.

By eight-thirty, Thax had already bagged and released a nice thirteen-inch brown trout and was looking for more. He stood silently between the two huge weeping willows, casting upstream to a rock ledge on the other side of the deep seam of water. Moments earlier a large rainbow trout rose to feed on a fly that had fluttered too close to the surface of the water. Thax hoped, as he cast upstream of the rocks, that he had accurately matched his fly to the hatch on the river. He delicately floated a size 18 blue-winged olive—a tiny mayfly with an olive body and light gray wings—just beyond some slower water sheltered by the stone ledge. The cautious rainbow rose and then rolled without taking the fly.

"Are you having any luck?" The loud voice came from another angler sloshing through the water behind Thax.

Thax turned and stared at the young man who had obviously missed a few classes on fly fishing etiquette.

"No. No luck today," Thax replied.

"Yeah. Me neither," the man echoed, still thrashing through the waters as he continued upstream.

Thax didn't think anything in fly fishing involved luck. What he did believe was that, just as it was when trying a case in a courtroom, preparation and skill yielded the best results. In trial, luck was what happened after you spent weeks preparing. Fly fishing involved the accurate selection of a fly, a perfect cast and the skillful presentation of the fly to the fish. No, he had no luck today, but he did land a stunning brown trout.

Thax worked the waters of the Little Lehigh for another hour, occasionally and momentarily shifting his focus to the scenic surroundings of the river. A pair of Mallard ducks floated by him. Even a Great Blue Heron glided effortlessly down the river under the canopies of the trees, searching for breakfast. He tossed his fly into the fast, rushing rapids just upstream from the towering willows. A trophy brown trout grabbed the fly as it hit the water. He set the hook but the enormous fish snapped the tippet—the line attached to the fly.

"Damn! That was a nice one!"

Thax looked across the river and saw Bob Freeman sitting in the old park bench. It seemed like a good time to take a little break anyway.

* * *

"Bob, how are you?" Thax asked as he approached the park bench.

Freeman seemed preoccupied by the river. "Hey, Thax. I'm okay. How are you?"

"Pretty good today, Bob. Pretty hard to beat this." Thax motioned toward the water.

"Did you catch anything this morning?" Bob asked.

"Caught a nice brownie upstream from here in the riffles. Nice fish.

"How about you, Bob?" Thax didn't see Freeman's fly rod anywhere. "No fishing today?"

"Not today, Thax. Today is my son's birthday."

Thax hesitated. "Well, I'm sure he wouldn't mind if you fished a little bit. You're down here. You should have at least wet your line." Thax tried to get Bob to smile. "Are you okay, Bob?"

Bob didn't answer but looked intently at the river.

"Thax, why do you love this stretch of the river so much?"

Thax sat on the bench next to Freeman and leaned his fly rod against the side of it.

"I don't know. I used to love coming here with my grandfather. We used to fish here all the time. Then, when I got a little older and I fished alone, I was actually afraid to come here. When I started to fly fish, I was afraid to wade out there in the fast water. I didn't know where all the holes were and was scared that I would step in one. That deep seam—I was afraid of that, too. Believe it or not, Bob, I was terrified that I was going to drown. I even had bad dreams about it. It took me awhile to get out there and get close to the drop off so I could fish that rock ledge. I love this place now and I know every inch of this part of the stream."

Bob listened.

"How about you, Bob? I see you down here but I never see you fishing. You don't like this area?"

"Thax, I've caught some great trout in this little piece of water. I used to fish here. A long time ago. This was my favorite spot. Long before it was a fly fishing area."

Bob looked at Thax.

"My wife and I . . . we've been away for quite some time. We lived up in Nazareth near my sister. We just recently moved back. I think I told you we live in the townhomes up the road on Brigett's Way."

"I've seen them. They look nice."

Bob continued, ignoring Thax's comment. "I usually fish downstream below the bridge. Ronnie has me hooked on throwing tricos into that fast water." He smiled a bit.

"That sounds like Ronnie."

Bob stood up from the bench. "Well, I'd best be getting home to the wife."

"How's she doing, Bob?"

"Thax, my wife has been sick for many years. She's had a lot of problems, mostly emotional ones. She's never really recovered from her nervous breakdown. She's had a rough go of it."

"I'm sorry," Thax said, trying to comfort his new friend.

"I'm sorry, too," Bob said. He turned to walk away.

"Take care, Bob." Thax waved.

"Be careful, friend." Bob waved back.

Nineteen

JIMMY KAROPOLIS WAS a drug dealer, but not a very good one. The problem with Jimmy was that he kept getting caught. Unfortunately, when he did, his father, who despised what Jimmy did, enabled him by bailing him out and getting him the best lawyers. After all, in John Karopolis's mind, that's what a good parent did—help his children—no matter what.

John's wife, Jimmy's mother, died suddenly from a brain aneurysm when Jimmy was fourteen. John had a great business and earned a good living. He worked many long hours to reap his good fortune. He had tried to raise his son to be a good man, but considered that he had failed miserably at the task. He tried to get Jimmy to work in his restaurant business, but his son was unreliable and hated hard work. At twenty-eight, Jimmy had already made two trips to the State Correctional Facility and was working on strike three.

And that was just the times he was caught.

Jimmy kept a small first-floor apartment at PennCrest Gardens on West Fairmont Street in Allentown. He didn't deal dope from there and tried to be respectful to his neighbors. The truth was he was seldom there and most neighbors probably wouldn't have known Jimmy from Mickey Mouse. His father, of course, paid the rent.

The crescent moon threw little light on the city as it settled overhead on this clear late Sunday evening. Jimmy sat alone in his apartment watching reruns of *Grey's Anatomy* on his old TV and eating a midnight snack of cold ravioli from a can. Dozing off in his old, worn recliner, he was awakened several hours later by a knock on the door.

"Police. Open the door."

The officer didn't shout. Jimmy had heard the shouting before, like when they executed a search warrant on his old apartment. This wasn't that.

Shit, Jimmy thought. *Did they get me again?*

"Just a minute," he called feeling panicked. A few more seconds passed.

"Open the door, Jimmy," the voice from outside spoke again.

He looked around and quickly stashed a half-burnt joint under a seat cushion on his couch, then walked to the door. When he opened the door, he felt a gloved fist smashing against his face with brutal force. He nearly lost consciousness.

"Evening, Jimmy," the first intruder spoke.

Another punch to his stomach and another to his face knocked him back onto the floor.

Two people wearing black clothes and black ski masks forced themselves into his apartment. The door closed behind them. Jimmy thought he started to scream but the punch to his stomach had knocked the wind out of him. He couldn't speak or hear a sound.

The same intruder jumped on top of him. Three or four more savage punches pounded his face while he lay on the floor—each punch violently bouncing the back of his head off the linoleum-covered concrete floor.

At the same time, Jimmy felt the second intruder stomp the heel of a shoe into his side, again and again and again. The excruciating pain from the breaking of his ribs coursed through his body. He tried to scream but felt only a gurgle as his mouth filled with blood. Another punch struck his face, snapping his jaw out of joint. He slipped in and out of consciousness. The pain and another hard stomp of a shoe to the side of his head was the last thing he felt.

"Let's get this piece of shit out of here," the first intruder said.

The second intruder pulled a blanket from the bed in the bedroom. They wrapped Jimmy in the blanket and hurried him out of the apartment.

"Let's go," the first intruder called out as they both threw the blanket holding Jimmy's body into the bed of the truck. The body landed with a loud thud.

* * *

Chrissy slid her soft, warm naked body under the sheet and across the king-sized bed. Thax was asleep, lying on his back. She nuzzled closer.

"Rise and shine," she whispered, kissing his face.

Thax partially opened his eyes and kissed her. She felt him under the sheet.

"Ummmm," she moaned softly. "Looks like all you need to do now is shine."

Thax smiled as Chrissy slid her body over his.

"You feel good." He pulled her close slowly pushing inside of her. Chrissy groaned and swayed her body, thrusting faster against him.

"Rock my world, mister."

Thax caressed Chrissy, pulling her closer.

Several minutes later, Chrissy's cell phone, on the night table, started to vibrate. Thax and Chrissy both heard it, but tried to ignore it. A few minutes later, it vibrated again then stopped.

"What time is it?" Thax glanced at his alarm clock. It was five-thirty.

"I need to look," Chrissy said, stopping her rhythm. "Nobody calls me this early unless something's wrong."

She lifted her body off Thax's and crawled on her stomach to her side of the bed. Thax rolled with her and held her, softly kissing her back while she retrieved a voice mail.

"It's work. They didn't say what it was, but they want me available for a live shot at eight o'clock this morning. It must be something big. I need to get ready."

"Hey, it's five-thirty. It doesn't take you that long to get ready." Thax pulled himself on top of Chrissy as she lay on her stomach.

"Can we just finish?" he whispered in her ear.

Chrissy stretched her arms out in front of her and raised her lower body, pulling herself to her knees. Thax moved with her.

"I've finished a bunch of times already, fly boy. I've been waiting for you." She turned her head and closed her eyes.

"The clock's ticking," she said, exhaling deeply and burying her face into her pillow.

* * *

Thax walked through his front door. His three-mile run was fast and invigorating. The morning air was cool for this time of year. He drew the bottom of his T-shirt up to wipe the sweat off his face. His cell phone on the kitchen counter rang. It was almost seven-thirty.

"Hey," he answered. It was Chrissy. "I just got back from my run and was going to turn on the news. What's going on?"

"Someone dumped a body at the federal courthouse," Chrissy said. "The guy's not dead but it doesn't look good."

"What?!" Thax couldn't hide his shock.

"Do you know anything about this?"

"Chrissy, I don't have a clue. Do you know who it is? Do you have a name?"

"No one is identifying him yet. Just a white man in his late twenties, early thirties, is the best anyone is saying."

"It could be anybody."

"Well, nobody's saying anything but some of my sources are thinking it must have something to do with a trial or something going on in the courthouse. I'm still digging." Chrissy continued. "I'm going live in thirty minutes so if you hear anything and can tell me, call me."

Thax heard a quiet beeping sound in his phone indicating another incoming call. He glanced at the caller ID and saw it was Shea Barrows.

"I've got another call coming in. I need to take this."

"Okay. I've got to go, too. Talk to you later." Chrissy hung up.

Thax answered the incoming call.

"Shea, what's going on?"

Thax grabbed a cold bottle of water from the refrigerator.

"Did you hear about the body at the courthouse?"

"Uh, I just did. What's going on?"

"I got a call from Scott Adkins at the U.S. Marshals' Office. Apparently Allentown P.D. responded to an anonymous call for assistance at about four-fifteen this morning and found the guy on the steps of the courthouse. I guess they thought he was dead and somebody called for homicide to respond. The flippin' media must have picked up the call on a scanner. They've been out there since five o'clock."

"Slow down Shea." Thax could tell she was frazzled. He had never heard her like that.

"It's Jimmy Karopolis." Barrows's voice tensed. "Adkins says the guy was beaten so badly he's never seen anything like it. He was shocked when the paramedics found a pulse. He said it was brutal. Absolutely brutal."

Thax took a deep breath and exhaled. He listened to Barrows.

"The Marshals have reviewed their surveillance cameras from that side of the courthouse and Adkins told me they have a short blurb—a few seconds—around two-fifteen where a truck pulled up and someone threw the body at the base of the side steps. No license plate on the truck and the guy had a hoodie or a mask on. They're looking at it more closely now. I'll stay on it."

"Okay."

"What's wrong with these people?" Barrows asked with frustration in her voice.

"Someone just sent us a message, Shea."

Barrows was quiet. "I guess we'll just wait to hear if he makes it."

"No, we're not going to wait," Thax said. "Get over to Lehigh Valley Hospital now. Call Chris and get his ass out of bed and have him meet you there. John Karopolis is going to be there and we need to be there for him."

"But what's the media going to say if they find out the FBI is there?"

"You're there because the body was found at the federal building." Thax was pissed. He thought for a few seconds. "You know what Shea, I *want* whoever did this—and I think we know who did—to know we're not going to let this go unanswered. Not only do I want you to go, I want you to wear something that says FBI on it."

Barrows regained her composure. "Got it."

"I'll be in the office in an hour. Keep me posted."

* * *

Thax showered and flipped on Channel 10. It was eight o'clock.

"Good morning. I'm Gina Mondalvo, and thank you for watching Valley 10 News," the anchor welcomed viewers. "Let's go right now to Chrissy Barnes who is at the federal courthouse in downtown Allentown for breaking news this morning."

The screen cut to Barnes who stood on the front steps of the courthouse.

"Authorities are not saying much about the badly beaten body of a young man who was found this morning on the side steps of this courthouse. What we know now is that Allentown Police patrol units responded to the courthouse early this morning where they found the young man and initially believed he was dead. Homicide detectives also responded but we know that so did paramedics who took the victim to Lehigh Valley Hospital. At this time, authorities have not released the identity of the victim or his condition; however, based on what we have seen and heard here at the courthouse, we believe his condition to be grave."

The anchor cut in to ask a question.

"Chrissy, are authorities saying anything about any connection they believe this might have to any proceedings going on in the federal courthouse?"

Barnes responded.

"Gina, at this point, the Allentown Police have not said anything and the United States Marshals Service, who has responsibilities for security here at the courthouse has not speculated on any connection. The Marshals Service did say they have increased the presence of deputy U.S. Marshals and court security personnel here today but have said nothing more. This is Chrissy Barnes in Allentown for Valley 10 News."

Twenty

JOHN KAROPOLIS SAT quietly in an exam room next to the trauma bay at the Lehigh Valley Hospital off Cedar Crest Boulevard in the West End of Allentown. Paramedics bypassed the closer but older Lehigh Valley Hospital on 17th Street because LVH-Cedar Crest was better equipped for this devastating trauma. After initial triage, Jimmy Karopolis was taken directly to the operating room. His injuries were life threatening and included extensive internal bleeding. The attending trauma surgeon, Dr. Reid Brennan, had spoken briefly to John before rushing with Jimmy to the OR. Brennan, having seen Jimmy's brutally battered body, told the young man's father he would do everything he could. Karopolis understood from looking into Dr. Brennan's eyes the outcome was probably not going to be good. He bowed his head into his hands and prayed for his son to live. It was all he could do now.

A soft knock on the door broke the relative silence in the room and ended John's prayer.

"Yes," Karopolis spoke.

Shea Barrows pushed the door open far enough to stick her head in. "Mr. Karopolis. Can I come in?"

Karopolis motioned for her to enter.

Barrows walked over to Karopolis, who stood up from an uncomfortable plastic chair. She hugged him.

"I'm so sorry, Mr. Karopolis." Barrows held the man just a little longer. "What have they told you about your son's condition? Please. Sit down." Barrows helped Karopolis to the chair.

Karopolis wiped away the tears flowing down his face with his hand. "He has lost a lot of blood. He has internal injuries. They wouldn't let me see him up close because I would get in the way of the doctors, but I stood close enough to see his face. It was so bloody and smashed I couldn't even recognize him." Karopolis wept some more. "They had so many doctors . . ."

"I know they are doing everything they can for him." Barrows tried to comfort him.

"I know. I know," Karopolis said through his tears.

Barrows handed Karopolis some tissues from the counter.

"Does anybody know who did this to my son?"

"Not yet, but we are working on it with all the manpower we have."

"Agent Barrows, I think we know who did this. The only question is why didn't they come after me. My son didn't do anything to them."

Barrows knew in her gut this was retaliation against Karopolis, but had no proof yet.

"Mr. Karopolis. We are going to find out for sure who did this to your son and when we do—"

"I hope you find them before I do," Karopolis threatened.

"We will."

Karopolis stood up and walked to the door. He opened it and looked down the hall. After a few moments, he closed the door and turned back toward Barrows.

"If these people think they can intimidate me, they don't know who I am," Karopolis said. "If you need me to testify about these men that came into my house, I will do it. These thugs are not going to hurt my family anymore."

Barrows pulled up the other plastic chair and sat down. Karopolis sat down next to her.

"Okay," Barrows said. "Let's get some good news on Jimmy first."

* * *

At eight fifty-five a.m., Thax walked the short distance from his Jeep to the employee entrance in the rear of the federal courthouse. Several media news trucks were still parked on Hamilton Street opposite the courthouse entrance. His phone rang.

"Hey," Thax answered. It was Chrissy.

"Okay. Tell me what you know about this guy Jimmy Karopolis."

"Well good morning. Nice live shot," he responded.

"Are you going to tell me?" Chrissy asked impatiently.

"What do you know?"

"Did anyone ever tell you that you suck at answering questions Thax Colby?"

"I think my mother told me that once or twice."

"Thax!"

"Okay. I know who this guy is and I probably know why he was beaten so badly . . ."

"But you can't tell me," Chrissy interrupted.

"No. I will tell you. Karopolis's father gave us some info on our bad cops. He identified one of them when they stole money out of his house. I don't know for sure that this is retaliation for that but I would bet Dorothy's ruby slippers that it was. That's what I know."

Chrissy was quiet.

"You trust me, don't you?" She sounded pleased.

"I need to go."

* * *

Dr. Brennan walked into the exam room where John Karopolis and Shea Barrows were waiting. The trauma surgeon, draped in OR scrubs, held his white mask in his left hand. It was eleven thirty-five a.m.

"Mr. Karopolis." Brennan walked closer. "Your son is still in surgery. He's lost a lot of blood. We had to remove his spleen and are trying to control the bleeding in his chest. He has numerous broken ribs. The paramedics placed a tube in his throat at the scene because his facial bones are severely fractured as is his jaw on both sides. He couldn't breathe without the tube. He has a cranial bleed." The doctor paused. "There's a lot going on, sir. I'm going back in there. I expect we'll be a while yet."

Karopolis tried to be strong. Barrows stood next to him and put her arm around him.

"Will he—"

"Will he live?" Brennan spoke. "If there's any good news, it's that he's still fighting."

* * *

"Good afternoon. I'm Robin Parker, and thank you for watching Valley 10 News," the anchor welcomed viewers. Continuing with our top story let's go out to Chrissy Barnes who is at the Lehigh Valley Hospital. What's new on this story, Chrissy?"

"Robin, a few minutes ago, Allentown Police Chief Scott Butler made a short statement where he identified the victim of this morning's brutal assault as Jimmy Karopolis. Chief Butler said his patrol units arrived on the scene at the federal courthouse early this morning to find the battered body of Karopolis. Chief Butler would not comment on any leads or reasons for this attack. He did ask that anyone with any information about this crime contact the Allentown Police tip line.

"Valley 10 News has learned that Karopolis, who is twenty-eight years old, has twice been convicted for narcotics offenses and has served time in state correctional facilities. While the Allentown Police and the FBI, who are at the hospital, search for clues in this vicious crime, sources here at LVH-Cedar Crest tell us that Jimmy Karopolis is still clinging to life. His condition is listed as critical. Back at the courthouse, the United States Marshals office told me this morning that they do have surveillance cameras outside the federal building and that they were reviewing footage from this morning for any information that might lead to the arrest of the perpetrators of this crime. At the Lehigh Valley Hospital, Chrissy Barnes, back to you Robin."

Twenty-One

"CHRIS AND SHEA are here. Do you want me to bring them back?" Abigail asked, stepping into Thax's office.

"Absolutely. Thanks."

A minute later Abigail returned with Campisano and Barrow.

"I'm headed out for lunch," Abigail announced. When she turned to walk away, Campisano stared at her ass in her tight fitting black skirt.

She turned abruptly and sneered at him.

"Done dreaming, Chris, or should I stand here a little longer?"

Campisano shrugged and grinned with delight.

"Busted, Chris." Barrows laughed. Abigail smiled and continued on her way.

"Can we do some work now?" Thax asked. "What do we know about Judge Harlin?"

Barrows opened her leather notebook and flipped a few pages of the legal pad.

"Eugene Harlin. Age fifty-seven. Elected to the bench six years ago in Northampton County. Looks like he ran unopposed. He presides mostly over criminal cases and has handled a few high-profile murder cases in the last few years. Before he was elected, he worked in a two-man firm, Harlin & Linderbacher. He did criminal defense and his partner did personal injury work. No bar complaints or anything to speak of that I could find. He was born and raised in Easton, so he's a hometown boy. Married with a couple of grown kids. He's involved with the Chamber of Commerce there in Northampton County and the Kiwanis Club. That's it."

"What's his connection to Allentown?" Thax asked.

"I have no idea, Thax. Like I said, all his family—everybody—they're in Easton."

Campisano frowned tightly and shook his head.

"Christopher? What's on your mind?" Thax asked.

"Okay. No offense, but, I mean, are we sure this is the same guy whose name is in the notebook. I mean, yeah, it's Harlin, but are we missing something? It sounds like this guy has nothing to do with our cops over here. I'm on board 100 percent, but we need to find something more. That's all I'm saying."

"I hear you," Thax concurred as he pulled out a copy of the notebook page. "Let's assume that Harlin *is* our guy and the $20,000 is some kind of payoff or bribe."

Campisano shrugged.

"I know. Play along. Humor me." Thax continued. "What do we think the numbers mean?"

"I think it looks like a date," Barrows said. "Look at the way it's written: 10 slash 12. How about October 12th? And E.S., that's who paid the money?"

"Or the defendant?" Thax suggested.

"How are we going to do this?" Barrows asked. "I know what you're thinking, but how are we going to look at all of Harlin's cases without someone in the Clerk's office getting suspicious? We know how tight knit the clerks are with the judges."

Thax spun around in his chair to access his desktop computer and began typing.

"There we go. Northampton County Clerk of Court." Thax wrote down the phone number. He turned back toward his desk and dialed the phone. Barrows and Campisano just watched. He dialed and put the call on speakerphone.

"Clerk's Office, this is Judy," a pleasant sounding woman answered.

"Hi Judy. My name is Thax Colby. I'm a federal prosecutor in Allentown. How are you today?"

"I'm fine. How can I help you?"

"Judy, I'm sitting here with a couple of federal agents, so I have you on speakerphone. I have a witness over here who has been trying to identify a bank robber for us and he just told us that he had seen the guy in court in Easton."

"Okay . . ." the clerk responded.

"Here's the problem. My witness is not real bright. All he remembers is that he was in court to speak for an acquaintance of his—he's not even really sure of that guy's last name—and he says he saw the man who robbed the bank in the courtroom. He says our bank robber was a defendant in another case over there in your court. He told us if he hears the guy's name he's sure he'll recognize it. He knows it was sometime between September and the end of the year."

"What year?"

"I'm sorry, Judy. This guy is really brain dead. All he remembers is that it was in the last three years."

"He doesn't know what judge's courtroom he was in?" the clerk inquired, some of her pleasantness starting to fade.

"I'm not even sure he knows what city he's in now," Thax joked. "How many judges do you guys have over there?"

"We have eight."

"Is there any chance you could run a search on your records for all defendants pending in say, October through December for the last three years." Thax braced for the verbal explosion.

"I should be able to do that," the clerk responded. "I'm not sure if I can get it done today though."

Thax expected the worst, that it couldn't be done at all or that it would take weeks.

"Judy, you are the best," Thax said. "I hope you just helped us catch a bank robber. When it's ready can you call the FBI agent who is working the bank robbery? Her name is Shea Barrows." Thax gave the clerk Barrows's cell phone number.

"I really, really appreciate it, Judy."

"You're welcome Mr.—"

"Colby. Thax Colby. Thank you so much for your help." Thax hung up.

"Nice." Campisano snickered. "Very nice."

Thax looked at the clock on his wall.

"I have a two o'clock hearing with Judge Matthai I need to get to." He walked to the door for his jacket. "We need to talk tomorrow about Jimmy Karopolis and Detective Schick. It's time for us to send our own message."

* * *

Thax left Judge Matthai's courtroom on the second floor and headed for the U.S. Marshals office on the first floor. He waved to the receptionist who buzzed him in the front door and headed down the hall to Deputy U.S. Marshal Scott Adkins's office.

"Thax, come on in buddy," Adkins greeted his friend.

"Scott. Talk to me. What's on those surveillance cameras?"

"I guess you don't want to tell me why you're so interested in this, do you?"

"We know this guy's father. We talked to him about being a witness in a case we're working. I don't think this was a coincidence."

Adkins held up his right hand. "I don't need to know any more." Adkins sat at his computer and pulled up a video screen. He played a four second video clip for Thax. The video showed a dark-colored pickup truck driving up to the side of the courthouse onto the pavement, stopping quickly and a person wearing dark clothes, face covered, sliding Jimmy Karopolis's body out of the bed of the truck. The vehicle then sped off. "These guys were fast, Thax. They knew we had cameras out there but they were smart enough and bold enough to do this anyway. The license tag was removed from the truck. My guys are still trying to figure out the exact make and model. We've done some freeze frames but it's kind of blurry. The guy who got out, there's obviously no identification. White, black, Hispanic, who knows? These guys were good. We aren't pulling any prints off the blanket either."

Thax tried to hide his frustration.

"I appreciate you working on this, Scott."

"No problem. I hear the guy is going to pull through, huh?" "I hope so."

"Hey, some reporter from Valley 10 is looking for a copy of this video. My boss didn't want to release it. She's called me a couple of times in the last few days trying to get it. What do you think?"

"Let's release it. Maybe someone will recognize the truck. Why don't you call her? Maybe we can get it on the news tonight."

"Will do."

"Hey, and if you pin down any details on that truck let me know or give Shea Barrows at the Bureau a call."

"You got it, man," Scott answered as he headed toward the door. "You been doing any fishing?"

"Every chance I get."

* * *

"Good evening, and thank you for watching Valley 10 News at seven o'clock. I'm Will Coburn. Let's go right to Chrissy Barnes who's at the federal courthouse in downtown Allentown for an update on what has been our top story for days. Chrissy."

Barnes stood on the side of the federal courthouse.

"Will, early this evening the United States Marshals Service released this video of the dumping of Jimmy Karopolis's brutally beaten body, several days ago, right here where I am standing. As viewers can see, what appears to be a dark-colored pickup truck pulled onto the sidewalk here and then at least one person can be seen pulling Karopolis's body from the bed of the truck. The vehicle then speeds off. Authorities say they have few leads on the identities of the assailants or the vehicle and they are asking anyone with any information about the vehicle or the identity of the person in the video to please call the U.S. Marshals office or the Allentown Police tip line.

"Today, Allentown Police Chief Scott Butler told Valley 10 News that Jimmy Karopolis was not, to his knowledge, a witness in any pending cases in Lehigh County Court. Federal authorities have been silent as to any connection to any federal investigations. Meanwhile, Karopolis remains in extremely critical condition at LVH-Cedar Crest. Reporting from the federal courthouse in Allentown, I'm Chrissy Barnes. Back to you, Will."

Twenty-Two

CAMPISANO AND BARROWS sat in Thax's office.

"Does John Karopolis know the shit will hit the fan when we do this?" Thax asked Barrows.

"I'm telling you, Thax, he is more determined now than ever. His boy is not out of the woods yet, and he's angry that they didn't come after him," Barrows answered. "And he doesn't know that we were surveilling his home and business in case they did try to go after him. Who thought they would go after his kid?"

"Well, I'm just going to let you testify in the grand jury, Shea. I'm not going to bring Karopolis in here. You can summarize what he told you and provide the evidence with the photo lineup. I don't want him getting cold feet when we get to trial."

"He'll be fine," Barrows said confidently.

"So what are we charging Schick with?" Campisano asked.

"Violating John Karopolis's civil rights by stealing his money," Thax explained.

"That's beautiful," Campisano said.

"It gets better," Thax continued to explain. "The Court of Appeals says that a civil rights violation is a crime of violence, even if no one gets hurt."

"What does that mean?" Campisano asked.

"Well, you know the statute that lets us charge a drug dealer who brings a gun to a drug deal with a five-year mandatory minimum sentence—carrying a gun during a drug crime?"

"Yeah."

"Well it applies if you carry a gun during a crime of violence, too. So, in addition to the civil rights violation which, unfortunately, isn't a very big hit—maybe a couple of years—there is a mandatory five-year *consecutive* sentence for the gun. Karopolis did see a gun on Schick, didn't he?" Thax confirmed what Barrows had told him before.

"Sure did. They all had guns," she answered.

"We can do that even if the gun he was carrying was because he was a cop?" Campisano asked.

"Yes," Thax answered. "Bad news for him. When you're committing another crime, the law doesn't care that you would otherwise be allowed to carry the firearm."

"When are we doing this?" Campisano asked.

"We'll indict him on Wednesday. That gives us a few days to put this all together and get the boss to sign off on it."

"And the arrest?"

"We'll talk about it, but I don't want to wait. We need to do this and do it soon." Thax looked at the agents. They both shook their heads in agreement. "Here we go."

Barrow's cell phone buzzed twice. She pulled it out of her purse and looked at it. "It's a text from Judy at the clerk's office. She just emailed me the documents on the judges."

"Looks like we're headed to my office, Chris." The agents prepared to leave.

"Let me know how that goes," Thax said as they walked out.

* * *

Thax answered his office phone. It was Chrissy.

"Hey, mister."

"Hey, yourself. Aren't you working?" Thax teased, looking at the clock on his wall. It was four forty-five.

"Of course I'm working. That's why I called. Anything new on Jimmy Karopolis?"

"I'll talk to you about it later," Thax said.

"We'll it's going to have to be much later. I'm headed to Easton. Looks like they have some more information on a possible suspect in the Murtaugh murder. It's going to be a late night. I think they're going to want me there for a live shot at eleven. I may just drive to my place and make sure no one has put it up for sale. It'll be midnight by the time I get done and drive back there. Besides, Easton may be popping tomorrow."

"Whatever," Thax replied.

"You'll miss me, won't you?"

"Maybe. But I do have my teddy bear," Thax chuckled.

"I'll see you tomorrow sometime," Chrissy said tenderly.

"Tomorrow's Saturday."

"I know. I'll see you when you get back from the river."

* * *

Thax's office phone rang as he walked to the door to grab his jacket.

Who's calling me now? he thought glancing at his watch. It was six-thirty p.m. "Leave a message," he shouted, turning out the office lights. He headed for the door. His cell phone rang. It was Campisano.

"What's up, Christopher?"

"You still in the building?"

"Not for long."

"You need to come to my office. Shea and I are looking at these records and we think we found something."

"I'm on my way down now."

* * *

Thax walked into the DEA conference room where Barrows and Campisano were examining the Northampton County records.

"What did you find?" Thax asked.

"Well, what we *didn't* find was any defendant Judge Harlin had on his docket with the initials E.S.," Campisano answered.

"Okay . . ." Thax replied.

"There are a few defendants with those initials that were on other judge's dockets, but nothing on Harlin's. This one is interesting though," Campisano said, handing one of the pages to Thax.

"This is Harlin's case. Victor Lord. Do you see the sentencing date?

October fifteenth, two years ago. October fifteenth was a Monday. The twelfth was the Friday before, so we're close." Campisano watched for Thax's reaction.

"Who is this guy?" Thax asked, sitting down at the table.

"Interesting. I just ran him in NCIC because these records don't tell me anything other than a defendant's name, the type of proceeding and a date." Campisano paused. Thax hated when Chris told a story.

"And . . ." Thax waited.

"Victor Lord was arrested by the Easton Police Department in July, two years ago, for possession of cocaine with intent to deliver. That's this case. He pled guilty. It shows the disposition as probation."

"Does this guy have any prior record?" Thax asked.

"That's the part that's really interesting. He's got *three* prior convictions for possession of cocaine. How the hell does a guy with three prior cocaine possession convictions get probation when he gets convicted of a more serious offense of possession with intent to deliver?" Campisano asked.

"Harlin gave this guy probation? Did you call Easton P.D.?" Thax asked.

"Not yet. I was waiting for you to come down. I knew you would have more questions. We have a guy from Easton P.D. on our task force. Do you want me to call him?"

"Yeah. Let's take this one step at a time," Thax cautioned.

"No problem, I'll just tell our guy from EPD that I'm looking at Lord for something else and we saw the arrest. Maybe he can get some details."

"Nice work, guys." Thax walked toward the door. "You can go home now. Have a good weekend!"

Barrows smiled. "You too, Thax."

* * *

Thax sat on his couch watching a rerun of *Columbo* from the 1970s. He savored the last few drops from a glass of good California cabernet sauvignon. At eleven o'clock, he turned to Channel 10.

The cameras cut to Chrissy at the Northampton County Courthouse. Thax admired how charming and alluring Chrissy Barnes really was. He was amazed that a national network hadn't scooped her up—not that he ever wanted her to go.

"Tonight, authorities here in Easton say they believe they are close to identifying a suspect in the brutal rape and slaying of Lafayette College sophomore Erica Murtaugh. The person of interest, who authorities believe goes by the name of 'Jimmie Lee', is a homeless man who police say was seen before the murder at the tip of Hugh Moore Park in Easton, where he is suspected of killing Murtaugh. Police have previously said Murtaugh died of blunt force trauma to the upper body. We have now learned through law enforcement sources familiar with the investigation, but who could not be identified, the gruesome details of this crime, that Murtaugh was strangled while she was raped, then her skull was crushed with a large rock. What authorities are not saying tonight is where Jimmie Lee is or if they know anything more about him. They have released this blurry cell phone photograph of him that we are showing on the screen and have asked the public to call Easton Police if he is encountered or to immediately call 9-1-1. Live in Easton, Pennsylvania, Chrissy Barnes for Valley 10 News."

Thax poured another glass of wine and rested his head on a large square pillow. As he drifted off to sleep, his cell phone rang. He reached the phone on the table next to him just before it stopped. It was Campisano.

"You're not in bed yet, are you?"

"No. What's up?"

"I thought you'd want to know this and I didn't want to bother you while you were fishing."

"What?"

"Victor Lord got popped on a traffic stop with a full brick of powder and almost half a kilo of crack. Probation for a kilo and a half of cocaine."

"Jesus," Thax said with disgust. "I bet there are some pissed off cops and a prosecutor somewhere over there in Easton. I think we need to talk to them."

"I'm on it," Campisano said.

"Monday. Have a good weekend." Thax hung up.

Twenty-Three

JOSH SCHICK HAD been a fitness fanatic since his days in the Marine Corps. Not much kept him from his daily appointed five mile run through the rolling hills of the Lehigh Valley countryside. He downed a small glass of cool water, fastened the band on his sports watch and said goodbye to his wife who was just grabbing her first cup of decaf.

"See you in a bit," Josh said planting a kiss on her cheek.

"Be careful," was Marlena's stalwart reply.

Josh bounded out the front door of their simple, but well-maintained, two-story home on Hilcrest Drive in Macungie. He waited to hear the clicking of Marlena locking the door behind him. He started slowly, warming up, as he turned onto Hill Street then right onto Fairview. His route took him down Fairview Avenue, a quiet country road, to Shoemaker and Macungie Elementary Schools and Eyer Middle School, where he would veer off onto Buckeye Road. Another mile and a half and a U-turn would bring him home.

He quickened his pace as he turned right onto Fairview. The street was peacefully quiet at six-thirty on this humid Monday morning. An occasional car passed him forcing him to hug the edge of the two-lane paved road. Approaching the parking lot for Shoemaker Elementary, a dark blue Ford Crown Victoria with flashing blue lights sped past him. The vehicle turned sharply in front of him blocking his path. He slowed when another Crown Vic pulled up next to him. A quick blare of a siren stopped him in his tracks. Shea Barrows jumped out of the passenger side door wearing her FBI raid jacket.

"FBI," she screamed, leveling her 9mm handgun at Schick's head. "Get on the ground now!" Schick raised his hands and dropped to his knees.

"Face down! Hands behind your head!" she shouted.

Schick, his heart racing, complied immediately.

"Don't shoot," he yelled out and dropped to his chest.

Three other FBI agents had followed Barrows toward Schick and trained their firearms on him.

Barrows kneeled down next to Schick, holstered her weapon and reached for her handcuffs. She pulled Schick's right hand from behind his head and snapped the handcuff around his wrist. She swiftly finished handcuffing him.

"Stay down," she directed.

Schick was wearing running shorts and a T-shirt, but Barrows, a creature of good habits, asked any way.

"Are you armed?"

"No," Schick replied.

Barrows and Agent Marco Martinez grabbed Schick's arms and lifted him to his feet.

Barrows leaned forward and looked into Schick's eyes.

"Detective Joshua Schick. You are under arrest for violating the civil rights of John Karopolis and for carrying a firearm during a crime of violence."

Schick looked stunned.

"You have the right to remain silent. Anything you say can and will be used against you in a court of law. You have the right to an attorney. If you can't afford one, one will be appointed for you. You have the right to have that attorney present during questioning. If you choose to answer questions you can stop at any time. Do you understand the rights I've just explained to you?" Barrow asked, knowing Schick had advised hundreds of suspects of the same rights as a police officer.

"Yes."

"Let's go." Barrows pulled on Schick's left arm.

"Can you please call my wife and tell her what's going on?"

"There's an agent at your house right now," Barrows said.

She guided Schick toward the vehicle. Before opening the rear passenger side door, she stopped.

"Just check him," Barrows directed her fellow agent to pat down Schick for weapons.

"He's good," Agent Martinez said, finishing his search.

"Watch your head," Barrows said, placing Schick in the back seat of the FBI vehicle. Martinez got in and sat next to him. Barrows got into the passenger's side while another agent entered the driver's side.

"Where are we going?" Schick asked.

Barrows turned toward Schick. "The federal building, my office, then the U.S. Marshal. I'm sure the magistrate judge will see you for initial appearance this afternoon."

Schick nodded.

The unmarked cars headed north on Brookside Road toward Allentown.

"Anything you want to tell me about the sham search warrant you and your boys did at Mr. Karopolis's home out in the West End?" Barrows asked pointedly. She hated foreplay.

"I don't know what you're talking about, so I guess I'll just remain silent."

"That's fine," Barrows replied. "Someday soon we'll talk. I'm sure of it."

* * *

"All rise! The Honorable Kellie Franckhauser presiding," the Court Security Officer called out as the United States Magistrate Judge took the bench in Courtroom 2B.

The packed courtroom remained standing until Judge Franckhauser settled into her robust looking black leather chair.

"Be seated and come to order," the CSO directed.

"Please call the case," Franckhauser asked the courtroom deputy clerk.

"United States of America versus Joshua Schick," the deputy clerk announced. "Will counsel please state their appearances."

Thax and Barrows sat at Government counsel's table. Thax stood to speak.

"Good afternoon, Your Honor, Thax Colby for the United States."

"Good afternoon Mr. Colby."

Jack Winthrop stood behind the defense table. A well respected criminal trial lawyer and a tough opponent, Winthrop was a lot more lawyer than any local cop could afford. Even a corrupt one.

"Good afternoon Judge, Jack Winthrop appearing for Mr. Schick."

"Afternoon, Mr. Winthrop," the judge replied.

Judge Franckhauser examined the indictment.

"Mr. Schick," the judge addressed the defendant.

Schick was prompted by Winthrop to stand.

"Sir, you have been charged in an indictment with two counts of alleged criminal conduct. It is not my intention to go over those charges with you today in great detail. Mr. Winthrop, I assume you have a copy of the indictment?"

"I do, Your Honor," Winthrop announced.

"Mr. Schick," the judge began, "I want to tell you that you have the right to remain silent. If you have already spoken to someone from the Government, you do not need to continue speaking with them. You have counsel with you today and you have the right to have counsel with you at each stage of this case. If you cannot afford an attorney, I will appoint one for you at no cost to you. Because you have been charged by an indictment, a grand jury has already made a determination that there is probable cause to believe you have committed these offenses, therefore, you are not entitled to a preliminary hearing. Do you understand what I've just explained to you?"

"Yes, Your Honor."

"You may be seated, Mr. Schick." Schick sat and the judge continued. "You are entitled to have bail considered and I am prepared to do that now. What's the Government's position on bail, Mr. Colby?"

Thax stood to address the court.

"Your Honor, the United States is requesting that Mr. Schick be detained without bail."

Schick's wife, Marlena, a petite, attractive and visibly pregnant young woman, sat two rows behind the defense counsel's table. She sniffled, brushing her long jet black hair away from her face.

"It's okay," Schick mouthed, glancing in her direction.

Thax continued.

"Your Honor, we are asking the Court to continue this hearing for three days until Thursday. Mr. Schick is an Allentown police detective and he is charged with a crime of violence and a firearms violation that carries a mandatory five-year consecutive sentence. This offense involved breaking into a citizen's home under the guise of conducting a search warrant to steal forty-thousand dollars from the man's house. Mr. Schick was armed as were his unidentified co-conspirators."

Thax made his argument, turning briefly toward the back of the courtroom to ensure he was heard. Seated in the last row, against the back wall of the courtroom were familiar faces and unexpected spectators. Detectives Rocco Morales and Steve Dailey sat side-by-side, joined by Detectives Thomas Gallon and Kathy Piper.

Thax made eye contact with each of them as he continued to address the court.

"Several days ago, Your Honor, that citizen's son, his almost lifeless body was dumped on the side steps of this courthouse. We are asking for the three-day continuance to give us additional time to further investigate that horrible crime and to determine, if we can, whether this defendant had anything to do with it. It's quite a coincidence that within days after Mr. Schick was interviewed by the FBI about the theft at Mr. Karopolis's home, that Karopolis's son was brutally beaten and his body dumped here at the same courthouse where Schick was interviewed."

"Mr. Winthrop?" the judge asked. "What is your position?"

"Your Honor, Mr. Schick is a narcotics detective here in this city. He has served honorably for thirteen years. Before that he served heroically as a United States Marine. He has lived here in this area for almost fifteen years. His wife," Winthrop turned toward Marlena, "is four months pregnant. We would ask that you release Mr. Schick on his own recognizance. My client is neither a flight risk nor a danger to anyone."

"I assume you oppose the Government's request for a three-day continuance?"

"We do."

"Well, I find that there is a good reason for the continuance and I'm going to grant it. We will reconvene Thursday at 3:00 p.m. Mr. Schick you will be detained until then. We're in recess."

"All rise," the Court Security Officer bellowed, as the judge left the courtroom.

Two deputy U.S. Marshals approached Schick from behind him to escort him in their custody.

Thax walked over to defense counsel's table where Winthrop was still standing next to Schick. Thax looked back at Marlena who glared at him through her tears.

"Jack," Thax addressed Winthrop, "can I speak to your client for a minute? I don't want him to say a word. I just want him to listen."

"He's not saying a word, but you can say whatever you want to him."

Thax set a letter size piece of paper in front of Schick—a colorful computer printed photograph of a school. Thax pushed it toward Schick.

"Do you know what that is?" Thax asked without expecting a response. "Right there, those windows lead into Ms. Bastian's second grade classroom where she teaches a room full of seven-year-old boys and girls."

Schick looked closely at the picture.

"You keep being a tough guy and that's where your kids are going to be when they first see their daddy outside of federal prison."

Schick glared at Thax.

"You need to do the right thing and cooperate. Forget about those people in the back of the courtroom. They aren't the ones going to do your time."

Thax pushed the paper closer to Schick.

"You can keep the picture."

* * *

Chrissy Barnes walked down the front steps of the federal courthouse. The camera zoomed in on her face. Glossy brick red lipstick courtesy of Dolce & Gabanna accentuated her sharp petite features. A light early evening breeze gently waved her gold-spun blonde hair.

"An Allentown Police Detective is under arrest this evening charged with federal civil rights and firearms violations. Joshua Schick, an almost fourteen-year veteran of the force and narcotics detective was arrested near his home early this morning by special agents of the FBI. In court today, federal prosecutors asked that Schick be detained without bail pending his trial on the charges. Magistrate Judge Kellie Franckhauser continued the hearing until this Thursday. Until then, Schick remains in federal custody.

"In the hearing this afternoon, federal prosecutors told the judge that investigators are still investigating a connection between this case and the brutal beating of Jimmy Karopolis almost two weeks ago. Karopolis remains in guarded condition at LVH-Cedar Crest. The charges in this case stem from a sham search warrant that was allegedly executed by Schick and other unknowns at Karopolis's father's home outside of Allentown earlier this year.

"Allentown Police Chief Scott Butler said today that he was shocked by these allegations and that his department would cooperate with the FBI in any investigation of this matter. Allentown Mayor and gubernatorial candidate Logan Branfield, who still holds a slim lead in the most recent statewide polls, was unavailable for comment about his city's police department. Live in Allentown, Chrissy Barnes, Valley 10 News."

* * *

"Goddammit, Richie." Logan Branfield smacked his hand on the top of his desk. "I thought this was going to be taken care of. We can't have these damn distractions. Not now!"

"Schick said he would take care of the problem," Sokol explained. "How did I know he would fuck it up so badly?"

"I don't care, I don't care." Branfield's cadence got louder and louder. "I don't care, I don't fucking care! If I have to listen to one more story about corrupt cops in this department. Do you think that's not going to bite us in the ass in November? My opponent is so happy with this he's playing with himself. And what's the story with this prosecutor? We don't need this guy digging around in our shit. It's bad enough the money has slowed down so much."

"I hear you, boss," Sokol lamented.

"Shut this shit down. Am I perfectly fucking clear on this?"

"I'll take care of this personally," Sokol assured his boss.

Twenty-Four

"Are you seriously agreeing to let this guy out?" Campisano asked Thax as he and Barrows sat in Thax's office discussing Schick's detention hearing. "That's exactly what he wants. I thought we were going to break this guy's balls."

"Christopher," Thax's voice got quiet. "A guy walks outside and he sees a deer in his yard. His yard is fenced and he knows the deer had to jump it to get in, so the deer can easily get out. So why hasn't the deer escaped?"

"Is this going somewhere?" Campisano asked.

"The guy opens the gate so the deer can get out. When he does, the deer starts racing around frantically running *away* from the gate," Thax continued. "You see, it's not that the deer can't get out, he's panicked because *he* knows there is a pack of wolves lying out there waiting him out. The danger is the open gate. The last thing he wants is for the man to open it."

Campisano grinned. "You think Schick really doesn't want to get out of jail?"

"I think he wants to be home with his wife, but he has to take us on at this hearing and win on his own terms. He can jump out of the yard, he just can't let *us* open the gate."

"So, if we agree to let him out everybody is going to think we got to him and convinced him to cooperate since Monday," Campisano interjected.

"Exactly," Thax said.

"In other words, we're feeding him to the wolves." Campisano shook his head.

"We're giving him a choice," Thax said. "He can stay inside the fence and cooperate with us and we'll protect him or he can face the wolves on the outside who will wonder how he managed to change our minds from detaining him to letting him go."

* * *

Spectators filed into Judge Franckhauser's packed courtroom. A few minutes before the scheduled three o'clock detention hearing, the rhythmic clanking of Josh Schick's leg irons announced his presence, escorted by two deputy U.S. Marshals into the courtroom. Schick wore the same drab orange jumpsuit worn by all prisoners held at the Lehigh County Jail. Without a federal detention facility nearby, the Marshals used the county jail for bed space for their federal detainees.

Marlena Schick sat in the first row behind the defense counsel's table. Despite the difficulties of the last few days, she managed a smile for her husband. Security policies didn't permit her to hug or even touch him. Seconds later, Jack Winthrop appeared, greeting his client and his wife.

Thax and Barrows made their way from the double wooden entrance doors to Government counsel's table. Thax walked to the defense table.

"Good afternoon, Jack."

"Afternoon, Thax," Winthrop responded.

"Any thoughts on what I spoke to your client about on Monday?"

"Honestly," Winthrop answered, "I don't think that's ever going to happen. We understand that he might get detained today but he's ready to fight this. I don't know what evidence you have other than this Karopolis guy, but my client doesn't know anything about this search warrant you're talking about. We'll just get the discovery materials you have and he wants to go to trial in thirty days so, if he is detained, he can get home to his wife before she has their babies."

Thax noted the intense interest in his conversation by Detectives Dailey, Gallon, Piper and Morales as they looked on from the back row of the courtroom.

"Detective Schick," Thax said quietly, so that only the detective could hear, "you're making a big mistake."

Thax walked back to Government counsel's table. "Here we go," he whispered to Barrows.

Magistrate Judge Franckhauser took the bench with the usual fanfare and began the detention hearing.

"Mr. Colby, are you ready to proceed with the detention hearing?"

Thax stood, looked over at Schick then toward the judge.

"Your Honor, at this time the United States is withdrawing its previous request that the defendant be detained. We have no objection to the defendant being released on his own recognizance."

The sound of hushed voices reverberated through the gallery. Thax's announcement caught Winthrop off guard.

"Let's have quiet in the courtroom please," Judge Franckhauser admonished the spectators.

"Mr. Colby," the judge spoke, "I understand this matter involves a firearms offense that carries a mandatory consecutive five-year sentence. Is that accurate?"

"It is, Your Honor. It is also my understanding that Chief Butler has, as of the time of Mr. Schick's arrest on Monday, placed this defendant on paid administrative leave and has prohibited him from carrying his city-issued firearm. I would ask that the terms of his release, if the Court is so inclined to follow our request, include that he not possess *any* firearm during his release."

Franckhauser had been a Magistrate Judge for almost six years. Before her appointment to the bench, she spent almost fifteen years as a federal prosecutor in the Philadelphia office. Thax Colby was her mentor. As a prosecutor, she had changed her position on bail many times when a defendant started to cooperate—the theory being that a defendant who was cooperating was a lot less likely to flee or become involved again in crime while on release. She didn't know if Schick was cooperating or not but she knew enough not to ask Thax why he had changed his position. At this point in the game, cooperation was something you didn't announce.

"Mr. Schick."

"Yes, Your Honor."

"Do you understand the United States has withdrawn its previous request that you be detained and has asked that you be released?"

"Yes, Judge. I do."

"Will you agree to abide by the conditions of release that I set?"

"I will, Judge."

"Mr. Winthrop, do you have anything you wish to say at this time?"

"No, ma'am."

"Very well then, Mr. Schick. I will release you on your own recognizance. That means you do not have to post any security or bond. It also means you agree to show up for all further proceedings in this case and to abide by the other conditions that I will set, including that you not possess any firearm while on release and that you not have any contact with any witnesses in your case. Do you understand?"

"Yes, Judge, I do."

"Very well. The defendant will be released. We're in recess."

After the judge left the bench, Thax stirred the pot a little more. He walked over to speak with Winthrop under the watchful gaze of all the spectators, particularly the four detectives. Schick was still seated next to Winthrop.

"Jack," Thax said, "call me before someone else who was involved in that sham search warrant with your client decides they want to talk to me first."

Winthrop had no reply.

"You don't think your guy is the only one I'm trying to get to talk to me, do you, Jack?"

"Have a nice day, Thax," Winthrop replied, unfazed. Jack Winthrop was seldom intimidated.

As Thax walked away, Winthrop leaned over to speak with Schick. As usual, he was all business.

"Alright, Josh. You get to go home. We'll talk sometime next week. Don't worry about a thing." Winthrop patted Schick on the back and packed his briefcase.

"Thanks," Schick responded. "But I have one question for you."

"What's that?"

"I know you didn't show up here because you like the scenery and I know I can't pay you. So who's paying your fee?"

"Josh. That doesn't matter. Let's just say it's someone who is looking out for your best interests. That's all you need to know."

Schick nodded.

As Schick and Winthrop talked, Thax and Barrows headed toward the exit doors where Thax spied Chrissy leaving the courtroom. By the time he reached the hallway, she was gone.

* * *

Thax's office phone was ringing when he walked in after the Schick hearing. He scrambled to reach it on the last ring.

"This is Thax Colby."

"Well I'm glad to hear that," Chrissy said cheerfully, "because you're just the man I want to talk to."

"You skipped out on me," Thax teased.

"I'm sorry. I had to call in the story. I'm going live in an hour on the Schick story. Anything else you can tell me?"

"Nothing you can report."

Chrissy didn't respond.

"What's going on?" Thax asked, sensing that something was wrong.

"I'm going to be a little late tonight. There's a producer in town from Fox News and he wants to take me to dinner," Chrissy said, uncertain of how Thax would respond. "I think they like me."

"What's not to like about you? Knock'em dead!"

Chrissy was unsure of the enthusiasm.

"Will I see you before I go to bed?" Thax asked.

"If not, I'll wake you when I get there."

Twenty-Five

At three-thirty in the afternoon, Louie's café, located a half mile east of the Northampton County Courthouse, was quiet and almost empty. The secluded business in an old tavern on Butler Street in Easton was marked by a single white metal sign hung above the door with the name "Louie's" painted in black. An old jukebox played hits from the sixties and seventies.

Seated at the back corner booth and facing the front door, Northampton County Assistant District Attorney Aaron Lewis anxiously awaited his guests. Minutes later, Easton police officer Hugh Coleman joined him at the table.

"Are these guys gonna show up?" Coleman asked.

"They'll be here," Lewis assured him.

A few minutes and one Linda Ronstadt song later, Thax and Campisano walked in.

"Nice place," Campisano cracked as they scanned the desolate restaurant, eventually spotting their party. At the back booth, they introduced themselves to Lewis and Coleman.

"Thanks for meeting with us," Thax said. "I know Chris was pretty vague about why we wanted to meet. I appreciate you guys taking your time to talk with us."

"What's this all about, Thax?" Lewis asked.

"It's about Victor Lord."

"What about him?"

"Well for starters," Campisano said, "can you tell us how you arrested him?"

"Hugh?" Lewis deferred to Coleman.

"Sure. Well, I was patrolling the downtown historic district. I don't remember the date, but it was summer a few years back. One of the other marked units responded to a prowler call near the Trinity Episcopal Church. They didn't find anybody there when they got there. An hour later, I was patrolling near there and I saw an older model gray Honda Accord parked in the back of the church. There's never anybody at the church that late, so I checked it out. There was nobody in the car so I walked around the courtyard. That's when I heard the tires screech as the Honda tore out of the lot. I got back to my unit and put out an alert for anyone to stop that vehicle. Twenty-five minutes later, a marked unit down by the waterfront put eyes on the car and they tried to stop it. The guy took off and we had a chase. I joined in and after taking us for a joy ride for fifteen minutes, I did a PIT maneuver on him and spun him out."

"Jesus . . ." Campisano sighed.

"That's not the end of it," Coleman continued. "He took off running and, this is west of here, over near Easton Hospital. He ran behind a rehab center over there and John Spitori, one of our K-9 guys, sent his dog after him. Tough, bad-ass little German Shepherd. Bit the shit out of Victor."

Campisano was glued to Coleman's every word. The guy could tell a story.

"Anyway, while Victor was telling Spitori how he was gonna sue him for letting his dog bite him, I was searching his car. He was under arrest and he abandoned his vehicle, so I searched it. On the back floorboard was a K-Mart bag with a full kilo of cocaine in it, plus about 400 grams of crack. I don't know what he was doing at the church, but that was pretty stupid to be dicking around like that while he was riding dirty with that much coke. No doubt that's why he ran though," Coleman finished.

"Wow," Thax said, "that's quite a story."

"Man, he sure was pissed at that dog," Coleman said reaching for his cell phone. "I think I still have a picture of his leg on my phone. Dog chewed him up really bad." Coleman searched his phone for the picture. "Here it is!" Coleman said, turning the phone screen to show Thax and Campisano.

"Jesus! That's a serious bite," Campisano said as he and Thax looked at a picture of Lord's leg from just above the knee down to his ankle. "The dog did some serious damage."

"He took eighty-five stitches. Poor son of a bitch." Coleman grinned.

"So Aaron, tell me what happened with this guy?" Thax asked, bringing the conversation back to its purpose.

"Well, as soon as he was arrested he lawyered up. He didn't say anything. He's a real hardass. We were set for trial in front of Judge Harlin. He's not our worst judge. At least I didn't think so then."

"What do you mean?" Thax asked, not yet ready to disclose the real reason for his interest in the case.

"I mean Lord's got a bad criminal history, especially for drugs," Lewis explained. "He's also been convicted of a few burglaries. Based on the state sentencing guidelines, he was looking at seven to fourteen years, so this was definitely going to be a trial. We caught the guy with the dope in his car."

"What happened?" Thax asked.

"Lord's attorney said he was going to trial. His defense was that someone else was driving the car for a week before Lord got the car early that night. I guess Lord was going to say he borrowed the car from this dude he didn't know and Lord didn't know anything about the dope being in the car. The attorney said Lord ran from the cops because he thought he had an outstanding warrant."

"I take it that wasn't true?" Thax asked.

"Not at all," Lewis answered.

"Then what happened?" Thax asked.

"On the Monday we're supposed to start trial, Lord came in with a big smile on his face. His lawyer told us he was going to plead guilty, that Lord just told him a few minutes before then that he was going to plead. The judge came on the bench and Lord told him he wanted to plead guilty and the judge took the guilty plea."

"He admitted the dope was his under oath?"

"He sure did," Lewis said. "Then everything went haywire."

"What happened?"

"Lord asked to be sentenced immediately. In the state system, you don't have to wait for a presentence report. You can ask to be sentenced right away, which is what he did. So his attorney asked the judge to go below the guidelines, down to three years and I asked Harlin to give him ten," Lewis explained. "The judge talked about how important it was that Lord had accepted responsibility for this crime and how he saved the Commonwealth the expense of trial, which is all bullshit. That happens every time someone pleads guilty rather than go to trial. Then he sentenced him to one year of probation. One year!"

"That's crazy," Thax replied.

"I wanted to appeal him on this one but my boss doesn't like to piss off the judges. He thinks when we appeal we're probably going to lose anyway and then we've just angered the judge we took up on appeal. He's the boss."

"I understand. Has Judge Harlin done anything like this before?"

"You know, Thax, not really. This one just didn't make any sense. He must have taken some crazy pills that morning. I don't know. Since when can we figure out why judges do what they do?"

"Hey, Hugh. Can I get a copy of that dog bite photo?" Campisano interrupted.

Coleman pulled the picture up on his phone and showed it to Campisano again. "What's your email?"

Campisano looked at the photo then took the phone out of Coleman's hand to look at it closer.

"What is it, Christopher?" Thax asked.

Campisano looked at the picture and zoomed in on Lord's leg. "Holy shit, Thax! Can you see what that tattoo down his leg says? I can't believe I didn't see that before."

"What?" Thax looked as Campisano showed him the picture again.

"What does it say?" Coleman asked.

"It says East Side," Campisano answered. "Like in East Side Boyz. We have a street gang in Allentown with that name."

"This obviously means something to you?" Lewis asked.

Thax tried to contain his excitement. "It sounds like one of our gang-bangers made his way from our town to yours, that's all."

Lewis looked at his watch. "Thax, I need to get back before someone misses me. Call me if we can be of any further help to you. Is DEA going to try to do something with this guy?"

Campisano nodded. "We might."

"You don't happen to know where Lord is hanging his hat these days do you, Aaron?" Thax asked.

"I know he finished his year of probation here. I heard he got popped over in Jersey on a burglary. I think he's doing some state prison time. At least someone locked this guy up for a while," Lewis said, as the four men rose from the booth.

"Where in New Jersey?" Thax asked.

"I think right over the line," Lewis responded. "Why? Are you thinking of trying to talk with him?"

"Maybe," Thax answered.

"Don't waste your time, Thax. This guy is a serious asshole. He's as hard-core as they get. He will tell you to go fuck yourself as sure as I'm standing here."

Thax nodded.

"I appreciate all of your help." Thax shook hands with the men. "We'll be in touch."

Coleman and Lewis walked out the front door of Louie's. Campisano looked at Thax.

"At least we know now what the initials E.S. stand for on Chip Meyers's notebook page," Campisano nodded. "East Side."

"Let's find Mr. Lord," Thax said. "I have a few questions for him."

Twenty-Six

Thax and Campisano walked through the front door of the New Jersey Mid-State Correctional Facility Annex. The storied complex, on Fort Dix Army Base in Wrightstown, New Jersey, was a short ninety-minute drive from Allentown for the two feds. A deputy warden, expecting their arrival, met them at the reception area and escorted them to a secure interview room well inside the confines of the prison. The small but adequate room provided a four-foot by three-foot rectangular steel table, with a single round metal stool on each of the longer sides. The stools were bolted to the floor. On the side closest to the large steel door, the table was outfitted with a steel ring to secure a prisoner with handcuffs. Solid stone walls fortified the room and most of the prison structure. New arrivals knew immediately that they were in prison.

Thax and Campisano stood waiting for their guest. A few minutes later, two correctional officers escorted Victor Lord into the room.

"Who are these guys?" Lord growled as the officers seated him at the table. Lord, wearing a tan prison jumpsuit with his home address emblazoned in black letters on the back—New Jersey State Prison—sat on the uncomfortable stool. One of the officers unlocked the handcuff from Lord's right hand and threaded the open cuff through the two-inch steel ring. Lord was immediately recuffed. The ring permitted the chain between the handcuffs to slide through the ring. The inmate was going nowhere.

"Thanks, guys," Thax said as the officers walked out.

Lord glared at Thax. "Who the fuck are you?"

Thax stared back a little longer before speaking.

"Mr. Lord, I'm Thax Colby. I'm a federal prosecutor in Eastern Pennsylvania, Allentown specifically, and this is Special Agent Chris Campisano from DEA."

"That's nice," Lord snapped. "Now get me the fuck out of here. I have nothing to say to you."

Thax ignored Lord's response. "Mr. Lord, you're not going anywhere. Not until I say you are, so your best bet is probably to shut up and listen to what I have to say."

"Officer! Officer!" Lord screamed for the correctional officers outside the door. Thax waited. Lord screamed again.

"Tell me when you're done, Mr. Lord. I've got all day."

Lord sat up, stared straight ahead, and said nothing.

Thax sat on the metal stool facing Lord.

"Mr. Lord, you need to listen to what I'm going to say because I'm only going to say it once. You don't need to say anything but one way or another, you are going to listen to me."

Lord said nothing but stared at Thax.

"I want to know how you got probation for your *fourth* drug conviction. Can you tell me that?" Thax asked without waiting for a response. "That doesn't just happen so I think you can enlighten us as to how it did. Would you like to tell us how that happened?"

Lord continued to stare at Thax.

"Okay, Mr. Lord, let me explain something to you. You had three felony drug convictions before you were caught with a kilo of coke and almost a pound of crack. You pled guilty to possession with intent to deliver that cocaine and crack and admitted it was yours. So here's your big problem now—"

"You're fucking boring me, man," Lord interrupted.

"Your first problem, Mr. Lord, is that you don't know when to shut up and listen. As I was about to say, I'm going to charge you with the same drugs in federal court and because you have at least two previous drug convictions, you're going to get a mandatory life sentence. Do you understand me, Mr. Lord? Life. You are never getting out. No parole, no early release. Life."

Lord laughed, followed by an evil grin.

"Hey, asshole." Campisano had put up with this guy's shit long enough. "You know what life is in the federal system? It means life. It means they're going to carry your sorry ass out of federal prison in a pine box. Get it. He's not fucking around."

"Fuck you," Lord snapped. "You can't prosecute me for the same crime twice. Everybody knows that's double jeopardy!"

"That's good, Victor," Thax responded. "I didn't know you were a lawyer. It's not double jeopardy. It's called dual sovereignty. That's a couple of big words us lawyers use to say that the state can prosecute you for violating its drug laws and the federal government can do the same for violating federal laws. For the same dope."

"I don't need to listen to this bullshit anymore. Get me out of here! Officer!" Lord screamed again with no response.

"Victor, tell me how you got probation in Northampton County for that much cocaine," Thax pressed.

"Fuck you," Lord responded.

"No, I think you're the one who's going to get fucked Victor. I'm done wasting my time. When I walk out of here I'm going to charge you with a mandatory life offense and you are going to die in prison. You're twenty-seven years old. You are going to spend the next fifty years in a federal penitentiary and you will never get out." Thax knew Lord fancied himself as a ladies' man so he played on it. "Do you remember the last time you had a piece of ass, Victor?"

Lord pulled hard on his handcuffs. Thax never flinched.

"I hope you remember it because that was the last time," Thax said. "Last time."

Lord continued to glare at him.

"You have one minute to tell me about your case in Easton. One minute." Thax looked at his watch.

"Man, this is coercion!"

"That's another big word, Victor. You have fifty seconds." Thax stood up.

"You can't put me in jail for life. That's bullshit!" Lord shouted louder.

"Life. You're leaving in a box Victor," Thax responded calmly and started walking for the door. "Thirty seconds."

"You can't do this to me! I'm Victor Lord. You can't screw with me like this! This is bullshit!" Victor tried to stand up.

"You've got twenty seconds."

"Man, shit! Why are you doing this to me?" Lord sat back on the stool.

"Ten, nine, eight . . . I'll see you in federal court Victor."

"I can't . . ."

Lord was breaking.

"I need a name Victor. Four, three, two . . . we're out of here."

"Okay. Okay," Victor pleaded. "Wait a minute . . ."

"One . . ."

"Morales," Lord shouted.

"Morales who?"

"Rocco Morales. Sergeant Rocco Morales, APD."

"What about him?" Thax pushed harder.

"It was his shit, man. We pick it up here in Jersey and drive it to Allentown. Then after we sell it, Morales gets the money, minus our cut."

"Who were you getting it from over here?" Campisano asked.

"I don't know. Morales didn't use the phone. He tracked me down with one of my boys and told me when and where to pick it up. It was never the same place and the shit was always there already. I never seen anyone."

"What happened in Easton?" Thax asked.

"I was rolling through there with the shit and I got a call from some bitch that I had been with a couple of times over there. She wanted me to meet her up at the church and get some. Bitch didn't show up so I drove around a little bit and drove back there. That's when the P.D. rolled up. I guess you know the rest of that story. Fucking dog."

"How long was this going on?" Thax asked.

"For a while, man. At least a couple of years before I got popped in Easton."

"Where's it coming from?" Campisano asked.

"Honest to God man, I don't know. Morales is really smart about this shit. He didn't share much," Lord told him.

"We'll get the details on the dope later," Thax said, looking at Campisano.

He turned back to Lord. "Okay, so tell me about your case. What happened?" Thax asked.

Lord took a deep breath and exhaled.

"Man, you gotta protect me."

"What happened?"

"Morales always had my back in Allentown. Me and the rest of my boys. When I got popped over in Easton, he couldn't help me. He lost his dope and his money. He was really pissed. All I know is he had one of my boys—Nicky—deliver a package to my judge's office. Asked to see the judge and handed it right to him. It was a padded envelope with twenty grand in it. I know 'cause my boy looked inside before he delivered it."

"When did this happen?" Thax asked.

"Morales gave him the envelope the Friday before my trial. After he dropped it off with the judge he got a message to me in the jail over the weekend. It was a piece of paper that said 'plead guilty, everything's good.' So I did. It was Morales taking care of me. He protects the East Side Boyz."

"Okay," Thax said. "Why this judge? What connection does Morales have with this judge?"

"I don't know. I don't know."

Thax sat quietly, assessing whether Lord was telling him everything.

"What happens now?" Lord asked.

"Now you can tell us all about the dope. Start from the beginning." Thax said.

Campisano sat down at the table with his notepad. "Don't leave anything out. Tell me everything. *Everything*."

"I'll tell you everything, but you have to protect me, man," Lord begged.

Thax looked at Lord. "Put me in touch with Nicky. Then we'll be back to see you."

"I can't do that."

Thax turned toward the door.

"I'm getting ready to leave again, Victor and I'm not coming back."

"What's Nicky's last name?" Campisano asked.

Lord looked down at the table and hesitated before he spoke. "Price. Nicholas Price."

"Is he related to Danny?" Thax asked.

"It's Danny Price's kid brother."

"If you talk to Nicky, Danny will know I gave his little brother up. I'll be done, man. I'll never be able to go back there again. They'll be gunning for me."

"How old is Nicky?" Campisano asked.

"Like twenty-five or around there." Lord looked at Thax. "Please, man, I was straight with you. Don't drop me in the grease."

"Who else knows Nicky paid the money to the judge?" Thax asked.

"Just me and Morales." Lord rolled his head back and looked toward the ceiling. "The judge, I guess, but he don't know Nicky's name."

"Victor, I'm going to try to keep you out of this as far as Nicky goes, but I can't make you any promises. I'll do what I can."

Thax and Campisano walked to the door. Lord buried his face in his hands. "You did the right thing, Victor." Thax knocked for the guards. "We'll be in touch."

* * *

Campisano turned his truck onto Route 309 heading north toward Allentown. The trip to New Jersey to talk to Victor Lord was extremely productive. Campisano and Thax discussed their strategy.

"We need to get Shea up to speed on all of this," Thax directed.

"I'll brief her as soon as we get back," Campisano said.

Thax's cell phone rang.

"It's Scott Adkins at the Marshals office," he said, looking at the caller ID. "Hey, Scott. What's going on?"

"Thax, I'm glad I caught you. I tried to reach you a couple of times today."

"I've been inside Mid-State over in Jersey all day interviewing a prisoner. No cell coverage in there. What's going on?"

"I've been working on this Jimmy Karopolis thing. You know me. I can't let anything go," Scott chuckled. "I figure whoever did this did it fast and then dumped him. APD said there was blood all over his apartment, so it obviously happened there. They didn't find anything else there to ID the guys who did it. Anyway, I figured the fastest way to the courthouse from his apartment on Fairmont Street was east on Route 22 and then south on 7th Street. APD has a couple of red light cameras coming down 7th."

"Red light cameras?" Thax asked. "Who the hell would run a red light with an almost dead body in the back of their truck?"

"Exactly, Thax. Who would?"

Thax paused.

"A cop," Thax answered. "Tell me . . ."

"Not on 7th Street. There wasn't anything on that route. But we pulled the photos for the light at 19th and Tilghman. Bingo! We got them, Thax!" Adkins's voice boomed with excitement.

"What?" Thax exclaimed.

"Same truck. About ten minutes before our camera picked them up at the courthouse," Scott advised. "And I saved the best part for last . . . no masks. I got a shot from the front and the back. A woman driving and a black guy as the passenger. The lighting's great at that intersection, even in the middle of the night," Adkins said excitedly.

"Holy shit! Let me put you on speaker phone, Scott. I have Chris Campisano from DEA with me."

"They got pictures of the people who did the Jimmy Karopolis beat down." Thax brought Campisano up to speed.

"Scott, I need you to get those pictures to Shea Barrows at the FBI as soon as you can."

"I'm surprised she hasn't called you yet," Adkins said. "When I couldn't get you, I called her because you told me to if I couldn't reach you."

Thax's phone beeped, indicating he was getting another incoming call. It was Barrows.

"Scott, that's Shea calling. Let me call you back, buddy. You're the best," Thax said, pressing the button connecting him to Barrows.

"Talk to me, Shea. That was Scott Adkins I was just talking to."

"It's Gallon and Piper," Barrows said. "No doubt. It's like someone was sitting on the hood of the truck taking their picture. They are done, Thax. Stick a fork in 'em."

"Shea, you keep this as tight as a drum. I don't want this getting out to anyone."

"Of course, Thax. What about Scott?"

"Don't worry about him. He was divorced for almost five years before anybody knew about it. He can keep a secret."

Barrows chuckled and changed the subject. "How was your trip?"

"Very productive. We'll talk when we get back."

"Okay. Sounds good."

"Hey. One more thing. Can you check NCIC to see if there are any active warrants for a Nicholas Price, white male, approximately twenty-five years old? And flag this guy's driver's license through PennDOT. I want to know if anybody runs him. I'll explain when we get back."

"Sure thing."

Twenty-Seven

"I WANT TO PRAISE our firefighters today for all of their bravery and sacrifices made in saving the lives of our citizens every day. My promise to you, the people of this great state of Pennsylvania, is that no firefighter will ever lose his or her job to budget cuts in a Branfield administration. Never! Let's rally this city around the thought that the Keystone State can be better than it has ever been!" Logan Branfield smacked his right hand on the top of the podium. "Better leadership! Strong support for our heroes! Let's win in November!"

The crowd of several hundred erupted with cheers, waving Branfield for Governor signs against the backdrop of the historic red brick firehouse, now the Pennsylvania National Fire Museum. Branfield basked in the outpouring of support from the Harrisburg crowd. The mayor walked from the podium, turning several times to engage supporters who continued to cheer him on. His path to his waiting vehicle led him into a small group of local reporters.

"Mayor," a young, smartly dressed woman holding a microphone shouted over the still energized crowd. Branfield stopped and turned toward her. "Alex Lee with WHTM here in Harrisburg. Mayor, to what do you attribute your almost four-point lead in the polls as we head into September?"

Lee thrust the microphone toward Branfield.

"I think the citizens of this great state are starting to see a clear choice. We have run an honest, straightforward campaign and the people can see what terrific things I have done in my home city of Allentown. Crime, especially violent crime, is down significantly, and our city looks beautiful!" Branfield spoke louder as the group continued to chant and cheer.

Another reporter, pushed forward.

"Mayor Branfield, Brian Tucker with the Patriot-News. Do you have any comment on the recent developments in your police department? A suicide of one narcotics officer and now an arrest of another. I know you tout your accomplishments there but is there a problem in your police department?"

Branfield glared at Tucker.

"Sadly and tragically, one of our officers ended his own life. There is no indication it had anything to do with his job or the superb police department that he worked for." Branfield started to walk away, ignoring the rest of the question.

Tucker pressed forward.

"What about Detective Schick, sir? What about the charges against him?"

Branfield turned sharply and looked Tucker in the eye.

"Mr. Tucker, I'm not going to comment on a pending case. As I am sure you know, Detective Schick is presumed innocent. We'll see how that all turns out, and we can talk about it then."

The candidate made his way to the awaiting black Lincoln Town Car and waved one last time to the crowd of supporters as he settled into the back seat. Richie Sokol who was walking next to him the entire time closed the door behind Branfield and got into the front passenger's seat.

"I hope that little piece of shit Tucker's tire isn't flat when he gets up for work on Monday," the mayor grumbled.

Sokol nodded his head in agreement.

"I bet all four of them are, boss," Sokol chuckled.

* * *

Marlena Schick leaned up against a wall of pillows on her bed trying desperately to get comfortable. Her husband, Josh, laid across the top of the bed trying to help, stuffing pillows here and there. When it looked like she had found a comfortable position, he started to get up from the bed. Marlena grabbed his hand and pulled him back.

"Give me your hand," she asked, pulling it toward her stomach. "These are our babies, Josh. Are you going to tell me anything about what that prosecutor said you did? You haven't said a word to me."

"What do you want me to say, Mar?" he asked defiantly.

"Well, how about start with did you do it?"

Josh was silent. He didn't like to lie to his wife. Marlena, like Kristin Meyers, knew they had more than they could afford on the salaries they both made, but never questioned her husband about the extra cash. She never asked, so Josh never had to lie to her.

Marlena pulled his hand harder into her stomach. "Our babies, Josh."

"What if I did?"

"Oh, Josh," Marlena shook her head.

The tough former marine's eyes welled up. He took a deep breath.

"We've all been taking money. For a long time. It started real small, fifty bucks a guy, so no one would notice. Then it just got out of control. There was so much money. These pieces of garbage had tens of thousands of dollars and they never worked a day in their lives. It was just too easy to take it from them and there was no way to say 'no' when everybody else in the unit was doing it."

Marlena squeezed her husband's hand and closed her eyes. She rolled her head back and began to cry.

"Don't cry, Mar," he said, regaining his composure.

"You've got to make this right, Josh. I don't want you to go to prison. I can't raise these babies on my own. You have to do something."

"What do you want me to do, Mar?" he asked, pulling his hand away from her. "How do I do it? The only way out is for me to plead guilty to something and to tell them the truth about this. How can I do that? I'll lose everybody, every friend I have at the department. I'll be a rat. They will say I'm a liar and I made it all up. I'll never have a badge again."

Marlena continued to cry.

"What will we do, Mar? How will we afford this house? Clothes and food for the babies? What will I do? Who is going to hire a convicted dirty cop? We won't even be able to live here. There's no way out, Mar. No way out. Chip Meyers took the only road out of Dodge. One shot."

"Stop it, Josh!" she shouted. "Don't you ever talk like that! You need to call your attorney and ask him what your options are. I don't care if you bag groceries. I love you and these babies need a daddy."

"And if I have to go to prison? You don't think they're going to let me just walk away do you?"

"Then we will face it and you will get out and we will go on," she said resolutely.

Josh sat on the edge of the bed listening to his pregnant wife. She asked him to make the toughest decision of his life.

"Promise me right now that you will call the lawyer on Monday morning?"

"Okay," Josh relented, "I'll call him."

* * *

Thax relaxed in his brown leather chair reading the latest issue of Fly Fisherman magazine. A quiet Friday evening was just the ticket after a stressful week at work. Chrissy wandered into the family room where Thax was unwinding, carrying two glasses of red wine. One of Thax's old blue dress shirts covered her low-cut boy short underwear.

"Whatcha doing, fly boy?"

Thax peeked over the top of the magazine at Chrissy standing in front of him.

"What are *you* doing?" he asked.

"Just thought you might want a little grape with your fishing stories," she said playfully, handing him one of the glasses.

"Thank you," he replied, then looked back at his magazine.

Chrissy took a sip of her wine. Thax continued reading.

"Are you ever going to ask me about my interview?"

Thax looked up again from his magazine.

"Oh yeah. How was your interview?" He played along.

"Well, since you asked, it went really well."

"Good," Thax said without looking up.

"Actually, it was amazing! The producer wants me to come to New York and to take over a one-hour slot on the Fox News national broadcast in the afternoon. He took me to an amazing restaurant over in Bethlehem—"

Chrissy spoke excitedly trying to get Thax's attention.

Thax turned the page of his magazine.

"—and to seal the deal, I gave him a quickie in his car just before he dropped me off . . . Thax Colby, are you listening to anything I'm saying?"

Thax calmly placed his magazine in his lap and looked at Chrissy.

"Jesus, the guy offered you an anchor position on a national broadcast and all he got was a quickie?"

"Thax?" she snapped back. "Seriously."

"Okay." Thax closed the magazine and set it on the table next to his chair. "Seriously. Tell me about your meeting."

Chrissy knelt in front of him and set her wine glass on the floor. She slowly rubbed her hands on the top of his legs.

"The meeting went really well. I think they're interested in me. They want me to get them my greatest hits DVD. You know the best clips from the stories I've done. I think they're looking for a general assignment reporter in New York."

Thax put his hands on Chrissy's.

"I think that's fantastic. I know that's one of your dreams. And you should follow it."

"Really? You really feel that way?" Chrissy wanted Thax to talk about their relationship. "New York's less than two hours away. We could make that work? Couldn't we?"

"Did they offer you this job?"

"Not yet. But I want to know what to say if they do."

"Come here." Thax motioned for her to sit in his lap. He gave her a big hug. "If they offer you that job, you tell them 'yes'." Chrissy hugged and kissed him.

"Tell me about that quickie again." Thax smiled. Chrissy unbuttoned her shirt.

"Why don't I just show you," she whispered.

* * *

Judge plopped his big German Shepherd head into Cole Hatten's lap.

"Hey, boy." Hatten scratched behind the big dog's ears. Judge let out a whine, then turned toward the front door.

"What's the matter, buddy?" Judge's ears perked up. Hatten glanced toward the door.

"Is there something out there?" Hatten got up from his old card-table-turned-desk in the kitchen. Judge barked twice sharply and ran toward the door. Hatten followed.

"Go check it out," Hatten commanded, opening the door just fast enough for Judge to charge through it.

Hatten saw the tail lights of a vehicle driving down the street. He watched the vehicle turn right and out of sight at the four-way stop. Judge stood on alert in the front yard growling quietly.

"It's okay, boy. Let's go in."

Judge stopped briefly to mark a bush before strolling back to the front door.

"Good boy," he said, lightly thumping Judge's shoulder.

He returned to his desk. The table was covered with photos of the Meyers crime scene. His Chief had told him to shut this investigation down. Unfortunately, there were other cold cases that needed his attention.

He stared at the photos of the back door. There was no sign of any forced entry there or on any door. If someone killed Chip Meyers, there were only a few possibilities. They got in through an unlocked door and locked it on the way out or unlocked it with a key. All the locks at the Meyers house were deadbolt key locks. Or, Hatten thought, there was another incomprehensible possibility. The killer was somebody in the house.

Hatten glanced at the time displayed on his cable box. It was past eleven p.m. Too late to call Kristin Meyers. He had more questions that needed answers.

* * *

Katie Meyers walked out of her bedroom and down the hall toward the office. She passed her sister's room on her left. Neither her mother nor her sister were awake at two forty-five a.m. When she reached the short hallway leading from the main hallway toward the back door, her pulse quickened, although she didn't know why. She glanced down the dark hall and thought she saw a brief flash of light, perhaps from a passing car. The light went away but her head was pounding. She took several more steps toward the office until she found herself looking through the door toward where she saw her father the night he died. She began to cry.

Since that night, she had been unable to even get this close to the scene. She closed her eyes and stepped into the office, flipping the light switch on the wall. A plain looking lamp on top of a beige metal filing cabinet illuminated the room. Her mother had the desk and chair removed from the office the week after her father died. A small, more modern desk set replaced them. Smells of new carpet and fresh paint permeated the room. Katie stared into the room, motionless, focusing on nothing in particular. Eventually she summoned the courage to walk further into the room.

On the credenza, she looked at a picture of her dad with her and her sister Erin on the beach at the Jersey shore. She picked up the frame and hugged it to her chest. She felt uneasy. Something was wrong. She heard a loud pop in her head and saw another bright flash of light. The room was spinning. She made her way to the hallway and grabbed the wall to hold herself up. She dropped to her knees and sobbed. Through her tears she looked down the short hall to the back door.

"No! No! No!" she screamed.

Her mother was awakened by the chilling screams of her oldest daughter. She ran down the hallway to comfort her. Erin cracked her door open to see what was wrong. She had become accustomed lately to her sister's early morning sobbing.

"Oh, Katie," Kristin said, dropping to the floor to hug her daughter.

"I'm sorry, Mom," Katie said. Her body shook. "I thought I could . . ."

"It's okay," Kristin reassured her, trying desperately to comfort her daughter.

"No, it's not Mom. It's never going to be okay."

Twenty-Eight

THAX SAT IN the passenger's seat of Barrows's dark blue Ford Crown Victoria waiting for her to exit the Lafayette Ambassador Bank on Butler Street in Easton, a mile west of the Northampton County Courthouse. The bustle of the morning rush hour had subsided on the busy road into center city. He looked at his watch. It was nine forty-five.

"I think you're going to love this," Barrows chimed as she entered the driver's side of the vehicle. She handed Thax a white letter size business envelope bearing the Ambassador Bank's emblem. He opened it and pulled out several pages of records the bank had just produced to Barrows in response to a federal grand jury subpoena.

"The top one is the best," she said, directing Thax's attention to the safe deposit box records of Judge Eugene Harlin.

Thax examined the first page. "Well, look at that," he mused. "The good judge went to his box on October twelfth. Looks like the man goes to his safe deposit box two or three times a year and he just happened to go on the day he was paid twenty thousand dollars."

"It gets better," Barrows said. "In the last two years since then he's made a total of six trips to his safe deposit box."

Thax studied the record then flipped to the remaining pages.

Barrows continued. "After each one of those trips to the box, he walked over to the teller and deposited three thousand dollars in cash."

Thax slipped the records back into the envelope. "I'd say his Honor has some explaining to do."

* * *

Thax pushed the button on the shiny steel face plate to the intercom outside of the door leading to Northampton County Common Pleas Judge Eugene Harlin's chambers.

"Can I help you?" a female voice responded.

Thax and Barrows looked up at the camera mounted near the ceiling to the right of the door.

"Yes, ma'am. My name is Thax Colby. I'm a federal prosecutor and I'm with Special Agent Shea Barrows from the FBI."

The buzzing of the door lock signaled Thax and Barrows to enter. They walked into a large office area where a middle-aged woman with short brown hair greeted them from behind her desk.

"How can I help you?" she asked politely.

"Good morning," Thax said, extending his hand to the woman. He peered to his right through a tall open solid oak door leading into the Judge's office. "We were hoping we might speak to the judge for a few minutes if he's available."

"Can I ask what this is in reference to," she asked suspiciously.

"Brenda. Send those two fine public servants in here please," Judge Harlin's voice bellowed from the inner sanctum of his chambers.

"Yes, Judge," she answered. "Go right on in," she said, directing them to the doorway.

"Thank you," Thax replied.

A gentleman with a small build and short graying combed-over hair met Thax between the doorway and his desk. "Eugene Harlin." The judge shook Thax's hand.

"Hello, Judge. Thax Colby. I'm an Assistant U.S. Attorney in Allentown. This is Special Agent Shea Barrows from the FBI."

"Good to meet you both," Harlin said as he shook Barrows's hand.

"Well, what can I do for you today?" the judge asked. "This is a bit unusual."

"Judge, we'd like to ask you a few questions if you don't mind. Maybe you can help us with something we are investigating," Thax said.

"Please, sit down." Harlin motioned to the two dark red leather chairs positioned in front of his desk. The judge sat in a matching tall-backed wing chair behind his large oak desk.

"Judge, do you remember a drug dealer you sentenced about two years ago, his name was Victor Lord?" Thax asked.

Harlin repositioned himself in his chair, clearly uncomfortable with the question.

"Mr. Colby, you're going to have to help me out with that. I have a busy caseload here. I sentence five to ten defendants a week. Quite a few of them are involved in drugs. Can you be any more specific?"

"Judge, I'll try to help, but I guess that means you don't have any independent recollection of this guy?"

"No, sir, I don't."

"Okay," Thax said, "Victor Lord pled guilty on the day of trial and you sentenced him right away. He was from Allentown. He was arrested by the Easton Police with a lot of cocaine."

"Do you have picture of him? That's not ringing any bells."

Barrows reached into her briefcase and pulled out a driver's license photo of Lord. "This is him, Judge," she said, handing the photo to Harlin.

Harlin looked at the photo, then reached for glass of water. He took a sip and swallowed hard.

"This man doesn't look familiar to me at all. But, as I said, that doesn't mean anything because I see so many of these guys in my court."

"Judge, this guy got bitten up pretty badly by a police K-9 when he tried to run from the Easton P.D. He had a kilo of cocaine and almost a pound of crack cocaine in his car. He had three prior convictions for possession of cocaine. You sentenced him to a year of probation." Thax was respectful, but stern.

"What is this all about, Mr. Colby? I don't understand. Surely you aren't here to question my sentence of this gentleman. Are you?" Harlin's voice cracked. He tossed the picture onto his desk.

"Judge," Thax began to speak.

"Mr. Colby. If I sentenced this man to a year of probation it was what I thought was a just and proper sentence after looking at all of the information I had before me at the time." Harlin leaned forward in his chair and looked directly at Thax. "That is my duty and my responsibility and unless an appellate court tells me I have done something wrong, then my word is the *last* word on it."

"Yes, sir," Thax replied.

"You still haven't answered *my* question. Why are you here asking me about this man's sentence? What does the federal government care about this?"

"Judge," Barrows interjected, "the FBI was investigating a corrupt Allentown police detective, who appears to have taken his own life. You may have heard the news reports. Chip Meyers was his name."

"I've heard something about that, yes," Harlin said, sliding back in his chair. "It was all over the news. Surely everyone heard about it."

"Well, the detective kept a notebook and this was in it." Barrows slid a copy of the notebook entry onto Harlin's desk. "We don't know who 'Harlin' is on that entry nor do we know what the other entries—20,000, 10/12 or E.S.—mean."

Harlin examined the piece of paper. "Surely you don't think it's me!" Harlin pushed the paper back toward Barrows. "What does this have to do with the person that I sentenced, this Lord person?"

"Judge," Barrows continued, "we don't know if one has anything to do with the other and for that matter we're certainly not suggesting that you've done anything wrong. We're just—"

"Grasping at straws it seems to me." The judge interrupted, shaking his head.

"Judge, did you know Detective Meyers?" Barrows asked.

"No," he snapped.

"How about any of the detectives he worked with?" Barrows asked.

"No."

"Do you know Meyers's supervisor, Sergeant Rocco Morales?"

"I said no, Agent Barrows."

The judge stood up from behind his desk.

"Mr. Colby, I'm still not sure why you came here today. I hope next time, if there is a next time, you will be better prepared. If there's nothing else, I'll show you out." Harlin walked toward the door.

Thax and Barrows rose from their seats and followed.

"Good luck in your investigation, counsel," Harlin said curtly as the agent and prosecutor walked out of his inner office.

Barrows reached for the door into the hallway. Thax turned toward the judge who was standing in the doorway to his office.

"Thank you for your time, Judge. I do have one more question though," Thax didn't give Harlin a chance to say anything. "Do you have a safe deposit box?"

Harlin smirked at Thax, turned and walked into his office closing the door behind him.

Thax and Barrows walked into the courthouse hallway.

Barrows looked pleased. "Perfect," she said.

* * *

Thax's cell phone buzzed as he and Barrows cruised westward on Route 22, south of the Lehigh Valley International Airport. It was Campisano.

"Talk to me, Christopher."

"How was your meeting with the judge?"

"As expected," Thax replied. "Are you calling because you miss me or do you have some news?"

"What time did you leave the judge's office?" Campisano asked.

"Eleven o'clock."

"Well, at three minutes after eleven the judge called Morales's cell phone. The call lasted for eight minutes. How do you like that?"

Thax repeated the information to Barrows.

"Nice call on the pen register order on the judge's office phone," Campisano said.

Before interviewing Harlin, Thax had asked U.S. Magistrate Judge Matthai to sign a pen register order which allowed agents to see what numbers were called from Judge Harlin's phone. The order allowed only information about the numbers called and the duration of each call. The agents couldn't listen to the content of the call.

"Has anyone ever done that before with a judge's phone?" Campisano egged on his friend. "Pretty ballsy."

"Thank God Judge Matthai had the balls to sign it." Thax laughed.

"I knew Harlin would call Morales as soon as we left. He's squirming like a fish out of water," Thax said. "But this one's not catch and release."

Twenty-Nine

THAX FOCUSED ON the red floss on the body of the Royal Coachman fly as it drifted into a swirling eddy just downstream from two partially submerged rocks. The golden pheasant tippets on the tail of the fly flashed reflecting the rising sun, now sufficiently above the horizon to light the Little Lehigh under the canopy of willows and sprawling oaks. A large wild brown trout rose in the whirlpool to investigate.

"Take it," Thax whispered anxiously under his breath.

The mature fish, likely having been caught before, rolled and then swam deep below the surface. Thax raised his fly rod, neatly picking the fly from the stream's surface. A crisp forward snap of the rod propelled the fly twenty feet upstream, where it lightly fell close to where Thax aimed it. He followed the fly again, watching it drift toward the rocks. As the fly moved past the rocks into the eddy's reverse current, a cool early September breeze rippled the water's surface giving cover to the large brownie as it flashed toward the fly.

Thax set the hook.

Now battling for its life, the seventeen-inch fish made a strong run for a fallen tree settled on the far bank of the river. Thax slowly pulled back and lifted the rod, keeping the fish from tangling the line in the tree's branches. The trout rose quickly, breaking the surface of the river, exposing the large, dark spots, outlined with pale halos on its sides as it tried to throw the hook. Thax let the fly line slide between the rod handle and his index finger, giving just enough so the line wouldn't break. After several minutes, he landed the trophy fish.

"You're a beauty," Thax said freeing the fly from its mouth. He returned the fish to the water and, holding its tail, faced it upstream so the water could flow through its gills. After several seconds, the large brownie snapped its tail and darted back into the stream. Thax fished for a few more hours then headed back toward the parking lot. Nearing the old stone spring house, he saw Ronnie holding court with several other senior citizen fly anglers at the picnic table just outside the front of the building.

"Are you all here to celebrate the trophy brown I just landed," Thax grinned, teasing the onlookers as he walked toward them. Ronnie usually responded to his ribbing but this time just quietly shook his head.

"What's wrong?" Thax asked.

Ronnie hesitated. "Bob Freeman's wife died. Skip here lives up on Brigett's Way a few houses down from Bob." Ronnie motioned toward an older graying man standing at the end of the table.

"She died yesterday afternoon," Skip confirmed.

"Poor Bob. He's got nobody now," Ronnie said, turning to get up.

"What about his son?" Thax asked, recalling his last conversation with Bob.

"His son?" Skip responded.

"Yeah, his son," Thax asked. "The last time I saw Bob he told me it was his son's birthday. He doesn't have a son?"

Ronnie looked at the two older men, then back at Thax.

"Thax." Ronnie paused. "I thought you knew. Bob's son died when he was just a little boy."

"What?"

"He drowned. He drowned right down there between the willows. Bob was fishing and his son chased a ball into the river. He slipped out there in the crease of deep water. It was horrible."

Thax stared at Ronnie. For the first time in a long time he couldn't speak. He stepped forward and sat on the end of the picnic table.

"Are you okay, Thax?" Ronnie asked, seeing that his friend was distressed.

Thax, clearly anguished, sat shaking his head. Finally, he was able to speak. "I didn't know."

Ronnie looked at Skip.

"It happened a long time ago, Thax. Late '60s or early '70s, somewhere around there," Skip explained. "Bob has suffered every day knowing that he took his eye off his son for just a few minutes and he was gone. Just like that. His wife, Evelyn, had a breakdown and never recovered. Bob always told me she would eventually die of a broken heart."

Thax stood up and headed toward the parking lot.

"Thax. Are you okay?" Ronnie asked again.

Thax stopped and turned. "It was 1969. July 1969."

Thirty

Logan Branfield looked out the back passenger-side window as the black Lincoln Towncar driven by Richie Sokol hurtled down the Schuylkill Expressway toward the next campaign stop in Philadelphia. His private cell phone rang. It was his longtime secretary Maggie Hill.

"Yes, Maggie."

"Jack Winthrop is holding. I told him you were on your way to Philadelphia and were probably busy finishing up your notes for your speech but he's pretty insistent that he talk to you."

"Patch him through," Branfield sighed.

"Will do. Do well today," she replied.

Branfield took a gulp from his bottled water as he waited.

"Logan," a voice came on the line.

"Hey, Jack. How the hell are you?"

"I'm good, Logan. I see you're doing well, too. The last polls I saw had you up by three."

"Well we've got to keep it going, Jack. We're getting close," the mayor replied, taking another drink of water. "So, what's on your mind? I know you didn't just call to shoot the shit. Is something wrong?"

"Well, that's why I'm calling. I had a meeting with Detective Schick this morning and I'm very concerned."

"What's going on?"

"He wanted to know what his options were with the case."

"Options? His option is to keep his damn mouth shut and do as he's told!"

"Pretty much what I told him, Logan. I told him he needed to stay calm and let me do my job. I told him I didn't think the Government had much of a case against him and that he should just relax and let's see what they have when they get me the discovery."

"What did he say to that?"

"Well, he said he could do that but . . ."

"But what?"

"He still wanted to know what his other options were. He wanted to know what he would get if he decided to plead guilty."

Branfield was agitated. "And why the hell would he do that? What would that accomplish? What's he going to say, that he did that bullshit search warrant by himself? Is this guy stupid?!"

Winthrop waited a few seconds for his old friend to breathe.

"Logan, I told him if he pled guilty, the judge was going to ask him that. Then I told him that I know this prosecutor and that as soon as the judge sentenced him, they would walk him down to the grand jury and compel him give up the other guys who were there."

"Can they do that?"

"Hell yes, they can do it. They rarely do but in this case, with this prosecutor, it will happen. Trust me."

"Shit," Branfield spoke under his breath.

"He also wanted to know about cooperation. He wanted to know if he could avoid going to jail if he sat down with the Government and told them what he knew. I told him that was *not* an option at all and he needed to settle down and start thinking like the smart cop that he is. I told him that no cop has flipped on him and none would because that's not what cops do to other cops. I told him to let me do my job with this witness, that I was confident I could take care of this guy and he would hopefully walk out of there and go back to being a cop."

"And?" the mayor asked.

"He said his wife doesn't want to raise their babies while he's in jail. I reminded him he wasn't in jail now, and that he should let me do my job to keep him out of jail. I told him, to try to get back on course, that if he was convicted after a trial, that we would explore his other options then."

"Are we okay with this guy? Bottom line?"

"Before he walked out of my office he asked me again who was paying my bill. I told him that didn't matter and he should be glad someone else is paying it because he obviously couldn't afford to pay me himself."

"And?"

"And that's why I'm calling. He said maybe he should get a lawyer who is really looking out for him."

"That son of a bitch," Branfield muttered.

"We're here, boss," Sokol announced, arriving at the campaign location in Philadelphia.

"I have to go, Jack. Thanks for the call. Take care of yourself."

"You too, Logan."

Thirty-One

"Good afternoon, I'm Robin Parker," the news anchor welcomed viewers. "We have breaking news this noon hour. For a Valley 10 News exclusive, let's go live to the Northampton County Courthouse to Chrissy Barnes."

Barnes walked down the last few steps of the cascading entrance way to the courthouse. A hard gust of cool September wind straightened and flapped the American flag on the pole behind her.

"Robin, moments ago special agents from the Federal Bureau of Investigation walked Common Pleas Court Judge Eugene Harlin down these steps in handcuffs, arrested on federal charges including bribery and lying to federal agents. The United States Attorney for the Eastern District of Pennsylvania released this press release and previously sealed federal indictment moments after Harlin's arrest. The indictment alleges that Harlin took a payoff or was bribed to impose a lower sentence on a drug trafficker in his courtroom and that in the course of the investigation, Harlin lied to an FBI agent when asked whether he knew an unnamed Allentown Police detective. The indictment does not name and authorities are not identifying the police detective at this time.

"They are not saying why they asked Harlin about this officer in the first place. It is also unknown at this time whether this arrest or investigation has any connection to the recent arrest of Joshua Schick, another Allentown Police detective, on charges of breaking into a citizen's home in what authorities called a sham search warrant to steal $40,000 from that citizen's home. Harlin is expected to appear before a federal judge for initial appearance later today."

The anchor broke in with a question.

"Chrissy, it's an unusual occurrence for a sitting judge to be arrested. What are court watchers saying, if anything, about the arrest of the judge at the courthouse and walking him out of the front door of the building?"

"Robin, it is indeed unusual for a judge to be arrested. Few employees at the courthouse would talk to us. Most looked shocked as one of their judges was whisked away in handcuffs by federal agents. As for walking the judge out the front door, one attorney I spoke with who appears regularly in federal court said, and I quote, 'this is the federal government sending a message. This has to be bigger than just one guy in a robe.' We will continue to follow this story. In Easton, Chrissy Barnes, back to you."

* * *

"I just heard," Sokol said as he walked into Branfield's office. He closed and locked the door behind him. The mayor sat on a small couch against the far wall of the office fidgeting with an unlit cigar.

"This is getting too fucking hot, Richie," Branfield cautioned. "We have forty days until the election. Forty days. And I have to wake up and listen to this bullshit?"

"I know, boss."

"My good friend Eugene Harlin did us a solid and now he gets dragged out of his own courthouse by a couple of federal agents. Jesus Christ, Richie. Somebody got to somebody. Who the fuck knew about this?" Branfield's voice got louder.

"I need to talk to Morales. I thought this was taken care of with no loose ends," Sokol answered.

"Well, apparently it wasn't," the mayor barked. "Somebody talked."

"Sounds like the judge talked. Talked enough to get himself in trouble."

"Don't put this on him. Gene Harlin is as rock solid as they come. Somebody else is talking, Richie. You need to find out who it is and what they're talking about. Someone's talking shit and you need to stop it. Permanently!" Branfield broke the cigar in half as he ranted. "I will not. I cannot have this happen now."

"I don't know who's talking, but I'll find out and I'll take care of it," Sokol assured the mayor.

"Richie, you're supposed to know everything."

Sokol didn't reply. He knew his boss was right.

"Well, don't just stand there. Get me some goddamn answers. I keep hearing 'I don't know' from you, which is fucking unacceptable. Get your ass out of here and don't come back until you do know." The mayor stood up from his couch. "You need to protect us."

"I'll take care of it," Sokol assured him. "I always do, don't I?"

"So far," Branfield answered. "So far."

* * *

Sokol headed south off Washington Street onto St. Lucas Street. After a hundred feet or so he turned his black Mercedes Benz Sedan into the black-topped parking lot of Muhlenberg Elementary School. He dimmed his headlights and pulled next to a silver Dodge Durango. The one-time playground behind the school was dark and desolate. Sergeant Rocco Morales got out of the SUV and opened the passenger side door of Sokol's car.

"Talk to me, Rock," Sokol greeted Morales as he got in and closed the door.

"Hey, LT," Morales said reaching for Sokol's extended hand. "I guess you saw the news," Morales said after a brief uncomfortable silence.

"Fuckin' right I saw the news, Rock. What's the story?"

"I don't know. You know, like I said back then, we had to help this guy. He played it straight up. He never said a word about where the shit or the money came from. Just said it was his. Period."

"The drug courier. What's his name again?" Sokol asked.

"Victor Lord. He's one of my boys on the East Side."

"Where is he now?"

"He's doing some time in Jersey."

"For what? What the hell was he doing over there?" Sokol asked angrily.

"LT, this guy's a certified bad ass, but women are gonna be the end of this guy. The night he got popped in Easton, he was on his way back carrying some weight and he decides he's gonna stop and get his rocks off with some broad he's been tapping. This probably wasn't the first time he stopped for some, knowing him. He got hooked up over in Jersey this time because he went looking for another broad. Turns out, she moved and Victor breaks into her house thinking he'll surprise her. He's not the sharpest knife in the drawer, but you'd have to stick a hot poker in his eye to get him to talk. Trust me. This guy *hates* cops. The only thing he would tell them would be to fuck off."

"Who carried the money to the judge?" Sokol asked.

"Little Nicky. He's East Side Boyz. He doesn't know shit. I gave him the package and five-hundred bucks to deliver it to the judge. The judge knew he was coming so he let Nicky in the office when he got there."

Sokol thought for a moment. "Listen Rock. Somebody's talking. You need to get to Lord and this Nicky kid and find out what's going on. Take care of it. Now."

"I will, LT."

Thirty-Two

Josh and Marlena Schick headed into Macungie to enjoy a relaxing Sunday night dinner at the Stoned Crab, their favorite local restaurant on Brookside Road. They were running a few minutes late for their eight o'clock reservations when a blue light flashed in their rear-view mirror. Josh slowed down and pulled his vehicle to the side of the road.

"I didn't think I was going that fast," he said, instinctively reaching for the badge he kept clipped to his belt, then realizing it wasn't there.

"Don't worry, I'll take care of this," he assured his wife.

He rolled his window down and watched the officer approach on the driver's side. He could only see a silhouette in the headlights of the vehicle. The man walked close to the vehicle stopping just behind the driver's door.

"Put your hands on the wheel! Now!" The man shoved the business end of a .45 caliber handgun toward Josh's head. "Don't move!"

Josh complied but Marlena screamed.

"Shut her up," the man shouted.

"Marlena! Stop! Just stop!"

"Tell her to put her hands on the back of her head."

Marlena heard the man and complied.

"What's going on officer?" Josh asked, trying to de-escalate the situation. "I'm a cop."

"Just shut up and do exactly what I say," the man grimaced, pushing the gun against Josh's neck.

"Okay. Okay," Josh responded. "Please don't hurt my wife. She's pregnant." He glanced at the side view mirror but couldn't see the man's face. This was definitely not a cop.

"Tell your wife to step out of the car. No funny business."

"Marlena," Josh said to his now almost hysterical wife, "you've got to calm down. Listen to what I'm telling you. Get out and do exactly what he says. Okay?"

Marlena got out of the vehicle. The man ordered her to step forward.

"Stop right there!" he shouted as she reached the front of the vehicle. "Don't move."

"Look, man," Josh said, "you're really scaring my wife. I've got a few hundred bucks on me. Please just take the money and go."

"Get out of the vehicle. Slowly."

Josh did what he was told.

"Face forward. Now walk up front there and stand next to your wife." Josh complied. "Hold her hand and walk away from the road, toward the high grass. Keep walking until I tell you to stop." The man followed them.

Josh squeezed Marlena's hand. "It's going to be okay," he whispered.

"Shut up," the man snapped.

The man stopped them fifty feet into the high grass. The area was dark, with little light from the scattered street lights.

"Take off your clothes."

"Come on, man," Josh implored. "Just take my money and let us go."

"Throw me your wallet," the man ordered.

Josh tossed the wallet back to the man who let it drop on the ground.

"Good. Now strip! Right now or I start shooting!" The man stepped closer pointing his gun at Josh's head.

Josh stripped down to his boxer shorts, then removed his shoes and socks.

"Just do it, babe," he told his wife.

Marlena undressed down to her bra and underwear.

"All the way!" the man demanded. "Now!"

Josh dropped his shorts. Marlena looked at Josh, who nodded. She quickly removed her bra and underwear, then crossed her arms over her chest. Her sandals were still on her feet.

The man stepped forward and took the cash from Josh's wallet.

"I'm sorry," he said.

* * *

Trooper Derek Lindsay had driven the four-mile stretch of Brookside Road south of Route 222 just west of Allentown a thousand times in his twenty-two-year career with the Pennsylvania State Police. The area was mostly rural with some nice homes and a few family farms along the way. The small town of Macungie, just west of the city, was quiet most of the time. Lindsay's shift was made up of accident calls and the occasional domestic dispute. At one time he longed for the excitement of investigating homicides but a bitter dispute with a commanding officer years ago condemned him to a career of patrol work.

Lindsay passed Brookside Country Club and its stately club house, continuing south past Macungie Memorial Park. When he passed Macungie Elementary School on his right, he noticed a blue Dodge Ram pickup pulled off the side of the road heading northbound. He slowed to take a look. *Maybe someone just ran out of gas*, he thought. It happened. More often than most people would believe. He didn't see anyone in the truck and didn't really think the situation called for his help. There were some houses nearby and he doubted anyone had climbed back into the thick trees and brush further back off the road.

I'll check on this on my way back, he thought, moving onto his next concern.

He sipped his coffee and continued southbound on Brookside Road which then became East Macungie Road.

"Echo three-four. Respond to a vehicle accident at Route 100 and Chestnut Street. Possible injuries. EMTs en route," the State Police dispatcher's voice crackled over the radio.

"10-4. I'm two minutes out from there," Lindsay responded.

Lindsay arrived on the scene of a two-car fender bender in the southbound lane of Route 100 just before the intersection with Chestnut Street. The drivers were already out of their cars exchanging insurance and driver's license information. The trooper pulled up behind the cars, activating his emergency lights.

"Everybody okay here?" he asked. Both drivers acknowledged him.

"I think we're fine," said a young, nicely dressed woman who was obviously one of the drivers.

"Does anybody need me to do a report?"

"No. I think we're fine, officer," an older gentleman said, handing the woman a piece of paper. The woman agreed.

"There's barely any damage," she said.

"Nobody's hurt?" Lindsay asked again.

"No, sir," the man responded. "I think I just need to pay better attention."

Lindsay told both drivers to be careful. Many moons ago he probably would have written the man a ticket, but not today.

"Lehigh PSP. Echo three-four is 10-2 on that accident. EMT is not on scene. Cancel their response." Lindsay looked at his watch. It was nine-fifteen a.m.

After a quick U-turn, he turned off his lights and headed north on Route 100, the same route he had traveled to the accident call. He turned back onto East Macungie Road, continuing northbound on the two-lane rural route. In the distance he saw that the blue truck he had passed earlier was still parked off the side of the road. *Better check this out*, he thought. He slowed as he approached the vehicle. There was nobody around. He checked behind him, activated his emergency lights and pulled his patrol unit behind the truck.

"Lehigh PSP. Echo three-four is gonna be out of the car on East Macungie Road near the elementary school. I think that cross street is Buckeye Road. I've got an abandoned vehicle. Can you run a registration on a blue Dodge truck, Pennsylvania tag KAT830? Kilo, Alpha, Tango, eight, three, zero."

Lindsay stayed in his car awaiting a response. Looking around the area behind the vehicle, he saw nothing unusual. A few minutes passed.

"Echo three-four. That registration comes back restricted. Do you want to call me from your phone?"

"10-4. I'm gonna check it out first."

Lindsay got out of his car and walked toward the truck. The driver's door was closed but not all the way. Nobody in there, he observed. He saw only a T-shirt and a backpack in the back seat. The door on the passenger side was also slightly ajar. Nothing else looked unusual.

"Lehigh PSP. This is Echo three-four. Can you send a wrecker out here to my 20?"

"10-4, Echo three-four. Wrecker is en route."

Lindsay looked toward the grassy berm off the road and into some thick brush approximately fifty feet from the vehicle. The dense growth was still moist with dew from the cool evening air. He walked through the clusters of tall grass, following a flattened path of grass into the thicket.

"What the hell . . ." Lindsay walked even deeper into the grassy berm toward an awful scene.

"Oh my God!"

Two bodies lay in front of him, face down with their feet pointed toward the road. The naked, lifeless bodies appeared to be a man and a woman. Scattered clothing littered the area around them. The trooper inched closer to where he could see more horrible destruction. Both victims had been shot at close range, in the back of their heads. He knew that checking for life was futile.

"Lehigh PSP. This is Echo three-four. We have a big problem out here," he departed from his usual radio communications protocol.

"Say again Echo three-four?"

"I have two deceased on scene. Gonna need back up, the coroner and a supervisor."

"Shit," he said in disbelief.

Lindsay moved closer to the bodies. The body closest to the road was the man's. He noticed a wallet in some shorter grass between the body and the road. With a small stick, he flipped the wallet over to examine any identification inside.

"Damn," he sighed. He recognized the name. "This is a cop." He moved to the other side of the male victim to view the woman's body, being careful not to disturb the crime scene. A flash of panic struck him when he saw the swollen abdomen of the deceased woman.

"Son of a bitch," Lindsay muttered under his breath as he observed the pregnant victim. "What kind of an animal . . ." He felt a flash of nausea looking at the devastating entrance wound on the side of the young woman's head.

"Echo three-four. What's the status out there?" the dispatcher called, not having heard from the trooper in a few minutes.

"Lehigh PSP. Echo three-four. I've got a police officer down and the second victim is pregnant."

Almost a minute passed before the dispatcher responded.

"Echo three-four. Call the Captain."

Lindsay reached for his cell phone and dialed his Captain directly—something he almost never did. Captain Reece Hutcheson answered the call.

"Captain. We have a double homicide off East Macungie Road near the elementary school," Lindsay advised his commander. "One of the victim's I believe is Detective Josh Schick from Allentown P.D. The detective the FBI recently arrested. The second victim is pregnant. I'm guessing from their wedding bands, probably his wife." Lindsay waited for the Captain's response. He heard nothing during that moment of stunned silence.

"Sir, this was an execution."

Thirty-Three

THAX FINISHED AN easy-paced three mile run and slumped lazily in his favorite lounge chair on his back deck. Unfortunately, he didn't get to enjoy it too often. The quiet relaxation of his well-deserved day off was interrupted by his ringing cell phone. He reluctantly reached for it. It was Chrissy.

"Hey, beautiful."

"Thax. I'm on my way to Macungie. The State Police are working a double homicide."

"What?"

"It's really bad, Thax. They're not saying a whole lot."

"What happened?"

"My info is that a trooper found two bodies on the side of the road. I don't know much more right now. We're just pulling up."

"Shit," Thax mumbled.

"I know. I gotta go."

* * *

Sergeant Jerry King looked at the crime scene from East Macungie Road. Minutes earlier he had parked his unmarked Ford Taurus among the numerous marked patrol units from the State Police and other surrounding municipalities. The immediate area looked like a festival of blue and red flashing lights. King, the senior investigator for State Police Troop M's Major Case Team, walked toward the blue Dodge Ram pickup truck while crime scene technicians methodically photographed the vehicle and dusted it for fingerprints.

"Anything I need to know about here?" King asked the lead tech.

"We're just getting started," the tech answered. "Not much inside the car that we could see on our first look. A backpack. It looks like the male victim's. Found a small black purse on the floorboard on the front passenger's side. Each of the front doors was slightly ajar, like someone got out and didn't completely close them. Nothing obvious around the vehicle."

King observed that the truck was parked partially on the blacktop berm of the roadway with the passenger's side straddled over the grassy area just off the roadway.

"I assume you didn't see any footprints around here before you started on the vehicle," King inquired.

"None. Just grass and blacktop. No tire tread marks in front or behind either. Wish I did," the tech replied.

King nodded, acknowledging the information. He looked back toward where the bodies were.

"Well, they obviously got from here to there," King said, surveying the trampled path through the high grass back to the victims. He observed another technician processing that area.

"We're on it," the lead tech assured King.

King walked outside the yellow crime scene tape, toward the bodies, carefully observing the area. The victims had obviously walked into the brush, from the truck, where they were killed. The veteran detective soon came upon the horrific aftermath of the double homicide. He looked at the two naked bodies, face down in some shorter grass. What appeared to be the victims' clothes were strewn around them. He moved closer to where he could see the body of the male victim. He crouched down to observe the fatal gunshot wound in the back of the victim's head. Two troopers, including Trooper Lindsay stood nearby.

"This was at really close range," King remarked. He observed that a portion of the victim's face was torn away, no doubt from the exit of a high-powered projectile.

"Any shell casings?" King asked Lindsay.

"I didn't see any, but I didn't want to disturb the scene," Lindsay answered.

King walked behind the female victim and searched the ground to the right. He crouched down and scanned the matted grass.

"Right there." He pointed at the gold casing. With a tweezer from his pocket he examined the shell. "It's a .45."

The senior investigator looked at the female victim's naked body lying half prone and within six feet of the male victim. Her distended belly—now a lifeless womb—was turned facing him. An entrance wound was visible just behind her left ear. Blood and brain matter soaked her long black hair. Nothing in his almost twenty-five years of investigating homicides had prepared him for this. King thought he had seen it all. This scene shook him to his core.

"What kind of sick bastard does this?" he asked, not directing the question to anyone in particular.

King looked at the clothes scattered around the bodies.

"Whoever did this took them from the truck, walked them back here, humiliated them by making them strip, then killed them. Probably him first. Then shot her when she turned to look. Why?" King pondered. To King, "why" was always the question. Figuring out why someone was killed would almost always answer the question of *who* killed them.

Lindsay pointed out the wallet on the ground ten feet behind the male victim. King examined it hoping to preserve any fingerprints.

"No cash in the wallet," King observed. "Kill two people for a couple of bucks?" He looked at the Pennsylvania driver's license in the wallet.

"Joshua Schick."

He removed a business card behind the DL.

"Detective Joshua Schick, Allentown Police Department." He pushed the card back into the wallet and looked at Lindsay.

"I assume the captain notified APD?"

Lindsay nodded.

Lehigh County Coroner Hilbert Chase appeared from behind King.

"Doc," King acknowledged the coroner with a nod.

Chase assessed the two victims.

"Looks like a large caliber projectile," Chase observed, looking at the entrance wound and gaping, destructive exit wound on the front of Josh Schick's head and face. "Close range. Two to three feet. Maybe closer."

Chase looked at the female victim. Without moving her head, he made a similar assessment.

"Single shot. Close range. Do you need a time?"

"When you can, Doc. We're thinking this happened last night," King answered.

"Pretty good guess, Jerry." Chase stood for a few seconds looking at the female victim then turned to walk away.

"Doc . . . how long?"

"Without oxygen from the mother, about four to five minutes. Is that what you were going to ask?"

King nodded. "Thanks, Doc." King walked back along the path of the crime scene tape toward the road scanning the grass field for anything that would help him. His partner, Gilberto Rolon, walked toward him from behind the truck.

"I don't see anything back there, partner," Rolon reported. "No tire marks. It's clean black top. The grass is rolled down, but it's like that all along the road. Our unit that rolled up on this was parked back there before calling it in."

King stared down the road from the front of the vehicle. He turned and looked behind him where he could see the press gathering for a briefing by State Police Captain Reece Hutcheson. He walked closer to the driver's door of the vehicle—far enough away that he couldn't hear whatever bullshit the Captain was going to tell the press. King was the lead investigator and had only been on the scene for ten, maybe fifteen minutes. *What could the captain possibly tell the press at this point?* he thought.

"Hey partner, come here a minute," King called to Rolon on the other side of the truck.

"What's up?" Rolon asked.

"What do we know about the vehicle?"

"Well, the plate comes back restricted, but it belongs to Joshua Schick."

"That's our male victim," King confirmed.

"Isn't he the—"

"—the APD detective the feds arrested recently. Yeah, that's him."

"And he wasn't packing?" Rolon asked.

"No. APD suspended him. No sign that he was carrying his gun. No holster. No gun with him or in the vehicle."

King motioned to a young crime scene tech who was standing on the passenger side of the vehicle. The tech responded.

"You find anything in that purse? Like an ID?"

"Yes, sir," the tech answered. "Marlena Schick. A DL and a couple of credit cards."

"Any cash in the purse?" King asked.

"Yes, but I don't think anybody counted it yet," the tech answered. "Not a lot from what I could see."

King thanked the young man.

"Let me ask you something," King addressed his partner. "This guy's a cop and he's with his wife, maybe heading out to the store or to get some dinner. He stops on the side of the road. No street lights anywhere near here. The area's dark. For what? No reason for him to stop. No car trouble, no flat tire. What's the emergency? And this just happens to be the place where someone else pulls over and decides to rob and murder him and his pregnant wife. For a few bucks in his wallet. I'm not buying it," King scoffed.

"I guarantee that's not what he's telling them," Rolon said motioning toward the Captain's press conference.

"Look at this truck. There's no sign of any collision or accident. The tires are all fine. It wasn't a flat that stopped them. What's here? Did she get sick? I don't see any sign that she got sick, either in the car or outside the vehicle. Why did they stop?" King pondered out loud.

"I don't know, Jer," Rolon answered.

King looked for another one of the crime scene techs and spotted one in the sea of police vehicles. He motioned for the tech, who responded.

"Yes, sergeant?"

"Did somebody start the engine? Is there anything wrong with the vehicle?"

"The key's still in the ignition, sir," the tech answered.

"Of course, it is," King said politely dismissing the CSI.

King walked around the vehicle again.

"Sergeant," the lead crime scene tech called for King. "I think you want to see this."

King walked toward the investigator. He was joined by Rolon.

"We found this cell phone in one of the plastic compartments on the side of the truck radio. There are a bunch of unanswered incoming calls starting at 8:35 p.m." the tech reported as he scrolled through the phone information. "It looks like the last outgoing call was at 7:19 p.m."

"That means our murders probably happened sometime in between there," King concluded. "Good catch."

"There's one more call I think you might want to see. It's from Saturday afternoon, around two o'clock" the tech scrolled through the calls. "Here it is. It's an outgoing call. I recognized the number. A few years ago I was working an investigation with an agent over there. It's the FBI."

"You remember the number?" King snickered with surprise. "How long was the call?"

"About thirty seconds."

"Don't even know if he got through, do we?" King thanked the tech.

King and Rolon walked back toward the vehicle. Dr. Chase accompanied the body of Joshua Schick as it was being carried on a stretcher to a waiting coroner's van.

"I'll get you a report after the autopsies. Probably tomorrow," Chase promised King.

While the press conference continued, some nearby news cameras panned toward the stretcher as it was carried by.

"I'll just never get those people," King muttered. "What if that was their mother?"

King walked back to the vehicle with Rolon. By now, word had spread through the law enforcement ranks that a cop was dead. If that information was still under wraps it wouldn't be for long.

"This cop stopped here for a reason," King said. "And whatever it was got him killed."

* * *

"Good morning! I'm Gina Mondalvo, with Valley 10 News," the anchor broke in to regularly scheduled morning programming. "We have breaking news this morning. Let's go straight to Chrissy Barnes who is in Macungie at the scene of a double homicide. Chrissy, what do you know?"

"Gina, we have just concluded a press conference with Captain Reece Hutcheson, the commanding officer of the State Police in this area. Early this morning, a trooper on routine patrol located a vehicle on the side of East Macungie Road and investigated. What he found was a horrific scene off the roadway with two dead bodies. State Police are not releasing the identities of the victims; however, our sources tell us that at least one of the victims may be a police officer. Captain Hutcheson would not confirm that information. There are, however, numerous police vehicles from neighboring municipalities, including Allentown, that are on the scene. Our sources are also telling us that both victims were shot at close range. Captain Hutcheson had this to say:

"At this time, what I can tell you is that there are multiple victims. I will not discuss how they died as this is an ongoing investigation. As for motive, we do not know for sure but investigators are looking at all possibilities including that this may have been a robbery. Our investigators are currently working this case. We will have more information as this matter moves forward."

"Gina, it appears that the police have little to go on. For now, that's what we know. Chrissy Barnes, Valley 10 News."

Thirty-Four

A crisp early October breeze brushed the surface of the Little Lehigh, sending a blanket of tiny ripples across the meandering limestone river. Thax waded cautiously into the quick moving current downstream from the two towering willows. A slip into the treacherous deep crease flowing through mid-river could result in severe consequences, especially now that the water had been chilled below forty-five degrees by the unusually cool autumn weather. Thax knew these waters like few others and skillfully navigated his way toward the hidden ledge. A mature brown trout held its position near a pool of slower moving water just beyond three barely submerged rocks. Thax snapped his Sage fly rod forward, propelling the blue-winged olive fly toward its target. The hungry trout rose to take the fly.

The early afternoon sun provided rays of warmth to offset the blustery air. After landing the fourteen-inch brownie, Thax looked downstream toward the bridge. When he was on the river, he was usually in another world, an escape from the responsibilities of his position. Today though, his peace was interrupted by thoughts of his early morning phone call from Chrissy about the double homicide. Even though the Lehigh Valley had changed since he was a kid in the 1960s, it was still a pretty safe place to live. Double homicides, fortunately, were rare.

His curiosity for the details disrupted his focus on fishing. On this rare day off, he purposely turned off his cell phone, although he kept it in the waterproof pocket of his fishing vest. He waded to the river's edge where he could see the silt bottom in the shallows near the bank. He unzipped the pocket of his vest and turned on his phone. He stood motionless listening to the first message:

"Thax, it's Shea," her voice quivered, "call me right away. It's urgent."

Thax hung up and called Barrows.

"Shea. Talk to me. What's going on?"

"Thax. Did you hear about the double homicide in Macungie?" Barrows asked, barely giving him time to answer.

"Yeah, I did. What's going on?"

"It's Josh Schick," she stammered.

"What?" Thax raised his voice. "Where did you hear that?"

"It's all over, Thax. It just hasn't been officially released. I heard it from a couple of sources since I called you. It's definitely him."

"Son of a bitch."

"They killed his wife too, Thax," Barrows whimpered. "Someone killed his pregnant wife. I just want to throw up." She sniffled then tried to speak. "I'm sorry. This is—"

"What happened? Does anybody know?" Thax asked.

"I don't know. It happened off East Macungie Road. All I know is that they found the bodies off the road. Both of them were shot in the head. They say it looks like a robbery."

"A robbery?"

"I know, Thax. I can't stop thinking we had something to do with this."

"Well, we had nothing to do with this," Thax replied.

"I didn't mean it that way. The timing on this—"

"I know, Shea. When did this happen?"

"Looks like it happened last night sometime. That's all I know."

"All right. Look. Give Christopher a call and let him know what's going on. I'm sure he's probably heard. I might have a message from him, too."

"Will do."

"Is this a state police investigation?" Thax asked.

"Yeah, they've already had a preliminary press conference but didn't have much to say."

"Well, let's let them work this and see what shakes out in the next twenty-four hours. Let's meet tomorrow, late morning or afternoon. Okay?"

"Okay, Thax."

"Call me if you hear anything more. Anything."

"Okay. Sorry to ruin your day off." Shea hung up.

Thax stood for a moment then retrieved his second message. The call was from Chrissy.

"Hey. You need to call me as soon as you can. I'm out here in Macungie. This is really bad. It looks like the victims are Josh Schick and his wife. They aren't publicly releasing the names until they notify family but that's who it is. We're going live with this at five, notification or not. I gotta go."

Thax called Chrissy and got her voicemail.

"Chrissy. Call me."

Thax grabbed his fly rod and walked down the gravel and dirt path along the river bank toward the riffles downstream from the bridge. He stopped at the weathered green picnic table and gazed at the river. The sun peaking from behind a partially cloudy sky reflected off the clear water. The quiet rushing of the river was soothing. Branches of a young weeping willow tree across the creek swayed in the breeze. Thax took a deep breath and soaked it in. *If only the rest of the world could be so peaceful*, he thought.

Thirty-Five

Chrissy readied herself for a live shot at the top of the five o'clock news hour. Her classic red London Fog trench coat shielded her from the damp chill in the air as the autumn sun slipped lower in the sky. She checked her lips, donned with glossy crimson lipstick.

"Perfect," she spoke to herself.

Barnes stood beside the yellow crime scene tape on the berm of East Macungie Road as the anchor cut to the live shot.

"This is Chrissy Barnes in Macungie where tonight the news of the death of a second Allentown Police Officer in recent months has rocked this community. Earlier this morning Pennsylvania State Police found the bodies of suspended Allentown Police Detective Josh Schick and his pregnant wife, Marlena, in this field, just feet from where I'm standing. What authorities are not saying is how this happened.

"Earlier this morning a truck, believed to belong to the victims, was parked on the side of the road near where the bodies were discovered. Allentown Police Chief Scott Butler spoke late this afternoon:

"All I can tell you at this point is the State Police are working every lead and following every piece of evidence to find the person or persons responsible for this horrific act. From what I know at this time, this appears to have been a random act, perhaps a robbery gone bad. We are asking that anyone who has any information or may have been in that area last evening to please contact the State Police."

The live shot came back to Barnes.

"Now, as I mentioned a few moments ago, Schick is the second

Allentown officer to die in recent months. The apparent suicide of fellow Allentown narcotics detective Chip Meyers months ago shook the local law enforcement community. After the recent arrest of Schick on federal charges, rumors have surfaced that perhaps both were the targets of a federal corruption probe. Valley 10 News contacted the United States Attorney's Office for comment. They would neither confirm nor deny such an investigation."

The anchor broke in.

"Chrissy, this is a terrible story and as you reported, the second Allentown police narcotics officer to die in a very short period. I know the Chief of Police spoke about this. Have we heard anything from Mayor Branfield?"

"Will, we know that earlier in the day the mayor was campaigning in Bucks County, but we have not yet been able to get any comment from him today about this. Chrissy Barnes, Valley 10 News."

* * *

"Goddammit, Richie, answer your damn phone," Logan Branfield screamed into his office phone. "Where the hell are you?"

Branfield slammed the phone down.

"Where the hell are you, Richie?" he mumbled again.

The mayor's office was dark but for the illumination from his one gold-plated desk light. He arched his back into his high-backed executive chair and closed his eyes. The Queen City's brash chief executive was this close to being Pennsylvania's next governor. The news of the murder of an Allentown police officer and his pregnant wife could not go without a comment from the gubernatorial candidate.

These sons of bitches in the media have had me on the ropes about the police department for too long, he thought. *Now I've got to go do something to fade the heat on these dead cops. I'm too close to the finish line.*

The ringing phone snapped him back to reality. He recognized the Pittsburgh area code and the number as his state campaign chairman's, Bo Hughes.

"Bo," he answered. "Talk to me."

"Evening, Govern—"

"Don't fuck with me Bo," Branfield said sternly, then grinned. "Give me the damn numbers."

"The Pittsburgh Post-Gazette poll is coming out at eight o'clock—"

"Just give me the damn numbers Bo."

"You're up fifty-one to forty-seven."

"Well hallefuckinglujah! I needed some good news today."

"Well, there you have it."

"What about the other two percent? What the hell are they waiting for?" Branfield snapped.

"Who cares? You're up by four points. Go have a drink, have a nice cigar and forget about this for the rest of the day. The next three weeks are gonna be a bitch."

"Have you talked to Richie tonight?" Branfield asked.

"No," Bo answered. "Why?"

"No, it's nothing. Just trying to find him. I'm sure he'll call me in a few."

"Good deal. Have a good night, Logan."

"I intend to. You, too." Branfield hung up the phone. He arched his back again in his chair and turned his head to look out the window. Just seconds passed before the phone rang again. It was his wife.

"Yes, darling," Branfield greeted Dana with feigned affection.

"Should I expect you home anytime soon?" she asked.

"I'm leaving here in a little bit. I've got one more thing I need to finish."

"Lovely. See you then."

Branfield hung up the phone and pressed the forward button so he wouldn't receive any more direct calls. He leaned back into his chair, his right hand stroking the long thick blonde hair of the beautiful intern who had been kneeling in front of him for the last ten minutes. He reached forward with both hands sliding them along the sides of her neck under her soft curled golden locks. His thumbs brushed against her face and gently pulled her head forward. Her mouth and lips moved faster, then in rhythm with his thrusts. He closed his eyes and exhaled.

"Don't stop, babe . . . Don't stop."

* * *

"Hit me again, Tommy." Richie Sokol swirled the ice in his glass. "Make this one count."

The bartender poured a four-count of Dewar's Scotch into Sokol's glass.

"You okay, Richie?"

"I'm fuckin' great, Tommy. Couldn't be better," Sokol slurred, then took a pop of his fifth drink.

Sokol sat on the middle of five bar stools in the small alcove adjoining Manny's Restaurant. One other patron shared the dimly-lit area with Sokol, seated two seats down to the right. Sokol, the patron, and Tommy looked to the TV in the upper right corner of the bar as the eleven o'clock news flashed across the screen. The lead story was the murder of a police officer and his wife. A reporter stood near the scene of the murders. Cameras panned back into the meadow on the side of the road where the carnage had taken place.

"Hey! Turn that up buddy," the other patron shouted to Tommy as the lead report continued. The barkeep complied. The live shot cut to tape from earlier in the evening.

"Tonight, after these senseless murders, Mayor Logan Branfield, the leading gubernatorial candidate had this to say."

Sokol took a gulp of his Scotch. Branfield stood in front of his home, impeccably dressed in his two-thousand-dollar navy Brooks Brothers custom-made suit, a white shirt, and a red power tie.

"Tonight, Dana and I are terribly saddened at the loss of a law enforcement officer of this city and the devastating and heinous killing of his wife in what appears to be a random act of violence and cowardice. A few moments ago I directed the Chief of Police here in our great city to assist the State Police investigation in every way possible. Also tonight, Dana and I are personally offering a $50,000 reward to any person who can provide information that leads to the arrest and conviction of the despicable individual or individuals who perpetrated these acts. I will not rest until those responsible have been brought to justice."

The newscast cut back to the live shot and the reporter.

"Now Jim, as you can imagine, the mayor's personal pledge of a reward has been met with a sharp response from his gubernatorial challenger, who a short time ago released this statement:"

'We are saddened by the homicides in Allentown's neighboring community. This is the second law officer from that great city to lose his life in such a short time on Mayor Branfield's watch. Both appeared to have been mired in some controversy, the extent of which is still unknown, and which may or may not have contributed to their deaths. The mayor's personal pledge of a reward for information, while seemingly generous, smacks of politics with just three weeks left in this campaign. We, too, are hopeful those responsible will be brought to justice.'

The live shot panned back to the reporter.

"In the Lehigh Valley, this is April Wentworth for ABC Action News.

Sokol stared at the TV screen. "I'm gonna need one more, Tommy," he called out lifting his empty glass. "At least one more."

Thirty-Six

Nicky Price grabbed his last handful of ass from Savannah, his favorite dancer at the Booby Trap strip club on Airport Road in East Allentown, before reluctantly saying goodnight. Price and the last few stragglers walked out the front door, fifteen minutes or so after the club's 2:00 a.m. closing time. Nicky and the rest of the East Side Boyz crew were regulars at the upstanding establishment and provided security for the club in exchange for a regular supply of liquor and sex. At twenty-six, Price had somehow managed to raise plenty of hell and havoc but, remarkably, had avoided seeing the inside of a jail cell. His brother Danny called most of the shots for the up and coming street gang and fiercely protected his younger brother.

A deep breath of cool October air filled Nicky's lungs. He hung a quick right between the strip club and the neighboring commercial building where he stopped for a few seconds to light a cigarette before continuing toward Marks Street and his apartment two short blocks away. Walking briskly through the small parking area behind the club, he continued down the sidewalk on the north side of the road. Nicky had made this walk hundreds of times amid the sparsely spaced city street lights. At this hour, there were few, if any, cars or residents around. Nicky's attention was drawn to the headlights of a slow-moving vehicle driving toward him. The silver sport utility vehicle slowed. The passenger's side window was already down. Nicky froze, his heart racing, as the vehicle abruptly stopped.

"Nicky," a voice called out from the SUV.

Price approached cautiously.

"Who's that?"

"Nicky. It's Rock. Get in."

Price still couldn't see the driver's face but recognized the voice. It was Rocco Morales. Nicky opened the passenger's door and got in.

"How the hell are you, Nicky?" Morales asked. He slapped and grabbed Nicky's shoulder. "You look good, kid."

"What's up, Rock? You scared the shit out of me. Don't you fuckin' sleep?"

Morales drove a short distance to the west end of Marks Street where he pulled into a dark, secluded parking lot near a playground and an old public tennis court a few hundred feet behind the strip club. He cut the engine and the headlights.

"Nicky, I haven't seen you in a while. I just happened to be over here on some other bullshit and saw you leaving the club. It's good to see you."

"I hope there ain't no shit going on with my club Rock, huh?" Price asked with concern.

"No, nothing like that," Morales added. He looked forward, momentarily taking his eyes off Price. "So, Nicky, I've been wanting to talk to you about something," Morales broke a short silence.

"What about, Rock?"

"You know that little delivery you made for me?"

"Sure."

"Well, there's been a little problem with that."

"What kind of problem?"

"Ah, the judge that got that package was arrested by the feds and somehow they know about the package."

"Well, shit, Rock! You don't think they heard it from me, do you? What the fuck!"

"I'm just asking, Nicky. I'm not saying you did. I'm just asking."

"I don't like the way this conversation is going, Rock. You think I talked to the feds? Are you crazy? Why would I talk to anyone? They got nothing on me. I don't even know what was in the package, Rock. I swear. This is bullshit!"

Price reached for the handle to open the door. Morales grabbed Nicky's left arm.

"Hey, Nicky. I ain't crazy so don't you get crazy." Morales tried to calm the situation. "I'm just asking. There are other people asking me. That's why I'm asking you. Somehow the feds know and it ain't good."

Price stared angrily out the side window.

"Now what?" he snapped.

"Now you go home and if anyone comes poking around here trying to ask you anything, you call me right away. You don't say shit. You got my number?"

Price reached into his jacket pocket for his phone.

"Shit. I left my phone back at the club."

"Listen. You don't need to call me. Anyone tries to talk to you, you *find* me. Understood?"

Price nodded.

"You didn't tell your brother you did this for me, did you?" Morales probed. "He'd fucking go ballistic if he knew I gave you that work."

"I told you. I didn't tell nobody. Nobody."

"All right, Nicky. Listen. No hard feelings?" Morales extended his hand.

"We're good." Price gripped Morales's hand. He started to open the door.

"Hey," Morales said, "tell you what. Can you take something to your brother for me? Save me a trip over here again tomorrow."

"What is it?" Nicky asked.

"It's just something he wanted from me. It's wrapped up in the back." Morales got out and opened the tailgate. Price met him behind the vehicle. Price saw a small cardboard box inside the cargo compartment.

"That's it," Morales said pointing to the package. "Can you get that out of there for me. My back's killing me."

"Sure thing, Rock."

Thirty-Seven

Court Security Officer Jeb Powers snapped a friendly salute as Thax's Jeep approached the gated secure parking lot behind the federal courthouse. The silver-haired former special forces officer and retired DEA agent greeted the prosecutor the same way every morning. Thax returned the salute and rolled his window down as Powers approached his vehicle.

"Morning, Jeb."

"Good mornin', Mr. Colby," Powers replied in his thick Brooklyn accent.

"You doing okay, Jeb?"

"I'm livin' the dream." Powers smiled convincingly. "Just don't wake me up. You?"

"Something like that." Thax smiled back.

"You have a visitor," Powers advised, motioning toward the parking area. "He said you weren't expecting him. He's been here for an hour. Since the building wasn't open yet and he checked out I let him pull in here."

"Who is it?"

"Jerry King. State Police. Hope that was okay."

Thax looked at his watch.

"He's been here since six forty-five?"

"At least that."

"Well, I better go see what he wants."

"Yes, sir," Powers responded, backing away from Thax's vehicle. "Have a good one."

Thax parked in his assigned spot and greeted King.

"Thax. How the hell are you?" The tired looking investigator reached out and shook Thax's hand.

"I'm good, Jerry. It's been a while. What's going on?"

"I caught that double yesterday."

Thax nodded.

"Can we talk in your office?" King asked politely.

"Sure. Let's go."

* * *

King scooted his chair up close to the front of Thax's office desk. He spread some draft reports and his notebook in front of him. Thax was curious why King was there talking to him and not out working the case. He also knew that if King was there to see him there was a really good reason. He listened intently as his old friend spoke.

"One shot each to the back of the head. Close range. Never saw it coming. They probably thought it was a robbery. Made them strip before they were shot." King was direct as always.

"Is that where this is going? It was a robbery?" Thax interjected.

"There was an empty wallet at the scene. I think that's where everyone else is going with this."

"Everyone else?"

"That's why I'm here Thax. I've been doing this for twenty-five years. Whoever did this, if I'm supposed to believe this was a robbery, executed two people—one of whom was a pregnant woman—for whatever cash was in that wallet. Now I don't believe that for a damn minute and for a lot of reasons but I'll show you one right now." King shuffled through a brown file folder containing some photographs. He handed one to Thax.

"Hope you haven't eaten any breakfast," King said.

Thax looked at the picture.

"That's the female victim. Marlena Schick," King advised.

Thax studied the photo. Schick's naked body was lying on her right side facing her husband. His right hand was visible in the photo. Thax could see the gunshot wound to the left side of her head.

"Do you see it, Thax?"

"I wish I did, Jerry. All I can look at is her stomach."

King slid another photo across the desk. It was an enlargement of Marlena's left hand.

"How about now?"

Thax examined the second photo. "Wow, Jerry. How could I not see that before? It's huge."

"Because you weren't looking for it," King answered. "It's almost two carats. I'm guessing five, maybe ten thousand dollars. You take the cash out of his wallet and leave her diamond ring on her hand? I don't think so."

Thax started to speak but King interrupted.

"Was Schick cooperating with you on whatever you're working on? I don't need to know any more than you can tell me, but I'd like to know that."

Thax looked surprised.

"No. He wasn't cooperating with us. Why would you think he was?"

"Because he called the FBI on Saturday."

"He did what?! How do you know that?"

"Thirty second call on his cell phone Saturday afternoon to the FBI's main number. Don't know if he left a message or not, but I know you'll check it out before I get out of the building," King replied. "Here's his cell number and the time of the call."

"Thax, I'm barely into this thing and it stinks. There's no physical evidence. No prints on the wallet or the truck, no tire tracks, footprints, and no witnesses. Just a lone .45 shell casing. There's absolutely no reason why Schick pulled off the road where he did. There was nothing wrong with his car, no evidence that he or his wife was sick. Shit, if they were, there's any number of places just up the road where they could have pulled over."

Thax listened to his friend.

"Someone caused them to stop there. I thought maybe he was forced off the road but there's no damage to his vehicle or maybe he stopped to help someone who just happened to be armed and prepared to execute them. Really? I don't think so."

"What do you think happened, Jerry?"

"That's the reason I'm here. This was no robbery. Someone got them to pull over in the most isolated area of that road, walked them back into that meadow and executed them. You could sit here all day and you won't come up with any reason to kill a soon-to-be mom. There isn't any. Unless you're killing a witness to a hit, which is exactly what I think this was. A hit."

Thax listened to King's theory. There was a reason anyone who worked with King wanted him as the investigator if they were ever murdered. He was, hands down, the best.

"If you're looking at cops, I'm not saying someone isn't capable of doing this to one of their own if they thought he was talking, but this is evil, Thax," King said, pointing to the photo of Marlena's body. "Whoever did this or ordered it is a vile, sick motherfucker and they've got *a lot* to lose if someone talks. This guy apparently wasn't talking but someone thought he was or was thinking about it. They just sent a clear message to anyone you're trying to get to cooperate."

Thax nodded as he picked up the photo and looked at it again.

"This is bigger than one rogue cop," King explained. "This hit came from the person who has the most to lose if the shit hits the fan. If you don't know, you need to find out who that is. And, if you don't, they just made it a lot harder for you to *ever* find out."

King stood up and gathered his papers.

"I hope to God you find out who it is, Thax," King said, turning to walk out. "There's a needle waiting for 'em."

Thax picked up the photos to hand to King.

"You can keep those if you want them," King said. "Thanks for your time, Thax. I've got to go. Sorry to drop this all on you but you needed to know it. I'll keep you up to speed on any developments but I don't think there are going to be many on my end. No leads right now. I think our best leads will come from you and your investigation."

"Thanks, Jerry. I'll walk down to the FBI office when you leave and check on that call. I appreciate your help more than you know." Thax shook King's hand. They walked toward the door.

"How's your uncle doing?" King asked.

"He's okay, Jerry. He's starting to forget things."

"We're all starting to forget things. Just not the things we'd like to." King paused. "Give him my best, would you? He's a good man."

"I will," Thax replied. "We'll be in touch."

* * *

The receptionist at the FBI office buzzed Thax through the secure entrance.

"Good morning, Martha." Thax smiled. "Is Shea back there?"

"She's back there." Martha returned the smile. She reached for a visitor's badge for Thax.

"I don't need that," Thax said, waving his hand as he walked down the hall. He stuck his head through an open door. Barrows was sitting at her desk sipping a large cup of Starbucks coffee.

"Did you get some for me?" Thax asked, startling Barrows.

"Thax. What are you doing here? Aren't we meeting later this morning?"

"We are." Thax pulled a piece of paper from his pocket. "Jerry King from the State Police is the lead on the Schick murders. He's a friend of mine. I just met with him a few minutes ago."

"What about?"

"Josh Schick called here on Saturday."

"What?" Barrows almost spilled her coffee. "Seriously? Who did he call?"

She looked at her phone. "I've got no voicemail messages. If he called, he didn't call me."

"Here's his cell phone number." Thax handed her the paper. "According to King, he called the main number at 2:17 p.m. on Saturday. A thirty second call."

"Thirty seconds?" Barrows repeated. "Our overnight message is long. He wouldn't have even had a chance to leave a message in thirty seconds." She paused momentarily. "Hang on a minute." Barrows dialed Martha.

"Martha. Do two things for me please. Pull a log of the incoming calls to the main number for this past Saturday."

"Okay," Martha answered.

"And were there any messages in the general mailbox this morning?"

"Just one for Marty Koenig. That's it."

"Did you listen to it?"

"Yeah. It was from the duty agent in Cincinnati asking for Marty to call him today."

"Okay. Check that log for me ASAP if you will," Barrows asked.

"Hang on. I'll check right now," Martha said.

Barrows put the call on speaker phone while they waited. She looked at Thax.

"Do you think our guy was having thoughts of cooperating?"

"Shea," Martha interrupted. "There were two calls on Saturday. The one for Marty from Cincinnati and another one from (610) 628-2231 at 2:17 p.m. No message."

"Thanks, Martha." Barrows hung up. "That's our boy, Thax." Barrows looked at the number on the paper. "He must have called but gotten cold feet."

Thax nodded in agreement and then briefed Barrows about the details of his conversation with Jerry King.

"Whoever is calling the shots on this operation thought Schick was going to talk and stopped him before he did. That's what I think, Shea." Thax started to walk out of Barrows office. "It's time for us to flush these rattlesnakes out of hiding and cut their heads off. I'll see you and Christopher in an hour. Brief him on what King told us. Okay?"

"I'll call him now to make sure he's up," Barrows chuckled.

"Good idea," Thax said.

Barrows took the last hit of her coffee.

"Need some caffeine?"

"No, thanks," Thax replied. "I need to make a call."

* * *

"Good morning, law offices of Jack Winthrop. May I help you?" a pleasant female voice answered.

"This is Thax Colby in the U.S. Attorney's Office. Is Jack in this morning?"

"One moment please, Mr. Colby. Let me check if he's available." A few seconds passed.

"Thax, how are you?" Winthrop answered. "To what do I owe this pleasure?"

"I'm fine Jack. I thought you would have been calling *me* this morning," Thax mused.

"About what?"

"About Josh Schick? I'm sure you probably heard. Seems somebody killed him and his pregnant wife."

Winthrop responded after a brief silence.

"I did hear that. It's too bad. Very upsetting to us all. What a nice young man and a pretty wife too."

Thax ignored the insincerity.

"I'm just curious when you were going to call me to tell me he wanted to cooperate with us."

"Cooperate? Who said anything about him cooperating? He didn't have anything to do with the things you all accused him of doing. He was an innocent man and I certainly expected him to be exonerated after a trial. He didn't have the slightest thought about talking to you or your agents. What would he cooperate about?" Winthrop scoffed.

"Well, that's not what he said when he called the FBI." Thax stirred the pot.

"What do you mean?" Winthrop snapped.

"I mean your client called the FBI on Saturday afternoon. A couple of hours before someone killed him."

"Well, what did he say?"

"Now, Jack, there's no need for me to get into all the details with you right now," Thax taunted.

"Thax, if my client made statements to the FBI before someone killed him I need to know what he said." Winthrop spoke louder and faster.

"Your client's dead. I think your attorney-client relationship has ended."

"Thax," Winthrop growled before he was interrupted.

"I'll tell you what, how about you tell me who was paying his legal tab, because I know he wasn't paying it himself, and I'll think about telling you what he said."

Winthrop laughed nervously.

"Thax, I've known you for a long time. I'm telling you, you don't want to go barking up that tree."

"You have known me for a long time which is why you know I'm not just going to bark up that tree. I'm climbing up the tree and I'm going to chew on someone's ass when I get up there and I'm going to saw off some rotten branches while I'm up there too. Now, you decide whether you want to be involved in that process or not because it's going to happen."

"I want to know what he said."

"I bet you do. Why don't you tell me who really wants that information and I'll tell them myself?"

"You need to tell me what he said or—"

"Or what, Jack? Are you threatening me?"

"I'm just telling you," Winthrop grumbled.

"Here's the way I see it. Somebody hired you to keep Josh Schick quiet. Somehow somebody thought he was going to talk so now he's dead. Only problem is that call to the FBI. I don't think they're going to be very happy with you if they learn that you didn't keep him quiet after all. Maybe you're the one who needs to look over your shoulder."

"Dammit, Thax," Winthrop stammered.

"You know how to find me, Jack. Have a good day."

Thirty-Eight

"YOUR AGENTS ARE here," Abigail announced peering around the doorway into Thax's office. Thax looked up from the report he was reading.

"Thanks. Can you send them back?"

"One step ahead of you. What I meant was they're right here."

"Great security up front, huh?" Thax chuckled. "Thanks."

Campisano and Barrows walked in. Thax stood up to greet them.

"Hey, brother. How are you doing?" Thax gripped Campisano's hand.

"I'm good." He and Barrows sat down.

Campisano dove right in. "Shea tells me PSP thinks this Schick thing was a hit."

"Jerry King is the lead investigator. *He* thinks it was a hit," Thax responded.

"I've heard the name but I've never worked with him."

"Jerry King is kind of a legend with homicide cops in this state. He's solved a lot of cold case murders over the years. About fifteen years ago, when you were still out in Arizona, they pulled him up to Meadville—a sleepy little college town just south of Erie—when they had a serial killer stalking coeds there at Allegheny College. He eventually solved the case. No one else could even get a decent lead before he got there. He's as good as they get."

"He worked with your uncle?" Campisano asked.

"Jerry started here as a rookie trooper around the same time I started in this office. One day he and a senior trooper who was his field training officer—Mac Hill—were working speeders up on the interstate. They had two patrol cars; Mac was clocking them and Jerry was stopping them. They'd been working for a couple of hours when Jerry got a call from his wife to meet her for lunch and Mac told him to go. A few minutes after Jerry left, Mac stopped a guy who was driving like a crazy son of a bitch. He got the guy out of the car. Turned out the guy was on PCP, angel dust. He resisted, tackled Mac and wrestled his gun away from him. Mac was down on his back pleading for the guy not to shoot him, but he did. It was horrible. Mac was like Jerry's father. Since it happened in Allentown, my uncle worked the case. He got Jerry through some really dark days. A couple years later, he and my uncle started the local Gold Shield Foundation for the families of cops who are killed in the line of duty.

"Anyway, that's how I got to know Jerry and if he thinks this was a hit, it probably was."

"So who are we looking at?" Campisano asked.

"I don't know. I called Schick's attorney before you guys got here. If Schick was going to flip, I would think he would have said something about it to his lawyer. Maybe not. I don't know. I think Jack Winthrop and whoever retained him to handle Schick's case are knee deep in this shit. Winthrop seemed like he was scared to death about Schick having talked to the FBI."

"You told him Schick called the FBI?" Barrows asked. "But Schick didn't leave a message."

"Well, I think I neglected to tell him that part. For all he knows, Schick spilled the beans about everything he knew."

"Nice." Campisano nodded. "I bet there are some puckered ass-holes somewhere."

"Right. But where? Thax asked. "And who are they? Who thought Schick was ready to cooperate and who killed him or had someone kill him?"

"What about Morales?" Barrows asked. "He's the sergeant over this crew. I think he's a good bet."

"I don't know, Shea. But I think we need to squeeze him hard."

"What's your plan?" she asked.

"Christopher, get a hold of Walt McConnell at ATF. Let's arrest Danny Price on a criminal complaint for those AK-47's. We'll charge him with being a felon in possession of firearms. Let's see if Morales is going to stick to the story that Price was an informant too. Do I think he will step up and really go to bat for Danny Price? My guess is he won't. If he doesn't stand up for Price, Price is looking at a shit load of federal time. If we're right that Morales was protecting the East Side Boyz, Price is going to be really pissed when Morales leaves him hanging. Then we flip Price, use Jack Sweeting's patrol stop of Price with Morales's business card and the missing coke and we use Victor Lord's testimony to bury Morales for all of the cocaine that Lord brought in here from Jersey for him. *That's* my plan."

"Excellent," Campisano said. "How much of the story do we tell Walt?"

"Walt already knows Morales wasn't right on this thing," Thax explained. "If we're going to use his case to work our investigation, I think we need to wire him in on where we're going and what we're doing."

"I agree." Campisano nodded.

"Me too," Barrows said.

Thax continued. "The next thing is Judge Harlin's trial. They want a speedy trial so we're set for early December. We need to move Victor Lord into protective custody at the prison. He's not going to like that but we can't afford to lose a witness if some unfortunate accidental stabbing should happen while the judge is waiting for trial. Morales might have some connections over in Jersey. I don't know. We need to keep our guy safe."

"Okay," Barrows answered.

"I'll tell you what. Better yet. Walk down and see Scott Adkins in the Marshal's office. We can writ Lord out of the prison in Jersey. Let's see if we can put him somewhere near here where we can keep him safe. The Marshals can do all kinds of shit."

"I got that one." Barrows smiled. "Scott likes me."

"Good." Thax took a breath. "What else? Nicky Price."

"Right," Campisano answered.

Thax continued. "We need to find Nicky and see if we can get him to talk about delivering the money to Harlin."

"You don't really think he's going to talk to us do you?" Barrows asked.

"Probably not. But if we can get his big brother Danny on board, we'll make Nicky's testimony part of the deal," Thax said. "It's worth a shot."

"Do we want to try to talk to Nicky before we arrest Danny?" Barrows asked.

"I've been looking for this kid for a few weeks," Campisano said. "I've got a few task force guys out looking for him too. We haven't found him yet.

Once we find out where he's laying his head at night, we'll be able to get to him whenever you need."

Thax agreed. "Let's find out where Nicky is but hold off on trying to talk to him."

"Anything else?" Campisano asked.

"What about Gallon and Piper?" Barrows asked. "Are we going to arrest them for trying to kill our witness? I know that would make Mr. Karopolis very happy."

"How's his son doing?" Thax asked.

"I spoke to his dad last week," Barrows answered. "They still have Jimmy in ICU but they think he's out of the woods. He's got a lot of surgeries ahead of him, mostly reconstructive stuff, and man, this kid was just torn apart by those pieces of garbage. We really need to slam those two."

"I agree," Thax said. "I'll try to work on an indictment so we can take a shot at them too. They're looking at a bunch of time plus state charges when we get done with them. Maybe we can flip one of them."

"Let's do it," Barrows said.

"All right," Thax replied. "Keep in touch. Let me know what's going on."

Campisano's phone vibrated for about the tenth time since the start of the meeting. He looked down at the phone.

"Will you please answer that now," Thax pleaded. "I'm tired of hearing it," he razzed his friend.

"It's one of our task force guys. Foster Cooke. Let me call him back since he keeps calling," Campisano said, stepping outside of Thax's office.

"What about Schick?" Barrows asked. "Do you want us to touch base with Jerry King or not?"

"I'm sure Jerry will keep me up to speed if anything new develops. Let's just stay out of the way for now."

Campisano walked back into the office. Barrows stood up to leave. He looked at Thax and shook his head.

"Well, we can scratch Nicky Price off the list."

"What do you mean?" Thax asked.

"Some kids just found his body in a wooded area near a playground over on the East Side. APD homicide is working it."

"Shit." Thax slammed his hand on his desk.

"You still want me to reach out to Walt to arrest Danny?" Campisano asked.

Thax thought for a few seconds.

"Get with Walt and be ready to go. Don't arrest him today. I'm pretty sure we'll know where to find him now."

"So tomorrow?" Campisano asked.

"What compassion you guys have," Barrows said.

Thax didn't skip a beat.

"My compassion for any of these guys is gone, Shea. Do you want to see the photos of Marlena Schick?"

"I know . . . I'm with you . . . Tomorrow." Barrows nodded.

* * *

Thax stared out of his office window over the roof of the U.S. Post Office on the other side of 5th Street. The lights of center city Allentown's Hamilton Street provided a soft warming glow to the cool autumn evening. Traffic was light but steady on the city's main thoroughfare. He thought about Nicky Price. Another potential witness was dead. Thax didn't believe in coincidences. As of a few hours ago, Allentown Police homicide detectives had no suspects in Nicky's murder. Detectives would only report to the media that the victim died of blunt force trauma to the upper body, police speak for any cause of death short of poisoning. They would keep the details—that Nicky was shot once in the back of the head—to themselves for now. No suspect or person of interest had been named. Thax's office phone rang. It was nine twenty-five p.m. He recognized the number.

"Hey, beautiful," Thax answered. "Where are you?"

"I'm pulling into your driveway," Chrissy responded. "Don't you answer your cell phone?"

Thax searched his desk for his cell phone then realized where it was.

"Sorry. I left it in my jacket."

"Well, I'm glad I found you. Are you coming home anytime soon?"

"It's going to be a while yet. I'm going to be pretty late."

"Well, I'm sad about that."

"Me, too."

Chrissy hesitated.

"Anything new going on with the Schick murders? No one at PSP is saying anything."

"Well . . . maybe they're not saying anything for a reason."

The stress in his voice was evident. She didn't push any further.

"Did you hear about the body they found over on the East Side?" Chrissy asked. "My sources are saying it was probably gang-related. Anyway, they gave it to someone else to run with since I've got this Schick thing. Which seems to be going nowhere."

Thax didn't respond.

"What's pretty late? I miss you."

"I'll get out of here in about an hour. It's been a long day."

"Mine, too. Time to pop the cork on a bottle of red. I'll save you a glass . . . maybe." Chrissy tried to lighten up the conversation.

"Okay."

"Hurry home, fly boy."

* * *

Katie Meyers sat on her bed, her legs crossed in front of her, squeezing the life out of a large stuffed puppy dog. Tears rolled off her face onto one of the dog's big floppy ears. A floor lamp in the far corner of the room provided adequate lighting for her to read Detective Cole Hatten's business card. She looked at the card and dialed his cell phone number. She tried to control her emotions as the phone rang.

"This is Detective Cole Hatten with the South Whitehall Township Police Department. Please leave me a message and I will call you back."

Katie was about to hang up when she heard the tone. She hesitated.

"Detective Hatten. This is Katie Meyers. I'm sorry." She began to cry again. "I saw a man at the back door. I *remember* seeing a man at the back door. I just can't remember any more than that. He was outside the door, walking away. I think. I don't know who he was . . . I'm sorry."

Katie hung up and set the phone down on the bed. The haunting image that took so long for her to remember, was front and center in her brain.

Thirty-Nine

"This is bullshit!" Danny Price smacked his handcuffed hands against the wooden table where he was seated in the DEA office interview room.

The leader of the East Side Boyz street gang—his hair and clothes disheveled from his early morning rendezvous with ATF agents—scowled at ATF agent Walt McConnell. Campisano and Thax sat at the opposite end of the table.

"My brother's body's not even cold and I gotta deal with this bullshit," Price raised his voice again. He buried his face into his hands, rubbing his bloodshot and swollen eyes.

"Let me take your cuffs off," McConnell offered in his mild Georgia drawl. He removed Price's handcuffs hoping to engender some goodwill before his questioning.

"Thanks," Price mumbled.

McConnell started the interview. "Danny, I'm sorry about your little brother."

Price didn't respond.

"You know why you're here," McConnell continued. "I read you your rights in the car and you said you understood. Right?"

"Right. I got it, but I don't know why you want to arrest me. I was helping out Morales. He told you that, didn't he?"

"Danny. We know a lot about what's going on with you and Morales and we know you weren't out there on some sanctioned operation, so don't even go there," McConnell tried to cut through the nonsense story.

"I was working for Morales."

"Why would a narcotics detective have you buying guns? That just doesn't add up, Danny. The whole story stinks. It stunk then. It stinks now," McConnell countered.

"Well, that's what you say, but that's what happened."

"All right, let's play it your way," McConnell said, still hoping to make the interview productive. "Walk us through it."

"Morales came to me and told me he needed my help. He was going to pay me $500. All I had to do was meet this guy Harman and order up three AK's. I'm was supposed to pay the guy a grand a piece. We had a couple of calls—"

McConnell interrupted.

"No. You got *called* a couple of times and you wouldn't talk about the guns on the phone."

"Wait a minute," Price interjected.

"No, you wait a minute," McConnell responded. "Are you telling me Morales was trying to make a case on this guy Harman and you didn't talk dirty to him on the phone?"

Price moved in his chair.

"Man. I don't talk shit on the phone."

"You just said you were working for Morales. What would you care about talking dirty on the phone?"

"I don't get you," Price responded.

"You're lying, Danny. What were you going to do with the guns?" McConnell's patience with Price was almost gone.

"Hey. I don't need no guns like that," Price responded.

"Who wanted the guns?"

"You're not hearing me." Price leaned forward. "They weren't my guns."

"You're not helping yourself by sticking to that story," McConnell warned.

"It ain't a story man. I was buying the guns but I was doing it for Morales. That's what he'll tell you. Shit, he already told you that the day it happened. You know that. Why are you arresting me? Come on, man. This is bullshit."

McConnell looked at Thax who moved to the seat next to Price.

"Mr. Price, listen to what I'm going to tell you," Thax said in a low voice, leaning closer.

Price leaned forward in his chair.

"Sergeant Morales does *not* back up your story."

Thax slid the government phone from the middle of the table toward Price. "Here's his number." Thax flipped a page over on his yellow legal pad and slid it in front of Price. "Let's call Sergeant Morales right now."

Price sat silently, his right foot nervously rocking his body back and forth. Thax picked up the receiver and handed it to Price, who refused to take it.

"Do you want me to dial?" Thax asked. "Take the phone."

Price declined.

"Rocco Morales has been running protection for you guys for a while now," Thax bristled. "He gets you and your boys out of jams and makes problems go away. He protects you because you're selling all his dope."

Price's eyes got big and wide. He continued to fidget in his chair.

Thax continued.

"You weren't out there working for Morales, you were out there buying guns for you and Morales was protecting you. Well, your pact worked for a while but that game's over. Do you really think Morales is going to stand up for you? He's got no cover on this one. He didn't have you make any recorded calls. I'm sure he didn't sign that three grand out from the department. There's no reports to back this up. This was a side deal Morales was protecting you on. The last thing anyone thought was that Harman was working for ATF. Morales isn't going to back your play. He can't. He's going to drop *you* in the grease."

"Man, you don't know that shit. If you knew any of that, Morales would be sitting here in handcuffs and not me."

"Call him," Thax said again, handing Price the phone. "If he says he's going to back up your story, I'll send you home. If he doesn't, you cooperate and tell us everything you know about Morales, the cocaine, the protection . . . everything."

Price stared at Thax, who pushed the phone closer.

"What's it going to be?" Thax asked sternly.

Price looked at McConnell.

"I guess you better take me wherever you need to so I can see a judge. I got nothing else to say." Price smirked and tried to stand up.

"Sit down." McConnell pushed down on Price's shoulder.

McConnell handcuffed Price then stood him up to walk him out of the office. Price, a no-good, fast-talking, dope-dealing, gang-banging punk, couldn't help himself to one more smart ass remark.

"I guess it's time for me to go home," he snickered, taunting Thax.

Thax nodded.

"You know, Danny, it's too bad we can't talk to your little brother Nicky about the money he delivered for your boy Morales. I would have liked to have heard that story."

"What are you talking about?" Price snapped. "Morales didn't do shit with Nicky. What are you talking about?"

Thax had pushed his button.

Price was agitated. "Nicky wasn't involved in anything with Morales." He paused, breathing heavily, trying to contain his anger. "Tell me what he did with Nicky."

"I'm sorry, Danny," Thax replied. "What was it you said? I've got nothing else to say."

"Tell me about Nicky." Price glared at Thax. He tried to turn back toward Thax as McConnell shepherded him toward the door.

Thax stared back.

"See you later, Danny."

The door closed to the interview room.

Campisano looked at Thax. "Is the judge going to release him on a bond today?"

"Yeah. He'll be out later today."

"How long do you think it will be before he reaches out to Morales? I'd love to be a fly on the wall for that conversation."

Thax nodded in agreement.

"I didn't see that one coming," Campisano commented on Thax bringing up Nicky's delivery of the money.

"Well, if he would have been straight with us and cooperated I wasn't going to bring it up."

"And the telephone thing?"

"What about it?"

"How did you know he wouldn't call Morales?"

"I didn't. But now you know for sure the whole story was bullshit, right?"

"You're full of surprises today, aren't you?"

Thax was pleased.

"And the day's not over yet."

Forty

Logan Branfield clicked the remote to turn off the forty-six-inch flat screen monitor on the wall of his office. Branfield and Sokol had just finished watching the first seven minutes of the local five o'clock news.

"This is what I'm talking about, Richie," the mayor began. "The top of the news around here—every fucking day—a cop committed suicide, a cop and his wife murdered, a body found in the woods. I know these things happen, and they're unfortunate, but I need to be the lead story! Me! Me! Me!" his voice got increasingly louder.

Sokol, uneasy and obviously unhappy with the mayor's rant, tried to speak but was interrupted.

"Me!" Branfield repeated tossing the remote into an empty chair in disgust.

Sokol shook his head.

"Can I talk now?" Sokol asked.

"Please," Branfield interrupted again. "Say something."

"Exactly what do you think is gonna happen when someone guns down a police detective *and* his pregnant wife. You think that's not going to be at the top of the news?"

"Shit," the mayor scoffed, sliding into his plush executive chair. "We've got two minutes left in the game and we have the fucking ball. Let's not blow this thing now. I'm out there spouting law and order and I have cops in my city committing suicide, being indicted, being killed. We've got a couple of weeks. I need attention, but not that kind."

"I hear you, boss."

"Don't just hear me Richie. *Listen to me.* For the next two weeks, *I* need to be the lead story. Can you make that happen or not?"

"Unless someone claims the reward you offered," Sokol replied sarcastically.

"Right." Branfield smiled twirling an expensive black French fountain pen on the top of his desk. "We'll just hope that doesn't happen."

Branfield stood up and looked out the window behind his desk. The calmer of his multiple personalities spoke with reserve, breaking the tension in the room.

"I got a call from Judge Harlin today."

"Oh, yeah? How's the judge doing these days?"

"Well, when I spoke to him he sounded like he was in pretty good spirits. He's demanded a speedy trial in his case. It's set for December."

"With one less witness," Sokol interjected, "now that Little Nicky's gone."

"Like I said, there's so much unfortunate news to hear lately," the mayor replied smugly. "A young man murdered and dumped like an old bag of garbage. Damned unfortunate news."

Branfield and Sokol shared a moment of conspiratorial silence.

"Are we done, boss?" Sokol asked. He limped uncomfortably as he made his way toward the door.

"How's the knee?" Branfield asked. "It doesn't look so good."

Sokol stopped and turned back toward the mayor.

"Probably as good as it's gonna get. I don't think I'll be running any marathons anytime." He continued walking to the door.

"Hey, Richie?"

Sokol turned as he stopped at the door.

"Yeah."

"You're going to love Harrisburg."

Forty-One

"THE ANSWER IS no, Cole," South Whitehall Township Police Chief Jay Moser said, sitting in his office behind his gray metal desk. "There's just not enough to justify keeping this thing open anymore. I gave you some room, but—"

"Chief, I think there is." Detective Hatten pleaded his case. "We talked to Katie Meyers and she's *sure* there was a man at the back door the night her father was killed."

"You mean the night he killed *himself*," Moser replied. "The coroner says it was a suicide."

"Chief, with all due respect to Dr. Chase, you know the physical evidence on this doesn't add up. There are too many questions that I can't answer and this latest breakthrough is a really good lead."

"Breakthrough?" the chief responded. "You've been pressing this traumatized young girl to remember something and now she thinks she remembers."

"No. She does remember."

The chief stood up and exhaled deeply.

"Cole. You're my best detective. I know you believe there's more to this than the suicide, but with just her statement that she remembers a man at the back door and without any further description and with everything she's been through, I just don't see this going anywhere. I'm not sure it's good to keep pushing her so hard."

"Chief," Hatten started to speak.

"Look," the chief continued, "if she calls you with more detailed information we'll talk about this again, but for now, it's closed. I don't see anything that you can do at this point, even with this new information. We've got other things that need your attention."

"Yes, sir," Hatten said, rising to his feet and snapping an informal salute. He stepped toward the door of the office.

"You've done everything you could possibly do on this one, Cole," the chief assured him. "Don't beat yourself up over it."

"Yes, sir."

* * *

"Tonight, State Police investigators are reporting little progress in the double murder of suspended Allentown Police Detective Josh Schick and his pregnant wife Marlena."

Chrissy reported at the top of the six o'clock news on the stalled homicide investigation standing outside the Troop M State Police Barracks, a two-story red brick building near Airport Road in Bethlehem. The thundering roar of a large passenger jet taking off from the adjacent Lehigh Valley International Airport interrupted her report.

She continued as the engine noise subsided.

"Captain Reece Hutcheson addressed the media today with this statement."

The story cut to the uniformed Troop Commander.

"We are asking anyone with *any* information about this crime to please contact the State Police. We believe that someone, anyone, who may have been traveling on East Macungie Road the night of these homicides might have seen a vehicle on the side of the road or might have heard something that could be related and helpful to our investigators. Please, if you were in that area that evening between six and ten p.m., contact us or the PSP Hotline to speak with one of our investigators. Thank you."

The live shot returned to Chrissy.

"Today, a law enforcement source who spoke on the condition of anonymity, stated there are no suspects and no leads at this time. That source also told me that police have identified no motive for this horrible crime. It appears that the trail of the killer or killers of this officer, his wife and their unborn children, has very likely gone cold. In Bethlehem, this is Chrissy Barnes, Valley 10 News."

Forty-Two

"WHAT ARE THEY hitting on this morning?" Thax asked, sticking his head through the doorway of the fly shop.

Old Ronnie, who was sitting at his work bench tying a fly, looked up over the top of his glasses.

"Well, they're probably not very hungry anymore," Ronnie said, looking at the small round plastic clock on the wall. It was almost eleven o'clock.

Thax nodded, acknowledging the lateness of the morning.

"I know. Just getting a slow start this morning," he responded. "You doing okay?" Thax noticed the building was as cool as it was outside. "Did you forget to pay the electric bill?"

Ronnie smirked.

"I'm fine. And it's not that cold in here."

"Whatever you say," Thax said, browsing through the collection of flies in the wooden slots on the front table. He grabbed a couple of flies from a bin—size 12 flying black ants.

"What are you going to do with those?" Ronnie asked sarcastically.

"I'm going to catch that twenty-inch trophy that sits out there sometimes behind that rough submerged rock pile."

"Well, good luck with that." Ronnie smirked again.

Thax threw six dollars onto Ronnie's work bench.

"Best money I spent this week," Thax teased. He turned to leave.

"There's somebody fishing in your spot," Ronnie said. "That's what happens when you get here at lunch time."

Thax chuckled. "There's a big river out there." He hooked the flies onto his vest. "See you later, pal."

Thax headed down the dirt and gravel path toward the giant willows. The cool weather made the smell of the grasses and shrubs along the way more intense and fragrant. The river was fast and clear. The late October sun had yet to show itself. The "partly cloudy" weather forecast was, so far, only partly right. When he reached the first giant willow, he noticed a man wading near the middle of the stream. He walked closer. The fisherman was focused on the river and didn't hear him approach. Thax stood and quietly admired the expert form of the senior angler.

"They said someone was fishing in my spot," Thax called out from the edge of the bank.

Bob Freeman turned his head.

"Thax? Is that you? How are you? Hang on a minute. Let me get out of here. I was just getting ready to leave anyway."

Freeman reeled in his fly and waded to the water's edge.

"How are you, Thax?" he repeated, reaching to shake Thax's hand.

"I'm good, Bob. How are you? I was sorry to hear about your wife."

Bob nodded.

"Thanks. I really appreciated the flowers you sent to the funeral home."

"Are you doing okay, Bob?"

"I am. Things are different without her here. I miss her every day but I know she's in a better place now."

"I thought you didn't fish in this spot anymore," Thax said, looking out toward the stream.

"I didn't. Not for a long time." Bob paused for a moment looking at the water. "It's a good spot. I thought I'd try it again. Caught a couple of nice brownies here this morning."

Bob looked back toward Thax.

"Your son," Thax asked, "what was his name?"

Bob glanced back at the river. He stared quietly for a few seconds.

"His name was Nathaniel. He drowned. Right out there. I avoided this place for so many years because of the memories of the day he—"

"I know, Bob."

Bob looked up at the towering willows.

"These trees sure have grown since then."

"I know." Thax hesitated. "The man who tried to help your son that day. That was my grandfather."

Bob listened. He gazed toward the river then back at Thax.

"The little boy?" Bob asked.

"That was me."

Bob reached over and grabbed Thax's arm.

"I'm sorry, Thax."

Thax nodded.

"It's okay, Bob. Life goes on. Sometimes it just takes us a lot of precious time to realize it."

Thax looked toward the river. A brief streak of brilliant sunlight shone between two masses of clouds—the first and only sun of the day.

"You take care of yourself, Thax." Bob started to walk away.

"You too, friend."

Forty-Three

Rocco Morales sat in his new sapphire blue Cadillac Escalade in the parking lot of Mahaffey's Irish Pub on the northeast corner of Plymouth Street and Hanover Avenue in East Allentown. A single street light barely illuminated the intersection. Above the side door of the pub, a small light cut through the darkness of the perpetually empty parking area. Looking west from the lot, the police sergeant surveyed the traffic on Hanover Avenue, a main thoroughfare through the East Side of the city into neighboring Bethlehem. The area was relatively quiet. The only daytime business nearby was a freestanding CPA office building just west on the avenue. The former Allentown State Hospital, set back hundreds of yards on its expansive grounds, was across the street.

Within several minutes of his arrival, Morales watched anxiously as he recognized Danny Price's vehicle traveling south on Plymouth Street toward the parking lot. Price pulled his white Ford Explorer into a parking space on the driver's side of Morales's SUV. He rolled his window down and looked into Price's vehicle.

"I thought you were coming alone," Morales remarked, looking at the attractive young woman with short dark hair sitting in the passenger's seat.

"She's just dropping me off. I assume you can get me back to my neighborhood when we're done," Price replied.

"Sure." Morales shrugged, his annoyance evident. "Get in."

The woman smiled at Morales then leaned over and gave Price a long deep kiss. Morales couldn't help but stare at the woman's long shapely legs and glittering rhinestone platform heels as she exited the passenger's side and walked around the vehicle. Price got out of the driver's side and walked to the passenger's side of the Escalade. The Explorer exited the lot and disappeared on Hanover Avenue.

"Who's the broad?" Morales asked. Price closed the door.

"She's a dancer from the club."

"That's nice," Morales responded curtly. "The next time you want to meet me, don't bring your fucking hooker girlfriend with you. You understand?"

Price turned in his seat to look at Morales.

"And another thing," Morales continued, raising his voice, "the next time you call and want to meet with me, don't fucking tell me you need me to stop what I'm doing right away because *you* have a problem. You work for me you little shit, not the other way around. Don't forget it."

Price stared out the front of the vehicle.

"You see this, Danny?" Morales pulled up the bottom of his brown leather flight jacket with his right hand, revealing a shining gold detective's shield attached to his belt. Price glanced at the badge. "I'm a cop. A detective. I'm in charge in this city. You don't demand anything from me."

Morales shook his head in disgust. He covered the badge and reached for the shift on the right side of the steering wheel.

Price turned his head to look at Morales.

"Fuck you, Morales!" Price pulled a Glock nine-millimeter handgun from his jacket pocket and fired a shot into Morales's stomach.

Morales lurched backward from the impact and grabbed his stomach. He let out a primal scream. Blood seeped through the jacket around the entrance wound.

"What the fuck!" Morales screamed through the smell of spent gun powder. "You shot me! Are you fucking crazy?"

Price leaned over the center console and shoved the muzzle of the gun against the center of Morales's chest. His left hand reached under Morales's jacket and grabbed the top of the detective's gun holster. He quickly unsnapped the holster and withdrew Morales's service weapon, pushing the Glock harder against his chest to deter any resistance.

"You motherfucker!" Morales groaned. "You fucking shot me, Danny!"

Morales tried to put pressure on the wound. Blood soaked his hands and jacket.

Price continued to train his Glock on Morales but moved back away from him with his back against the door.

"What are you doing, Danny," Morales tried to speak, writhing in pain from the gunshot wound.

"You were supposed to back me up," Price said, raising his voice. "Fucking ATF arrested me on those AKs. You were supposed to have my back!"

"Danny, I don't know anything about that. I do have your back."

"The fuck you do. That's not what the prosecutor said. Told me to call you and if you backed me up he'd let me go home."

"What?" Morales struggled to speak. He continued to bleed.

"I knew then that you had fucking sold me down the river. You son of a bitch. All the shit we've moved for you. You couldn't back me up on this one."

"Danny . . . I swear . . . listen to me . . . I never . . . they were lying to you. They never, ever asked me about this after the day it happened . . . I swear Danny," Morales gasped for breath.

Price glared at Morales.

"You have to believe me, Danny. Please . . . help me. There's my phone," Morales pointed to a slot in the console where his phone was placed. "Please . . . call for help . . . please!"

Price shook his head then reached into his left jacket pocket.

"Here," Price said, tossing a cell phone at Morales. "Why don't you use that phone."

Morales grabbed the phone to dial but realized the phone was turned off.

"Do you know whose phone that is?" Price asked angrily as Morales tried desperately to turn it on.

"No, Danny, I don't. Please just help me." Morales struggled, now coughing up blood.

"That's my little brother Nicky's phone," Price said defiantly. "The night my brother was killed, he left his phone at the club. The dancer who showed up with me tonight, she was taking the phone to Nicky at his apartment. Except when she was walking through the cut behind the club she saw someone forcing Nicky toward the woods with a gun at the back of his head. She ran back to the club for help but heard a shot and realized it was too late."

"Danny—"

"Shut up!" Price shouted. "Tonight, when she looked at you and kissed me, that's when I knew it was you."

Morales squirmed, gasping for air.

"He never did nothing to hurt you," Price said, his fury building. "Nothing."

Price pointed the Glock at Morales's head.

"Danny, please," Morales begged, reaching toward Price with his right hand.

"Go to hell, Morales." Price pulled the trigger again and again and again until he had emptied every one of the seventeen rounds in the magazine into his target.

He opened the door. His ears were ringing. He pulled a paper bag from the inside pocket of his jacket and tossed it in the vehicle.

"That's for Nicky," Price mumbled under his breath.

Forty-Four

ALLENTOWN POLICE HOMICIDE Detective Harlan Kinnebrew looked through the shattered driver's side window of the blue Cadillac Escalade. A trio of crime scene techs maneuvered around the vehicle snapping photographs and dusting the exterior for fingerprints. Kinnebrew's partner, Pete Walker, pointed the beam of his flashlight into the vehicle. The morning sun was still comfortably tucked below the horizon. The pre-dawn darkness left a damp chill over the Lehigh Valley.

"I haven't seen anything this bad since Fallujah," Kinnebrew, a steely homicide detective and Marine veteran, observed. "Jesus."

The two detectives examined the bullet-riddled body of their fellow officer. Walker, a relative newcomer to homicide, felt a short spell of nausea as he stared at the carnage. Kinnebrew walked to the passenger's side of the vehicle and stuck his head through the open door. The senior detective had investigated murders for almost fifteen years—before and after his military deployment. One thing about this scene was certain. Whoever murdered Sergeant Rocco Morales was really angry. This had rage written all over it. Morales was shot at least four times in the face and head. Kinnebrew couldn't even count the other entry wounds in the officer's torso, but there were many. Blood and brain matter were splattered everywhere.

Kinnebrew scanned the passenger's side for anything that would tell him what happened. The floor was littered with spent 9mm casings. He counted eight on the passenger's floor and seat. There were surely others he didn't yet see. From the position of the body and the entry wounds, he knew that Morales had been shot from the direction of the passenger's seat.

A brown paper lunch bag lying in the victim's lap drew the veteran cop's attention. The top of the bag was rolled down tight. Parts of the bag were soaked with blood.

"Are you done with photos?" he asked the lead crime scene tech.

"Yes, sir," the tech answered.

"Great." Kinnebrew removed a pair of disposable latex gloves from his jacket pocket and put them on. He reached for the bag and opened it.

"Son of a bitch," he mumbled as he looked at the contents of a plastic bag inside the paper sack.

"What is it?" Walker asked, still peering through the driver's window.

"What does it look like to you?" Kinnebrew turned the top of the open bag toward his partner.

Walker shined the beam of his flashlight at the bag. "Looks like cocaine to me. A bunch of it."

Kinnebrew rolled the bag closed and set it back in Morales's lap.

"What are you thinking?" Walker asked.

No Allentown cop, regardless of rank or position, was unaware of the rumors of corruption in the narcotics unit of their own department. While no good cop wanted to believe it, the allegations were getting harder to ignore. For some, the smoke had already turned to fire.

"He's got a half a pound of coke in that bag. Where did that come from?" Kinnebrew asked. "This wasn't a drug deal gone bad. There's not one backup or surveillance detective around. None. He was out here flying solo. This is bullshit."

"So he's out here off the clock," Walker started.

"Off the clock?" Kinnebrew repeated sarcastically. "How about off the damn chart."

"I don't know, Harlan. I'm just trying to give this guy the benefit of the doubt."

"Okay," Kinnebrew interrupted, "so how do you think this went down?"

Walker sensed his partner was on the defensive. He walked to the passenger's side of the vehicle to be closer to him. Officers from Allentown and nearby Bethlehem P.D. had arrived and continued to arrive at the scene. Many were posted up along the cordoned off crime scene. Others waited near their vehicles to show support and to assist in apprehending a suspect.

The sharp staccato bark of a police K-9 echoed over the sounds and activity of the arriving patrol units. Crime scene techs were still close by to the vehicle. Neither detective wanted to share his thoughts with the bystanders.

"Well?" Kinnebrew asked.

"Maybe he was meeting with someone to set up a deal later on."

"Come on, Pete. You meet with someone, you have backup. You don't do this alone. This guy was out here running his own pass patterns."

"I don't know." Walker shook his head. "What if he just happened to see someone he wanted to talk to and they got into his vehicle to talk? Or maybe someone called him late and there was no one around to back him up?" Walker struggled to make some sense—any sense—of this.

"And what? They get into an argument and someone kills him and leaves the dope in the car? When has that ever happened? If the person who did this brought the dope to the meeting, do you really think they would leave it after they shot and killed Morales? There's thousands of dollars' worth of coke there Pete."

"I don't know," Walker responded. "Maybe? I don't know. Maybe the guy was showing Morales the dope, the shit hits the fan, the guy panics and can't stop shooting. He runs off so fast he's not thinking and leaves the dope. He's afraid to come back to get it. I don't know. I'm just trying to give Morales the benefit here."

Kinnebrew shook his head again.

"Well, what do you think happened?" Walker asked, growing impatient with his partner.

Kinnebrew looked inside the vehicle again to scan the passenger compartment and the body of the dead detective.

"Do you see that?" Kinnebrew asked. The light from his flashlight shimmered off the bottom of Morales's badge. Part of the shield was visible at the bottom of his jacket. "When's the last time an undercover detective wore his badge on his belt to a drug deal?"

Walker didn't answer.

"They took his gun," Kinnebrew observed. "Do you see it anywhere?" Walker again walked to the driver's side window area and scanned the scene from there.

"I don't see it," Walker answered.

"Was his gun taken before or after he was shot?" Kinnebrew pondered. "I've got a lot of questions. If someone took his gun after he was shot, why didn't they take the cocaine?"

"I don't know, Harlan," Walker replied. "Maybe someone killed him then planted the dope on him to make it look like he was dirty."

"Or to confirm it," Kinnebrew answered.

Walker didn't respond.

Kinnebrew reached for an iPhone that was tucked into a small space in the console. He tried to turn it on. A password screen stopped him from opening it. He continued his inspection of the scene. A few seconds later, his eyes were drawn to another older cell phone lying on the floor near Morales's feet. He picked it up by the edges. The power on the older phone was off. He turned it on.

"Does this look like Morales's cell phone?" Kinnebrew asked skeptically, holding up the older phone for Walker to see.

"That phone? I doubt it," Walker responded.

"Well, let's find out," Kinnebrew said. He walked to where Walker was standing.

"How are you going to do that?" Walker asked.

Kinnebrew used the older phone to dial his own cell phone number. He pulled his phone from his pocket when it rang. He grinned tightly as the caller ID feature on his phone displayed the number for the incoming call.

"Check it out," he said, turning his phone display toward Walker. "Now watch this," he said as he returned the missed call. The older phone rang. Kinnebrew listened to the voicemail greeting.

"Yo, this is Nicky, lay it down and I'll holler back. Out."

Not even a week had passed since Kinnebrew answered the call on the Nicky Price homicide. There were few leads in that murder.

"You think that might be Nicky Price?" Kinnebrew asked.

"Might be," Walker answered.

"Well, if it is, what the hell would Morales be doing with Nicky Price's phone?"

A throng of onlookers had gathered outside the bright yellow police tape. The scene looked like a gangland slaying and the curious locals were snapping pictures with their cell phones.

Allentown Police Chief Scott Butler arrived on the scene in full uniform and approached Kinnebrew to be briefed.

"Give it to me straight, Harlan," the chief said, obviously aware that his detective was dead and out in the field with no cover units. Butler peered through the blood-spattered windshield at Morales's body.

Kinnebrew looked at his chief.

"Chief, he was hit ten, fifteen times. Maybe more. His weapon was taken. He was here alone. No indication that he was on the job when this happened."

Butler interrupted. "So you're telling me this was retaliation or something personal?"

"I didn't say that, Chief," Kinnebrew continued. "I said there was no one out here and this looks like it was off the clock."

Kinnebrew respected rank and the chain of command, but he didn't think much of Butler as a leader or an investigator. Butler was politically savvy. Probably the reason he was the chief. Kinnebrew knew it was time to drop the bomb.

"Chief, there's more. We found a bag with half a pound of cocaine in his lap."

Butler closed his eyes and exhaled deeply. Kinnebrew noted the outward absence of shock or surprise.

"Anything else?" the chief asked.

"Yes. Looks like he may have had the cell phone of our most recent murder victim, Nicky Price, in his possession, too. No explanation for that right now. We're still trying to confirm that."

"Do we have any idea where this cocaine came from?"

"No, sir. Not yet," Kinnebrew answered.

"Who knows about the dope?"

"Just us," Kinnebrew said gesturing to himself and Walker. "I don't think crime scene collected anything yet and as far as I know, no one photographed the contents of the bag. We're the only ones to look in the bag."

"All right," Butler said. "You take the drugs into your custody for now. And the cell phone. No leaks on this—to anyone—until we find out what the hell was going on here. Understood?"

"Yes, sir," the detectives answered.

Butler started to walk away.

"Chief?" Kinnebrew spoke up. Butler turned toward him without answering.

"How are we going to run at this?"

"How are we going to run at it?" the chief repeated back. His anger was evident. "Someone killed one of my cops . . . *another* one of my cops. We going to find out who did it. *That's* how we're going to run at it. Got it?"

"Yes, sir," the detectives replied.

Butler walked away, frustrated.

Kinnebrew and Walker returned to the passenger's side of the vehicle where they stood, silent.

"You guys done in there? Can we bag and tag?" The lead crime scene tech interrupted the silence, wanting to secure the evidence in evidence bags.

Kinnebrew looked at his partner.

"Give us a minute," Kinnebrew answered.

The anxious tech shrugged and walked away.

Kinnebrew stepped closer to Walker and spoke so no one else around could hear him.

"I don't know about you, Pete, but I'll be goddamned if I'm going to let that empty suit fuck up my career. I like wearing this badge. You can say whatever you want about this," Kinnebrew said, pointing toward Morales, "but this is a bad scene. I hear the rumors and I *believe* them. At least with this guy I do."

Walker listened to his partner.

"I'm not taking that cocaine with me. And I'm not taking the phone. That's bullshit," Kinnebrew said, trying to keep his voice down.

"What are we gonna do?" Walker asked. "I'm with you. I guess I can always be a chef or something, when this doesn't work out."

"Don't flatter yourself Pete," Kinnebrew smirked. "You can't cook worth a shit."

Kinnebrew saw the coroner's wagon pulling up closer to the vehicle.

"Go stall them for a minute or two," Kinnebrew directed. Walker headed in their direction.

"Hey, Chet," Kinnebrew called for the lead tech.

"Yes, sir," the tech responded.

The senior detective walked to the open passenger's door.

"You see that bag?"

"Sure," the tech answered.

"The contents are important to this investigation, but I don't want you to open it."

"But I have to inventory everything in—"

"Chet," Kinnebrew interrupted. "It's *very* sensitive. Chief's orders. Secure it in a plastic heat seal bag. You can mark on it 'to be inventoried later.'"

"Chief's orders?" Chet asked.

"Just do it, Chet. That's between you and me."

"Okay, Harlan. I'll take care of it right now, before the coroner gets in there."

"Thanks," Kinnebrew replied. "I appreciate it."

Kinnebrew walked to where Walker was standing talking to the deputy coroner and few other officers.

"You know where we need to go, partner, don't you?" Kinnebrew asked.

"I sure do. Let's get moving."

Forty-Five

CHRISSY STOOD IN front of an old, two-story white frame house a hundred feet west of the chaotic crime scene. Marked patrol units packed three and four cars deep, surrounded the area around the fallen officer's vehicle. With flashing red and blue lights behind her, she delivered the breaking news to the early rising residents of the metro area.

"Allentown detectives responded to this scene behind me earlier this morning after the discovery of the body of Allentown Police narcotics detective Rocco Morales. What we currently know is that Morales was killed in his vehicle. Chief Scott Butler spoke to reporters a few minutes ago. All Butler would say was that Morales was shot multiple times and died at the scene. At this time officers are being tight-lipped about what happened. The chief did not say whether there are any suspects or persons of interest in the slaying. Detective Morales has been with the APD for twenty-three years. He was married and had two adult children."

Chrissy paused, turning her head back toward the murder scene, then back toward the camera.

"This is the *third* Allentown narcotics detective to die in six short months. In East Allentown, Chrissy Barnes, Valley 10 News."

* * *

Dana Branfield walked from her bedroom and into the family room of her luxury home in Allentown's swanky West End. Thousand-dollar Derek Rose silk pajamas complimented her tall, fit, fashion-model body. A tousled mane of long fiery red hair tumbled over her shoulders toward her mid-back. A faint glow of light from the recessed lighting highlighted her cheekbones and narrow nose. She was beautiful even without makeup.

Her husband stood motionless in front of the TV.

She stopped before walking into the kitchen for her morning coffee.

"Bad news?" she asked.

"Yeah. You could say that."

Dana could see the flashing lights on the TV screen.

"What happened?"

"Looks like they killed another police officer."

Dana poured a cup of coffee, stirred in some cream, and joined her husband.

"That's terrible. Do you know who it was? What happened?"

"Rocco Morales. A sergeant in narcotics. Someone shot him."

Dana reached for her husband's arm to offer support as he turned toward the kitchen.

"I better get going. It's going to be a hell of a day," he grumbled, pulling away.

Dana sat down on the edge of a sofa and watched the news report about the dead officer. Her husband walked to the kitchen and poured a second cup of coffee.

"Don't you have some place to be this morning?" he growled. "It's Thursday you know."

Branfield really didn't have to remind his wife that the election was on Tuesday. In the last days before the election they would campaign separately in the southeastern part of the state. Dana was thinking about responding to her husband's snide remark but decided to let it go.

"I need to be out there getting votes today," he snarled. "Not dealing with another dead cop." He walked toward the bedroom. The home phone rang. Dana answered it. Her husband stopped, anticipating that the call was for him.

"It's Chief Butler," she said holding out the phone. "Urgent he says."

* * *

Thax's cell phone rang as he walked from the quiet elevator lobby to the eight-foot solid entry door into the U.S. Attorney's Office. He stopped to answer it.

"Good morning."

"Really? Have you seen the news?" Campisano asked his friend. "Morales is dead."

"Why do reporters know about a cop getting murdered before we do?" Thax asked. "Don't you think there's something wrong with that, Christopher?"

"I don't know."

"You know, I kinda like to get the first phone call," Thax said.

"I hear you," Campisano replied.

"Do you know anything more?"

"Just that he was capped in his vehicle over on the East Side. That's all I heard. Apparently, they've got no suspect. At least that's what they're saying right now."

"Really?"

"I know what you're thinking," Campisano replied.

"Yeah?" Thax keyed in his security code and walked into the office. "There's no way this isn't related to our investigation. Not a chance in hell."

"Find out what the hell they know, Christopher. I'm going to do the same. I'll call Shea and see what she's heard. Call me back."

Forty-Six

"OPEN THE DOOR, Danny," Detective Kinnebrew shouted, banging his fist on the front door of a modest single-story brick-framed house in the 1500 block of East Tremont Street on Allentown's East Side. A row of newer townhomes completed the city block. An aging and rusted six-foot chain-link fence surrounded a small industrial complex across the street.

Danny Price's yellow Ford Mustang GT was parked on the faded and cracked macadam driveway in front of the residence. Kinnebrew and his partner had taken a statement from Price the night his brother Nicky was murdered. A devastated Danny Price had identified the body. Surely, the detectives thought, Danny could identify Nicky's voice on the cell phone's voicemail message. Kinnebrew knocked again while Walker walked down a thin concrete sidewalk toward a covered side entrance.

"He ain't here," a female voice shouted from behind the red front door.

"Allentown Police," Kinnebrew announced. "Just open the door, ma'am."

"I said he ain't here," came a more agitated reply.

Kinnebrew banged on the door again. "Open the door."

A few seconds later, the front door opened just far enough for a young woman with long dark straggly hair to peek her head through it. She squinted when the bright morning sun hit her face.

"I told you he ain't here," she repeated. "I don't know where he's at. He didn't bother coming home last night."

"What's his car doing here?" Kinnebrew asked, cautiously looking into the residence as the young woman opened the door a bit further.

"That don't matter. He got so many people that give him rides."

Kinnebrew looked at Walker who was returning from walking the perimeter of the house. Walker shook his head indicating he didn't see any other activity in the home.

"We need to find him," Kinnebrew said.

"Is he in some kind of shit?"

"No," Kinnebrew answered. "We just need to talk to him for a few minutes. It's about his brother."

The woman hesitated.

"I guess you could try looking at the Trap. You know the strip joint up on Airport Road."

"Okay, we'll check there. If you see him, you tell him to call me at that number." Kinnebrew handed the woman a business card.

"What's your name?" Kinnebrew asked.

"Ellie."

"You have a last name Ellie?"

"Harper."

"Thanks for your help Ms. Harper."

"Yeah. You're welcome. If you see him first, tell him to get his ass home."

* * *

Detectives Kinnebrew and Walker pulled their dark brown Ford Crown Victoria into a parking spot in front of the canopied entrance to the Booby Trap strip club. The parking lot was relatively empty. In another hour, patrons of the gentlemen's establishment would be enjoying a free lunch buffet complete with a selection of tits and ass. The detectives approached the double silver entry doors. Walker pulled on the door handle of the locked door, ignoring the sign that said "closed."

"I've never knocked on a strip club door before," Walker chuckled.

"That's more information than I needed to know, Pete." Kinnebrew laughed.

Walker banged the heel of his palm against one of the front doors. No one answered. The second time he banged harder. A tall, muscular young man in a tight black T-shirt, with the tact of a good bouncer, opened the door.

"Don't youse read?" he grunted in his south Philly accent. "The sign says we're closed."

"I'm sorry," Kinnebrew responded flashing his badge in the bouncer's face. "We're cops. Everybody knows we can't read."

The man stopped for a moment to think.

"What do youse want?"

"Who is it, Max?" a woman's voice projected from behind the door. A hard-looking middle-aged woman wearing a short black dress with a plunging neckline pushed the bouncer to the side.

"I'm sorry, officers. I'm Dixie," she announced, flipping her bleached platinum blonde curls. "I'm one of the managers here. What can I do for you today?"

Kinnebrew looked past the woman into the dimly lit club. Music played quietly in the background. A few fixed spot-lights illuminated the center stage.

"We're looking for Danny Price," Walker responded.

"He's not here."

"Are you sure?"

A subtle, instinctive turn of Dixie's head toward the inside of the club gave her away.

Kinnebrew stepped forward pushing the door open further. Toward the back of the room he spotted a solitary figure sitting at one of the square tables hugging a bottle of whisky and a shot glass. It looked like Danny Price.

"Danny!" Kinnebrew called out, as he and Walker pushed past Max and Dixie. Price, startled, threw the bottle in the direction of the advancing detectives then ran toward a hallway at the back of the club.

"Danny! Stop!" Kinnebrew shouted. He and his partner dodged the broken glass from the bottle. "We just want to talk to you!"

The detectives chased Price through the narrow hallway where he ran into the men's room. Not knowing whether Price was armed, Walker and Kinnebrew positioned themselves on the sides of the doorway—Walker to the left and Kinnebrew to the right. Kinnebrew reached for the levered door handle. The door was unlocked.

"Jesus, Danny," an out of breath Kinnebrew called through the door. "We just want to talk to you. What are you running for?"

"I know what you want to talk to me about," an obviously intoxicated Price screamed through the door. "I fucking know."

"Danny," Kinnebrew replied. "Just come on out."

Price shouted over Kinnebrew.

"That son of a bitch! That fucking son of a bitch! He made me do it!"

"Danny," Kinnebrew spoke firmly. "Who are you talking about?"

"That fucking son of a bitch . . ." Price's voice trailed off as he broke down crying.

"Danny, just come out. We only want to talk to you," Kinnebrew assured him.

The detectives could hear Price sobbing uncontrollably.

"You know why I killed that piece of shit?" Price rambled.

"What are you talking about Danny? Who are you—"

Price yelled out. "Because he killed my Nicky."

"Who killed Nicky, Danny? Who killed Nicky?"

"Morales. Morales killed him. That's why I had to kill that fucking piece of shit."

Kinnebrew and Walker looked at each other. They hadn't planned on solving *two* homicides today.

"That piece of shit killed my little brother and I gave him what was coming. Now you're going to take *me* to jail? That's fucked up." They could hear the anger rising through his tears.

"Danny. Listen to me. Just open the door and come on out. It's going to be okay," Kinnebrew promised, trying to de-escalate the increasingly tense situation.

"No, it's not going to be okay," Price yelled. "It's never going to be okay!"

"Come on out, Danny," Kinnebrew demanded.

The detectives waited for a response.

Six quick gun shots through the wooden men's room door broke the tense silence. Shards of wood flew everywhere, the door shattering more with each shot. The reports of the semi-automatic handgun reverberating in the small tiled washroom and the confined hallway were deafening. Kinnebrew and Walker dove for cover and drew their weapons. Neither returned fire when the shooting stopped.

"Danny," Kinnebrew shouted from his position. "What are you doing? Put the damn gun down and get out here!"

"I'm not going back to jail! I'm not going back!"

Price fired two more shots, this time through the drywall inches above Walker's head just to the left of the door jamb.

"Shit!" Walker yelled as he fell back and scrambled on his back to get further from the door.

"Pete!"

"I'm okay," Walker replied. "What the fuck!"

Price fired two more times through the door then, seconds later, the door opened. Price charged through it firing wildly. Walker thrust his weapon forward toward the doorway and fired four rounds at Price's chest. Price stopped instantly and dropped to the ground. Kinnebrew immediately stood over him with his gun pointed at Price, covering himself and his partner. Walker did the same as he reached to move the weapon away from Price's reach.

Danny Price was dead.

Forty-Seven

A visibly shaken Walker leaned forward in one of the padded wooden chairs pushed against the side wall near the back of the strip club, his head in his hands resting on his knees. Kinnebrew tried his best to help.

"You did what you had to do, partner. There wasn't any other way around it. You saved both of us."

Several crime scene techs passed by the detectives on their way back to the bathroom area. Walker lifted his face from his hands. His eyes followed them back to where Danny Price's body lay.

"I know, Harlan," Walker replied. "What the hell was he thinking?"

"He wasn't. And if he was, he wasn't expecting to walk out of here alive," Kinnebrew answered.

Detective Rick Fletcher, one of the two detectives working the shooting, walked toward Kinnebrew and Walker. Kinnebrew had already given them a preliminary rundown on what transpired.

"Hey, Pete," Fletcher spoke. "If you're up to it, I have a couple of questions for you. Won't take more than a few minutes."

Walker looked at his colleague.

"Sure, Fletch. Give me a minute."

"Whenever you're ready, give me a shout," Fletcher said, heading back toward the bathroom.

Kinnebrew looked toward the front of the business. Max, Dixie, and a couple of scantily clad strippers, ready for work, stood behind the yellow crime scene tape at the front doors. The house lights illuminated the interior of the club. An occasional patron arriving for "lunch" was turned away by uniformed officers. Kinnebrew recognized the walk of the next person through the door. Chief Scott Butler strolled decisively in the direction of his detectives.

"Is this the guy that killed Morales?" he asked, looking past the officers down the crowded hallway.

"That's him. Danny Price. East Side Boyz," Kinnebrew answered. "He had Morales's gun."

"How did this go down, Harlan?" the chief asked.

"We came here looking to talk to him. He saw us and took off for the john. We tried to get him to come out so we could talk to him but he popped off half a dozen rounds through the door. Tried to get him to give up and put the gun down but he shot a few more rounds through the wall—those almost hit Pete. We dropped back and he came through the door shooting. Pete put him down. It was a clean shoot."

Walker listened while his partner recounted what happened.

"You have anything to add to that?" Butler asked, looking at Walker.

"No, sir."

"Perfect," Butler said. "Sounds like this turd got what was coming to him." The chief walked past the detectives and into the hallway where he surveyed the shooting scene. He turned and walked back to Kinnebrew and Walker.

"Anything else, gentlemen?"

Kinnebrew stepped closer to the chief.

"Yeah, there is, Chief. The reason we couldn't talk this guy out is because he said he killed Morales."

"You already said that, Detective," the chief interrupted.

Kinnebrew paused.

"He said he killed Morales because Morales killed his little brother Nicky. Nicky Price."

"And you believe that?"

"Yes, I do, Chief." Kinnebrew nodded. "I absolutely do."

"Well, that's interesting, Harlan," the chief said derisively. "But I guess the only witness to that is dead so this is how this is going to go." Chief Butler grabbed Kinnebrew's right arm with his left hand and pulled him closer.

"One of my detectives," the chief began, "the sergeant in my narcotics unit, was ambushed this morning and shot to death by a violent gang banger. His gun was stolen and the perpetrator was identified and pursued to this fine establishment where he fired upon two other detectives who narrowly escaped with their lives. They were forced to shoot and kill this piece of shit who cut down my detective in the prime of his life and career. That detective will be buried with full honors next Monday. That is exactly what the mayor and I will announce this afternoon when he gets back from Harrisburg."

Kinnebrew stared hard at the chief.

"Now you get this wrapped up and get out of here. I don't want to see or hear from either one of you until Monday. Wear your dress blues," the chief scowled. Butler turned and walked purposefully out of the building.

"That was pleasant, Harlan," Walker remarked.

Kinnebrew grabbed hold of the gold detective shield that swung from a black lanyard around his neck.

"Pete, this badge doesn't mean anything if the person wearing it doesn't do the right thing." He gripped the shield tightly.

Walker looked at his badge that was still clipped to his belt. He was still reeling from the shooting. His hand trembled as he snapped the badge off his belt.

"I agree Harlan. I agree." Walker looked at his partner. "So, what are we going to do about it?"

Forty-Eight

THAX'S OFFICE PHONE rang. His secretary Abigail was calling.

"I've got a Detective Kinnebrew from APD Homicide on the phone. He wants to know if you can talk to him for a minute. He said it's important."

"Sure. Put him through."

"You'll have him when I hang up."

Thax answered the call.

"This is Thax Colby."

"Mr. Colby, Harlan Kinnebrew from APD Homicide. My partner and I caught the Morales murder this morning. We shot Danny Price—the guy who killed him."

"I heard the news reports. I'm glad you're okay. Aren't you guys still in the middle of all of this?"

"Yes and no," Kinnebrew answered. "We *really* need to talk to you. Today. We just need a few minutes."

Thax sensed concern in the detective's voice.

"I've got whatever time you need, Detective."

"We'll meet you in the parking lot behind the old King George Inn on Hamilton Street if that's okay. In about an hour?"

"I'll be there."

* * *

Thax walked through the metal doorway into Chief Scott Butler's office.

Butler, dressed in uniform and looking tired, stood up from behind his large oak desk. The natural light from two floor-to-ceiling windows on the wall behind him lit up the office.

"Chief, thanks for seeing me on such short notice," Thax said, standing in front of the desk. Neither man reached to shake the other's hand.

"Well, your secretary told mine it was urgent, so—"

"Well, it is," Thax interrupted.

Campisano followed Thax into the office.

"Chief, this is Special Agent Chris Campisano from DEA. You don't mind if he sits in on this, do you?"

"I guess not," Butler said. "I don't know what this is about—"

Thax interrupted again. "Well it's—"

"I've got five minutes," the chief cut Thax off. "The mayor and I have to get ready for a press conference at three o'clock. You do know we lost an officer today, don't you Mr. Colby?" the chief asked, sensing a modicum of disrespect from his visitor.

"I do," Thax replied curtly.

"Sergeant Rocco Morales. He was a good man," Butler said.

"Well, that's why we're here, Chief. To talk to you about Detective Morales," Thax replied.

"What about him?"

"Well, you can't have a police funeral and bury him with full honors," Thax said.

"And why in the hell not?" Butler snapped.

"Because Morales was corrupt. He was a cocaine trafficker. Lots of cocaine."

"What are you talking about, Colby?" Butler fumed, now forgoing the formalities.

"What I'm telling you is that Morales was bringing large shipments of cocaine from New Jersey into Allentown and members of the East Side Boyz street gang—including Danny Price—were his distributors."

"What's your source for that?"

"It doesn't matter who my source is, Chief. I'm telling you that within the next month there will be testimony about it in a federal courtroom and I don't think anybody's going to be very happy about it. But it *is* going to happen. And the mayor's not going to be happy when he finds out that you knew about this and let him stand up and praise Morales as a 'fine officer'."

The chief opened the top front drawer of his desk, where he retrieved his keys.

"I need to go," he announced, "if there's nothing else."

"Well, actually, Chief, there is something else."

"And what would that be," a clearly annoyed and angry Butler asked.

"You spoke to Detective Kinnebrew today. When was the last time you two spoke?"

"Kinnebrew? Why would you ask me that? I saw him this morning. He and his partner shot Morales's killer."

"That's not what I asked you, Chief. I want to know when you *talked* to him last."

"I don't know," Butler stammered. "I *don't* remember."

"Chief, in the federal system we call that a lie," Thax said coldly.

"A lie? Just what the hell is this, Colby? You come into my office, tell me the detective who was murdered this morning is a drug dealer and now you're calling me a liar." Butler, indignant, rose quickly from his chair. "You get the hell out of my office," the chief shouted pointing toward the door.

"Sit down, Chief," Campisano said sternly, stepping toward the desk. Butler hesitated, then wisely backed down and eased back into his chair. Campisano placed a small digital recorder on the desk then looked at Thax. Thax nodded. The agent pressed the play button. Harlan Kinnebrew's voice was heard on the recording:

"Chief, I'm calling because the crime scene tech was going through the evidence and found the cocaine in the paper bag."

"Goddammit, Harlan, I told you to take that shit and to make sure it didn't make it into evidence."

The chief recognized his voice on the recording.

"I know you did, Chief," the recording played.

"You figure out a way to get that stuff out of there, Detective. I don't want this showing up in a report or an evidence voucher. Just fix it!"

"Yes, sir, Chief."

Campisano clicked off the recorder. An uncomfortable silence permeated the room.

"*That* was the last time you talked to Kinnebrew today. When he recorded that call to you late this morning. I'm pretty sure tampering with physical evidence is still a crime in this state. Isn't it, Chief?" Thax asked.

Butler combed his left hand through his thick brown hair and pushed back into his chair.

"What do you want me to do?" a dejected and bitter sounding Butler asked.

"No funeral with honors for Morales."

"Okay," Butler reluctantly acquiesced.

"And your resignation—before three o'clock today," Thax demanded.

"My resignation? Are you out of your goddamn mind? Or what?" Butler hissed.

"Do you really want to find that out?" Thax fired back. "Do you think the mayor's not going to fire you when he hears that recording? Especially when he hears it on the six o'clock news."

Butler gritted his teeth.

"You're a son of a bitch," Butler mumbled under his breath.

"Now *that's* the truth," Thax said smugly.

Campisano picked up the recorder and put it back in his jacket pocket. He gave Butler a hard look as he and Thax turned to leave. Campisano hesitated and turned back toward the chief.

"Why were you protecting that piece of garbage?" Campisano asked the chief, referring to Morales.

"I thought you federal boys were smarter than that," Butler snickered through his contempt. "I wasn't protecting Morales."

* * *

"Good evening and welcome to the six o'clock edition of Valley 10 News. I'm Gina Mondalvo. Thank you for joining us. A violent and tumultuous day in Allentown today. Let's go straight out to Chrissy Barnes, who is in Easton tonight."

Barnes stood at the entrance to Hugh Moore Park, on the island flanked to the north and south by the forked Lehigh River. The illuminated downtown Easton skyline was her backdrop. She could see her breath through the crisp frigid November air as she delivered her report.

"Just days before what is anticipated to be the closest gubernatorial election in the history of the Keystone State, tragedy and turmoil have blanketed the City of Allentown and its police department. This morning at six forty-five a.m., detectives responded to a scene off Hanover Avenue, a parking lot, where they found a solitary vehicle. Inside was the body of Allentown narcotics detective Rocco Morales—riddled with bullets. Detectives have yet to say why Morales was there or what he was doing when he was murdered.

"At ten a.m., homicide detectives investigating Morales's murder confront Danny Price, a known gang member, at a strip club a mile and a half from where Morales was murdered. Price fired multiple shots at officers, who returned fire, killing Price. Neither officer was injured. A short time later, Price is identified as the suspect in the murder of Detective Morales.

"Then, at two p.m. reporters gathered for an anticipated three o'clock press conference at City Hall with Chief Scott Butler and Mayor Branfield are told that, due to developments in the ongoing investigation, the mayor and chief would not address the media at that time.

"At two twenty-five p.m. Allentown Police spokesman Lindsay Epstein, reads a short statement to reporters: 'After twenty-one years of honorable service as a law enforcement officer, Chief Scott Butler has resigned, effective immediately.' Deputy Chief of Police Kelly Vaughn is appointed Acting Chief.

"Next, at three p.m. several law enforcement sources who spoke to Valley 10 News on the condition of anonymity confirmed growing rumors that Detective Morales may have been under federal investigation for trafficking in narcotics. A United States Attorney's Office spokesperson will neither confirm nor deny such an investigation.

"Finally, at three-thirty p.m., Acting Police Chief Kelly Vaughn released a statement that plans for a police funeral on Monday for the fallen officer have been changed and the family will now make private arrangements for his burial.

"Tonight, Gina, in this swirling sea of controversy, Allentown Mayor and gubernatorial hopeful Logan Branfield has chosen to avoid reporters in his home city and to speak here, in Easton, amidst a swelling crowd that has gathered to hear perhaps his last 'tough on crime' message to supporters and potential voters before next Tuesday's election. It is fitting, his aides say, that

Branfield speaks here on the day of the unveiling of this oversized billboard along Interstate 78. A billboard that was erected with funds raised by the Branfield campaign, asking all motorists who pass through this busy area to help identify the blurry cell phone photograph of the person of interest in the horrific rape and murder of Lafayette College freshman Erica Murtaugh.

"Live in Easton, Chrissy Barnes, Valley 10 News."

* * *

The elevator stopped on the first floor of the federal courthouse. Thax glanced at his watch as the doors opened. He loosened his tie. It was seven p.m.

"I knew you'd still be here," Barrows said. "I was just on my way up to see you."

"What about?"

"We have some unfinished business. I didn't know if you still wanted to do this Monday or if you wanted to wait until later in the week," Barrows asked, "with the election and everything happening next week."

Thax chuckled.

"Yeah. Unfortunately, I'm starting to pay a lot more attention to this election than I'd like to."

"No kidding."

Thax paused for a moment.

"Let's do it Monday. We have the indictment and the sealed arrest warrants. It's time. Are your people ready to go?"

"We're ready," Barrows replied. "I talked to Chris and he said DEA's ready anytime."

"Good. Monday it is."

"You look tired, Thax."

Thax looked back at Barrows and nodded his head.

"It's been quite a day, hasn't it?"

"It sure has."

"Time to go home." Thax was tired. "Have a good night, Shea."

"You too, Thax."

Forty-Nine

Detective Kathy Piper sat in a padded wooden chair in the FBI interrogation room. She wore jeans, an old T-shirt, and a comfortable pair of slip on shoes. Her dusty brown shoulder length hair was unbrushed. Blotches on her face and bloodshot eyes painted the emotion of her current predicament. The cold handcuffs around her wrists were tighter than she thought they should be. She yawned nervously, looking at the round metal government clock on the far wall. It was seven-thirty a.m.

Barrows and Thax entered the room. Thax took a seat on the opposite side of the small table in the room while Barrows, still dressed in her tactical gear, sat in a chair next to Piper.

"Detective Piper, I'm Shea Barrows from the FBI. We met earlier this morning. This is Assistant U.S. Attorney Thax Colby."

Piper acknowledged them by nodding her head.

"Do you know why you're here?" Barrows asked.

"Well," Piper leaned forward, toward the table, "since you woke me up before my alarm clock did and dragged me in here without even letting me put on some makeup, I'm hoping you've got a good reason."

"Good," Barrows said curtly. "Being a smart ass will definitely help you out today."

Piper smirked.

"You're charged with retaliating against a witness." Barrows advised. "Specifically, you're charged with attempting to kill Jimmy Karopolis to prevent his father from testifying. His father's the guy you and your fellow narcotics detectives ripped for forty grand with that bogus search warrant out in the West End."

"That sounds bad but I don't know what you're talking about," Piper replied.

"Oh, you don't?" Barrows asked. "You and Detective Gallon went to Jimmy's apartment, beat him within an inch of his life, threw him in the back of a pickup truck and then dumped him right outside here next to the courthouse. You don't remember that?"

"That's bullshit," Piper scoffed sitting back in her chair.

"Yeah, it is bullshit," Barrows responded.

Thax spoke after a brief silence.

"Kathy—"

"Are you going to be the good cop now, 'cause that shit's not going to work with me." Piper grew more agitated and hostile.

"Detective, I don't have time for your games this morning," Thax spoke calmly and deliberately. "You're looking at thirty years in federal prison and when we get done with you the DA is definitely going to want to charge you with attempted murder. So if you want to keep up the attitude, that's fine."

"I don't know what you're talking about," Piper answered.

"Shea, show her the picture."

Barrows took an eight by ten photo from a folder and pushed it across the table in front of Piper. The detective leaned forward to look at it. She tensed when she viewed the picture; her eyes widened. She nervously exhaled a long breath.

"That's you and Thomas Gallon taken by a red light camera the morning you tried to kill Jimmy Karopolis," Thax informed. "You're supposed to stop at red lights."

Piper leaned back and restlessly rocked her body in her chair. She looked toward the ceiling and shook her head in denial.

"Detective," Thax said, sensing an opportunity, "you've got two choices. Cooperate and try to reduce your sentence or don't talk and probably spend the rest of your life in prison. It's one or the other. This isn't a game show. There is no door number three."

Piper reached forward and pulled the photo closer with the extended fingers of her cuffed hands. She exhaled again as she stared at the clear shot of her face. The anxiety coursing through her body tightened her stomach. She tried to breathe. She knew she was done.

"That was a bad idea. It wasn't mine."

"Whose idea was it?" Barrows asked.

Piper fixed her eyes on Barrows, then looked at Thax.

"They're killing cops, you know." Piper twisted with uneasiness in her chair.

"Who's killing cops?" Thax grilled. "Who are you talking about? Chip Meyers? Schick? Morales was killed by a gang banger? What are you talking about?"

Piper continued to shift nervously in her chair.

"What are you talking about?" Thax asked again.

"You know what I'm talking about," Piper responded. She looked down at the photo and pushed it away from her.

Thax took a photograph from his file. He stood and moved closer to Piper. He placed the photograph of the blue notebook in front of her.

"What do you know about that?" Thax asked.

Piper picked up the photo and held it. She examined it closely. She glanced at Thax's face, then back at the photo.

"That's LT's notebook," she answered hesitantly.

"LT? Who's that?" Barrows asked.

"Lieutenant Sokol. Richie Sokol. He's retired from APD. He used to run our unit. He works for the mayor now as his bodyguard."

"Why would Chip Meyers have Sokol's notebook?" Thax asked.

Piper stared at Thax.

"Son of a bitch," she mumbled to herself, shaking her head.

"What?" Thax asked.

"Chip Meyers had that notebook?"

Thax didn't answer.

"So he *was* going to talk," Piper said. "He must have taken LT's notebook. LT kept it in the office."

"What do you mean Meyers was going to talk?" Thax pressed.

"Son of a bitch," Piper mumbled again, moving her hands toward her mouth. She shook her head and closed her eyes.

"What was in the notebook?" Thax asked.

"What do you mean?" Piper answered with surprise.

"There were pages ripped out of it. There was nothing in it," Thax answered.

Piper looked at Thax.

"I can't do this."

"You're already doing it, Kathy," Thax responded.

"If I keep talking, I won't even last a week out here. I won't even make it to sentencing, let alone prison." Piper tried to push back from the table.

"We'll keep you safe, Kathy," Thax said.

"Really?" Piper smiled nervously. "And what are you going to do after that? Reduce my sentence to twenty-five, maybe twenty years? The DA is going to drop another twenty on me? Do you know how long a cop is going to last in a federal prison—any prison—where they're going to send me? You think I'm going to do all that time in segregation? I *can't* do this."

After a short silence, Thax spoke.

"We're going to find Thomas Gallon. We're looking for him now. When we do, do you think he's going to go to prison for thirty years to save you? He's going to flip on you so fast."

"No, he won't. You're wrong." She smirked. "When Thomas heard about Morales, he packed a bag and took off. He's sitting on a beach somewhere in Mexico sipping a margarita. He's *never* coming back."

Thax and Barrows looked at each other.

"Yeah. He asked me to go with him. I guess I messed that up, too." Piper laughed nervously. "I guess it's time for me to get a lawyer. We're pretty much done here."

Thax agreed.

"I guess we are."

Fifty

THE RAUCOUS CROWD erupted with shouts and applause at the Starlite Ballroom on South Front Street in center city Allentown. The once reserved crowd of supporters had waited until now—almost two o'clock in the morning—to hear the announcement from campaign manager Bo Hughes. The supporters, their number having barely dwindled over the course of the evening, had watched the incoming election results from around the state on a large TV screen for the last seven hours. No major station in the Commonwealth had yet called the race.

"If I can have your attention please, ladies and gentlemen," Hughes tried to speak over the noise and cheers, repeating himself several times until it appeared that he had the crowd's attention.

"It is my distinct honor and privilege to present to you the next governor of the Commonwealth of Pennsylvania, Logan Branfield!"

The enthusiastic chanting of "Branfield! Branfield!" became deafening. Election signs swayed above the heads of the hundreds of gathered faithful and loyal supporters. Patriotic music could barely be heard over the thunderous roars filling the room. Huge clusters of red, white and blue balloons were released from storage bins around the ballroom. In the midst of the fanfare, Logan Branfield, his left hand clasping the hand of the future first lady of the State—his wife Dana—strolled triumphantly onto the stage. His teenage son and daughter, along with other close friends and family converged behind the Governor-elect and his beautiful wife. Branfield raised his right hand and flashed the victory sign. The crowd continued to chant and cheer as the Branfields paced from one side of the small stage to the other, waving to the tired but exuberant supporters. He returned to the podium in the middle of the ballroom stage then kissed Dana who stepped behind him and stood with their children.

"Thank you." Branfield tried to quiet the crowd several times. He eventually got them to settle.

"A few minutes ago, I received a call from my opponent, who congratulated us on a well-run campaign and conceded this incredibly close election. I expressed my gratitude to him for a fair and valiant effort and asked him and his supporters to join us as we all seek a new, vibrant, thriving and safer Pennsylvania."

The crowd cheered wildly after each sentence uttered by the newly elected chief executive.

"There are so many people I want to thank . . ."

* * *

The picture on Thax's TV flickered in the almost complete darkness of his family room. The volume was turned down low enough so Chrissy could sleep without being disturbed. She had surrendered to exhaustion several hours ago.

"Whisper in my ear who won when you come to bed," she said before slipping off to the bedroom.

Thax watched as Logan Branfield stroked and worked the crowd. In spite of the corruption in his police department and the unexplained and mysterious deaths of three narcotics detectives, his political star continued to rise.

Thax clicked the remote, turning the TV off. In the stark silence of the early morning, he couldn't get the words of a dishonorable and incompetent chief of police out of his head.

I wasn't protecting Morales.

Kathy Piper's information was equally disturbing. The notebook on Chip Meyers's desk belonged to the former lieutenant in charge of the corrupt narcotics unit, Richie Sokol. The mayor's bodyguard. The same notebook that contained the information about the payoff to Judge Harlin. That meant Sokol had to be dirty, too.

What else was in that notebook and where are the missing pages? he thought. *What if Meyers was going to testify?* Thax grew more restless. *Cole Hatten didn't believe Meyers killed himself. What if someone—maybe Sokol—found out Meyers took the notebook?*

Thax's brain raced as he pondered all of the ugly possibilities.

It was almost two-thirty.

He walked into the kitchen to get a glass of water and glanced at his cell phone sitting on the corner of the kitchen counter. He had a voice message. It was the middle of the night. It could wait until tomorrow. He drank the water and placed the glass in the sink then headed toward the bedroom. He stopped at the bedroom door and returned to the kitchen.

"Damn voicemail," he mumbled, acknowledging his unhealthy reliance on technology. He listened to the message:

"Thax, it's Shea," the agent's voice was barely audible. "Kathy Piper is dead. She hanged herself in her jail cell. They found her around midnight. They couldn't revive her . . . goddammit."

Thax looked at the clock, then started to call Barrows. He stopped and set his phone down. Another police detective was dead and there wasn't a damn thing he could do about it.

Fifty-One

CHRISSY STOOD BEFORE the steps leading to the front doors of the federal courthouse. It was just after noon. The warmth of the sun took the edge off the cold, late November day. She looked into the camera as the anchor tossed her the lead story.

"Gina, in a surprise revelation today at an unrelated news conference just three weeks after his election, Mayor Logan Branfield told reporters that Judge Eugene Harlin was with him in Las Vegas on official business on the day federal prosecutors say Harlin was in Easton accepting a payoff to fix a drug case. Branfield gave no specifics except to give his assurance that he would testify on Judge Harlin's behalf at the trial scheduled to begin next week. The U.S. Attorney's Office offered no reaction to this bombshell disclosure. Matt Greyson, Harlin's attorney, told us that his client has always denied any involvement in a payoff and that this information should give the U.S. Attorney's Office great pause in going forward with the prosecution of a well-respected jurist. Greyson called for prosecutors to dismiss the indictment ahead of jury selection next week.

"Live in downtown Allentown, Chrissy Barnes, Valley 10 News."

* * *

Thax turned out the light on his desk in his home office. He swirled his wine glass—the last remnants of the cabernet he had been nursing for the last hour—and swallowed it as he walked into the family room. Chrissy stood in front of the fireplace, staring into the flames while basking in the warmth of the slow crackling fire.

"You're quiet tonight," he said wrapping his arms around her from behind.

Chrissy turned her head and pushed back into the security of his embrace.

"I know. I'm sorry."

Thax knew something was wrong.

"Are you okay?" he asked, gently nuzzling her hair.

"I really didn't want to bother you with this while you're preparing for trial." Chrissy turned her body toward him.

"Bother me with what?"

She looked into Thax's tired blue eyes.

"I got a call from the network."

"And?" Thax asked anxiously.

"They offered me a job."

Thax didn't see Chrissy smiling.

"In Denver. They want me in Denver."

"Denver? What happened to New York?"

"I don't know. All I know is they want me in the Denver Bureau."

Thax was quiet—his usual defense mechanism. Chrissy hugged him tightly.

"Say something, Thax."

"What do you want me to say? This is your dream. You have to go."

"Say you'll come with me. Please say you'll come with me."

"I want to. You know I do, but I can't." Thax's mind flashed back to what seemed like another lifetime when his now ex-wife tried to get him to leave Pennsylvania.

"Thax . . ."

"Chrissy, this is where my work is. How can I leave? Especially now. I'm in the middle of this investigation. Everything I know is here. My uncle. He's not well anymore. I'm all he has. How could I leave him now? I thought with New York we could make it work for a few years until I retired, but Denver . . ."

"I know," Chrissy said acknowledging his concerns. "We can try it though. I can come here and you can come there. I know we can make it work."

"Chrissy, I already have my dream. You have to chase yours."

"Just tell me you don't want me to go and I won't go," Chrissy started to break down. "Tell me not to go. I love you. Just tell me . . ."

Thax held her as she sobbed.

"I love you, too. But if I tell you not to go, someday you are going to know it was me who stopped you. And I'll always feel guilty for telling you not to go. I can't do that."

Chrissy cried some more while Thax tried to comfort her.

"When do they want you in Denver?"

He wiped the tears from her face.

"They want me there right away. I told them I couldn't come until the judge's trial is over."

"That's only a couple of weeks."

"I know," Chrissy said sadly. "I know."

Fifty-Two

RETIRED COURT WATCHER Mabel Fox leaned forward in the third row of Courtroom B—the ceremonial courtroom on the fourth floor of the Edward N. Cahn U.S. Courthouse in downtown Allentown. She could have been enjoying a game of gin rummy with her girlfriends at the Lehigh Country Club but ditched them this crisp December day for a seat at what she described as "the best show in town." Mabel was lucky to get a seat. Judge J. William Ciccone's beautiful dark mahogany paneled courtroom was packed full for the fifth day of the corruption trial of Northampton County Judge Eugene Harlin.

"Will there be any further direct examination of this witness, Mr. Greyson?" Judge Ciccone inquired of Harlin's counsel.

"No, Your Honor."

"All right then. Let's take twenty minutes for our mid-morning break. Let's get the ladies and gentleman of the jury out." Without hesitation, the Court Security Officer bellowed, "All rise for the jury!"

Everyone in the courtroom, except Judge Ciccone, rose to their feet as the members of the jury filed out of the jury box on the left side of the courtroom into an open door leading to the jury deliberation room.

"Anything else?" Judge Ciccone inquired of counsel. Hearing nothing, the judge stood up to exit through the door behind the bench.

"All rise!" the CSO spoke in a deep, loud voice, as the judge disappeared into his chambers.

Thax stood behind Government counsel's table conferring with Barrows. He turned to look into the spectator area of the courtroom.

Through the crowd of onlookers filing out of the double wooden doors at the rear of the courtroom, he spied Chrissy. She looked stunning in a dark red skirt suit with an off-white, seashell-colored blouse. Of course, she wore matching red heels and lipstick. She smiled at Thax, motioning for him to meet her outside. He rushed to meet her outside the courtroom doors.

"Hey," she beamed, grabbing his suit jacket. "Nice touch with 'federal' blue today," Chrissy ribbed him about his suit.

"And the red tie . . . nice accessorizing," she teased.

Thax almost always wore a blue suit, white shirt, and a red tie when he was in trial.

"Did you want something? I'm in the middle of a trial, you know." Thax smiled playfully.

"I need to talk to you. Privately." Chrissy looked toward a witness interview room down the hall and motioned for Thax to follow. "Come with me."

The crowd outside the courtroom had thinned out almost completely. Chrissy tugged on Thax's sleeve as she headed toward the witness room. The light was on in the room. She knocked on the heavily frosted glass window of the door. When no one answered, she opened the unlocked door. The room was empty except for the three by six-foot wooden table and two padded swivel chairs. Chrissy looked furtively down the hallway, prompting Thax to come into the room. She locked the door behind them.

"What's going on?"

Thax barely finished his question when Chrissy embraced him and kissed him passionately. She unbuttoned her jacket and tossed it at one of the chairs then started to pull Thax's suit jacket off.

Thax took a breath and hesitated. "Hey. We're in a courthouse."

"Just kiss me," she demanded. Thax tossed his jacket on the nearby chair. As they continued to embrace, Chrissy pushed her right hand down the front of Thax's pants.

"Chrissy." Thax resisted.

She grabbed his tie, pulling it toward her as she backed up to the edge of the table.

"I want you," she whispered, pulling up her skirt.

"I can't. Not here." Thax glanced toward the door.

Chrissy reached behind him with both hands and pulled him against her. She kissed him again.

"Come on, Thax," she begged.

"I can't."

Chrissy leaned forward and hugged him.

"This is crazy, Thax. I don't want to let go of you."

The moment was interrupted by a loud rap on the glass that startled them.

"Colby!" CSO Bill Carpenter called. "If that's you in there, the judge is coming on the bench in five minutes."

"Thanks, Bill," Thax shouted back.

"I need to go put myself back together," Chrissy said, sliding off the table. "Do you think I can get out of here without anybody noticing?"

"Not if you walk out in that G-string."

Chrissy tried to smile.

"Let me get out of here first. Then you can make a break for it," Thax said.

"See you in a few," she replied.

"You better hurry up." Thax donned his jacket and straightened his tie. "You're not going to want to miss this."

Fifty-Three

United States District Judge J. William Ciccone, looked to Thax Colby at counsel table. "You may proceed with cross-examination counsel."

Thax stood. "Thank you, Your Honor." He approached the lectern, holding no notes.

"Good afternoon, Mayor," he began, his heart still racing from the clandestine midmorning interlude.

"Good afternoon, Mr. Colby," Mayor Branfield replied. "And you can call me Governor-elect."

Thax pursed his lips. "Mayor Branfield, how long have you held your current office?"

Branfield smirked at the perceived disrespectful tone.

"Almost eight years. Two delightful and accomplished terms."

Thax ignored the extraneous information.

"Are you married, sir?"

"Well, I'm sure you know that I am. My beautiful wife is seated in the second row behind Judge Harlin's table," Branfield said smiling, pointing to his wife. "In the lovely yellow chiffon dress."

The attention of the courtroom focused on the former beauty queen. Her eyes sparkled as she scanned the jury box. Describing them as blue was sufficient, but not accurate enough, to capture their beauty. They were deep. Penetrating. With just a brief glance the panel couldn't help but feel connected to her.

"How long have you had the pleasure of being married to Mrs. Branfield, sir?"

"Almost eighteen wonderful years," he answered, gazing again toward his wife.

"Now sir, you have testified that on October twelfth, two years ago, the day that Judge Harlin is accused of accepting payoff monies, that he was with you on a business trip to Las Vegas. Is that your testimony?"

"Yes, it is."

"Your testimony is that he could not have received money that day because he was with you and because he was not in Easton where the payoff allegedly occurred, correct?"

"That's correct."

"And you are certain that it was October twelfth you and Judge Harlin were in Las Vegas?"

"More than certain."

"Why are you so sure?"

"October twelfth was my sister's fiftieth birthday and I distinctly remember calling her from Las Vegas. That's why I am so certain, Mr. Colby," the mayor said arrogantly.

"I assume you flew a commercial airline to Vegas, Mayor. Didn't you?"

"Of course, I did. The mayor doesn't have a private jet."

"Mayor Branfield, did the City of Allentown pay for your trip to Las Vegas?"

"I think I said it was a business trip. Judge Harlin, who is also a member of the Northampton County Chamber of Commerce, and I were going there for a city revitalization seminar. That's my business." Branfield looked at the jury. "Taking care of our city, and soon our state."

One older woman in the front row of the jury smiled politely.

"Where did you and Judge Harlin stay in Vegas?"

"I'm sure we stayed at the Venetian."

Thax looked for the jury's reaction. The Venetian was the most expensive hotel on the Vegas strip.

"Do you have a business credit card that you used to make flight and hotel reservations?"

"I do. An American Express card."

"Is the card in your name?"

"Of course it is," Branfield replied, not sure where Thax was going with this line of questioning.

"Do you carry that card in your wallet?"

"I do."

"Can you please take it out?"

Branfield looked at Judge Harlin's attorney for guidance. The attorney nodded. The mayor pulled his wallet out and removed the American Express card.

Thax walked a few steps back to the Government counsel's table where Barrows was seated. She handed him a document.

"May I approach the witness, Your Honor?" Thax asked, consistent with the rules and etiquette of the court.

"You may," Judge Ciccone permitted.

Thax walked to the witness box, situated to the left side of the bench, and handed Branfield the document. "I want to show you what has been marked as Government's Exhibit thirty-three. Do you know what that is?"

Branfield examined it while Thax walked back to the lectern.

"Yes. It's a copy of my American Express card bill for October of the year we are talking about. It's dated November second."

"Your name is on the bill?"

"Yes."

"Does the card number on the bill match the number on the card in your wallet?"

Branfield examined them both. "It surely does, sir."

Thax glanced at the jury. They eagerly awaited his next question. "Mayor," Thax said curiously, "can you show us on your statement where the charges appear for your flight and the hotel?"

Branfield examined the bill. After reading the first page he moved to the second. He looked again at the front page. He seemed flustered.

"Well, obviously American Express screwed this up. I don't see those charges anywhere on here. There must be some mistake," the mayor squawked, talking very quickly. "Let me look at this again."

The mayor continued to look at the pages of the bill. Thax interrupted his examination. "It's not on there, Mayor, is it?"

Branfield tossed the documents on the table part of the witness box. Obviously frazzled, he quietly replied, "No."

Thax paused momentarily.

"Are we done with this bill now, Mr. Colby?" the mayor said. He picked it up and motioned for Thax to retrieve it.

"Not quite yet." Thax stared at Branfield.

Thax continued his cross.

"Mayor Branfield, do you have interns in your office?"

"Of course. At any given time we have as many as three or four interns in the office."

"College students?"

"Mostly," the mayor responded. "Occasionally a law student."

"Mayor," Thax asked curiously, "do you know a Mark Wolfe?"

The mayor contemplated his answer.

"Mark Wolfe was an intern in my office several years ago."

"Do your interns have credit cards issued by the City?" Thax asked glancing at the jury.

"Of course not. They would have no reason to have a credit card. Besides, they are all volunteer positions. Their compensation is that they get to work with me."

"Sir, what is the address of your office?"

"You know that, Mr. Colby. My office is at City Hall," Branfield snipped.

Judge Ciccone interrupted sternly, "Mr. Branfield. Just answer the questions that are put to you."

"Yes, Judge," Branfield replied without looking back at the judge.

"My address is 435 Hamilton Street."

Thax looked over to Barrows who handed him another document. Thax stepped back to the lectern looking back into the seating area of the courtroom. For a second he caught a glimpse of Chrissy.

"May I approach the witness, Your Honor?" Judge Ciccone granted permission.

Thax approached the witness box and handed Branfield the document. "I want to show you what has been marked as Government's Exhibit thirty-four. Do you have any idea what that is?"

The mayor looked at the three-page document, page by page, then looked at Judge Harlin's lawyer. Branfield was noticeably angry that the attorney wasn't helping.

"I have never seen this before in my life," Branfield said vehemently.

Thax walked back to the lectern then turned to face the mayor.

"Mayor, that's an American Express bill addressed to your office at City Hall, isn't it?"

Harlin's counsel stood. "Objection, Your Honor. He said he's never seen it before."

"Overruled. I'll allow some inquiry. Answer the question Mr. Branfield," the judge instructed.

"This American Express bill is addressed to my office, yes. Yes, it is."

"In fact, it's addressed to Mark Wolfe at your office, isn't it?"

"It appears to be. Yes."

"And it is for the same time period as the previous bill, Exhibit thirty-three, that you have identified as your bill. Is that correct?"

"Yes."

"Do you see on page two of Mr. Wolfe's bill a charge for three nights at the Venetian in Las Vegas for October eleventh through thirteenth?"

Branfield looked at page two of the document. He reached for the water pitcher on the witness stand. His hand shook as he poured water into a white Styrofoam cup. He took a small sip of the cool water.

"Yes, I see it. I don't know what it is or anything about this card, but I do see it. Yes."

Branfield was coming unhinged.

"Was your intern, Mark Wolfe, married?"

"No, he wasn't."

Thax retrieved another document from Barrows and asked for permission to approach the witness.

"I have another exhibit I want to show you, sir. It's Government's Exhibit thirty-five." Thax handed Branfield a four by six-inch white paper card.

"Have you ever seen this?" Thax waited patiently by the witness box.

Branfield's face turned red.

"I don't know what you're trying to do, Colby, but this is outrageous." Branfield raised his voice.

The judge cut him off. "Mr. Branfield, this is the last time I will warn you. This is my courtroom, not yours. You will conduct yourself accordingly. Do you understand?"

Branfield said nothing, but nodded his head. He glared back at Thax.

"What is Exhibit thirty-five?" Thax asked again.

Branfield picked up the card, then tossed it down in front of him. "It's a guest registration form for the Venetian—"

"Dated?" Thax interrupted.

"October eleventh."

"In what name is the room registered?" Thax looked at the jury as he awaited the response.

Branfield looked toward his wife Dana then, looking down at the card mumbled, "Mr. and Mrs. Mark Wolfe."

"I'm sorry sir, I couldn't hear you," Thax shot back. "What did you say?"

"I said, Mr. and Mrs. Mark Wolfe."

Branfield was done but Thax was not. Not yet.

Thax walked back to the lectern and turned toward Branfield. "Mayor Branfield, are you aware that the Venetian has security cameras in its lobbies, hallways, and all over the hotel?"

Branfield was speechless. Thax looked at Barrows who handed him some photographs. Thax flipped through them. Branfield had no idea the photos were of Barrows and her family at Disney World.

"You have to answer, Mr. Branfield," Judge Ciccone directed.

"I assume they do," Branfield said just loud enough for the jury to hear. The entire jury was leaning forward in the jury box.

"Who were you with at the seminar, Mayor Branfield? Tell us her name," Thax pushed for an answer, holding the photos in his hand.

Branfield looked again for his wife, who sat with her head down and turned toward the far wall of the courtroom. Dana Branfield knew her husband was secretly a cheat and a liar but she tolerated his antics for her own personal good fortune. She didn't anticipate this public flogging.

"Her name was Wendy Carlson." Branfield let out a deep breath.

"Wendy Carlson?" Thax repeated.

"She was an intern in the District Attorney's Office." Branfield looked for his wife who was visibly more embarrassed than hurt.

"I'm sorry," he mouthed.

Now Thax was done.

"I have no further questions for the *Governor-elect*."

Fifty-Four

Richie Sokol rested his back on a few pillows laying against the headboard of the king-sized bed in his suite at the Allentown Hilton near the Lehigh Valley International Airport. Still naked from a fresh hot shower, he climbed into bed and pulled the covers over his lower body. He grabbed the remote and switched on the TV on the credenza at the foot of the bed. He changed to Channel 10 and listened to the reporter standing in front of the federal courthouse.

"This is Chrissy Barnes at the federal courthouse in Allentown where, today, the corruption trial of Northampton County Common Pleas Judge Eugene Harlin took a serious turn against him when Allentown Mayor and now Governor-elect Logan Branfield was forced to admit to an affair with a former District Attorney's Office intern. Branfield, who earlier in the day had provided an alibi for Judge Harlin—that he and Harlin were in Las Vegas on the day a payoff was allegedly made to Harlin to fix a pending drug case—essentially recanted the crucial testimony when confronted with documents showing that on the day before the payoff, Branfield and the former intern registered at the Venetian, a five-star Las Vegas resort using an alias. The courtroom went silent as the prosecutor grilled Branfield about the illicit affair two years ago. Leaving the courthouse this afternoon, with his wife Dana still at his side, Branfield refused to speak with reporters regarding his testimony or the affair. The trial continues tomorrow with closing arguments expected to begin early next week. Branfield's inauguration will take place in Harrisburg on January eighteenth. Back to you, Will."

"Don't you want to watch this, baby?" Sokol asked as he reached down with his left hand and ran his fingers through a head of naturally red, long wavy hair. He massaged the upper back of the stunning woman who laid under the sheets. The woman pulled closer to Sokol until her head was on top of his lower body.

"You're amazing," Sokol groaned, closing his eyes and pressing his head back against the pillows. He pulled the sheet down off the woman's head. She looked up and smiled playfully at him.

"You really are amazing," he repeated, softly stroking Dana Branfield's face. He set the remote on the night table next to him. "Now, your fuckin' husband. He's an asshole. That prosecutor kicked the living shit out of him today."

Dana pulled her body up so she was face to face with Sokol. She embraced him and turned toward her back, pulling him on top of her. Publicly, Dana Holmes Branfield had been humiliated by the testimony of her husband's extramarital fling. Privately, the soon-to-be First Lady of Pennsylvania did whatever she wanted—or *whoever* she wanted.

And right now, she wanted Richie Sokol to screw her brains out.

Fifty-Five

Judge Ciccone surveyed his courtroom to assure that everyone and everything was in order.

"Ladies and gentlemen, there will be no outbursts of any kind when the verdict is read," he warned.

Judge Harlin sat stoically at defense table next to his high-priced mouthpiece, Matt Greyson. The jury of seven men and five women deliberated for just over four hours. Not one of the twelve had made any eye contact with Harlin when they returned to the courtroom moments earlier to deliver their verdict. Greyson leaned over to whisper something in his client's ear. Harlin nodded.

Judge Ciccone addressed the young CPA sitting in the first seat of the jury box. The man had been selected by the other jurors as their foreperson. "Mr. Morgan, I understand that the jury has reached a verdict."

The foreperson rose to his feet.

"We have, Your Honor."

"All right," the judge responded. "Mr. Carpenter, please retrieve the verdict forms from the foreperson."

The Court Security Officer secured the papers and handed them to Judge Ciccone.

Thax and Barrows sat anxiously at Government counsel's table. The courtroom spectator area had swelled to capacity. Thax's boss, Wes Hodges—the United States Attorney for the Eastern District of Pennsylvania—sat in the first row, directly behind Thax. A former Assistant United States Attorney, Hodges looked confident as the judge reviewed the verdict forms.

"Madam Clerk," Judge Ciccone addressed his courtroom deputy clerk, "please publish the verdicts," he ordered, handing her the verdict forms. She stood and read the verdict.

"In the United States District Court for the Eastern District of Pennsylvania, United States of America versus Eugene Harlin, verdict, Count One, as to the offense of extortion under color of official right—bribery—we, the jury, find the defendant Eugene Harlin guilty."

A mild hush came over the charged Courtroom. Judge Ciccone reached for his gavel, then hesitated as the room became quiet again. Harlin's wife, a plain looking, almost sixty-year-old, woman sitting in the first row of bench seats behind defense counsel's table, buried her face in her hands and quietly sobbed. The defendant stared forward at the clerk as she continued.

"Count Two of the Indictment. As to the offense of making false statements to a federal law enforcement officer, we the jury find the defendant Eugene Harlin, guilty. So say we all. Your Honor the form is dated and signed by the foreperson."

The clerk was seated. The judge addressed Harlin and his counsel.

"Mr. Greyson, does the defendant wish to poll the jury?"

Harlin leaned over and spoke to Greyson for a few seconds, then shook his head.

"No, Your Honor."

"Very well then," Judge Ciccone continued. "I will ask the defendant to stand."

Harlin stood and faced Ciccone, looking toward the jury then back toward the judge. Greyson stood next to his client.

"Eugene Harlin, the jury having returned verdicts of guilty as to Counts One and Two of the Indictment, this Court does now adjudge you to be guilty of those offenses. Sentencing will be set for March first at nine o'clock."

The judge thanked and excused the jury.

"Mr. Colby." Thax stood as the Court addressed him.

"Yes, Your Honor."

"I take it there is no objection to the defendant remaining on bond until sentencing?"

"No objection."

"Very well. And so it shall be."

Judge Ciccone conferred with his courtroom clerk.

"If there's nothing further counsel, we will be in recess." The judge stood to leave the courtroom.

"All rise!" CSO Carpenter's loud voice brought everyone to their feet. As the judge disappeared through a side door of the courtroom into his chambers, Carpenter announced that court was in recess.

Local reporters scurried to leave the courtroom, eager to get their stories out. Harlin's family huddled around him behind the defense table. The U.S. Attorney, the Special Agent in Charge of the FBI, and the Resident Agent in Charge of DEA congratulated Thax and Barrows, who were joined at counsel's table by Campisano. Thax graciously accepted the accolades but was clearly distracted. He searched eagerly through the commotion in the spectator area of the courtroom until his eyes met Chrissy's. She had stopped at the back of the room waiting for Thax's glance. They had said their goodbyes the night before. Chrissy forced a smile, trying desperately to hold back her tears. Thax managed to smile back.

"I love you," Chrissy mouthed.

Campisano grabbed Thax's arm and started to speak, unknowingly interrupting the moment. Thax turned then looked back. Chrissy was walking out of the courtroom doors. His heart hurt more than he thought it ever would as he watched her walk away.

"Nice work, brother," Campisano congratulated Thax, slapping his back.

Thax, still distracted, glimpsed back toward the courtroom exit.

"Thanks, Christopher. You and Shea deserve all the credit for putting this case together." Thax thanked his friend again for the kind words.

Campisano, sensing something was wrong looked toward the doors at the back of the courtroom where Thax was looking.

"Where's your girl?"

"She's gone, Christopher," Thax said somberly. "She's off to Denver . . . and dumbass me let her go."

Fifty-Six

"COME ON IN, Thax."

United States Attorney Wes Hodges waved his right hand toward Thax standing in the doorway to Hodges's office. He grasped his blue ceramic coffee mug with the other hand. The large corner office, just down the hall from Thax's office in the Allentown federal courthouse, was reserved for when the boss was visiting from the main office in Philadelphia. The aroma of freshly brewed hazelnut coffee wafted across the room.

Thax walked into the office. Hodges rarely made the sixty-mile trip north unless it was to deal with something important. Appointed by the President two years earlier, his politics were relatively simple: he hated politics, but it didn't hurt to know the right people at the right time. His stellar, albeit short, career as an Assistant U.S. Attorney didn't hurt either.

"What's going on, Wes?"

Thax and Hodges had been colleagues at one time and had maintained their friendship through the years.

"Shut the door, will you Thax?" Hodges took another long sip of his coffee.

Thax closed the solid wooden door leading to a small alcove outside the main office where a legal assistant could be stationed. He walked back toward Hodges's dark cherry government-issued executive desk and sat in one of the two plush leather chairs positioned in front it.

"Did I do something wrong, Wes?" Thax joked.

"Not this week." Hodges grinned.

"Well good. I've got that going for me, then." Thax chuckled.

Hodges opened a folder that was sitting on his desk.

"Thax, I'm putting you in for a Director's Award." Hodges picked up a letter from the folder. "You know that's the highest honor an Assistant U.S. Attorney can get from the Department. You've done a hell of a job on this corruption investigation."

"Thank you," Thax said. "I'm flattered."

"Well, hell Thax, there's no need to be shy about it. You deserve it. That's why I nominated you."

"I appreciate that," Thax said. "I have some great agents working this investigation with me."

"I know. Really good people."

"Unfortunately, I have a lot of bodies and not so many defendants," Thax lamented.

"Yeah. Well, stats are overrated." Hodges laughed.

"I guess so."

"Anyway, I wanted to tell you about the nomination." Hodges hesitated.

Thax sensed that his boss was uncomfortable about something.

"I thought they didn't nominate people for those awards until the case was over. I still have the sentencing of Judge Harlin and we have a pretty active ongoing investigation, Wes."

Hodges leaned back in his chair and ran his fingers through his short, prematurely grey hair. Behind him, the American flag and the U.S. Attorney's flag flanked a credenza with some of his personal photographs.

"They usually don't, Thax."

Thax listened, leaning forward and closer to Hodges. His instincts were right. Something was wrong. He tried to be calm.

"You didn't drive up here to tell me about an award, did you, Wes? What's going on?"

Hodges shook his head and chugged some more coffee.

"Thax, I think we . . . you have exposed the corruption in APD's narcotics unit. Bodies or defendants. Either way. I don't care. God knows how long this was going on here. You found it and put that unit out of business. When they get a new chief, I know they'll get that shit straightened out. This community should be sincerely grateful for your efforts, but—"

"But we've got other things to do?" Thax interrupted. "More important than this?"

"What do you want to do, Thax? Indict the damn governor for lying about screwing an intern? His wife was sitting there listening to him testify for Chrissakes." Hodges continued. "He lied to save his ass."

Thax couldn't believe the words coming out of Hodges's mouth.

"What are you saying Wes? It's okay to lie under oath as long as you're doing it to save your ass?"

"No. It's not," Hodges answered tersely. "You know damn well it's not."

"When someone walks into court and raises their right hand, I don't care who they are," Thax said

"I agree, Thax. I agree."

"Well, then . . ."

"We are not indicting the governor, Thax."

"He's not the governor yet," Thax scoffed.

"Well, he will be a month from now—whether we indict him or not," Hodges grumbled.

Thax looked out the window. It was starting to snow.

"Thax," Hodges took a deep breath, "we need to shut this down. Now."

Thax bristled at the directive. "There are other people out there too. I don't know yet who was calling the shots on this but they've got blood on their hands. Do you want to see the pictures of Marlena Schick with her brains blown out? She didn't do anything to deserve that. Her husband was a dirty cop, but she was going to be a mom. Somebody needs to account for that. This is bullshit, Wes!"

Thax realized that he was pushing back hard. Hodges was Thax's friend so he listened to him vent.

"Thax . . . I'm sorry."

"Is that all?" Thax rose to his feet.

"Sit for another minute," Hodges said, trying to calm Thax.

Thax sat anxiously on the edge of the chair. No one was going to like this. Not the FBI, DEA, or ATF.

"You and I did not have this conversation but I really do need to explain. I've been *directed* to shut this down. I hear everything you're saying and I agree with you. You know me. The last thing I want to do is to shut this down, but I don't have a choice."

"Where's this directive coming from?"

"Jesus, Thax," Hodges answered. "It's coming from the same people you don't need to know about. People who are already plotting for elections years from now. People who think this new governor will be a strong candidate for U.S. Senator in six years. That's who."

"Senator? Seriously?"

"That's the word."

Thax was pissed.

"Well, the word I have is this guy can't keep his dick in his pants for six weeks so six years is going to be a real challenge."

"We are *not* indicting the governor."

"I heard you the first time," Thax relented.

"You know, I already had to do some damage control. I guess they didn't like you tearing this guy a new asshole on cross." Hodges smirked.

"What does that mean?"

"It means I'm proud of you. But it also means shut it down. Everything except Judge Harlin's sentencing."

Thax stood up and walked toward the door.

"I thought we were the untouchables."

"We still are," the U.S. Attorney replied.

"No. We're not," Thax said with disappointment. He opened the office door and glanced back at Hodges. Through the large windows he could see it was snowing harder.

"Be careful driving back, Wes."

Fifty-Seven

JEAN MURTAUGH TURNED her silver Volvo sport utility vehicle off Belvidere Road through the open, black wrought iron gates of the Fairview Cemetery in Philipsburg, New Jersey two miles from Easton, Pennsylvania. Her vehicle crept north up a worn blacktop driveway that wove through the rolling, well-manicured grounds. She stared at the rows and rows of headstones and monuments. At a fork in the road she turned right, passing a sturdy oak tree, its branches now bare on this frigid January morning. After reaching another landmark, she pulled her vehicle over and stopped. Her stomach ached and she felt nauseous. She sat, breathing deeply. Leaving her vehicle, she walked some twenty-five yards to a small plot under a nearly leafless canopy of young red maple trees. She recalled how hauntingly beautiful they were the first day she saw them. She placed a dark blue wool blanket on the cold, damp ground in front of a flat granite headstone.

"I'm here, sweetie. It's Mom," she said softly. She wondered how many other mothers had come to this cemetery to bury a child.

Murtaugh's gloved hands gently pushed the fallen leaves off the pink-hued grave marker so she could read her daughter's name. Erica Lynn Murtaugh.

"I brought you a rose," she whispered, placing a single long stem red rose on the headstone. "We miss you so much, baby."

Murtaugh sat on the blanket and talked to her daughter. After almost an hour, she got up to leave.

"Goodbye, Erica. I'll be back next week. I love you," her anguished voice quivered.

* * *

Jerry King's metal desk on the first floor of the Troop M State Police Barracks in Bethlehem looked like a cyclone had hit it. Fortunately, the seasoned homicide investigator could locate just about anything on the disaster that was his desk at any time.

Today, he enjoyed the relative calm of the quiet squad room as he focused his investigative experience on his most challenging open case, the murder of Josh and Marlena Schick. After hundreds of hours of running down half-baked leads, he was nowhere closer to solving this horrific crime. Offers of rewards for the public's assistance had yielded nothing. With no witnesses and next to no physical evidence, he found himself in a place he had rarely ever been. This case—this horrible case—had gone ice cold. He remained convinced that the murder of the disgraced Allentown narcotics detective, his pregnant wife, and their two unborn babies was not a robbery—it was a hit. But that was just his opinion. *Amateur criminals leave behind evidence,* he thought. *Something to go on. This one left next to nothing.*

King opened the case file. Paging through reports from dead-end leads he came upon a color picture of Marlena Schick that had been retrieved from the Schick home sometime after her murder.

"I'm so sorry," King said, looking at the picture. "You didn't deserve this."

* * *

"Katie?"

Kristin Meyers looked down the short hallway toward the back door. Katie stood staring in that direction.

"Katie," she called louder.

Katie Meyers turned her head, acknowledging her mother's presence.

"I'm okay, Mom," she said. Kristin hugged her from behind.

"You're trying too hard, sweetie."

"I can see something, Mom. A man. I know he was here. I just can't see him clearly. Every time I think I can, it's just a blur. What's wrong with me?"

Kristin turned Katie toward her. She grabbed her arms and pulled her closer.

"Katie, I don't know what to say to you. I just don't know."

"Did he kill Dad?"

"Katie," Kristin tried to answer.

"What if he killed Dad and I can't ever see him clearly? I feel so guilty, Mom. Why can't I see him? Why?" Katie became more agitated.

Kristin felt helpless. She struggled with her own emotions. She didn't want to think that her husband would take his own life, but the thought that someone had broken into their home and killed him was equally terrifying. Her heart ached for their loss and the torment that her daughter was going through. Were her daughter's visions real or just a coping mechanism after the sudden tragic death of her father?

Kristin held Katie close.

"Katie, we have to move on. Dad is gone. We have to try to keep going." She didn't know what else to say.

Katie hugged her mom tightly.

"I know, Mom. I love you."

"I love you, too."

* * *

Logan Branfield stood proudly on the inaugural platform on the steps outside the east entrance to the Pennsylvania Capitol. He gazed out at the thousands of supporters who braved near freezing temperatures and a light rain on this January day to witness his swearing in. Branfield's black wool overcoat and a black scarf would keep him warm enough for the swearing in and the short ten-minute speech he would deliver afterward.

The Chief Justice of the Commonwealth's Supreme Court, Elizabeth Kay, stepped forward as the crowd grew silent. Dana Branfield stood between her husband and the Chief Justice. She raised and held out an old Bible that belonged to her husband's great-grandfather, upon which Logan Branfield squarely placed his left hand. Raising his right hand, he repeated each phrase of the oath of office as the Chief Justice requested.

"I, Logan Branfield, do solemnly swear that I will support, obey and defend the Constitution of the United States and the Constitution of this Commonwealth and that I will discharge the duties of my office with fidelity, so help me God."

Richie Sokol, the soon to be new Commissioner of the Pennsylvania

State Police, looked on from the front row of the hundreds of spectators huddled in cold folding chairs in front of a large fountain in a granite amphitheater on the Capitol's east side. As Branfield spoke the last words of his oath—"*so help me God*"—Sokol looked toward the dark cloudy Harrisburg skies for a lightning bolt.

Five years later . . .

Fifty-Eight

THE TWENTY-ONE-YEAR-OLD ALBRIGHT College senior strode confidently through the second-floor main hallway of the south wing of the Pennsylvania State Capitol building. The resonant click of her black high heels on the granite floor blended with the other sounds of the many Commonwealth employees making their morning trek to work through the busy thoroughfare. A handsome young page, working in the House of Representatives, slowed his pace to admire the co-ed's long toned legs that disappeared under her mid-thigh length navy overcoat. The rest of her small body wasn't too bad either. He stopped, watching her continue down the hallway until only her long straight blonde hair was visible before she turned the corner toward the entrance to the governor's office.

Executive Secretary Carlotta Magnanti greeted the young woman just inside the double oak doors leading to the governor's office.

"Good morning," Magnanti said brightly, walking around the front of her desk. "How can I help you?"

"Good morning. I'm Katie Meyers." The young woman reached to shake Magnanti's hand.

"Well, of course," Magnanti replied. "Our new intern. Welcome, Katie. I'm Carly. I'm the governor's secretary. It's wonderful to have you here."

Katie beamed a perfect smile. She felt welcome immediately. "I'm so excited to be here. Thank you."

"Well," Magnanti responded, "take off that coat and let me show you to where you'll be working."

Katie slipped out of her overcoat and neatly folded it over her left arm.

"Follow me," the sleek-looking middle-aged secretary said, advancing toward a long hallway that ended at a ten-foot oak-paneled door leading into the governor's private inner sanctum. The hallway, with its towering ornate ceilings, was evenly punctuated with office doors on both sides. Katie curiously peeked into several of them as she passed. A tall, balding man walked from an office several doors in front of them, his tie loosened and shirt sleeves rolled up tightly.

"Kirk," Magnanti said as she stopped. "I'd like you to meet our new intern, Katie Meyers. Katie this is Kirk McDonnell, the deputy chief of staff."

McDonnell stopped and gave Katie a welcoming handshake.

"So nice to meet you, Katie."

"Good to meet you, too," Katie replied.

McDonnell continued to edge toward the front of the office trying not to be rude. "I'm sorry. I have to run out for a minute. I'll catch up with you in fifteen, maybe thirty minutes," he said, looking at his watch. Magnanti continued down the hallway.

"This is the hub of the whole Capitol building, Katie. Things move fast here. Real fast." Magnanti stopped just outside a doorway four doors down from the governor's private office. "And don't let anyone tell you they're in charge here." Magnanti motioned with her head toward the big door at the end of the hall. She cracked a sassy grin. "Even *he* knows who's really in charge."

The secretary showed Katie into the office where they had stopped.

"This is yours," Magnanti said, following the intern through the doorway. "Desk, computer, telephone. You can hang that coat right on the back of the door. Now the important stuff. The restroom's outside the front door on the other side of the hall. Coffee pot's in the break room on the other side of my desk. Settle in and Kirk will be back soon to get you set up with the computer, a key card, and all the other good stuff you'll need. There's a phone list with all the extensions right next to your phone. Call me if you need anything, or you can just walk down and find me. Okay?"

"Absolutely," Katie said, trying to take it all in. "Thank you so much, Carly."

Magnanti nodded.

"This is going to be a great experience for you."

"I surely hope so," a booming male voice interrupted them from just outside the door. Logan Branfield stepped into the office. Katie's stomach fluttered wildly as she locked eyes with the handsome, dark-haired leader of Pennsylvania.

"It's Katie, right?"

"Yes. It is. Katie Meyers."

"I'm Logan Branfield," he said, with all the charm he could muster. He stepped closer and grasped her hand. "Welcome to my office."

Katie gushed with pride. "It's a pleasure to be here, Governor."

"Katie's an honor student at Albright. Communications major," Magnanti interjected.

"Well," the governor glanced at his secretary then back at Katie, "I must tell you. My staff somehow manages to keep hiring interns that are smarter and prettier than I could ever imagine." Branfield considered himself a connoisseur of beautiful women and the one standing in front of him was pretty stunning.

Katie tried not to blush. She was so taken by Branfield's charisma that she seemingly ignored the inappropriateness of his comment.

"Where are you from, Katie?" he asked.

"I'm from Allentown."

"Really? Well, you probably know then that's my city. My hometown."

"I do."

"You probably don't remember much about me being the mayor there, do you?"

"A little bit," she responded. "Actually, I remember the beautiful flowers you sent my mom when my dad died."

"Oh, I'm sorry." The governor moved closer. "Remind me how I knew your father?"

"He was an Allentown Police Detective. Chip Meyers was his name. They say he killed himself. Your flowers were a wonderful kindness to my mother."

"Chip Meyers," the governor said curiously. "I do remember that. Of course. I was sorry that happened. Very sorry."

"Me, too," Katie said sadly.

"Well," Magnanti said, interrupting the few seconds of awkward silence, "let me get out of here. Katie, if you need anything, come see me."

"Thank you, Carly."

"I need to go, too," Branfield said, turning toward the door. "If you need anything, I'm in the big office down at the end of the hall. Glad to have you here."

"Thank you," Katie answered.

Fifty-Nine

THAX MADE HIS way from the parking lot toward the water's edge, slightly downstream from the old stone building. The early morning sun threw light and welcome warmth through the overhanging willows and other native trees on this crisp, early March day. With no late winter hatch, flying insects were scarce. Thax knelt down and scanned the shallow water just off the river bank looking for anything to help him with his fly selection. Before leaving the parking lot, he had tied on a parachute black ant—a dry fly ant pattern with an off-white hackle and white parachute for visibility. As he surveyed the gin clear open water in front of him, well downstream from the two willows, an enormous brown trout, its colors having relinquished some brilliance from the well-past autumn months, slapped its tail as it gobbled its breakfast. The monster fish held its position facing upstream just below the surface, looking to feed. Thax knew even his slightest movement would spook the fish.

From the kneeling position, he quickly but quietly stripped fly line from the reel and prepared to cast upstream from his target. His cast was perfect. As the line flew across the water and straightened, he extended his arm and rod tip upstream, throwing a mend into the line before the fly landed like a feather ten feet upstream from the hungry trout. The fly's drift matched the speed of the current, following every swirl and ripple of the water without any drag from the fly line—dead drift. Seconds later, the wild trophy brown rose and slashed the ant from the surface.

Thax set the hook.

* * *

Thax stood at the end of the picnic table outside the fly shop. Old Ronnie walked from the door of the shop clenching a slightly aged eight by ten black and white photograph.

"Do you see this here, Thax?" He held up the picture and flapped it back and forth.

Thax was amused.

"This is a damn photograph. It's a picture of the heretofore biggest brown trout anyone's ever taken from these waters." Ronnie's voice got louder and more intense. "See, when someone catches a trophy trout they usually take a damn picture of it. That way people have some proof that the person claiming such a feat actually caught the damn fish!"

Thax tried not to laugh as Ronnie tossed the photo of a much younger and slimmer Ronnie, holding a twenty-two-inch brown trout, onto the table.

"Twenty-five inches you say?" Ronnie snorted and shook his head in disbelief.

"Well, you're right buddy. It may not have been twenty-five. I was just estimating. It could easily have been twenty-six, maybe even twenty-seven."

"Do you not have a camera on that cell phone of yours?" Ronnie asked sarcastically.

"You know, since I retired, I rarely carry that thing with me. It was like cutting off a ball and chain."

"So I guess we're just supposed to take your word for it then?" Ronnie snapped up his photo from the table. He brushed some remnants of dirt and crushed leaves from the back of it.

"I guess so."

"Maybe we can just draw a picture of a fish, put your name on it and hang it on the wall in there? We'll say it was twenty-five inches. How would that be?" Ronnie continued to needle his friend.

"Sure. I don't see why not," Thax mused.

"No one else saw it, huh." Ronnie turned toward the fly shop.

"Well," Thax replied, "it was pretty early this morning. There used to be a time when other guys would have been out here that time of day, but

I guess they were still in bed or home feeding their cats while I was out here fishing."

Ronnie didn't respond to Thax's jab. So what if he liked cats? He took a few steps, stopped at the door, then turned toward Thax.

"Some of us aren't as young as we used to be either." Ronnie paused. "What did you catch him on anyway?"

"I guess it doesn't matter, does it?"

"No, I guess not," Ronnie said, shrugging his shoulders. "I guess not."

Sixty

Polk County Sheriff's Detective Andy Morefield stepped out of his unmarked black Dodge Charger and approached the Subway sandwich shop at the end of a strip center on Havendale Boulevard, south of U.S. Highway 92 in Auburndale, Florida. The parking lot seemed empty. The fragrant smoke from a nearby barbecue joint permeated the cool evening air. Morefield, a local boy from the small town an hour east of Tampa, had work to do. The veteran detective tugged the front of his light jacket back exposing the silver star-shaped Sheriff's badge on his belt to the two uniformed PCSO deputies who stood watch securing the crime scene outside the glass front entrance door to the establishment.

"What do we have, gentlemen?" Morefield asked in his strong southern drawl.

The senior uniformed deputy briefed him.

"Witnesses say two young men—white men—came runnin' out of here in a hurry. Jumped in an old green Chevy pickup and took off like a bat outta hell, headin' south down Havendale. One of the witnesses got a partial tag off the truck. We already put out a BOLO with their particulars—best we could get. Both of 'em about six-foot tall, 'bout 180, 190. One with dark hair, the other one was wearin' a ball cap. They cleaned out the register. Don't know how much they got. One of the workers was in the back cleanin' up the refrigerator. She ducked for cover when she heard the shot. She was the lucky one. She's right over there." The deputy pointed to a teenaged girl with a ponytail leaning against a marked patrol cruiser parked outside the business. A female uniformed deputy tried to console her.

"The other kid out front here wasn't so lucky, though. Looks like he took one to the chest. It's pretty awful, Detective," the deputy said shaking his head. "My oldest boy's about that age."

Morefield acknowledged the deputy's angst. The experienced investigator focused on the grim task ahead him.

"Crime scene?" Morefield asked.

"On their way. Medical examiner should be here, too, any minute," the deputy answered.

Morefield thanked the deputies and walked through the front door. An open and emptied cash register drawer on the other side of the glass divider caught his eye. A young male victim lay on the floor behind it. The detective walked to the end of the counter and accessed the work area through a door marked "for employees only." He approached the victim. Bright red blood soaked the young man's green Subway polo shirt making the entry wound barely visible. What seemed like the rest of the teenager's blood pooled beneath him. A single shell casing lay on the floor. Morefield wouldn't need the medical examiner to determine the cause of death. After further examination of the crime scene, he stepped back outside.

"Do we have an ID on this boy?" he asked the senior deputy.

"The girl says his name is Eddie Wallace. Lives down the road a bit. That's his silver Ford Taurus parked right out there," the deputy added, pointing toward the back of the parking lot.

Morefield nodded. "Does the owner know what's going on here?"

"I'm pretty sure he does." The deputy pointed to the business owner who had just arrived. Other deputies prevented him from entering the store.

"Right," Morefield replied. "Go talk to him." Morefield had seen the video surveillance cameras in the store on his walk through. "Tell him I need the video from inside this store as fast as he can get it. Walk in with him and don't let him touch anything except what he absolutely needs to. And make damn sure he doesn't call this kid's parents."

"Yes, sir," the deputy answered.

Morefield looked up and saw a local news van pulling into the parking lot.

"And will someone get me an address for the parents right away. Before you take him in there. Run the tag on the kid's truck if you have to. We don't need mom and dad finding out about their kid on the news."

As the deputy set out on his mission, another detective, Tommy Steadman, Morefield's partner, arrived on the scene.

"Talk to me, Andy," Steadman dispensed with his usual humor. They turned to walk into the shop.

"We have a dead kid, Tommy. One shot to the chest for I'm guessing maybe a few hundred bucks. Sounds like a couple of locals to me. I'll never understand this shit as long as I live. We need to find these guys—fast. Either way, we're fixin' to have one hell of a long night."

Sixty-One

Katie Meyers stared past her computer screen through the single window to the left of her desk and gazed at the darkened Pennsylvania sky. The bright lights of Harrisburg's bustling Capital District blighted her usually clear view of the traffic traversing the Harvey Taylor Bridge over the Susquehanna River. With eyes glazed over, she blinked and tried to refocus on the almost-finished memo she was working on for the deputy chief of staff. Usually she left before dark to catch an early bus across town to her townhouse apartment but today's responsibilities caused her to work into the early evening. It was almost seven o'clock and most, if not all, of the governor's staff had packed it in for the day. She enjoyed the solitude of the evening; it was the complete opposite of the frenetic environment in the chief executive's suite during normal working hours. Katie was working hard and learning more than she ever imagined. Her internship was a blast. She was having the time of her life.

"You're still here?" Katie focused her tired eyes in the direction of the voice in her doorway.

"Trying to close this place down tonight?" Logan Branfield asked, stepping through the threshold to her office.

Katie reclined in her chair and swiveled to face Branfield.

"Just trying to knock this memo out before I leave."

"Well, I don't know what it is, but I doubt the whole state is going to crash and burn if you don't get it done tonight."

"I'm sure it won't. But I did promise that I'd get it done, so—"

"Well," Branfield interrupted "a promise is a promise." He turned to leave. "*Promise* you won't stay too late."

"I won't." Katie yearned for the governor's attention. In the almost three months of her internship, she and the governor had developed a comfortable relationship, sometimes playfully touching each other when others were not around. She was more than smitten by his affection toward her. As for the governor, he had real feelings for Katie, unlike the rest of his female interests who merely provided him with instant sexual gratification. At times—like now—the emotional tension between the two of them was palpable. She watched Branfield linger into the hallway. She turned back toward the computer.

A few seconds later, she felt the governor's strong hands on her shoulders. He rubbed and massaged her neck. She tossed her long blonde hair over her left shoulder and rolled her head back.

"I like that," she purred, closing her eyes. "Your hands feel amazing." Branfield leaned over her, softly kissing her neck. She felt his warm breath on her face and the top of her chest. He drew her face toward him with both hands, pulling her closer as they kissed. She rose from her chair.

"Should I stop?" he whispered, hoping she wasn't uncomfortable with his advance.

"No." She turned her head to kiss him again.

Branfield hugged her from behind, cupping her breasts through her pink silk v-neck blouse. His hands wandered lower on her body, caressing her as he pulled her closer. Katie turned to face him. She wrapped her arms around his waist. He kissed her again. Her hands reached for his belt.

"Not here," he said in a hushed voice, putting his hands on top of hers.

"Let me take you home."

Sixty-Two

"SHOULD I ASK where this came from?"

Branfield fondled the almost one-inch thick stack of new fifty-dollar bills Richie Sokol had tossed on his desk.

"Does it spend any different if you know?"

"Of course not." The governor grinned.

"Then why do you fuckin' care?"

"You're right, Richie. I don't fucking care." Branfield thumbed through the bills. "Why should I care when my State Police Commissioner gives me, what—"

"Ten grand. There's ten grand there," Sokol interrupted.

Branfield held the stack up to his nose and inhaled deeply.

"I love that smell. New money. Never get tired of that smell." Branfield took another whiff then tossed the money into his top desk drawer.

"I always think it's best if you don't know anything about where it comes from. Just trying to protect you."

"Well, that's good thinking, Richie," Branfield said, nodding in agreement. "Humor me anyway."

Sokol leaned forward in the leather chair in front of Branfield's desk. He glanced back at the main door to the office, instinctively checking to be sure they were alone.

"There are ten troopers—detectives—that do a lot of traveling, so they have all kinds of expenses. You know, meals, hotels, all that stuff."

"Okay." Branfield listened.

"These troopers, the thing is, they aren't real. They just exist on paper.

Theoretically they're traveling all the time and submitting vouchers for their expenses which are paid to them by check by direct deposit. Only, since they don't actually exist, their checks get diverted to another account, which is controlled by another person who sort of has a fake identity. That person has access to the account and withdraws the cash from the account."

"How—" Branfield started to speak.

"I got a broad who works in the budget office. You don't need to know all those fuckin' details, but let's just say she was sucking up to me—"

"Sucking what?" Branfield laughed.

"Exactly. I told you, you don't want to know all the details." Sokol grinned. "Any way, what we do is create fake employment profiles for these phantom troopers, then submit fake vouchers and cut checks that get diverted into an account that she controls. It's an undercover account. Once the money goes in there, she takes it out and gives it to me."

"What's in it for her?" Branfield asked, reaching for a still-packaged cigar on his desk.

"I take care of her."

"I bet you do you." Branfield smirked, twirling the cigar in his fingers. "I bet you do."

"Like I said, I don't guess you need to know all those details," Sokol said, sliding back in his chair.

"Please. Spare me," Branfield replied.

"That's what I thought," Sokol said.

"Just don't get fucking stupid," Branfield snapped.

"Listen," Sokol replied, "she thinks this is some secret special operations fund and that she's doing a service for me and the great state of Pennsylvania. That's why I told her we needed to set this up. She doesn't have a fuckin' clue the money's being skimmed."

"Really?"

"Blonde. Big tits. Not that smart. Trust me, she doesn't know."

Branfield opened his top drawer and grabbed the stack of fifties. "I do love that smell though, Richie." He lifted the bills toward his face. "Love that smell."

"I heard you the first time," Sokol said bluntly. He stood up and walked toward the door. The row of portraits of former Pennsylvania governors encircling the office above the top trim line of the office doors caught his attention. Wood pilasters framed and separated each portrait into its own compartment. He turned toward Branfield and motioned with his head toward the portraits.

"You think any of these guys did this shit?"

Branfield popped out of his chair and walked from behind his desk. His right hand slapped Sokol's back as he looked him in the eye.

"You're fucking kidding me, right?"

Sokol shook his head. He didn't think his pondering about the possibility of previous governors being corrupt would evoke such a strong response.

"I'll forget you just asked that stupid question, Richie. Now get the hell out of here."

Sokol reached for the door.

"Oh, and Richie, Benjamin Franklin was my favorite governor. Actually, he was the sixth *president* of Pennsylvania."

"That's nice," Sokol responded.

"I like him so much better than that fucking Ulysses Grant, if you follow me," Branfield snickered.

Sokol was a quick study. "I follow you, boss."

* * *

As corrupt as Sokol had become, there was still something distinctively vile about his boss that he could never shake. Branfield's greed was unsurpassed by anything Sokol had ever known or seen. Sokol knew his own rise to the Commissioner's spot—and his continued prosperity—was tied hand-in-hand with Branfield's election as the chief executive, but there were days, like this one, when he just wanted to walk away from it all. He remembered the days before he was a dirty cop, when he was just hard-charging and kick-ass; when he was trying to make a difference and doing the right thing. Even when he started taking money from drug dealers, he justified it because they were the scum of the earth and he was one of the good guys. Amazingly, he now spent part of each day trying to figure out how to keep his boss flush with illegal cash. He knew in his heart he had no way out. If anyone ever exposed even a small part of the corruption he and Branfield had been involved in over the years, it would mean decades of incarceration—probably a lifetime. There was no turning back or jumping off. He hung his head in disgust as he hobbled down the main hallway of the governor's suite, his stride still so many years later impeded from his line-of-duty injuries. He passed two staffers in the hallway, one of whom followed his every movement down the hall.

* * *

"Jesus Katie," Deputy Chief of Staff Kirk McDonnell said, grabbing Katie Meyers's arm as she stared at the departing police commissioner. "You look like you've just seen a ghost. Are you okay?"

Katie's face was flush as she watched Richie Sokol disappear through the doors at the entrance to the governor's suite. She leaned back and grabbed the wall for support.

"Katie. Katie," McDonnell spoke louder. "What's wrong? Are you okay?" He quickly ushered the trembling intern into his office where she slid into a chair.

McDonnell kneeled in front of her. "Katie. What's wrong?"

"I'm okay." She inhaled a short breath, struggling for the next one. "I'm okay," she stammered unconvincingly.

"I don't think you are," McDonnell replied. "You don't look okay at all."

"No." She tried to breathe. "Really. I'm okay."

"What just happened? Are you sick?"

"Who was that?" she gasped, ignoring McDonnell's question.

"Who was who?"

"The man. The man in the hallway." Her thoughts raced faster than she could speak. "The man with the limp. The one that just passed us. Who was that?"

"You mean the Commissioner?"

"The guy with the limp?" she shouted.

"Settle down, Katie. It was the State Police Commissioner. Commissioner Sokol. Richard Sokol. Why?"

A cold shiver shook her to her core.

"Sokol?" She quivered. "Where's he from?"

"He's from Allentown. Your hometown. He was the governor's

right-hand man when he was the mayor there," McDonnell answered. "Why are you asking, Katie? What's going on? Do you know him?"

"It's okay," she said quietly. "It's okay. Can you please get me some water?"

McDonnell grabbed a bottle of water out of his refrigerator in the corner of his office.

"Here, Katie." He twisted the cap and handed her the bottle. "Take a drink."

"Thanks, Kirk."

Katie sat silently for a few minutes, sipping on the water.

McDonnell watched with concern. "Are you going to be okay?"

"I think so," she answered tentatively.

"It's almost four o'clock," McDonnell said. "Why don't you get out of here. Go home."

She turned and hugged McDonnell.

"Thank you," she mouthed. "I think I will."

"Are you sure you're going to be alright?"

"I think so," she said. She approached the doorway and looked down the hall. "I'll see you tomorrow."

* * *

Katie pulled the small wooden box from the bottom of her foot locker. It was one of her few treasured items from home. She carried it over to her bed where she sat leaning against the pile of pillows that lined the headboard. A light on a nearby night table glowed in the darkness of the room. She brushed her hand across the front of the box.

Detective Charles "Chip" Meyers
Medal of Valor

Her eyes welled up with tears when she opened the lid and looked at the ornate gold medal lying against soft blue velvet backing. The few times before that she had brought herself to open the box the writing on the engraved gold plate blurred behind her tears.

"I miss you, Daddy," she said, drying her eyes with a wad of tissues. She read the words on the inside of the top of the box.

Medal of Valor
For exhibiting exceptional courage, bravery and extraordinary decisiveness above and beyond the call of duty and without regard for his own personal safety, while saving the life of Lieutenant Richard A. Sokol.

Katie sobbed uncontrollably. She set the box on the bed and reached for the phone. She retrieved a business card from her wallet and dialed the number on the card.

"Hello," a man answered.

"Detective Hatten?"

"No. This is Detective Long. Who's this?"

"I'm sorry." she apologized. "I had this number for Detective Hatten. Cole Hatten."

"Yes, ma'am. Detective Hatten retired about a year ago. I got his old phone number. Is there something I can help you with?"

"Do you have any way to reach him?" Katie asked. "It's really important."

"Ma'am, I'm sorry. All I know is he moved to North Carolina, up in the mountains somewhere. I don't think anyone's got a contact number for him."

"It's okay. Thank you, Detective."

Sixty-Three

KATIE KNOCKED ON the closed door leading into the governor's office. She knocked again when she didn't get an immediate response.

"Come in," the governor's voice called through the door.

Upon opening the door, she saw that Branfield was on the phone. He motioned for her to come in.

"Look, we'll just have to finish this up another time Jim. I've got to go. I'll talk to you soon." He ended the call. Katie walked closer.

"How are you?" he asked.

She shook her head without responding. She tried hard not to cry like she had promised herself she wouldn't. It was obvious she was not okay.

Branfield met her in front of his desk and hugged her. She felt secure in his embrace.

"What's going on? What wrong?" he asked.

"I need your help, but—"

"But what?" he interjected. "If you need something you know I'll do anything for you." He reached for her hands and held them. "Anything. What is it?"

"I need to sit down." she said, sitting in one of the chairs in front of Branfield's desk. The governor sat in the other one.

"Tell me what's wrong," he said pulling his chair up close to hers.

Katie tried to get herself together. She took a deep breath and slowly exhaled.

"My father." She looked into Branfield's eyes. "I was there the night he died. Everyone said he killed himself. All these years." She struggled to speak.

Branfield listened.

"The thing is, I never believed that he did it. I never believed that he took his own life. My dad had so much to live for. He would never have done that to us."

"Katie, I'm sorry. I know how painful it is for you to relive this, so why are you doing this to yourself?"

She tried to compose herself and continued.

"That night, I saw my dad. He had been drinking and I said goodnight to him. I went back to bed, but something woke me up. I'm sure now it was the gunshot. I just didn't hear it then. But it woke me up. I got up because I thought maybe my dad was still up. When I walked toward the office, I looked down the hallway toward the back door. I saw someone. I saw someone walking away."

"Katie, have you ever told anyone this?"

"No. Because I couldn't remember. So many years have passed and I haven't been able to recall anything about the person in the hallway. Even my mom thinks I'm making it up as some sort of defense mechanism."

"It's okay. You don't need to trouble yourself with this. I know it's still painful, but struggling like this is not going to bring your dad back to you. I know it's hard but—"

"I know who did it," she interrupted sternly. "I know."

"What do you mean?"

"I know. I saw the man who killed my father. I saw him."

"Saw him where?"

Katie stood up. She felt her heart pounding. Her pulse quickened. Her palms were moist.

"I saw him here. In this office."

"Here? What are you talking about, Katie?"

"It was Commissioner Sokol. The State Police Commissioner."

Branfield stood in silent disbelief.

"My father saved Sokol's life. He won the medal of valor for it. Then, for some reason I'm sure I'll never know, Sokol came to my house and shot my father. Shot my father." Katie's rage overtook her. She bit her lip. Her voice got louder and angrier. "I saw him limp down the hall after he left your office. It was like I was seeing a ghost. I'll never forget that limp. Ever. That's the man who was leaving my house who I saw walking down the hallway. That's him."

Branfield was stunned. He struggled for the words to respond.

"Katie, I know you think it was him."

"I *know* it was him."

"Just calm down for a few minutes," Branfield's voice crackled. "Sit." He stepped behind her and guided her back to the chair, then kneeled beside her.

"Okay. I'll look into this but you can't go around telling people that the State Police Commissioner murdered your father. You can't do that."

She nodded in agreement.

"Who else have you told about this?"

"Just you," she whispered.

"Good. Let me investigate this. Give me a few days then we'll take it from there. Okay?"

Branfield pulled Katie's head against his chest. "Okay?"

"Okay," she relented. "I love you."

"I love you, too," he assured her. "I love you, too.

* * *

Branfield swirled the half-melted ice cubes at the bottom of his cocktail glass. He stared out his office window toward the bustling capital city. He pondered his rise to the governorship and hopefully, his continued upward political trajectory. *Senator* Branfield had a damn nice ring to it. Or more—Branfield set no limits for himself. Nearly nothing he did was left to chance. When he did fall, he got up. Logan Branfield was a winner. A brash, egotistical, cheating, sometimes maniacal bastard. But always a winner.

Unfortunately for Branfield, beautiful women were his Achilles heel. His wife Dana had long ago stopped sleeping with him because of his philandering. No one could fathom why she stood by him through his perpetual womanizing. Some perhaps thought her weak for not leaving him, but most saw her as a victim of his indiscretions. Who could blame her for staying with him and at least enjoying all the other benefits of being the State's First Lady?

Handsome and powerful, he didn't care whether Dana shared his bed. He was getting some of the nicest ass around, even if it wasn't his wife's. Luckily, he had dodged the disclosures of his affair with a District Attorney's Office intern before his gubernatorial election. Had Judge Harlin's trial happened months earlier, undoubtedly the good people of the state would have soundly rejected him. Four years later, having kept his illicit affairs much more discreet and with many political successes, he decisively won a second term by a virtual landslide. One thing he hadn't planned on was Katie Meyers.

He walked to a liquor cabinet next to the window. He opened the door and retrieved an almost empty bottle of top-shelf Russian vodka. He poured about an inch into his glass, then took a drink.

"Goddammit," he said to an empty office.

He thought Katie would be just another fling, but she wasn't. She was charming, beautiful, intelligent, funny and incredibly sexy. Who wouldn't fall in love with her? He cherished every minute of his time with her. There was never enough. She had never asked for more—until now. Now she had identified the man she thought was her father's killer, Richie Sokol, the one man who knew almost all of Branfield's *real* secrets. Now, she wanted him to intervene and to help her bring Sokol to justice. Sokol was as loyal as anyone could be, the governor hoped. What they had done together had certainly bonded them for life. But confronted with a murder rap? Perhaps the death penalty? Who could know what Sokol would do under that kind of pressure. Would he spill all the beans to try to cut a deal? Branfield's stomach knotted up as he pondered his precarious position.

He gulped the rest of his vodka, wincing from the burn of the liquor rolling down his throat, then slammed the empty glass on the top of his desk. The most powerful man in Pennsylvania's world was careening out of control.

Sixty-Four

WINTER HAVEN, FLORIDA Police Officer Bob Stiles checked the double-wide three-foot high chain-link gates that stretched across the concrete driveway in front of his patrol vehicle. The fencing guarded a small, poorly maintained home on Ave. R, N.W. in the small but thriving city of Winter Haven. The gates were closed and latched but not locked. He keyed the mic of his shoulder radio.

"Bravo twenty-one is out at 1278 Ave. R. on that welfare check."

"10-4," his dispatcher replied. "Be advised that the daughter called from out of state. Her elderly mother hasn't answered phone calls for over a week."

Stiles acknowledged the info. He opened one of the gates and walked a short distance to a white door with a window located under a dilapidated car port. He knocked loudly on the door.

"Hello! Hello! Winter Haven Police! Is anybody home?"

After waiting several more seconds, he knocked again with no response. He peered through the large glass pane on the door but couldn't see anybody inside—only a dirty, unkempt kitchen. The officer walked to his left, down the side of the home, attempting to see inside through some partially closed window blinds. He saw nothing but the same filthy interior. Stiles called out, announcing his presence as he continued to investigate. Turning the corner near the back of the home, he saw another door—a solid aqua blue door that matched the rest of the hideous looking trim on the house. He tried again to get a response from anyone inside.

"Winter Haven Police! Please open the door," he yelled checking to see if the door was locked. The knob turned as he did. He yelled again and pushed the door open. The stench of rotten food and human waste made him gag. He swallowed hard.

"Police! Hello? Anybody home?"

Shielding his nose from the awful odor, he stepped further into the living room. An old TV was turned on but there was no sound coming from it. Half-eaten food and other waste littered the poorly lit room.

"Jesus Christ," he mumbled, observing the mess.

"Hello," he called out, walking into a small depressing looking bedroom. An elderly woman, startled by his presence, twitched as she sat in an antique rocking chair.

"Ma'am, I'm the police. Are you okay?" he asked, walking closer.

"What?" the woman asked.

"Are you okay?" Stiles asked again, this time in a much louder voice.

The old woman shook her head from side to side.

"I'm going to get some help, okay?" He requested EMS assistance using his shoulder radio.

Stiles realized the woman was unable to get out of the chair and had relieved herself—many times—right where she sat.

He retrieved a glass of water from the kitchen.

"Here, drink this."

She thanked him.

"People are coming to help you," he assured her, touching her on the shoulder to comfort her. The woman nodded. Her shoulders moved as she quietly sobbed.

* * *

While EMS units attended to the distressed woman, Stiles headed back to his patrol unit. In the corner of a small cluttered grass yard he observed the outline of a truck draped in a worn brown canvas tarp. He knew the older woman couldn't drive. He wondered who would park their vehicle there when the woman's only child was out of state. He investigated, pulling back the tarp. The older model, faded dark green Chevy truck looked drivable. In fact, the fast food wrappers haphazardly tossed on the back seat looked fairly new. He pulled the tarp back further, exposing the bed and rear of the truck. He didn't remember why, but something about the truck was pinging his brain. Then it hit him.

"Winter Haven, this is Bravo twenty-one. Wasn't that a green pickup truck involved in that homicide at the Subway over in Auburndale?"

He waited for a reply. Auburndale was six miles from where he stood.

"10-4. Possible make of the vehicle involved is a green Chevrolet truck."

"Didn't they get a partial tag on that vehicle?"

Stiles waited impatiently for the response.

"10-4. Partial tag is E-Echo, five niner. Echo five niner."

The patrolman's heart raced when he looked at the tag on the truck. FDY-E59.

"10-4. Can you contact PCSO Homicide? I think I may have found their truck. And can you run this tag for me? I'm outside my vehicle. FDY-E59."

* * *

"Mrs. Holcomb," Officer Stiles said, kneeling next to the elderly woman who now, thanks to EMS, was breathing oxygen through a nasal cannula and was being prepared for transport to Winter Haven Hospital.

The woman acknowledged him and reached to put her hand over his.

"There's a green truck parked in your yard. Do you know who it belongs to?"

The woman looked at Stiles with an empty stare, then nodded her head.

"Might be Ollie's," she responded.

"Who's Ollie?"

"Oh, that's my grandson. Is he here?" The woman looked around anxiously.

"No, ma'am," Stiles responded. "But we'd sure like to find him to tell him you're going to be okay. What's Ollie's last name?"

"Hickshaw." She coughed and tried again. "Hickshaw," she repeated.

"Do you know where he lives?"

The woman closed her eyes and shook her head, indicating that she didn't know.

"That's okay," Stiles tried to comfort the old woman. EMS was ready to go. "You're going to be okay."

Stiles stood by as EMS placed eighty-three-year-old Bernice Holcomb onto a stretcher for transport.

"Bravo twenty-one," he heard from his shoulder radio.

"Go ahead."

"That tag comes back to an Oliver Hickshaw with a Winter Haven address. Do you want to copy the address?"

"Yes," he answered. "Have you notified PCSO?"

"10-4. Detective Morefield is on his way to your location. Asked if you could stand by there and secure the scene."

"Tell him I'll be here."

Sixty-Five

Katie Meyers hadn't eaten much in days. Her stomach was in knots, tumbling and churning noisily. She felt like shit and didn't think she looked much better. Three days after her revelations to the governor, she found herself back in his office demanding answers. She didn't like the ones she was getting.

"That's impossible," she raised her voice. "I know what and who I saw and it was Sokol. He killed my father!" Katie stood in front of Branfield's desk. He had taken refuge behind it.

"Katie, the night your father died Richard Sokol was out of town. He was in Hershey on city business for me. I checked my old calendars and he wasn't anywhere near Allentown that day."

Katie was so furious she could scream. "I don't care what your calendar says. I saw him at my house. What would he be doing in Hershey anyway? He killed my father and now you're going to cover for him."

"Cover for him?" the governor responded. "What does that mean?"

"Exactly what I said. I know he was your bodyguard, your right-hand man when you were the mayor. Don't think I don't know that." She leaned over the desk. "I thought you were going to help me. I trusted you."

Branfield walked from behind his desk to where Katie was standing. She turned her back to him, but didn't walk away. He embraced her from behind.

"Please don't fight me on this," he whispered. Her body tensed. She tried to pull away. He held her back.

"I told you I would find out what happened. I'm telling you Sokol has an airtight alibi. Airtight. He was *not* at your house the night your father died. If somebody killed your father, it wasn't him."

Katie struggled again to pull away.

"It was not him, Katie. You think it was but it wasn't. It's been a long time and now you think you can identify a man by his limp? You want me to ruin the State Police Commissioner's career—his life—because you're seeing ghosts?"

Katie finally broke his grasp and pulled away. She faced him with fury.

"I've never seen a ghost, but I'm as sure as anything I've ever done or seen that it was Sokol leaving my house after my father was killed. If you're not going to help me, I'll have to do this myself."

Branfield scoffed. "What are you going to do, tell the South Whitehall Township Police that the State Police Commissioner killed your father."

"Maybe I will," she snapped.

"And then what will you do when they stop laughing? And who will protect you then? When you threaten the livelihood and reputation of the most powerful police officer in this state?"

"Are you trying to scare me?" Katie gritted her teeth.

"I just asked who would protect you," he responded.

"You will," she answered. "Because, if you don't, then maybe the press will find out about this little secret of ours."

"It looks like you're threatening *me* now," Branfield countered.

"You promised to help me. Sokol killed my father. You take care of it. Now." Her voice was stern and clear.

"Or what?"

Katie headed for the door then turned before she walked out.

"I just don't think the people of this state will elect you as their senator when they find out you've been screwing another one of your interns."

Branfield had never seen this side of Katie. It sounded like she had just drawn a line in the sand. He didn't like it.

Nobody threatened Logan Branfield.

Sixty-Six

BRANFIELD RETREATED FROM his reception room to the solitude of his office after a brief early afternoon press conference. The lack of sleep from the night before made his announcement seemingly unimportant. He was agitated and edgy from the blow-up with Katie the previous day. He didn't take any questions.

The governor knew that he had to tell Sokol about Katie. He couldn't afford for him to get caught off guard if she tried to do something stupid and made good on her threats. Sokol knew too much. He could bury Branfield if he ever flipped. His feelings for Katie hadn't changed. He still loved her even if, in her grief and anger, she had threatened to expose their relationship. Deep down, he didn't really think she would do it. He also knew he could never leave his wife Dana—not with his political aspirations. He feared that if he told Sokol he wouldn't be able to protect her. There was no good solution, not even for a powerful governor. He resolved to make it work. He would tell Sokol about Katie but he would call him off at the same time. He called Sokol's private office phone.

"Yes, sir?" Sokol answered.

"I need to see you. Meet me at Bricco on South Third Street. Five o'clock. I'll have a table in the back.

"Is everything okay?"

"No, it's not okay. Just be there at five."

* * *

Only a celebrity or powerful politician could score a choice table at Bricco on such short notice. At five o'clock on any given night, the best Mediterranean-Italian restaurant in the city was packed. Branfield sat at a table for two with his back to the wall near the back of the establishment. The fragrant aroma of garlic and herbs wafted from the open kitchen. He ordered a second drink before finishing the first one. At a few minutes past five, the hostess escorted Richie Sokol to the table.

"Can I get you something from the bar?" she asked.

"I'll have what he's drinking," Sokol answered.

Branfield raised his glass. "Grey Goose. Cold and neat."

"Right away," the hostess said before she walked off.

"What's going on?" Sokol slid into his seat.

"We have a problem."

"What's that?"

Branfield leaned forward so he didn't have to publicly broadcast his problems. "There's an intern I've been seeing—"

"Jesus Christ, you didn't knock this broad up did you?"

"Just shut the fuck up and listen, Richie," Branfield snapped. "Like I was saying. There's an intern. I've fallen pretty hard for her. Really hard."

"So what's the problem? Other than your wife?" Sokol offered little comfort. He would have loved to have told Branfield that he was screwing his wife every chance he got.

"I'll tell you the problem. She saw you limping down the hallway last week in my office."

Sokol listened impatiently.

"She says she's seen that limp before, Richie."

A waitress delivered Sokol's drink along with Branfield's second. Branfield waited as she set the drinks on the table. He politely waved her off.

"Her name is Katie Meyers. She's from Allentown. Chip Meyers—*Detective Chip Meyers*—was her father."

Sokol didn't know what to say. He leaned back in his chair. He struggled to hide his disgust for Branfield. "You sure live in a tangled fuckin' web, don't you?"

"She says she saw you walking out of her house on the night Meyers died," Branfield continued. "She's sure it was you. She thinks you killed her father."

"And what?" Sokol asked.

"And she wants me to have you arrested or she says she's going to the police."

Sokol smirked nervously. "Well, neither one of those things is gonna happen. Are they?" Sokol leaned forward with his hands clasped together, his elbows on the table.

"Richie. Look. I needed to tell you this because I didn't want you to get blindsided, but I've got this under control. I've told her you have an alibi—that it couldn't have been you. I will handle this. I'm going to talk to her again tonight. She just needs some time to accept it. Is that understood?"

"So you're telling me this broad is hell-bent on having me locked up for killing her father but not to fuckin' worry about it? Is that what you're asking me? Not to worry?"

"That's what I'm *telling* you Richie. Is that a problem?"

"You're goddamn right it's a problem! It's not your ass she wants strapped to a gurney or rotting away in a fuckin' hole somewhere. It's a problem that needs to be taken care of before it festers."

Branfield reached across the table and dumped the rest of his vodka into Sokol's glass. Sokol's eyes popped with surprise when Branfield spilled the 80-proof drink on the table and into Sokol's lap.

"What the fuck?" Sokol pulled back from the table and looked at his soaked pants. When he looked up, Branfield had grabbed the candle from the center of the table and menacingly dangled it over the vodka soaked tablecloth. The rest of the patrons of Bricco were too engaged in their own affairs to notice.

"You're fuckin' crazy." Sokol stared at the flame.

Branfield spoke just loud enough for Sokol to hear him. "You haven't seen crazy. I'm promising you she won't turn you in. And, I swear to you, if that beautiful woman even catches a cold while you're thinking about her, I'll take care of you myself."

Branfield set the candle down and stood up. He reached into his pocket, pulled out a fifty, and threw it on the table.

"And clean yourself up for Chrissakes," Branfield leaned in and spoke into Sokol's left ear as he started to leave. "You're the goddamn State Police Commissioner. You look like you pissed yourself."

Sixty-Seven

Ollie Hickshaw stared at the concrete walls of an interrogation room inside the Polk County Sheriff's Office. The dimly lit room was cold and damp. The inside building air was stale. Hickshaw took a deep breath—as much as his pack-a-day smoker's lungs could pull. One of the fluorescent lights on the ceiling flickered occasionally—just enough to get on his nerves. His chair wasn't very comfortable. It wasn't supposed to be. His cuffed hands rested on a plain looking metal table. A chair, identical to his, abutted the table on the opposite side. A solid metal door behind him opened. He had heard it before.

"Alright, Ollie, this is your last shot to make this work for you," Detective Andy Morefield spoke as he closed the door and walked the few steps toward the table.

"I told you, man," Hickshaw whined, "I don't know shit but you just don't want to hear that, I guess."

Morefield had been questioning Hickshaw for more than two hours. He'd been stonewalled, lied to and disrespected by the twenty-four-year-old asshole. Hickshaw had admitted only that the dark green Chevy truck discovered at his grandmother's home was his but nothing more. He claimed that sometime before the robbery-murder at the Subway his truck had been stolen. Several days later he found it abandoned on the side of the road in Lake Alfred, a city northeast of Auburndale. Morefield could tell from Hickshaw's body language that he was full of shit. Plus, his story had way too many holes in it to give it any credence. Unfortunately for Morefield, the two robbery suspects had covered their faces with bandanas before entering the store. One of the guys on the video sure looked like Hickshaw but it wasn't a lock. The identity of the other guy—the shooter—was still unknown. None of that was disclosed to Hickshaw. Not that it would have helped.

Morefield stood next to his prisoner and leaned in close enough so Hickshaw could feel the detective's breath on his face.

"You're lying to me, Ollie. You need to get straight right now."

This wasn't Hickshaw's first dance. His first ride in the back of a patrol car was at age sixteen when he was charged with aggravated battery with a knife. He was no stranger to the police station, the jail, or even cops getting in his face. He didn't budge from his position.

"Am I free to leave now?" he asked blowing his own foul-smelling breath toward Morefield.

"Not a chance," Morefield answered curtly.

"I think maybe I need to talk to a lawyer."

* * *

Morefield and Sergeant Hank Cressman gathered in Cressman's office a few doors down from the interrogation room.

The detective briefed his supervisor. "He's not budging from his bullshit story. What do you want to do?" Certainly no one wanted to have to cut Hickshaw loose. While they considered their lot, a familiar voice echoed from outside Cressman's office.

"Did you get that guy from the Subway on board yet?"

Cressman knew that voice anywhere. It was David Squires, a veteran Florida Department of Law Enforcement Special Agent assigned for several decades to Polk County. Squires and a few of his FDLE colleagues worked closely with the Sheriff's Office and local police departments especially on drug and homicide cases.

"Jesus, they'll let just about anybody in this place I guess," Cressman said, as Squires stuck his head through the office door.

Morefield spoke to his old friend.

"He's being an asshole, David. A complete asshole."

"You want me to take a run at him?" Squires asked, stroking his graying brown mustache.

"You'd just be wasting your time, buddy," Morefield answered.

"Give me a few minutes. What could it hurt?" Squires shrugged.

"Well, that sounds great but he just invoked so we can't talk to him until his attorney gets here," Morefield advised.

"He asked for an attorney?"

"He said he thought maybe he should talk to one."

"Well he can think all he wants," Squires replied. "Unless he said he definitely wants one we're still in the game. Aren't we?"

Cressman nodded. "So what's your plan, David?"

"I'm gonna read him a couple of verses from the Book of the Snake."

"What?" Cressman asked.

"Just give me five minutes." Squires headed toward the interrogation room.

* * *

"Ollie Hickshaw, I'm David Squires with FDLE."

Hickshaw started to speak.

"Just shut up and listen. I'm not asking you anything since I understand you're thinking about talking to a lawyer."

Hickshaw started to speak again.

"Shut up. I mean it. Just shut up," Squires said firmly. "I want to tell you something. Listen up."

Hickshaw sat back in his chair and puffed out his chest.

"I've been next door in another room talking to your partner in the Subway robbery. He was a tough nut to crack. Thing is, when I explained to him that since this was a murder in the course of a felony, and the shooter was going to death row, he immediately gave you up. Said you were the one who shot the kid. He says he had no idea you were going to do that when you guys walked in there. He's over there now writing it up. The only thing is, he says since you killed the kid, you're the one who knows where the gun is. I told him I thought that was bullshit and he knew where the gun was too. So while he's thinking about that, I thought I'd just let you know that it looks like you're pretty much screwed. Since he's the first guy to give it up and since you're the shooter, we don't really need to talk to you at all.

"Anyway, they'll be in here in a few minutes. They're fixin' to pack you up and take your sorry ass over to the jail," Squires finished.

Hickshaw pulled his cuffed hands into his lap. He nervously rolled his shoulders forward.

"You ain't got nobody next door. I think you're lyin' to me. How do I know you're not lyin' to me?"

"I guess you don't." Squires pulled the second chair around so it was next to Hickshaw. He turned it and straddled it, folding his hands on the top rail. "The question is, are you willing to bet your life on it? I didn't come in here to hear you talk. I just came in here to tell you you're screwed and that your partner shit all over you. If I'm not retired by then—sitting on the beach drinking one of them fancy drinks with the little umbrella—I'll see if I can get up to Starke to watch you get the needle. I'm done here."

Squires stood up to leave. In about one minute he had puckered Hickshaw's asshole shut.

"Hey," Hickshaw yelled as Squires reached for the door. Squires stopped but didn't answer. "Hey! What did you say your name was?" Squires stepped back toward Hickshaw.

"My name is Squires and you don't get to ask any more questions."

"Alright," Hickshaw said. "You know all that shit you just laid out. That's all bullshit!"

"I've already got my confession, Ollie. I don't need to talk to you."

"I want to tell you what really happened, Squires. That son of a bitch ain't putting this on me. I didn't shoot nobody. That son of a bitch."

"I'll be right back." Squires left the room and returned with a legal pad and a pen. "Write it down. From start to finish. Don't leave anything out, including where the gun is."

"What about Cabot, that lyin' son of a bitch?"

"Don't worry about him. I think he's just shit the bed. I had a feeling he was lying about not being the shooter."

"Damn straight," Hickshaw replied.

"Write it down. Everything. I'll be back in a few minutes."

Squires walked out of the room where Morefield and Cressman stood by.

"Well?" Cressman asked.

"Your other guy's name is Cabot something or other. I'll know his last name in a few minutes."

"You flipped him?" Morefield asked incredulously.

"The Book of the Snake, boys. Quote chapter and verse. He's writing his confession now."

Sixty-Eight

"SHUT THE FUCK up," the intruder snapped.

Katie Meyers felt the cold leather gloved hand snap her head back, choking her. The other hand pulled hard against her bare stomach, jerking the glass of white wine from her hand. It dropped and shattered on the floor.

"Do exactly what I say. No fuckin' problems. Got it?" The man's voice was muffled and disguised. He pulled back harder.

"Get in the bedroom," he demanded, grabbing her left wrist and forcing her arm behind her back. She grimaced from the pain. "Move!"

A streak of light from a nearby street light penetrated a narrow opening in the heavy drapes covering the bedroom windows. The man slammed Katie against the edge of the queen-sized bed, forcing her face into the comforter. She struggled against him.

"Don't . . . I will kill you."

Ignoring his threat, she fought back. Her small but fit body arched back, resisting the man who now laid on top of her. "Why are you doing this?"

"Stop," he said, pulling his left forearm tightly against her neck. "I told you to shut up!" he shouted. "Shut! Up!" His arm pulled tighter against her windpipe with each word. Her lungs labored for air. She tried to scream. She was choking and losing consciousness. The intruder released his throttle on her neck just before she passed out, then slammed his knee into the middle of her back. The sound of a buck knife snapping open behind her left ear startled and terrified her.

"Should I slit your throat now? You won't be talking then."

The intruder held the knife blade against her face. "One more sound and I *will* kill you." He pressed the cold blade harder against her cheek.

"Stop resisting me." He forced his knee harder into the middle of Katie's back, demanding submission. He folded the knife and slid it into his pocket. The intruder grabbed Katie's long blonde ponytail and yanked her head back. With his other hand, he reached in front of her and snatched her cut-off T-shirt, pulling it back over her head and down her back. His knee still anchored her small frame to the bed. He crudely bound her wrists with the shirt just above the small of her back. He pulled tight on the makeshift handcuffs.

"Please. You're really hurting me," her voice trembled.

The man laid his much heavier body on top of her, his face inches from hers.

"You should have left well enough alone," he snarled. He pounded his fist into the side of her face, opening a deep gash in her lip. The taste of warm blood filled her mouth and soaked the comforter under her face.

"Please," she sobbed hysterically.

Katie resigned to survive. The longest two minutes of her life were about to get worse. With his body lying on her left side, his right hand grabbed the back of her underwear. Her body stiffened when he pulled them to her knees.

"Oh, please don't," she pleaded.

Katie's anguish paralyzed her. The assailant's hand pressed against her—his gloved thumb penetrated her forcefully, then repeatedly. Each thrust was more painful. His pace quickened.

"You need to keep your fuckin' mouth shut. Do you understand?" he warned as he continued to violate her. The pain had overcome her mind and body. She prayed and closed her eyes. After several more torturous minutes, he stopped and rolled his body off of hers. His hands gripped and tightened around her neck. She struggled for air until she could breathe no more.

* * *

When she awoke, Katie felt nothing. She lay motionless. Her lungs spasmed, her body heaved as she desperately gasped for air. She freed her hands. There was no resistance. No intruder. With all of her heart she had fought and survived. The sound of the front door opening made her heart race.

Thank God, she thought. "I'm in here! Please help me!"

Sixty-Nine

Carly Magnanti, the governor's secretary, watched the clock on the wall in front of her. Well into her third cup of coffee, she paced near her desk, hoping desperately to see Katie walk through the doors. Something wasn't right. It didn't feel right. Katie had never missed a day at the office but she was a no show yesterday. Carly worried then but thought that maybe Katie just didn't feel well and needed the day. The chief executive's secretary didn't live in a bubble, though. When Katie left, now almost two days ago, she was visibly upset about something. Carly knew that whatever drama had transpired had happened in the governor's office. Her short graying hair and the wrinkles around her eyes said she was getting older, but she wasn't blind. She had worked for Logan Branfield since his first day as governor. She was loyal, perhaps in her mind, to a fault. She had long ago buried her distaste for his philandering—there were so many other things in life to worry about.

At ten-thirty she summoned Kirk McDonnell, the deputy chief of staff. A few minutes later he appeared at her desk.

"Have you seen Katie today?" McDonnell asked.

"No, Kirk, I haven't. That's why I called you. I'm really worried about her. She left Tuesday afternoon. She looked furious. She didn't even say goodbye. Yesterday, she wasn't here and didn't call. No call today either."

"That's strange," Kirk responded with concern.

"It's more than that, Kirk. I have a bad feeling about this."

"Look," Kirk said trying to reassure Carly, "I'm going to take an early lunch. I'll head over to her apartment and check on her. I'm sure she's okay.

Maybe she just got upset about something and went home to Allentown. I'll call you when I find out what's going on."

"Thanks, Kirk. I appreciate it more than you know." Carly sighed.

"I'll call you." McDonnell grabbed his suit jacket from his office and headed for the door.

* * *

McDonnell's stomach churned as he traversed the short walkway to Katie's front door. His increasingly louder and anxious knocks went unanswered. His heart thumped wildly when the door opened with a turn of the knob.

"Katie! Katie!" McDonnell shouted, moving further into the eerily quiet apartment.

"Katie? It's Kirk," he called again, hoping desperately for a response. Passing the kitchen, his right foot crunched something on the floor. Shattered fragments of a wine glass littered the faux wood floor. The floor was sticky and smelled sour. His concern grew greater. *Katie wouldn't leave broken glass on her floor*, he thought. "Katie!" he called again. He made his way toward the bedroom. The dark drapes made the room beyond the threshold too dark to see. He felt for a light switch on the wall next to him and flipped it on. The headboard of the bed abutted the wall to his left. A light blue comforter covered the empty queen bed. His pulse quickened when he saw bare legs, from the calf down, lying on the carpet on the far side of the bed.

"Katie!" he screamed, rushing toward the bed. He stopped when he saw the horrible sight. Katie Meyers was dead. She lay prone and nearly naked on the floor, her arms out to her sides. An amorphous pattern of dried blood encircled her head and upper body. When he stepped closer he saw clumps of dried blood on the back of Katie's head, matted into her long blonde hair. Her eyes were open and fixed in a ghastly stare.

Kirk felt nauseous and ran for the nearby bathroom. After wiping the remnants of his vomit from his lips with a wad of toilet paper, he took his cell phone from his pocket and did what any good political aide would do.

The phone rang once.

"Governor Logan Branfield's office," Carly Magnanti answered.

"Carly, it's Kirk." Still stunned at his discovery, he tried to breathe normally. His queasy stomach still swirled.

"Katie's dead."

"What?" Carly said in disbelief.

"She's dead, Carly. I need to call 9-1-1."

Carly felt a sharp, piercing pain in her chest.

"Oh my God . . ."

Seventy

"CAN I HELP you, sir?" Carly Magnanti asked, stepping out from behind her desk.

"Yes, ma'am. Detective Vincent Rodgers, Harrisburg Police Department. I have an appointment to see the governor."

"Of course, Detective," she responded. "I think he's ready for you. Just let me check." Magnanti stepped behind her desk and made a quick call to the governor. Rodgers, a tall, clean-cut former Army ranger, stood by waiting patiently.

"Right this way," she said, leading the way down the hall. Rodgers, an all-business, eighteen-year veteran of the department, followed a few steps behind. He straightened his burgundy and blue striped tie and buttoned the top button of his dark gray suit. He followed the pleasant scent of Magnanti's perfume down the hall.

With a quick knock, Magnanti gained access to the governor's inner sanctum. Branfield was waiting.

"Detective Rodgers, you said?" The governor extended his hand. Rodgers gripped it firmly and shook.

"Good to meet you, sir," he responded.

Magnanti excused herself, closing the door on the way out.

"Please, come in and have a seat," Branfield said, inviting the officer to sit in one of the two chairs opposite his desk. He sat in the other one. The lawman looked around, admiring the grandeur of the governor's private digs. He had never been this close to a governor before.

"What can I do for you, Detective? I sensed some urgency in your request to see me."

"Sir," Rodgers said respectfully, "I'm sorry to meet you under these circumstances. I hope you'll accept my sincere condolences for the loss of your intern, Ms. Meyers."

"Well, thank you, Detective," Branfield replied. "She was a bright star here in this office. It's a tragic loss to us and to everyone who knew her. A very tragic loss. I'm distraught about it."

"I understand, which is why I'm also sorry I have to ask you some of the things I have to today. I hope you'll forgive me ahead of time."

Branfield listened. "Well, go ahead, Detective. Ask away. Anything I can do to help you find the person who killed her."

Rodgers contemplated the governor's demeanor.

"Governor, what was your relationship with Ms. Meyers?"

"She was our intern. She'd been here for a short time. Two, three months. Very smart, but personable."

"Excuse me, sir," Rodgers interrupted. "I know you're a very busy man. They actually keep me pretty busy too, believe it or not." Rodgers gave a quick tight smile. "I don't want to waste our time."

"Was there something—"

Rodgers interrupted again. "I just want to know what *your* relationship was with Katie Meyers."

"She was my intern."

"Governor, we found a picture of you and Ms. Meyers in her apartment. A picture of the two of you together. It sure looks like the two of you are . . . well . . . together. Is that your answer, sir?"

"I'm not sure where this is going, Detective."

"Sir, I'm just trying to find out if you had any personal relationship with Ms. Meyers outside of her work. That's all."

"I understand what you're asking, Detective." Branfield bristled. "I have a personal relationship with everyone on my staff."

Rodgers, sensing resistance, hesitated before moving on.

Branfield seized the moment to change the subject.

"How else can I help you, Detective?"

"Well, sir, there's no good way to ask you this but we'd like to get a DNA sample if we could, just so we can quickly rule you out as a suspect."

"A suspect?" Branfield acted surprised. "Why would I be a suspect?"

"Sir, like I said," Rodgers spoke in a matter-of-fact tone, "just to rule you out. That's all. I'd just need to take a swab or two of your cheek inside your mouth. I can do it right now."

"Well, I don't see why that's necessary," Branfield protested, then reluctantly acquiesced.

"Alright. I'll do it before you leave . . . What else?" Branfield asked.

"Governor, do you own a firearm?"

"I do."

"What kind?"

"It's a Walther PPK .380. Can I ask why you want to know that? No one said Katie was shot. Was she shot?"

Rodgers could tell the governor was getting upset.

"Sir, the cause of death hasn't been released publicly."

Branfield stood up.

"Well, Detective, I've been cooperative with you. You come in here to my office. I voluntarily agreed to speak with you. I've agreed to give you a DNA sample, though I'm not sure why, and now you want to know about my gun, but can't or won't tell me if Katie was shot. I am the goddamned governor in case you've forgotten. You don't have to release it publicly to tell me. Just tell me. Was she shot?"

Rodgers tried his best to stay calm and professional.

"Sir, I'm sorry. I don't have the authority to release that information. That's not my decision. I'm sorry."

"Well who in the hell's decision is it then," Branfield snapped.

"That would be the District Attorney, sir."

Branfield thought about getting a drink. He damn sure needed one but rejected the idea. He tried to settle down and returned to the chair.

"Okay. So, do you want to see my gun?"

"I would, sir."

"It's at the mansion. I'd be glad to give it to you. I assume I'll get it back. If someone stops by in the morning, I'll make sure it's unloaded. You can do the DNA swab then, if that's okay."

Rodgers nodded. "That would be great. Oh-seven-hundred?"

Branfield looked unsure.

"I'm sorry, sir." Rodgers caught himself. "Is seven a.m. okay?"

"Yes. Perfect," Branfield responded. "Anything else, Detective?"

"Governor, just one more quick question. Again, I apologize for having to ask this but, have you ever been inside Ms. Meyers's apartment?"

Branfield had hit his limit. He rose from his chair.

"Detective, I'm as sad as anyone about Katie's death, and I think I've been more than cooperative with you. I hope you catch her killer. I really do. But I assure you, you are not making any progress to that end by being here with me. It seems to me that this meeting should be over."

Branfield waved his hand toward the door, directing his now unwelcome visitor to leave.

Rodgers got up and walked toward the door.

"Sir, I thank you sincerely for your time. I'm sorry for the inconvenience and for some of my questions."

"Good day, Detective," Branfield said, ignoring the apology. He motioned toward the door. "You get out the same way you came in."

Seventy-One

THE BRILLIANCE OF the rising sun reflected off the waters of the Susquehanna River, welcoming the inhabitants of Harrisburg to the magic of another beautiful Saturday morning. Nearly a mile wide, the glistening expanse flowed south through Pennsylvania's capital city. A.J. Scarlett, the duly-elected District Attorney for Dauphin County, headed north on Front Street in her restored 1965 red Mustang convertible. She flipped her custom aviator-style sunglasses from the top of her head to her face to block the glare of the sun dancing off the river to the east, leaving her long chestnut hair flowing freely in the breeze. Dressed casually in a pair of tight fitting skinny black jeans and a white button-down blouse, she punched the gas and passed a slower moving vehicle in front of her. Her destination—the governor's mansion—was just a mile away.

Katie Meyers had been dead for almost three weeks.

* * *

"Ms. Scarlett, please come in," Governor Branfield welcomed his guest. He had agreed to meet the first term county prosecutor at his residence rather than at his office to avoid unwanted attention, especially by the press. Scarlett promised only that she had important confidential business to discuss with the Chief Executive. The governor led Scarlett to an office not far from the front door.

"Please, sit down," he said cordially. "Can I get you something to drink?"

Scarlett politely declined.

"Well, Ms. Scarlett, to what do I owe this pleasure?"

The District Attorney felt Branfield's lecherous stare undressing her with his eyes.

"No pleasure today, Governor," she replied. "Sorry if that disappoints you." She had little time for games.

Branfield managed a tense smile.

"So, what does A.J. stand for?" he asked, not easily dissuaded.

"It's just A.J.," she replied tersely. Her parents and the few men she had shared her bed with called her Andie. She didn't think anyone else needed to know.

"Well, A.J., what can I do for you?"

"I'm here to talk about Katie Meyers."

"What about her," Branfield asked. "Have you found her killer yet?"

"I think we have."

"You have? Well? Please tell me."

Scarlett continued without answering.

"Governor, we found your fingerprints all over Katie's apartment. All over. The kitchen, the bathroom, the bedroom." Scarlett looked for a reaction. "The *headboard* in the bedroom."

Branfield listened, but said nothing.

"There are neighbors who saw you coming and going from Katie's apartment. Late at night, early morning. They saw you using a key to get in. You lied to Detective Rodgers. You told him you had never been to her apartment."

"I said no such thing. No such thing. He asked me and I didn't answer him. I didn't lie."

"Well that's great, Governor," she replied, "are you now saying that you have been to her apartment?"

Branfield took a deep breath. "I've been there. Yes. A number of times, and yes, she gave me a key."

"Do you want to elaborate?"

"No. I don't. Is that what you came here to tell me? That my fingerprints were in her house?"

Scarlett contemplated her next disclosure.

"The coroner says Katie was forcibly assaulted. She had some tearing and abrasions. She was raped."

Branfield rubbed the back of his neck. "I didn't know that," his voice trailed off. "That's terrible."

"Your semen was inside of her. I assume that means you were, too."

Branfield lowered his head and closed his eyes.

"I'm not finished. Shall I go on?" Scarlett asked.

Branfield looked up. His hand nervously tugged at the collar of his blue-striped polo shirt. "I cared deeply for Katie. I could never have hurt her. Never."

"Really?" Scarlett said, her patience waning. "Then maybe you can explain how a bullet from your gun smashed through the back of her skull and ripped into her head."

"That's impossible," Branfield protested. "Just impossible."

"No, Governor. That's the truth. Katie's killer got into her apartment without forced entry. You have a key. She was raped. Your semen was found inside her. Then she was executed with a shot to the back of her head with your gun. I won't even waste my time talking to you about the text messages that show how pissed off she was at you the day she was killed. That's what I'll leave you with." Scarlett stood to leave.

Branfield followed her through the office door, silently seething at the prosecutor's allegations. His rage got the better of him by the time she reached the front doors.

"You forget, Ms. Scarlett," Branfield shouted, "I'm the governor of this state. I'm not afraid of you."

The prosecutor turned and walked back to Branfield.

"My advice to you is to find the best lawyer you can," Scarlett said, standing nearly eye-to-eye with the man she suspected of murder. "The next time I see you I'll have an arrest warrant." She glared at Branfield.

"I'm not afraid of you either."

Seventy-Two

THE JET-BLACK CHEVY Suburban with dark tinted windows navigated the narrow sloping driveway off Fish Hatchery Road down past the old white cattle barn and into the gravel parking lot. The driver pulled the vehicle to the west end of the lot beyond the only two other vehicles parked there. The large SUV stopped on the grass beyond the gravel, almost in front of the stone fly shop building. The sound of the powerful V-8 engine so close to the shop got Old Ronnie's attention. He stood in the wooden frame doorway as a tall black man, sharply dressed in a dark charcoal suit, appeared from the driver's area of the vehicle. The man locked eyes with Ronnie and walked closer.

"I'm looking for Thax Colby," he announced.

Ronnie didn't know who the man was, nor had he bothered to say. Part of him wanted to protect Thax's privacy. The other part saw this as something official. He didn't sense anything threatening.

"Upstream about a hundred yards," Ronnie answered, pointing in that direction. "I'm sure he's in the river."

The man nodded and thanked him. Ronnie watched the man walk in the direction of the two huge willows.

The sweeping crowns of the willow trees provided broken cover from the rising midmorning sun. Moments earlier, Thax had delicately landed a blue-winged olive fly slightly upstream from a small group of smooth bowling-ball-sized submerged rocks. The water swirled ever so slightly as it rushed over them. In a slither of slower water behind the rocks, a decent sized wild brown trout waited. Then, in a microsecond, the surface of the water erupted as the hungry fish gobbled the fly. Thax landed and released it. He started to wade further upstream.

"Thax Colby?" a voice called from the river bank. Thax turned to see the man in the suit. He took a few steps closer.

"Who wants to know?"

"I'm Trooper Clarence Woodson, Pennsylvania State Police. I'm terribly sorry to disturb your fishing. Can I please have a minute of your time?"

His curiosity piqued, Thax waded to the edge of the river.

"Trooper Woodson, before I get out of the water, do you want to tell me why you're here?"

"Yes sir, Mr. Colby. Actually, I'm Governor Branfield's driver and bodyguard. He's in the parking lot in the car. He'd like a few minutes of your time, sir."

"Really?" Thax bristled.

"Sir, I don't know the history. I heard of you when I was a road trooper. I know who you are. I know you're one of the good guys. I also know it was a silent ride from Harrisburg this morning. There's a lot of tension sitting in that vehicle back there."

Thax nodded.

"If you don't talk to him, sir, it's going to be a really long ride home for me." Woodson shrugged his broad, athletic shoulders.

"Do you know what this is about?" Thax asked.

"No, sir."

"Okay," Thax responded. "Do you see that old green park bench over there?" Thax pointed to the bench just upstream from where they stood. "I'll talk to him there. Just him. Tell him he's got five minutes. I'm going to walk up the path for a few minutes. He needs to be here when I get back."

"I'll get him now. Thank you, sir," the trooper said before he took off running back to the governor's vehicle.

* * *

Thax walked up to the bench where the governor stood anxiously awaiting his arrival.

"Mr. Colby." The governor extended his hand. "Thank you for seeing me."

Thax reached over and leaned his fly rod on the bench, ignoring Branfield's outstretched hand.

Thax looked at his watch. "Your five minutes is ticking away. What do you want?"

"A.J. Scarlett, the District Attorney of Dauphin County, is about to charge me with murder."

Thax put his hand to his face to hide his grin.

"I had an intern in my office," Branfield continued. "Her name was Katie Meyers. She was murdered. I'm sure you remember her father Chip Meyers. He was an Allentown narcotics detective who killed himself when I was the mayor here. She was going to school in Harrisburg and was my intern."

"Your intern?" Thax snickered.

"I obviously know what you're thinking, Colby, so I'll tell you right now. I guess we've been down this road before. She and I were . . . intimate." Branfield turned and looked toward the water. His voice crackled as he spoke. "I know it sounds wrong, but I loved her." Thax studied Branfield's emotional response. "I really loved her."

"I'm sorry," Thax said. "I'm sorry that she's dead. I'm sorry that you preyed on another college girl—"

"Just stop, Colby," a perturbed Branfield interrupted. I didn't come here for a goddamn lecture. I came here because I need the best lawyer I can find in this state, and unfortunately, you're it. I don't like you one bit and I know for certain you don't like me."

"Then why would you think I would represent you, Governor?"

"I know one thing about you," Branfield answered. "I know that you don't care about politics or anything else when it comes to making sure that justice is done. You just want the truth."

"So why would I represent *you*?"

"One reason. Because I didn't do it," Branfield said emphatically.

Thax looked in the governor's eyes and held the gaze.

"Your five minutes are up."

"Thank you for your time," an exhausted-looking Branfield said, again extending his hand toward Thax. Thax reached for his fly rod. Branfield turned and walked away. When he was ten yards down the path, Thax called to him.

"A million dollars."

The governor turned and walked back to Thax.

"One million dollars is my fee. A cashier's check delivered within three days. It will be placed in a trust account. That's not negotiable and it is not refundable," Thax informed him.

Branfield listened.

"The defense is done my way and only my way. No exceptions."

Branfield stood on the path listening.

"Yes or no?" Thax asked.

Branfield nodded. "Yes."

Seventy-Three

Andy Morefield cracked the cap off an ice-cold Bud Light from the refrigerator in his garage. Half the bottle was gone before he could feel the cold liquid rushing down his parched throat. He held the bottle against his forehead, an old trick his dad had taught him when he was a kid as an attempt to battle the oppressive central Florida heat. Of course, back then it was a bottle of Coke. Morefield wasn't sure he was enjoying this day off anyway. Before heading back out to finish trimming the hedge of sweet viburnum between his and his neighbor's property, he checked his cell phone. He was elated at the news from Sgt. Hank Cressman.

Cabot Patterson in custody. Gun and money seized. Call ASAP.

Patterson's capture was long overdue. Morefield had searched for him since Ollie Hickshaw had identified him as the Subway shooter—as he was now known. Morefield called his boss.

"We got his ass," Cressman proclaimed happily. "A marked unit stopped him down near the high school in Eagle Lake. He had a .45 in the car along with a few hundred dollars and some weed."

"Is he talking?" Morefield asked.

"No. According to the deputy who arrested him, he hasn't said shit. I told him not to even try until you have at him. Just get your ass in here."

"Will do, Sarge."

"Oh, hey," Cressman continued, "I'll tell you more about this when you get here but I also got a call from ATF over in Tampa. They've got some national ballistics database or something like that. Looks like they matched our shell casing to a double homicide up in Pennsylvania. Same gun they say. I don't know how they did it but that's what he told me. Anyway, it sounds like this guy has a lot of explaining to do."

Morefield set his beer down. "I'll be there as soon as I can."

* * *

Morefield sat across the table from Cabot Patterson in the PCSO interrogation room and listened to the young man speak.

"Me and Ollie was just trying to hit a quick score. We didn't mean to hurt nobody. I don't know what happened. One minute we was in the door and the next I felt the gun going off. It was like a bad dream, man. A bad dream."

Patterson hung his head and rubbed his cuffed hands around on the table.

"I'm really sorry about the kid behind the counter. He just didn't move very fast. I shoved the gun forward and it must have gone off when I did. I wasn't aiming to kill nobody."

Morefield had heard so many excuses in his years as a detective and most of them were bullshit. He didn't think much of this story, one way or the other. It was a confession. It wouldn't bring his victim back but it might provide some solace to his family. At least they wouldn't have to relive their nightmare in a courtroom, except to see Patterson sentenced.

"What happens now?" Patterson asked.

"Now you can tell me about Pennsylvania, that's what happens."

"Pennsylvania?"

"Yeah. Pennsylvania," Morefield pressed.

"Man, what about it? I ain't never been there."

"Come on, Cabot. You've been straight with me so far. Don't lie to me now."

"I don't know what you're talking about. Honest. I ain't never been to Pennsylvania. I ain't never been out of Florida except for once when we visited my Grandpap up in Georgia. That was a long time ago. I was like eight or nine. Pennsylvania. No sir. Never been there."

"Look, your gun, it was used in a crime in Pennsylvania. Now I know that for a fact."

"Man, I got this gun at a pawn shop a few years ago. I ain't never committed another crime with it and I damn sure haven't been in Pennsylvania. I'm being straight with you, Detective. I swear."

"What pawn shop did you get the gun at?" Morefield asked.

"It's the one right there off of Main in Auburndale."

"Just down past the do-it-yourself pest control and the laundromats?"

"That's it. That's the one," Patterson confirmed.

* * *

Two bells tied to a shoelace banged against the top of the glass door to Scrubbs Pawn Shop announcing Detective Morefield's arrival. A few seconds later, a bearded man in his early thirties appeared from a room behind the long glass display case.

"Can I help you?" the man asked.

Morefield flashed his badge.

"I'm Detective Morefield. Polk County Sheriff's Office. I need some information on a gun you sold a couple of years ago."

"That's a long time ago, Detective. You know I don't need to keep those records longer than sixty days." The man resisted. "What are we talking about?"

"You sold a .45 Smith & Wesson to a guy named Cabot. Cabot Patterson." Morefield showed the clerk a mug shot photo of Patterson.

"That's not ringing a bell," the man replied.

Morefield pushed a photo of the gun across the glass counter top. "How about that?"

The clerk nodded and looked at Morefield.

"I assume this guy's in some kind of trouble or you wouldn't be asking," the clerk fished for information.

"Look, this guy sent us here. You're not getting anybody in trouble. If anything, you're helping him out."

The clerk contemplated his response.

"You remember him, don't you?" Morefield asked, sensing the clerk's reluctance.

"Not really. I do remember the gun though."

"What about it?"

"It was a nice gun. It was almost new. The guy who pawned it's been coming in here for several years. He's a good friend of my sister."

"Who's the guy?" Morefield pushed. The clerk hesitated. "He's not in any trouble either," Morefield assured him.

"Well, I guess it doesn't matter any way. The cancer's probably gonna take him any day now. If it hasn't already."

"What's his name?"

"Jimmie Lee Powell."

"Do you know where we can find him?"

"Yeah," the clerk said somberly. "I'm pretty sure I do."

Seventy-Four

"CALL YOUR NEXT witness, Mr. Colby."

Thax stood to address presiding Dauphin County Common Pleas Judge Robert Nescott. All eyes in the overflowing capacity third-floor courtroom focused on the governor's defense counsel.

"The defense calls Logan Branfield."

The courtroom reacted with hushed whispers. Thax turned his head to look at his client who sat stunned and motionless, just an arm's length away. Branfield's eyes darted contemptuously toward his attorney.

"May I have a moment, Your Honor?" Thax asked, quickly sitting next to Branfield.

"What in the hell is this, Colby?"

"You're going to testify, Governor."

"About what?"

"You're going to tell them everything. *Everything,*" Thax answered. "And you're going to do it now."

"What are you doing, Colby? You can't just call me up there," Branfield fumed. "We haven't prepared. I don't know what to say or how to answer."

"Let's try the truth this time, Governor."

"You can't do this goddammit," Branfield protested.

"I can. And I just did. My way. Remember, Governor?" Thax started to get up but Branfield grabbed his arm.

"Don't fuck me over," he growled, thinking only of how this would affect his political future.

Thax seethed at Branfield's arrogance. He stared into the empty soul that was Logan Branfield. "No one's ever been elected senator from state prison. Now get up there."

"Mr. Colby? Is everything okay?" Judge Nescott inquired, having waited long enough.

"Thank you, Your Honor." Thax repeated himself. "The defense calls Logan Branfield."

Thax's direct examination quickly covered the introductions and dispensed with what he considered extraneous matters. He was never one to waste the court's time.

"Governor, what was your relationship with Katie Meyers?"

"She was my intern."

Thax waited for more.

Branfield hesitated. He searched the front row of the gallery for Dana, who looked on stoically. All of the drama of the Harlin trial swirled in his brain. Uncontrollable anxiety coursed through his body.

"And . . . she was my lover."

The courtroom erupted at his disclosure. A few reporters rushed out hoping to be the first to report the salacious news.

"For how long?"

"About three months."

"Had you been to her apartment?"

"Yes. Numerous times. I had a key."

"Did your security detail know?"

"No. It was always a secret visit, if you will."

"Did you go to Katie's apartment on April 5th, the day she was killed?"

Branfield looked toward the floor then back at Thax.

"I did."

"Why?" Thax pressed.

"To make up?"

"Make up for what?"

"We had a fight. We both said some things we didn't mean. There were a lot of texts going back and forth." Branfield looked at the jury. "You've seen some of them."

"She threatened to expose your affair, didn't she?

Branfield nodded. "Yes, she did."

"And you weren't very happy about that, were you?"

"No. I wasn't."

"So you had a blow up?"

"Yes."

"Tell us why she threatened to expose the affair."

"Well, it was complicated."

"We've got time, Governor." Thax leaned against the lectern. "Explain it to us."

Branfield tried to make eye contact with the jurors. Most looked disgusted but intrigued. "Katie's father was a police detective in Allentown when I was the mayor there. They said he committed suicide. She never believed that. She said that she saw a man leaving her house the night her father was killed. She told me she had seen the same man, after all these years, and she wanted my help."

"Help to do what?"

"To have him arrested."

"And you couldn't do that?"

"It wasn't that simple."

"Why not?"

"Because the person she thought did it was someone . . . a public figure and a friend. Not an accusation you make lightly."

"Who was it, Governor?"

"Objection, Your Honor," A.J. Scarlett pounced to her feet. "I object to anything she told him as hearsay."

"Sustained."

That was fine, Thax thought. He'd do it another way.

"Do you know the person she accused?"

"Yes, I do."

"Did you tell this person that Katie had identified them as her father's killer?"

"Yes, I did."

"Did you tell this person that you were having an affair with Katie Meyers?"

"I did."

"Is that the only other person you told about your affair with Katie Meyers?"

"Yes."

Thax turned toward the jury. "Governor, who did you tell about your affair?"

Scarlett sprang to her feet. "Objection. Hearsay."

"No. I don't think so Ms. Scarlett." Judge Nescott replied. "Overruled."

"You can answer, Governor," Thax directed.

"I told Richard Sokol. The State Police Commissioner."

Thax waited to ask his next question. Several jurors leaned back in their chairs as they absorbed the governor's testimony. When Thax was sure that everyone had connected the dots he moved on.

"When you went to her apartment on April 5th, were you still fighting?"

"No. Katie had settled down. She wanted me to come over for make-up . . . so we could make up."

"Were you going to say make-up sex, Governor?"

"I guess you could call it that."

"I just did, Governor," Thax responded. "Would you call it something else?"

"No, I guess not."

"What time did you get to Katie's apartment?"

"Six o'clock."

"Did she send you a text earlier telling you what time to come?"

"She did."

"When you arrived was Katie alive?"

"She was."

"Did you have sex with her?"

"I did."

"Rough sex?"

"No."

"Consensual sex?"

"Of course. We had made up. She agreed to give me some more time to investigate her identification."

"Did you have a gun with you?"

"Absolutely not."

"The .380 handgun you voluntarily surrendered to the Harrisburg Police, where did you normally keep it?"

"In my home. We keep it in the closet."

"Governor Branfield, did you hurt Katie Meyers in any way either on April 5th or at any time since you had met her?"

"No. Never."

"Before you left her on April 5th what was the status of your relationship?"

"Katie was relieved. She believed I would help her. We were happy. We told each other 'I love you'."

"Was Katie alive when you left?"

"Very much so."

"Last question, Governor. Did Police Commissioner Richard Sokol know you were going there to see Katie Meyers on April 5th?"

"Yes, he did."

The realization of what had just transpired hit Branfield like a ton of bricks. He felt ashamed, but relieved.

"I have no further questions for this witness, Your Honor,"

Thax announced, exchanging a look with Scarlett.

Scarlett stood for cross-examination. She passed Thax on her way to the lectern. Her rock-solid case was cracking. Thax whispered a few words to his opponent.

"I think we're almost done. Don't you think so, Andie?"

Seventy-Five

Richie Sokol pulled up his plain white boxer shorts and sat on the edge of his bed. What was supposed to be twenty minutes of mind-numbing sex with the governor's wife had failed on almost all accounts. He stared out of the pair of six-foot high windows in his upscale condo on the East Shore, north of downtown Harrisburg.

"Chip Meyers wasn't supposed to die," he said, shaking his head.

Dana Branfield slid her still naked body across the bed and hugged him from behind. A folded one-page document on his night stand held his attention. The trial subpoena, served on him by a county constable at Thax Colby's request, directed him to appear tomorrow in Judge Nescott's courtroom to testify in the governor's murder trial. He picked it up to crumple it, then stopped and tossed it back on the table.

"What are you talking about?" Dana probed, sitting up next to him. "What does Chip Meyers have to do with this?"

"Chip Meyers is the reason for all of this," he continued.

Dana listened while Richie struggled to reveal more.

He nervously folded his fingers together. "Meyers was on the take, like we all were. The feds subpoenaed him to the grand jury. I didn't think he was going to talk, but he was distraught and scared. I called him at his home the night he . . . he was obviously drinking. I thought he was okay but then he said something that made me think he was going to kill himself."

Dana reached for his hands but he pulled away.

"I was only a few minutes away from his house. I had a copy of his house key. I made copies of all my guys' keys. They left them in their desk drawers and jackets. I guess I was just paranoid, but anyway . . . I was really concerned for him. I got there and walked around the house. I'd been there a bunch of times for different shit. I knew his office was in the back. There was a light on and I couldn't really see through the cracks in the blinds but I figured he was in there. I unlocked the back door and walked to his office. The house was quiet. Real quiet. When I walked in he was passed out with his head laying on the desk. His gun was sitting there too. It looked like he had passed out before he could do it or had decided not to. Who knows? I was so damn relieved that he hadn't killed himself."

Sokol folded his arms and tilted his head back, momentarily closing his eyes.

Dana put her hand on his thigh. "What happened?"

"I just stood there for a few seconds. Then I saw it. My notebook. He had stolen my fuckin' notebook. That notebook had entries for every penny we'd taken over the years. I don't even know how Chip got his hands on it. I kept it in my office. I was so goddamn mad. I was enraged. I felt like he had betrayed us all and was going to give us all up along with the notebook. It had everybody's name in it. I mean *everybody*. He was going to rat us out."

Sokol stood up and walked toward the sliding doors. A nearly full moon illuminated the rolling landscape behind his home.

"So I panicked. I grabbed the gun and pulled him back and sat him up in his chair. He rustled a little bit. I don't think he really opened his eyes. Then . . . then I put the gun in his hand, put it to his head and I pulled the trigger."

"Oh my God." Dana sat in shocked silence.

"I know." Sokol shook his head. "There was blood and brains everywhere. On me, too. I lifted the notebook from where is was on the desk, holding it by the edges. I was going to take the whole notebook but there was so much blood and shit everywhere. I was afraid the gunshot woke someone in the house. I didn't know what I was going to do then. I knew if I took it there would be something missing on the desk. It would be suspicious. All this was running through my head in a few seconds. I just had to get the hell out of there. I grabbed the metal binding, tore the pages out and put the notebook back on the desk. I heard Chip gurgle. I don't know if he was still alive or if it was just his body . . . Jesus Christ. I can't believe I'm telling you this."

Dana didn't know what to say so she didn't say anything.

"Katie Meyers was just a kid then, but she said she saw me limping out of their house. I left there so fast I wouldn't have seen her if I had tripped over her. Logan told me she saw me limping down the hallway in his office and told him it was me who killed her father."

Sokol walked around the bed to his closet where he opened a small black floor safe. A few seconds later he came out of the closet.

"These are the pages from the notebook."

Dana walked around the bed and picked up her underwear off the floor. She put them on then reached for her T-shirt that she had flung over the arm of a chair in the corner of the room on top of her jeans.

"Are you leaving?" Sokol asked, expecting that his confession had been too much for her to hear.

"No, I'm not leaving."

She slid into her jeans and snapped her long red hair into a ponytail. Sokol felt relieved.

"So, how bad did that asshole husband of yours drop me in the grease today?" he asked.

"Pretty bad. More than pretty bad, in fact. He said Katie Meyers had identified you as the man who killed her father. That he told you about it and that you knew he was going over to her apartment that night."

"Implying what?" he asked.

"Implying that *you* killed her because she was going to identify you. That's what."

Sokol had just come clean about Chip Meyers. Despite his bravado, his nerves were still raw from his disclosure. He damn sure wasn't taking the fall for killing Meyers's daughter.

"Well, guess what?" Sokol said angrily. "I did go there. And I roughed her up pretty good. I told her she needed to keep her mouth shut. But I *didn't* kill her."

"Well, you can say whatever you want, but tomorrow, when Logan's lawyer gets done with you, they're going to believe you did it. And he's going to walk out of there."

"Like hell he is!" Sokol furiously gripped the pages of the notebook. "I'm tired of all of this bullshit." He released his death grip on the notebook pages and shuffled through the first couple of pages. "I'm not falling on my sword for him again. He can spend the rest of his life in prison. I'm not doing this shit anymore. No more."

"What does that mean?" Dana stepped closer. "What are you going to do?"

"I'm going to talk to the DA. That's what I'm going to do. I think she'll be very interested in what I have to say." He held up the pages from the notebook. "What these have to say. Your husband got his cut on every one of these scores. Every single one. While our guys were kicking in doors and getting shot at, he sat on his ass, collecting his cut. How do you think he bought all that nice shit for you? On the mayor's salary? He thinks he's going to drop me in the grease. Fuck him! I'll bet the U.S. Attorney would love to see these too."

"You can't do that," Dana warned.

"The hell I can't. Why not?"

"Because I can't let you."

Sokol couldn't believe it. "You're really going to protect him?"

"I've always protected him. I can't let you do it. It will destroy him."

Sokol was incredulous. "You can't *let* me?"

Dana retrieved her purse from the nearby dresser. "No, I can't."

Seventy-Six

Bailiff Eddie Jones open the courtroom doors and called for the next witness.

"Richard Sokol." He waited momentarily for a response. He called again. "Richard Sokol."

Jones looked for the witness to appear from the moblike gatherings of hopeful spectators throughout the hallway for whom there was not yet an available seat in the packed courtroom. He walked in both directions of the hallway summoning the witness without a response.

"Richard Sokol," he bellowed one last time before returning to the courtroom.

All eyes were fixed on the retired lawman-turned-bailiff when he entered the courtroom and stood at attention near the doors.

"Your Honor," he announced, "the witness has not harkened to my call."

Judge Nescott thanked the bailiff.

"Ladies and gentlemen," the judge addressed the jury, "I'm going to send you back to the jury room for a few moments. We have some legal matters to discuss outside your presence."

The anxious audience looked on in anticipation as the jury filed out of the jury box back to their appointed quarters.

Thax's eyes met Scarlett's glancing in his direction. They exchanged a warm smile.

"All right," Judge Nescott began after assuring that the jurors were out of the courtroom, "how do you wish to proceed, Mr. Colby?"

"Your Honor, I was informed last night that the constable was able to serve the witness with my subpoena after court concluded yesterday. The witness is the State Police Commissioner. He certainly knows the consequences of not appearing for a subpoena."

"Well, I would hope so, Mr. Colby. I would hope so," Nescott commented.

"I would ask the Court to issue a bench warrant for his arrest."

"Anything you want to add, Ms. Scarlett?" the judge inquired.

"No, Your Honor."

"Well, based on what the Court and the jury heard from the defendant yesterday, if believed, it would appear that Commissioner Sokol may have a whole host of reasons for not wanting to appear and subject himself to examination under oath. The warrant will issue."

Branfield listened intently as Judge Nescott spoke. He gripped a ball-point pen in his right hand, nervously clicking the cap on and off. He looked at his wife who still sat behind him. Although they hadn't spoken a word to each other since his testimony, he still looked to her for support. She managed a small, uncomfortable smile. He nodded, acknowledging her presence.

"Are you ready with your next witness, Mr. Colby?" Nescott asked.

"Your Honor, if we could maybe take fifteen minutes, I'm sure I'll be ready to go. Obviously, I wasn't anticipating Mr. Sokol's nonappearance."

"Very well. Let's all be back and ready to go at ten o'clock."

Seventy-Seven

"THE DEFENSE CALLS Abigail Sutton," Thax announced standing behind defense counsel's table.

The courtroom spectators focused on Abigail as she entered the courtroom and walked confidently up the center aisle toward the front of the judge's bench. She was dressed conservatively in a knee length navy blue buckle dress—her trademark stiletto heels replaced with some less flashy navy pumps. Her long, curly brunette hair was set in an up-do. She gave the jury a friendly smile as she stepped into the well of the courtroom.

"Please come forward to be sworn," the courtroom deputy clerk directed.

Having been sworn and seated in the witness box, Abigail focused her attention on Thax standing at the lectern between the two counsel tables.

"Good morning, Ms. Sutton."

"Good morning."

"Ms. Sutton, so everybody knows, you and I know each other, don't we?"

"We do." Abigail nodded.

"Tell the jury how we know each other, please."

Abigail looked at the jury.

"I was Mr. Colby's legal secretary for almost fifteen years at the U.S. Attorney's Office in Allentown."

"What did you do before you worked in the U.S. Attorney's Office?"

"I worked for my father. He owned Sutton Jewelers on Hamilton Street in Allentown. He ran the business for thirty-eight years until he retired a few years ago."

"How long did you work for your father?"

"Almost eight years."

"And what did you do at the business?"

"Well, for the first year or so I sold jewelry, mostly diamonds, but some other rare gems as well. After that, my father wanted me to learn the business, so I learned it from him and eventually I started buying and appraising diamonds."

"How long did you do that?"

"For about six years."

Thax walked toward the clerk's table where he grabbed a clear plastic evidence bag and approached the witness box.

"Ms. Sutton, I am showing you what has been identified and admitted into evidence as,"—Thax stopped and read from the label on the bag—"miscellaneous items from victim's bedroom floor. That's Commonwealth's exhibit twenty-eight."

He handed the bag to Abigail.

"You'll see that there are a number of different items in that bag Ms. Sutton. Do you see any jewelry in there?"

Abigail manipulated the bag to view the contents.

"Yes, there appears to be an earring in the bag."

"Only one?" Thax asked.

"It appears so."

"Anything else?"

Abigail again looked through the numerous items in the bag.

"No other jewelry," she responded.

"On the label on the front of the bag, under where it says miscellaneous items, does it list the items in the bag?"

"It does. Do you want me to read it?"

"Does it say anything about jewelry?"

Abigail held up the bag.

"It says costume jewelry, one piece."

Thax retrieved the bag and walked toward the prosecution counsel's table.

"Your Honor, may I have Detective Rodgers open the evidence bag and get the earring out?"

"You may, Mr. Colby. Detective, could you please assist us?"

A.J. Scarlett rose to her feet.

"Your Honor, while Detective Rodgers is doing that may we approach sidebar?"

"Come on up," Judge Nescott responded.

Thax and Scarlett walked to the side of the judge's bench opposite to the witness box to have a private conversation out of earshot of the witness and the jury.

"What is it counsel?" the Court inquired of Scarlett.

"Judge, I haven't objected to this witness or to the line of questioning but I'd really like to know where this is going."

"Mr. Colby?"

"Judge, I've provided the District Attorney with Ms. Sutton's qualifications and told her I may call her to examine and give her opinion about some costume jewelry that was collected at the crime scene. She's never objected. I'm just asking this witness about the Commonwealth's evidence at this point. I'm not required to give the prosecutor a full road map for my defense. I'm not sure what she thinks has been objectionable."

"Me, either," the Court replied. "Do you have an objection, Ms. Scarlett?"

"Not yet." Scarlett answered.

"Well, when you do, I'm sure you'll let me know. Let's continue," the judge directed as the short sidebar conference concluded.

"Where's this going, Thax?" Scarlett asked as the two attorneys walked away from the bench.

"I guess we'll see, Andie. Don't worry, I'll connect all the dots," Thax quipped. Scarlett smirked at his coyness.

The court returned to order.

"Do we have that earring out?" the Court asked.

Thax continued.

"Ms. Sutton, could you please take a look at this earring?" Thax handed the earring—a yellow-colored stone in a simple gold setting—to the witness. Abigail examined it for a few seconds.

"May I use my jeweler's loupe?" she asked, referring to a 10x magnification eyepiece commonly used by jewelers.

"You may," Judge Nescott answered, now sitting forward in his chair listening intently.

Abigail retrieved the loupe from the small purse she had carried with her to the witness stand. She examined the yellow stone.

"Ms. Sutton, what can you tell me about this costume jewelry?"

"This isn't costume jewelry at all. This is a yellow diamond—a *real* diamond. About a carat and a half. The setting appears to be fourteen carat yellow gold."

"A real diamond?"

"Yes."

"And if I had the matching earring—"

Abigail interrupted.

"You would be able to make some woman very, very happy."

The courtroom erupted with laughter.

"What would that pair of earrings cost, approximately?"

"Well, if I was doing a real appraisal I would need to do this in a shop with a lot more detail, but approximately, this pair would be somewhere around twelve to fifteen thousand dollars, maybe more."

"Something your average college student could afford?"

"Objection, Your Honor." Scarlett jumped to her feet.

"Sustained."

Thax continued without skipping a beat, acting oblivious to the anticipated objection. He walked to the clerk's table again, this time shuffling through a stack of crime scene photos.

"Ms. Sutton, I apologize for asking you to look at these photos but if you could just examine this one—Commonwealth's exhibit forty-seven. It's a photo of the victim laying on the floor alongside her bed. Could you look at it, please?"

Thax handed the photograph to Abigail.

"Could we please pull this up on the jury's screens so everybody can look at it?" he asked.

With the assistance of the paralegal sitting at the prosecutor's table, the photo was projected onto monitors in the jury box and on the judge's bench.

While the jurors looked at the photo, Thax continued.

"Ms. Sutton, can you see the earring that you just talked about in this photo?"

"I do. It appears to be up at the top of the photo between her body and the wall. A few feet from her right hand."

Thax returned the photograph to the clerk's table. He walked back to defense counsel's table where he retrieved a sixteen by twenty-four-inch photograph he had marked as a defense exhibit.

"May I have a moment, Your Honor?" he asked as he motioned for Scarlett to look at the photo.

"You may," the Court responded.

Scarlett and Thax stood between the counsel tables discussing the photo. The prosecutor nodded in apparent agreement with Thax then returned to her seat.

"Your Honor, I would offer defense exhibit seventeen, which the Commonwealth stipulates is a photograph of Governor Branfield on the steps of the federal courthouse in Allentown leaving with his wife Dana after his testimony in Judge Eugene Harlin's trial approximately five years ago."

"I take it that's what the two of you just spoke and agreed upon, Ms. Scarlett?" the judge inquired.

"Yes, Your Honor," Scarlett answered. "No objection other than relevance."

"Alright. Your objection to relevance is overruled. It will be admitted. Please proceed Mr. Colby."

Thax walked toward Abigail and handed her the rather large photograph.

"Ms. Sutton, is Dana Branfield wearing any jewelry in this photograph?"

Abigail studied the picture.

"Yes. She appears to be wearing a pair of earrings with yellow stones that appear to be the same size and in the same setting as the earring I just examined and testified about."

Scarlett stood to object as Abigail answered but no words came out of her mouth. She felt like the air had been sucked out of her lungs. For a few brief seconds, the courtroom was silent. A.J. Scarlett, the powerful, high-profile district attorney had the governor's fingerprints, his semen, his gun, and text messages—compelling evidence, she thought, that he had raped and murdered Katie Meyers, but she and her team of detectives had overlooked a goddamned yellow earring. An earring that belonged to a woman who had every reason in the world to kill Katie Meyers—the young, beautiful intern who was screwing her husband.

Thax looked at the jury. Every one of their eyes was glued to him. He turned and stared toward Dana Branfield, who shifted nervously in her seat. He continued the hard stare for several seconds into the eyes of a now trapped and wounded animal.

"I have no further questions of this witness, Your Honor."

A.J. Scarlett glanced toward Thax and the governor, then toward Abigail, and finally at Judge Nescott.

"I have no questions, Your Honor."

The judge thanked the witness and asked her to step down.

"Call your next witness, Mr. Colby."

The governor sat with his head bowed. His faced was strained, his forehead creased with anger. He motioned for Thax, who leaned in to speak with him.

"Please don't do this, Colby," he pleaded.

Thax turned toward the gallery.

"The defense calls Dana Branfield . . ."

Seventy-Eight

THE STANDARD COUNTY office building fluorescent lighting illuminated Judge Nescott's chambers. A damp odor of old books from the wall of Atlantic reporters and Purdon's Pennsylvania Statutes permeated the room. A lingering aroma of Captain Black cherry pipe tobacco blended with the already stale air, despite smoking of any kind having been long since banned from the building. Judge Nescott leaned back in his chair and fingered his unlit pipe.

A.J. Scarlett stood next to Thax in front of the judge's desk.

"Judge, Mr. Colby had to know what a mess this was going to cause when he called Dana Branfield. He had to know she was going to refuse to testify." Scarlett shook her head. "He had to know."

"Have a seat counsel," the judge directed. "Mr. Colby?"

"Judge, first of all, we don't even know if she's going to refuse. You haven't asked her yet."

"Oh, come on, Thax," Scarlett interrupted.

"Well, that's the reason I called you all in here. I assume that's what she's going to do. Don't you think?" Nescott pressed Thax.

"I think you should ask her, Judge," Thax answered. "She might have a perfectly reasonable explanation for how her seven-thousand-dollar earring ended up next to Katie Meyers's dead body. Maybe she's going to say my client had it in his pocket for some unknown reason and accidentally dropped it when he was there to rape and kill the woman he loved. I don't know."

"Do I have to listen to this sarcasm, Your Honor?" Scarlett asked angrily.

Nescott calmly put the pipe to his lips and dry-puffed, observing a few de-escalating seconds of silence.

"Who's your next witness, Mr. Colby?"

"I'm done, Judge. We're going to rest."

"Ms. Scarlett?"

"Yes, Judge."

"Do you have anything in rebuttal?"

"No, Judge."

"Ms. Scarlett, let me ask you something. Do you think that Ms. Branfield will refuse to testify because she will incriminate herself?"

"Yes, Judge. She doesn't have a lawyer but I don't think we can let her make that decision without one."

"Well, I certainly wouldn't proceed without her having the advice of counsel," Nescott responded. "Don't I have to believe that her testimony might *actually* tend to incriminate her to let her assert that privilege? I mean I can't just let her say it so she doesn't have to bear the extent of Mr. Colby's examination? Don't you agree with that?"

"I agree, Your Honor," Scarlett answered.

"I agree too, Judge," Thax replied.

"Well, Ms. Scarlett, let's say I determine after speaking with her that indeed her testimony would incriminate her. Mr. Colby, I assume you want to ask her how in the hell her diamond earring got there?"

"Yes Judge. Among other things. Actually, I'm going to straight out ask her if she killed Katie Meyers with her husband's gun."

"Ms. Scarlett?"

"Judge—"

Thax interrupted. "If Ms. Scarlett is so sure she will incriminate herself, I think the question is why she believes my client is guilty. I think if that's the case, then she should dismiss the charges against Governor Branfield and prosecute the real killer. It seems to me that's Dana Branfield."

"What about it, Ms. Scarlett? You don't think they both killed her, do you?"

"No, Your Honor. I don't."

Thax shrugged his hands. "I think it's time for the District Attorney to fish or cut bait."

* * *

A.J. Scarlett's murder case against the governor was in shambles. She knew the political repercussions when she charged him. Who knew what would happen if, after almost finishing the trial, she would dismiss the case against him. There was personal fallout as well. While no one in the press had dug deep enough, surely when this case was Monday morning quarterbacked and dissected, someone would wonder why she dismissed the biggest case of her career, a case where the opposing attorney was also her ex-husband. Whatever those concerns, as the chief prosecutor for the county that was home to Pennsylvania's capital, she was compelled to do the right thing. Dana Branfield's single yellow diamond earring lying two feet from Katie Meyers's body was unexplainable and raised a reasonable doubt about Logan Branfield's guilt.

As she stood in front of Judge Nescott, the jury, the governor, Thax, Dana Branfield and a hundred and fifty or so of her constituents, she announced her decision.

"Your Honor, the Commonwealth moves to dismiss the charges against Logan Branfield."

Judge Nescott smacked his gavel repeatedly when the courtroom erupted, trying to bring the room to order. Eventually he did and he granted the oral motion.

"Governor Branfield, you are free to go," he announced.

In the pandemonium both inside and outside the courtroom, Scarlett locked eyes momentarily with Dana Branfield, who stood with her arm entwined with her husband's. Despite the earring, Scarlett would never be able to prove in a courtroom that Dana Branfield was Katie's murderer. She would never know that Richard Sokol had arrived at Meyers's home after the governor and Katie's make-up sex or that Sokol sexually assaulted Katie, leaving her apparently lifeless body for dead. Nor would she learn how Dana Branfield followed her husband to Katie's apartment that day and waited until he and Sokol had left there to confront Katie about her threats to expose their affair—details she learned about by reading her husband's text messages when he was in the shower. Finally, she would never find out that Dana Branfield confronted and struggled with Katie, losing her earring in the fight, before shooting her dead with her husband's gun. The discovery of Commissioner Sokol's bullet-riddled body in his home a few days later would only fuel the mystery.

Seventy-Nine

THE CRUNCHING OF wet gravel under Thax's felt bottom wading boots interrupted the peaceful silence of the early morning along the Little Lehigh. He walked purposefully across the parking area past the fly shop and onto the dirt path leading to the spot between the two willows. He was ecstatic to be back to the river after a long two weeks in trial. An hour into his day, though, he realized that he had made a terrible mistake. He had forgotten to leave his cell phone in his Jeep.

The phone vibrated in his back pocket. By the time he managed to retrieve it from under his waders the vibration had stopped. He recognized the 717 area code of the missed call but didn't recognize the Harrisburg number. The caller left him a voicemail.

"Hey, Thax, it's Andie. I'm sorry things got a little tense at the end of the trial. You did a great job. Congratulations. I was wondering . . . I'm heading out to Montana for a few days to unwind. Anyway, I was hoping you might want to come along. It was nice seeing you every day. Call me."

Thax's memories of a time long ago brought a smile to his face. At one time Andie Scarlett was everything he wanted and needed. But not any more. He erased the message.

Before he could tuck the phone into his fishing vest, it rang again. Another 717 call. He reluctantly answered it.

"Hello. This is Thax."

"Colby," the governor's voice boomed, "I didn't get a chance to thank you. You disappeared on me."

After the dismissal of the charges against Branfield, Thax snuck out while Branfield tried desperately to salvage his political clout outside with the press.

"Well, Governor, I never was much for those festivities."

"I understand. I understand. Anyway, I wanted to thank you and I was hoping maybe my tremendously large legal fee—which you rightly deserve—came with a free fly fishing lesson there on your river."

The last thing Thax wanted to do was to spend another minute with Logan Branfield—especially fly fishing with him. He decided not to share that sentiment with the governor.

"Sure, Governor," Thax said, "I'll call you to set it up."

"Well, that sounds great. I'll certainly look forward to your call. All right then. We'll talk."

"Goodbye, Governor."

* * *

After a few hours of undisturbed splendor on the river, Thax took a break for lunch. He checked his phone for messages. There was one from an old friend, Lieutenant Jerry King.

"Thax. It's Jerry King. I'm at the office. You need to call me right way. You've got to see this."

Thax had never heard King's voice tremble as it did. Something was wrong. Thax hurried to his vehicle foregoing a return call. He headed straight to the State Police barracks.

* * *

Jerry King played the video emailed from Detective Andy Morefield of the Polk County Sheriff's Office. A sickly-looking man, draped in a hospital robe and bald from chemotherapy, appeared on the screen. The man adjusted himself in a chair next to a bed. Thax watched as the man struggled to speak.

"My name is Jimmie Lee Powell. I'm here at the Good Shepherd Hospice in Lakeland, Florida."

Each short sentence was followed by a strained gasp for air.

"I don't have much time left. Stage four lung cancer. I'm making this statement freely and it's all true. It's terrible, but it's all true. I worked at

Bethlehem Steel before I got badly injured on the job. I was also an auxiliary Allentown Police Officer working part-time, you know, for parades and such. After my work injuries, I couldn't work for almost a year. I lost my wife, then my home. I ended up living on the streets or anywhere I could. I broke into places, any place I could to keep warm and dry. Back when I was in the auxiliary, I knew Mayor Branfield. After I lost everything, I would see him downtown some days when he was out for lunch. He recognized me and tried to help me out with a few dollars now and then."

Powell swallowed hard. His breathing was increasingly labored. He tried to sip some water from a small paper cup.

"About six years ago, some guy who said he was a close friend of Branfield's tracked me down. He said he needed me to do something for the mayor. It would be worth my while. The mayor was running for governor and he was down in the polls, he told me. He needed something to kickstart his position that he was tough on crime. That's how the girl from the college got killed. I'm sorry."

Powell grabbed some tissues and dabbed the tears from his eyes. He coughed violently, the tissues streaked and blotted with bright red spit and mucus from his mouth. After a minute, he resumed.

"A desperate man will do desperate things. This I know. A man who's hungry, who sleeps in an alley, who's so filthy he can't stand his smell . . . I was cold. I hadn't touched another person for so long . . . I didn't want to kill her, but they wanted something horrific. So that's what I gave them. Bashed her head in. Not a day goes by that I don't see that young girl's face. Not a day.

"I got five-hundred dollars so he could win an election. They even took me over to Easton to find someone at Lafayette College. I guess because he didn't want it to happen in his city."

"What about the gun?" Morefield asked.

"A little while had passed since the girl and one day I saw a car drive up and this time it was the mayor in the backseat. There was no one else around so he told me to get in. He had another problem he needed taken care of. A bigger problem. He said he would pay me five-thousand dollars and get me out of there to wherever I wanted to go. The same guy who approached me before gave me a gun—a .45 Smith & Wesson. He got me a hotel room with a hot shower too. He set me up with an unmarked police car so I would look like a cop and I could pull this guy over. I guess without suspicion. They told me where he lived, so I watched him until I knew I could do it. The mayor told me the guy had threatened to kill him and it was just going to be like self-defense. The mayor's the one who said if his wife was with him when I pulled him over to kill her, too. No witnesses. He told me to shoot her in the stomach. I didn't know until she got out of the car that she was pregnant. I shot them both in the back of the head. No way I was shooting her in the stomach. I'm not an animal."

Powell took another sip of water. His wheezing was getting worse, but he continued.

"They put me on a plane to Florida with an envelope full of cash. They would have done me a whole lot more good if they would have told me to stop smoking."

Eighty

OLD RONNIE GRABBED his worn gray metal lunch bucket from the passenger's seat and maneuvered his body out of his dark blue 2004 Ford pickup. He inhaled deeply as he made the short walk from the gravel parking lot to his "office" in the old stone building. The morning air was still crisp at seven-thirty—a refreshing respite from the warm summer afternoons. He stopped as he noticed a black Lexus LS 460 with dark tinted windows parked on the far end of the small lot. He knew almost every fisherman considered an early riser on that part of the Little Lehigh. This vehicle was unfamiliar to him. Besides that, he didn't know anyone who had a car that was worth more than his house. He scanned the river in front of him and downstream toward the bridge—in the direction of the Lexus—but he didn't see anyone fishing there.

After opening the door and turning on the lights in his thriving fly shop, he slowly walked the dirt path headed upstream toward the two towering willows. Along the way, he didn't see a single angler in or near the water. The heavy rains from the night before made the river high, fast and a little muddy, certainly not the ideal conditions for fly fishing. Passing the first willow, he observed something laying on the worn wooden park bench to his left—a small black case, not even half the size of his lunch box. He picked up the pack and unzipped it. Inside he found a cell phone. The bag, made of nylon and weathered canvas, wasn't wet. Even an amateur detective could see that the bag hadn't been there overnight or it would have been soaked by the heavy rains. Ronnie walked closer to the river, looking up and down the turbulent waterway. He saw no one. He closed the bag and returned it to the bench. *Maybe the owner is further downstream,* he thought.

As he approached the fly shop, he was overcome by his curiosity. He walked to where the Lexus was parked. The dark window tint kept him from seeing anything inside. He continued downstream toward the bridge then trampled down the short bank on the other side of it.

The usually tranquil waters in that part of the river roared from under the bridge raging over the rocky shallows just downstream. Ronnie admired the power of the fast-moving water as it funneled through the rock beds toward the widening river. He looked up and down the river. Then something caught his eye.

"What the hell," he spoke under his breath.

Just then, he heard a vehicle door closing in the parking lot. He scurried up the bank and saw a familiar young man wearing waders walking from his car toward the fly shop.

"Hey!" Ronnie yelled, out of breath from running up the inclined bank. He yelled again, finally getting the man's attention.

"I need your help," Ronnie yelled.

The man walked quickly toward Ronnie.

"What's wrong? Are you okay?" the young man asked with concern.

Ronnie realized his cry for help was perhaps too dramatic.

"Yes, I'm fine," he assured the man. "I just need your help. I don't have my waders on."

"What is it?" the man asked, now curious himself.

"Come here," Ronnie said motioning toward the water.

The man followed Ronnie down the bank.

"There." Ronnie pointed.

The man looked toward the rocks. Without saying another word, he waded into the fast, shallow water and retrieved a fly rod. The leader and fly line had wrapped around a pile of exposed rocks stopping the rod's drift downstream.

"Here you go," the man said, handing the rod to Ronnie as he returned to the bank.

"Someone lost a damn nice rod," Ronnie observed. "That's a Sage outfit. It's worth at least eight-hundred bucks."

The man chuckled. "Is this finders keepers?"

Ronnie continued to examine the rod ignoring the young man's comment. It was brand new. *The reel was only lightly scratched, probably from bouncing over those rocks*, he thought. He gathered up the line and saw the fly that was tied to the tippet—a size 24 trico pattern.

"Whoever owns this rod has fished here before," Ronnie announced. "And I probably know them."

"How's that?" the man asked.

"Because they knew to throw 24 tricos. That's the only way to catch trout in these parts."

The man nodded.

"I guess I better pick up some more of those before I hit the river."

Ronnie agreed. "Probably not such a great day for fishing today, though."

The man smiled. "I'd still rather be here than anywhere else today."

Ronnie looked back toward the river. More than four decades ago he had barely finished high school. At one point in his life he briefly tried community college. He wasn't a Rhodes Scholar by any measure, but he knew fly fishing and he damn sure knew people. Those talents had earned him a respectable living over the years. The $75,000 car in the lot, the abandoned phone case and now the expensive fly outfit on the rocks. Ronnie's alarms were going off big time. The young man stood by as Ronnie walked back down to the river's edge. He looked at the river, this time taking in every detail and nuance of the water. He took a few more steps downstream and then he saw it.

"Shit!" he gasped.

The young man turned and looked in the direction of Ronnie's stare.

"Shit!" Ronnie shouted as he ran downstream on the bank toward the end of the rocky waters, the hair raised on the back of his neck.

* * *

Thax stood next to the granite countertop in his kitchen preparing his lunch of a turkey hoagie with Swiss cheese, tomato, lettuce, and some red onions. Out of the corner of his eye he noticed a breaking news banner trailing across the bottom of his TV in the adjoining family room:

Second Term Pennsylvania Governor Logan Branfield
Dead in Presumed Accidental Drowning

He walked from his kitchen to the family room and turned up the volume. The anchor acknowledged a reporter from the local FOX affiliate at the scene. Thax listened.

"This is Marty Bracewell," the reporter began her report, "I'm standing here in Allentown on the bank on the Little Lehigh River, where authorities are telling us that early this morning the body of Pennsylvania Governor Logan Branfield was found in this river, a victim of what appears to be an accidental drowning. While authorities have said that it appears that Branfield may have drowned after losing his footing in the river while fishing, they have not said why Branfield was here at this location, some eighty miles from his current home in Harrisburg. One law enforcement source who spoke on the condition of anonymity told us that Branfield's new waders did not appear to have been equipped with a wading belt—an amateur mistake which may have cost him his life. Branfield, who was the mayor of Allentown before ascending to the Governor's mansion, was recently acquitted on charges that he killed his intern-lover. Just one day later, despite the revelations in his trial, he declared his intention to run for retiring Senator Edbert Williamson's United States Senate seat. The investigation into what exactly happened here continues. Reporting from Allentown, Marty Bracewell, Fox News."

Thax pondered for just a minute how quickly Logan Branfield must have made it to hell after his watery demise. A brief smile came over his face as he took a bite of his hoagie.

* * *

Lieutenant Jerry King arrived at his office on the first floor of the Troop M State Police Barracks in Bethlehem at his usual early hour. As King set his cup of black coffee down on his desk he realized he could actually see part of his desk pad—something he hadn't seen for years. A single white business envelope addressed to "Lt. King" was propped up against his tape dispenser. King opened the letter with his state issued letter opener. Inside, he discovered a single white sheet of paper, folded to fit the envelope. He read the five words typed on the paper.

For The Gold Shield Foundation

As he unfolded the paper, a cashier's check fell into his lap. King nearly fell out of his chair when he read it.

Pay to the Order of:
The Gold Shield Foundation—$1,000,000.00.

Eighty-One

THE RISING LATE morning sun glistened against the rippling, fast water of the Henry's Fork River as it forged its way southward through the Henry's Fork Ranch, a working cattle ranch just south of Ashton, Idaho. Long, broad patches of wispy white clouds painted the Western skyline. Thax Colby waded into the river and paused as he looked to the east, drawing in the masterful elegance of the enormous Grand Teton mountain range forty-five miles in the distance, still snow-capped at places even this late into the summer. A cool morning breeze swept through the open landscape over the surface of the river and against his face. It was exhilarating. The sounds of the stained, cascading water soothed his soul and delighted all his senses. A rising native rainbow trout distracted him from the wonderment. He cast his Chernobyl Ant hopper fly in the direction of the hungry fish.

"Catch anything, fly boy?" Thax heard a familiar voice from the river bank behind him. He turned toward the sound.

"Oh my God! Chrissy? I thought I was having a dream. What are you doing here?" His heart raced wildly as he sloshed as quickly as he could over the rocky bottom toward the river's edge.

Chrissy met him at the bank and threw her arms around him. He felt her heart pounding as he hugged her tightly.

"It's so good to see you, Thax," she said, hugging him again.

"What are you doing here? How did you find me?" Thax asked, trying to catch his breath. "It's so good to see you. God. Look at you. You look great."

"You look great, too." Chrissy tried to catch her breath. "We decided to come up here for a few days to chill out. I heard you were here." She smiled. "I've got good sources."

Thax laughed. He set his fly rod down on the grassy bank.

"You said we?" Thax asked as he looked around. He noticed a young boy scampering around a short distance behind Chrissy. The boy held a small, plastic fishing rod in his right hand—a hookless fly attached to a piece of string was tied to the rod's tip.

"That's my son, Thax," she said affectionately. She and Thax both gazed at the handsome, energetic brown-haired, blue-eyed boy.

Thax glanced at Chrissy's left hand. He didn't see a ring.

"He's beautiful," Thax said looking into Chrissy's eyes. He paused for a moment as he watched the boy swinging the rod.

"What's his name?"

Chrissy tensed as she looked back at her son.

"His name is Jeffrey," she said proudly.

Thax exhaled and smiled. "That's a good name."

"I thought so too."

Only a few people knew Thaxter Jeffrey Colby's full name.

"He's a great little boy," she bragged.

Thax glanced again at her left hand.

"Are you married?" he asked.

"No."

"His father?" Thax caught himself, then apologized. "I'm sorry. I probably shouldn't ask all these questions."

"It's okay. His father is a wonderful man. I love him dearly."

Thax's heart sank to his stomach. "That's good." He steeled himself as he looked into Chrissy's eyes. "I knew you would meet someone in Denver who was good for you."

She reached for Thax's left hand and pulled it to her chest. "I didn't meet him in Denver," she said in a hushed voice. "I met him in Allentown when he spilled my coffee on me outside the elevator." Tears rolled down Chrissy's face.

Thax's heart and head were ambushed with emotions.

"Are you—"

"He's your son, Thax. I wanted to call you when I found out I was having him, but I knew you didn't want to leave Allentown and I know you said you wanted a clean break and that you didn't want to keep me from having the career I wanted and—"

Thax put his finger to Chrissy's lips to stop her rambling. She grabbed his hand.

"I'm so sorry. I should have called you the thousand times I picked up the phone. I should have but I couldn't."

"Does he know?" Thax asked, looking toward the boy.

"I have told him so many things about you but he doesn't know it's you."

The young boy ran to his mother when he saw her crying. She hugged him against the side of her leg.

"It's okay," she said comforting him. "It's okay."

"I'm so sorry, Thax. Please don't hate me."

Thax brushed his right hand over Chrissy's face, wiping away her tears with his thumb. He hugged her and pulled her close.

"I don't hate you. I love you. And you're never going to leave me again."

The young boy looked up at Thax.

"So, you're Jeffrey?"

"Uh huh," the boy replied.

"How old are you?"

The boy raised his left hand and extended all of his fingers.

"I'm five," he said proudly.

"Do you like to fish?"

"Uh huh."

"Let me show you something." Thax reached for his son's left hand. "Come here for a minute."

The boy looked at Chrissy who nodded with approval.

Thax guided Jeffrey to the water's edge where he knelt behind him with his left arm around the boy's waist.

"I've got you," Thax assured him. "You won't fall in."

Thax put his right hand on the boy's right hand holding the fly rod.

"You throw it like this," Thax said moving Jeffrey's hand back then pushing it forward. The fly flew just a few feet into the river.

"Let's try that again," Thax said as they repeated the cast.

Jeffrey looked back at Thax.

"My daddy's a fly fisherman," the boy said proudly.

"Yes, he is," Thax swallowed hard and hugged his son tighter. "Yes, he is."

About the Author

For more than 30 years, **Jeff Downing** served as a federal prosecutor in the Middle District of Florida—one of the largest federal districts in the country. Assigned primarily to the Organized Crime Drug Enforcement Task Force, he prosecuted international and domestic drug trafficking, organized crime and gang defendants. For several years he supervised all public corruption prosecutions in the district. For a short time, he was the lead Organized Crime Drug Enforcement Task Force attorney in the District of New Hampshire.

Born in Allentown, Pennsylvania, Jeff graduated from William Allen High School. He received his B.A. degree in political science from Allegheny College in Meadville, Pennsylvania and his juris doctor degree from Duquesne University School of Law in Pittsburgh. He is an avid fly fisherman.

Made in the USA
Middletown, DE
16 March 2025

72762193R00217